D1509127

BLACK CROWN

THE DARKEST DRAE: BOOK THREE

KELLY ST. CLARE & RAYE WAGNER

1

I just needed a few more minutes to get this perfect. Taking a deep breath, I splayed my hands on the moist and squishy surface. The distinct smell billowed around me, and I grinned with anticipated triumph.

"Miss Ryn, are you in here?"

The muffled voice broke my concentration, and I clenched my jaw. Couldn't a Drae-Phaetyn find *any* solitude?

"No," I called back. I was inside the royal garden in Gemond, working on the pinnacle creation of my career. I couldn't stop now; I was so close. "I'm definitely *not* here."

The person—one of King Zakai's plebes I assumed—cleared his throat. "Your travel companion, Ambassador Dyter, asked me to pass on an urgent message."

I had a fair idea what that message entailed, and it could wait another ten minutes. I concentrated on the moss-green Phaetyn mojo traveling down my arms into the now-rich soil. Lani had given me a few tips, and I'd set myself to restoring the garden to its former glory. That occupied me for a few days, but once the garden was done, I'd become . . . side-tracked with a *project*.

The plebe continued without a reply, "Ambassador Dyter insisted you were informed all relevant parties are currently waiting

1

for you in the royal hall. This includes: Zakai, King of Gemond, and his son, Zarad; Lani, the rightful queen of the Phaetyn; Dyter himself; and your mate, Lord Tyrrik."

No! I grimaced. Dyter, my mentor, friend, and crotchety old coot, dropped the *mate* card? That would be like me making a joke about his gimpy arm, or how Zakai was skinny, or . . . or how Lani was an orphan. Courtesy demanded he wait before going there. It was a rule, like maybe Rule Number Ten: Wait a suitable amount of time before laughing about emotionally intense stuff.

The mate card was . . . true. Really true. So true, I wanted a size-able stint before the term was just bandied about. A timeframe longer than seven days. Even engagements lasted longer than *seven days*.

But engagements were nothing like mate-bonds. I hadn't seen Lord Tyrrik since this morning when I awoke next to him. The stronger bonds between us made separation difficult as in a little uncomfortable. My plan: to stretch the bond like sugar-taffy in the hopes I'd lose the *I-always-want-to-be-around-you thing*. So far, totally ineffective.

I lifted my head and studied my orange surroundings. Despite the personal satisfaction, I'd been in better, less stringy places recently. Then again, I'd also been in worse, and I had a goal to accomplish.

"How much room is left to the door?" I shouted. My voice echoed back at me in the confined space.

"About four inches," the person answered and then murmured to himself, "Does it matter?"

The barrier between us didn't muffle his voice enough for me to miss his baffled tone. I focused my Phaetyn mojo one last time, shooting my powers into the squash. Because yes, it did matter. "Now?"

"That'll do it, I reckon," he said. "You've filled the room."

Beaming, I stood inside the pumpkin and pushed the pale-orange fibers away, dodging a string of gigantic almond-shaped pips. The largest pumpkin that ever lived. In a trembling voice, I whispered, "My life's work."

I wrinkled my nose as I waded through the slimy guts of the cavity, the fibrous strands sliming me with their goo. I reached the inside of the shell to where I guessed the entrance to the royal garden to be and stared at the inner wall of the pumpkin.

"How are you going to get out?" the person asked.

Who was he? Emperor Obvious?

"Easy," I replied, attempting to dust my hands. Instead, I just smeared the sticky goop onto my skin in an even coat. "I'll use my talons."

Had I managed to partially shift without threat to my life yet? Nope. Transformations took practice, especially partial shifting. According to my *mate*, I hadn't practiced nearly enough in the three weeks since becoming a Drae. Unless one counted panicked instinct, in which case, I was a complete master. But left alone in the quiet? I'd rather grow things or take a nap.

"Are you doing the talon-thing yet?" the smart-aleck messenger asked.

"No," I grumbled. *Some people.* Closing my eyes, I began blocking out my senses. In this form, my Phaetyn form, I was only able to engage my Drae-heightened sense of smell, so I targeted this first. Tuning in to the moist pumpkin aroma, I pushed it back and reached for other smells. Remnants of Tyrrik's scent clung to my skin. I breathed in the damp fabric of my aketon and the soap I'd used on my hair last night. Good, good. I could do this. I imagined the squishy feeling under my bare feet and the sound of my breathing flittering away into open space.

Talons, I summon thee.

I focused on my fingers, willing them to sharpen and lengthen into the fierce blades of my Drae form. I envisioned how my claws looked, how they felt, their weight and strength, the power of the deadly weapons and what I'd be able to do with them here—make a door in this huge pumpkin. I focused my entire being on my hands and then smiled and opened my eyes.

My smile flipped in a second, and I scowled at my fingers. *Drak.* I thought I was in the zone.

I licked my lips, tasting raw pumpkin. Knocking on the thick wall, I shouted, "Hey, could you grab Lord Tyrrik real quick?"

"Are you stuck in there?"

I was done with Messenger Genius. "What I am is a Drae-Phaetyn who is able to grow sharp fangs," I snapped. "I've been hurt bad, so my temper is volatile. I don't even want to think about how unstable I am or who I might hurt if I get mad." When I didn't hear him leave, I snarled, "Hop to it, Mister Brilliant. Now."

"Y-yes, Mistress Ryn."

I smirked grimly at the pounding footsteps. Maybe Tyrrik was right; I should practice this shifty-hoo-ha. It'd be nice to save myself from future embarrassment . . . and death.

Khosana, are you okay? Tyrrik spoke through our bond, his voice filled with concern.

I rested my forehead against a pip. *Yes, but I'm trapped.*

Inside a pumpkin. Yes, I heard.

Was he concerned? Or was that suppressed laughter? Tyrrik better get rid of that humor I detected pronto. *Does everyone know?*

No, the messenger pulled me aside. But . . . how did you get in?

I shrugged, physically and mentally. *I just grew it around myself.*

I should've asked the pumpkin to grow a way to let me out.

As he drew closer, our bond began to pulse. The twisted onyx and lapis lazuli ropes thickened, the glow of the strands intensifying, their color blazing. I was certain it meant something. The bond liked Tyrrik being close and probably not for a game of hopscotch. I had a love-hate relationship with the mate-bond, depending on the circumstances and *possibly* my honesty on any given day.

I blew out a breath as the Drae came to stand on the opposite side of the squash-wall. Through the bond, I saw him lengthen his talons with barely a thought.

I've had time to practice, he reassured me.

I smiled, my mood brightening. Tyrrik was one hundred and

nine years old, so he'd had a lot of time to practice. *You only got the hang of it last year?*

Yes, Khosana, he immediately said. *You'll get the hang of this much faster I'm sure.*

He was stuffed full of potatoes, but I appreciated the boost to my ego, considering I was inside a pumpkin prison of my own making.

Stand back, mate.

The M-word. Again. "Wait, wait, wait," I screeched, seeing where he planned to cut. "I don't want you to just slice it up any ol' way."

"She wants a specific shape," he muttered on the other side of the orange wall.

I shivered as his low voice reached me. I squeezed my eyes shut and mentally described what I wanted.

Get that? I asked, taking a healthy step back from the wall.

Message received, he thought back in a strangled voice.

I jumped as Tyrrik's talons drove through the pumpkin as though the shell were a pancake. The razor-sharp blades sung as they sliced all the way to the inside. Crossing my arms, I watched with a critical eye as the Drae created a curved door. When he'd finished, he plunged the talons from both claws into the middle and pulled the new exit free, throwing it aside in the gem-encrusted hall.

Holding my head high, I stepped out of the pumpkin and met Lord Tyrrik's eyes with a dignified expression. Mum used to say, "People don't remember the mistake itself; they remember the grace with which a person handled it."

He reached for me, and I held my breath. But instead of pulling me in for a steamy kiss, he dragged a long, sloppy strand of pumpkin fiber from my silver hair.

I scowled at him as he pressed his lips firmly together. His eyes watered, and he tossed the stringy mess away.

"Not laughing doesn't really work when you're in hysterics in your head," I scolded. Jabbing a finger at my head, I continued, "I can hear you."

I stomped toward the garden exit, cheeks flaming.

He latched a hand around my wrist. "Forgive me, *Khosana*. You make me forget my worries is all." … *inside a pumpkin*, he mentally continued, laughing through our bond. "You always surprise me."

I appreciated his verbal effort, and truthfully, Tyrrik had so many worries and scars I was happy to help him forget his heartache for a moment. Even if it involved moderate levels of humiliation for me.

"It is the biggest pumpkin I've ever seen," he added, glancing back, still not releasing his hold on my wrist.

I grinned at the pumpkin which completely filled the royal garden in the previously barren area. It *was* a big pumpkin. "Do you think it's the biggest one ever?"

He nodded seriously. "Most definitely. And such a deep orange."

I slid him a suspicious look, but his expression didn't falter, and the bond didn't tell me otherwise. "Thank you." I smiled widely. "It is a nice color."

Tyrrik shifted his grip and intertwined our fingers, sending a pulse of his admiration through our bond.

My heart skipped a beat. *Holy pancakes.*

We walked out of the gardens in the direction of the meeting room, and I tried to settle my erratic pulse from Tyrrik's touch. A touch was simple to most people, but after everything in Irdelron's dungeons, people in my personal space didn't feel simple to me even if the person was Tyrrik.

He stroked the base of my palm with his thumb. "Dyter is not happy with you."

"Have they made any decisions yet?" I asked, hopefully. I sucked in another shallow breath and focused my attention on the rubies and sapphires. His touch even distracted me from shiny objects. That was a feat in itself.

"No, they await your presence."

"*Drak.* I'd hoped to show up when it was done." There were big decisions to make with even bigger consequences. I was eighteen, not an expert in any of the areas being discussed, so why did my voice matter so much?

Tyrrik smiled and pushed back a few fallen strands of his black hair. I stared for a moment at his sculpted and perfect face before forcing my eyes away.

He spoke again. "You are an important player in the war against the emperor, Ryn. More than that, you connect many of the people in that room together."

"You and Dyter," I mumbled. I'd rather they just gave me a summary to sign off on afterward.

"And Lani," he said.

Right. The *potential, and rightful,* Phaetyn queen. We'd saved her from a large army of Druman a week prior. I did feel a kinship with her, not only because I was part Phaetyn, but her mother, Queen Luna, had sacrificed herself to transfer her ancestral powers to me while I was still in the womb, ensuring I would live. My Phaetyn mojo knew Lani, and I felt super protective of her. I wasn't her mother; in fact, Lani was nearly fifty, though because Phaetyn's bodies matured slowly, she had the appearance of a child, and I felt a bit motherly toward her. Tyrrik was right: I did connect many of the people in that room.

I'd even saved the Gemondian king from starvation. Well him, his family, and his kingdom. He did seem pretty pleased about that. Understandably. Not everyone could do Phaetyn mojo and make things grow.

Tyrrik grinned at me.

"What's funny?" I asked.

He shook his head. "Nothing in particular."

Weird. "Okay."

The gold-wearing guards ahead bowed as we approached. As one, they opened the gilded doors for our entrance.

"So nice of you to join us," Dyter called, his voice filled with sarcastic bite.

2

The ceilings of the council chamber were low, like most in Gemond, and encrusted halfway up with priceless gems. The gems sparkled, spreading the minimal light so the room appeared bright despite being located several levels below the surface of the outside realm.

"No problem," I replied to Dyter as I walked into the room. I wasn't going to feel guilty for taking a minute for myself. Waving to the others as we approached the rectangular stone table, I couldn't help smiling at Lani who nodded regally in return. I swear the queen stuff was in her veins. I hoped the other Phaetyn would accept her because she was every single thing they needed.

I sat and peeked up at the glowering Dyter.

"Keep your hair on," I told the bald man. As the redness creeped over his scalp, I added, "Respectfully."

He snorted, and his shoulders dropped. The redness disappeared, and I knew I was off the hook. The old coot believed in this whole rebellion pretty strongly and got his apron tied in knots about the entire situation. I was on board with overthrowing the emperor and definitely wanted us to win. I just also appreciated down time.

"Ryn the Most Powerful Drae," King Zakai said from the top of the table, dipping his head. His son, Zarad, sat on the king's right.

"Hey Zakai," I replied.

"*Ryn*," Dyter said with a shake of his head. He gave me a meaningful look, mouth pulled down.

Really? He was telling me off about that too? I hadn't called Zakai king in ages—like never—and was pretty sure Dyter and I had already come to an understanding about kings and titles and such.

I turned to share my exasperation with Tyrrik and jumped slightly as he swept his hand over my shoulder in a movement that would be only a blur to the others. I squinted at the bit of pumpkin string now in his hand then turned my glare on Tyrrik. The Drae's expression was smooth and impassive, a look I knew well. To everyone else, he looked like an impenetrable, terrifying monster right now. *They* couldn't hear him slapping his stupid thigh in his stupid head.

"Al'right. What's happening? What do we need to discuss?" I asked, ignoring their baffled looks.

Lani spoke, "I must go back to Phaetynville."

I hadn't the heart to tell her Phaetynville wasn't *actually* what the Phaetyn called their home in the Zivost forest. I'd need to clear that up before she left.

"Yes, I agree," I said. If that was the only decision to make, maybe this wouldn't be as difficult as I—

"We left the Phaetyn in the midst of turmoil," Dyter said, leaning forward over the table, meeting each of our gazes in turn. "Kamoi and Kamini planned to restore peace to the forest, but we have no confirmation that has occurred."

"It would be foolish to send Lani into questionable conditions and hope for the best," King Zakai added.

Dyter nodded.

Umm . . . Right. I sat back. I really hadn't thought about that, but he was correct. My stomach twisted as I thought of the night we'd left Zivost. What if Lani went back only to encounter resistance? She really didn't know anyone there. Yes, the Phaetyn child-adult was Kamini's elder sibling and possessed ancestral powers the rest of her kind desperately needed to restore their defences against the emperor. But the Phaetyn hadn't exactly been the accepting, peace-loving, prancing people I'd envisioned. Last I'd seen, they'd been shoving blades dipped in Drae blood into each other.

I wasn't letting Lani go into that alone. "I'll go with her."

"No," Tyrrik said flatly, all traces of humor gone. "You will not."

My M-word often said no to things, lots of things, really. I decided then and there to translate the word as *yes* from now on. I said to Lani, "Great, so when do we leave?"

Tyrrik stood, his chair grating on the stone floor. Towering over me, he growled, "Whenever you transform into a Drae, the emperor gets a reading on your location. You're not going back to Zivost."

"*General* location," I corrected. "And I *am* going."

"We killed his Druman. Do you think Draedyn is stupid?" Tyrrik asked the table though I knew the words were directed my way. "Over a hundred of his Druman are dead in the last few weeks. Some in Verald, some outside of the Phaetyn forest, and then a whole hoard of them right outside of Gemond. Do you think he hasn't put two and two together? If Irdelron knew a rebellion was afoot before he died, do you think the *emperor* has somehow missed the signs of his starving and embittered Realm gathering to revolt? Even if Draedyn did, there aren't many creatures that can slaughter dozens of Druman at one time. There's only one."

Tyrrik had a point, but that didn't change the fact we'd need the Phaetyn later. And the best chance of us uniting them sat right next to us. "The likelihood of our success against Draedyn is best *with* the Phaetyn. If Lani goes by foot, the trip will take her weeks. Weeks that she'll be vulnerable." I hastily shot her a look. "I mean don't get me wrong; your trick of shooting roots through people is great, but you were in big trouble when we met."

"No offense taken," she said, her violet eyes twinkling.

I admired her sense of humor. Little eight-year-old girl-adult laughing at the two Drae arguing. But this wasn't really funny, and I wondered if anyone had pointed out the obvious, like plebe-brilliant who stood by the door. I turned to Lani, but the questions were to make a point. "Would you be able to harm your own people if they attacked you? Could you escape if dozens of Druman found you again?"

"I'll go then," Tyrrik said in a menacing voice. "If we need to get her there safely, I can do that. With relish."

You just proved why you shouldn't go. This isn't a revenge mission. The Phaetyn hadn't exactly treated him kindly when we were there. They'd sliced him with knives while he was injured to get his blood to use on weapons. Tyrrik might be still nursing a grudge. *I'd* be nursing a grudge except I'd already squashed the Phaetyn responsible.

Of course, Lani had the courage to disagree out loud. "I think it unwise, Lord Tyrrik. Drae are our natural enemy, and while *you* are not my enemy, the rest of the Phaetyn have not yet seen you as an ally. Since I will be appearing to them as a stranger and asking to be Queen, I'm not sure showing up with you by my side will endear them to listen. Even having Ryn there will present challenges."

I was certain we'd be fine as long as Kamoi and Kamini were in charge.

"It has to be Ryn," Dyter said with a grim face, and quickly added, "Just Ryn."

Tyrrik exploded. "You'd have her go out there alone? After everything? Are you insane?"

Kudos to Dyter. Though he paled significantly in the face of Tyrrik's snapping anger, he didn't back down. "No, Lord Tyrrik," he said softly. "It is *because* of what she's been through that I know she'll be okay."

I stood and rested a hand on Tyrrik's arm. He tensed under my grip, and his pulse feathered in his neck, but he didn't otherwise acknowledge me. I could feel his anger and underneath it, his fear.

"Tyrrik could come with me." I glanced around the table. Zakai and his son were halfway between sitting and rising, their eyes frozen on the Drae beside me. "He can wait outside the forest until we're done."

"You'd be giving Draedyn the perfect opportunity to ensure Gemond can't join the rebels," Dyter said, shaking his head. "The emperor must know there are two Drae by now and probably that you're both in Gemond. When his Druman confirm both Drae have left the kingdom—because you know there are more out there—I can't see why he'd hesitate to attack us."

"Then how are you proposing Ryn gets away safely?" Tyrrik snapped, a dark undercurrent to his words. "They're still going to see her."

The king straightened, looking much healthier now than he had a week ago, but it was his son, Prince Zarad, who said, "Decoy."

"Decoy?" Lani repeated, silver brows drawn as she looked from the father to the son.

"That is how we've evaded the emperor's Druman in the past," King Zakai explained. "Some of us pop out on one side of the mountain range, intentionally being spotted by Druman. The Druman follow them, and a few usually split off to report our movements to the emperor. While on the other side of the mountain range, our real traveling party sneaks off, undetected."

"My father is proposing Tyrrik stay here as a decoy to fool the Druman when Ryn leaves. His continued presence in Gemond will also discourage the emperor from attacking us," the prince interjected softly, flicking a look at his father. The Gemondian was around my age, maybe a few years older. Short and stocky, like most of the mining people here, and kind like his father.

Perhaps, once the young man got used to my unique sense of humor and stopped being nervous around me, we might be friends.

Tyrrik still stood, leaning over the table. He gripped the edges, the exposed muscles of his arms coiled and tight though his unfocused gaze was fixed on the stone table. "He'll feel her when she transforms remember."

"Yes, but you pose the greater threat to the emperor," Lani put in, already nodding.

The Drae released the table and curled his fists. "Ryn is the greater prize. She is a female Drae and his daughter. The emperor will go to great lengths to secure her."

King Zakai smiled at the Phaetyn who seemed unperturbed by Tyrrik's anger. If she could feel how near to the boiling point he was, she may not be so calm.

Tyrrik, I thought at him. *It will be fine. It takes one-and-a-half days to fly to the forest. If you go out and distract the Druman, they won't follow. If Kamoi and Kamini have resolved the Phaetyn war, getting Lani settled won't take long. If they don't accept her, I'll bring her back. I'll be returning in four or five days, either way.*

Ryn, I don't know if I'm physically capable of letting you go.

Well *that* stumped me. I understood his qualms. I didn't completely relish the idea of trying to stretch the bond that much. If being apart from him within the confines of Gemond was uncomfortable, I wasn't sure how I'd manage being a two weeks' walk away. *One-and-a-half days' flight,* I reminded us both.

He'd turned to me, and the others continued their conversation while Tyrrik and I discussed the matter separately.

If we cannot bear it, we'll only be the better part of a day from seeing each other if we leave at the same time. I paused, knowing this was where my reason would help overcome his instinct. This wasn't only our best option; it was our *only* option, which meant we had to make it work. Doing my best to lighten the mood, I quipped, *Although, I'm faster, so we'd meet a little closer to you, like maybe sixty-forty.*

He narrowed his eyes as he appraised me. *Sixty-forty? You think you're that fast?*

Didn't you hear what King Zakai called me when we arrived? I teased with a smirk.

Tyrrik sat down again, and we looked into each other's eyes. The conversation dwindled to a murmur around us.

You said if we cannot bear it, Tyrrik thought. *Did you mean it?*

What if I did say we? I held my breath for his answer, unsure what I wanted him to say in response.

"I hate it when they do this," Dyter muttered, covering his eyes with his sole arm.

I would not survive if anything happened to you, Tyrrik thought.

I swallowed as the bond between us began to pulse, glowing brighter than the sun, and I was inordinately glad no one else could see it. Because judging by the heat deep in my stomach, the bond connected to a certain part of my anatomy.

I blushed and broke Tyrrik's gaze. *I'll be careful, but we need the Phaetyn. They'll be healing all the humans, and you saw Lani fighting. I need to do this. It'll be worth the risk.*

Nothing is worth risking you.

Yeah, well, you're probably biased, I grumbled. He leaned closer, and my breath hitched.

That's because you're mine, he thought, and I blinked at the vibrating conviction behind his words. There was nothing he believed in more. Nothing in the world could shake his certainty that he was mine and I was his.

Tyrrik had accepted the bond wholeheartedly. Even before he knew me, he risked a lot to keep me alive in Irdelron's dungeons. Since our bond intensified, Tyrrik had flung the doors to his mind wide open even after confessing he feared what I'd find. His instincts had shown him we were mates, and that was enough for him.

I was sure about Tyrrik; really, I was. I just wanted to know him better before I gave everything to him. When my body was a broken mess, my mind had somehow survived, not unmarked, but it survived. I didn't worry what he'd find would scare him off; I had nothing to hide. But letting him have my soul, mind, and body just because instinct told me so? I'd pushed my Drae energy into him, knowing we'd be bound tighter. I knew letting him in my mind completely, letting my instincts take over, would bind us tighter again. I wanted to be sure I'd thought it all through before granting him unfettered access.

Will we still be able to talk like this? I asked. *Even when I'm in the forest?*

Yes, that will not diminish with distance. That will be my condition. If you are to go to Zivost without me, I'd like to be allowed to check up on you whenever I want.

I dipped my head as I acquiesced. *Understandable.* Reasonable even. *I accept your condition.*

Actually, his stipulation might give me exactly what I was looking for, a way to get to know Tyrrik without his proximity turning me into a donkey who had headbutted the stable door too many times.

Tyrrik broke off our stare, and I sagged forward as though released from a physical grip.

"Ryn will accompany Lani to the forest, and I'll act as a decoy. The duration of their visit is to be no longer than five days—"

My head shot up. Five days. That was more of a passing remark than a hard clause in our separation contract.

"—and if Ryn is in danger, I will leave this place immediately and get her." He stared down Lani. "And burn down your forest."

I gasped. "Tyrrik!"

Lani met his gaze. With an equally serious expression and tone, she answered, "Lord Drae, if the Phaetyn are so far gone as to put Ryn in any danger, you have my blessing to destroy them all."

3

"*Y*ou fear becoming dependent. You think dependency makes you weak."

We sat in our room on his bed *talking*. I was supposed to be packing, and when he offered to help, I'd hoped that was code for kissing. But no. Instead, Tyrrik did this. Talking.

I rolled my eyes at his comment. He used to call me out in a subtle way: a look, a veiled comment. Now, he just came right out with it. I *hated* it. I hated that he was right even more.

And why did we need to talk about *my* feelings—I'd much prefer to discuss a random stranger's. "Aren't men supposed to not like chinwags? I'm sure there's a book on that. Why are you mushy inside?"

Tyrrik raised his brow. "I had a lot of time on my hands. I spent a fair amount of it studying humans' behavior."

"I'm not human," I said, crossing my arms.

Tyrrik chuckled, a low sound that rumbled in his chest and bounced around in my head before settling in the deep cavity underneath the left side of my ribs, which I strongly suspected was my heart. Or possibly a terminal disease.

"You were raised to think like a human. Like a mortal. That is part of why you're having a hard time with accepting the

16

mate-bond even though you carry my mate mark on your neck."

I froze, blinking at him before remembering to keep up my cool facade. There he went with the M-word again. And the *double* M-word. I had a small onyx mark on the side of my neck where Tyrrik first touched me. It showed up after I'd accepted him as my mate a week ago when we saved Lani. Like I belonged to him.

"Think of our sister moons," he said. "What is the purpose of our moons?"

Was this a lesson? I shrugged. "They light up the night."

Surprisingly, Tyrrik nodded at my answer. "Does the brightness of one moon take away from the other?"

"No." This was stupid. "I see where you're going. But we're not sisters, and we're not moons." He needed to get better examples if we were going to be a M-thing.

"You're right; we're Drae, and we are mates. Being mates does not make either of us less than we were. It just is."

Ouch. The cavity under my ribs panged again. I thought I'd been doing the whole mate thing pretty well. At least well enough that Tyrrik didn't suspect my lingering fears. Clearly, I'd failed.

His face softened. "When you're in Zivost, please keep yourself safe. It is painful to my heart and mind for us to be apart, but if this is what you need to appreciate what being a mate means, I will do it. For you, not because those pointy-eared idiots need a leader."

That terminal disease spot in my chest panged *again*. Maybe there was something wrong with me. I wasn't sure what to say, so I peered around the chamber I shared with Dyter and Tyrrik, hoping the Drae would break the heavy silence.

I wanted this; I needed the time and space away from Tyrrik, enough so that I knew what I felt for him wasn't just attraction or instinct or the mate bond or whatever. I wanted my heart, my head, and my body to be on the same page because *I* chose it, not because of a black mark on my neck.

Deciding to grow a pair of potatoes, I forced my eyes to meet his. Tyrrik studied my face as though memorizing every curve, and then

KELLY ST. CLARE & RAYE WAGNER

leaned forward, brushing his lips against mine. His scent swirled around me, smoke and pine, just long enough to make my head spin before he pulled away.

That's it? I threw his way. *I'm going away for days, and you're going to give me a little peck? I thought you said I meant something to you.*

This time, I met him halfway, scooting closer when our lips met. My mouth melded against his, and I sighed, clutching his shoulders.

The bed covers bunched between us, and I growled, swiping them aside to crawl onto my knees and bring us closer still.

Tyrrik's lips were firm and warm. No one else knew that but me. Everyone else thought he was cold and hard, but I knew better. When his arm circled my waist to pull me closer, I grinned, peeking up at him as I bit my lip. He nipped at the spot when I released it, and I opened my mouth to him again. His tongue brushed and then tangled with mine, tasting of the sweetest nectar. His heat seemed to stroke me, luring me flush against him. The colors bouncing in the gem-encrusted room were augmented by the glow of our bond. The air around us crackled, and the steady smoulder in my belly exploded into something far more frantic. Tyrrik pulled me onto his lap, and I circled my arms around his neck, running my fingers through his midnight hair. *My midnight.*

Tyrrik's hands dropped to my waist, and I sucked in a breath, my hands twisting in his aketon. Heat and passion swirled between us. Right now, I couldn't feel what was mine and what was his.

I love you, Ryn.

His words hit my heart. The rawness within them brought me back to reality with a resounding boom. That was why I was going. I wanted to be able to say those words to him. I wanted to be able to assure him that I felt as strongly for him as he did for me, but I wouldn't say the words until I was absolutely certain of their truth.

Want and need were not the same thing.

A knock at the door interrupted us, and Tyrrik groaned as I scrambled off his lap.

"You're not the one who could be caught by your pretty-much dad," I reminded him then winced and said, "Again."

"I need to see Ryn," Lani said in her child-like voice, but the undercurrent tone wasn't childlike at all. "We need to practice something before we leave."

Lovely.

"She's busy," Tyrrik drawled, tugging on the hem of my aketon.

"Too busy to learn how to project a shield that will hide us from everyone but other Phaetyn?" Lani asked.

Tyrrik's eyes narrowed.

Point one to Lani. I bounced off the bed, patting my hair and adjusting my aketon as I walked toward the door. My lower lip felt distinctly swollen, and I could still taste nectar on my tongue. I hadn't felt so sheepish since hiding from Mum when I was six to drink a whole jar of honey syrup. Or maybe getting caught by Dyter.

"I'm here," I called, halfway to the door.

"I know. I could hear your heavy breathing from the level below. Get dressed, and meet me in the garden."

Get dressed? I stopped so quickly I tripped over my own feet. What did she think we were doing in here? I blushed even though there was no one but Tyrrik to see.

"I love when you blush," he said, crossing the room in a blur to stand next to me. *I love it even more when I'm the reason for it.*

"I'm still here," Lani called. "I'm pretty sure your breathing is getting heavy again, Ryn."

The burning in my cheeks intensified as I glared through the door in Lani's direction. I knew for a fact that Phaetyn didn't have super-hearing; that was a Drae power. I listened to the Phaetyn retreat down the passage, her musical laugh echoing in her wake.

Pretending to wipe my nose to hide my burning cheeks, I turned back to Tyrrik. "Looks like I'm . . . needed."

"Looks like." He smiled, though it didn't reach his eyes. *"We need* to find some time alone, uninterrupted, when you get back from Zivost." He tugged on my aketon again. "Maybe without so many clothes."

Whoa. My heart thundered in my chest, and I gaped at Tyrrik a moment and then sputtered, "Umm-m, yeah. Yes. Right. Awesome."

He arched a brow.

I stared up at him, mind blank. I jerked my thumb at the door and said, "Well, people to see, tricks to learn."

I hightailed it out of the chamber, congratulating myself on a mostly seamless exit from my M-word.

When I reached the royal garden, the workers were still harvesting chunks from the massive pumpkin I'd made. Of course they were. I'd made it. The air smelled of winter squash, and the bread-loaf sized seeds were scattered in the dirt. More than half of the gourd remained, and I smiled. A lot of people were going to bed with full bellies because of me.

I rounded the corner and spotted Lani cross-legged on a high ledge.

"I need to teach you how to veil before we leave," Lani said.

"Yeah," I replied, plopping myself on the ground below her. "When were you going to fill me in on that?"

"Now."

Helpful. "Is that how you remained hidden for so long?"

Lani closed her eyes, tipping her head back to bask in the stream of sunlight pouring into the garden—one of the perks of its location at the top of the mountain.

"It is, but I got careless. I was out foraging to replenish my supplies, and a group of Druman came over a hill and saw the disturbance in the water. One of them caught the scent of my trail. The gold veil has the obvious perk of keeping you hidden but only where it's covering. It's probably a smaller version of the golden barrier you described that previously protected the Phaetyn in Zivost. But as you'll see, erecting and maintaining a veil is taxing, and using it can leave you weakened until you get used to the effort."

Honestly, hearing that Lani knew how to put the golden barrier up was a huge relief. When I killed Queen Alani, the barrier came down, leaving the Phaetyn exposed to the emperor from above.

While the royal family could move the rock barrier circling the perimeter of the forest up and down, no one else knew how to put the veil up—Alani had only been able to sustain it, and barely at that. Ancestral powers were the strongest, and while I had ancestral power, my attempts to resurrect the wall hadn't been successful.

"You have to put the barrier up when we get to the forest," I blurted. I was not risking a repeat of last time.

"Yes, so I'll need my strength. Which means you'll need to cover us on the journey there. I think it's a good idea if we leave Gemond under veil so any Druman around can't see us."

Definitely. Even after our victory, I still hated the crossbreeds. And if the veil cloaked us from everyone but Phaetyn, that was the only defense I'd need.

I thought of Lani out on her own for the last twenty years. "How did you find out you had that kind of power?"

Lani smiled. "I drank a whole jug of honey syrup one time—"

Huh. I wondered if that was a Phaetyn thing.

"I heard my aunt arriving back before I'd hidden the evidence. Next thing I know, there's a golden net around me. My aunt strolled right by where I stood in the middle of the cellar, covered in honey. Learning to control the net beyond myself took time, but for what you want to do . . . You should be good to go within a minute or two. Protecting ourselves from danger is one of the strongest instincts we possess."

"It is?" I wrinkled my nose, wondering why the net hadn't worked when *I* stole honey syrup. Perhaps actually knowing I was Phaetyn would've helped. Still, Lani had hinted at more. "What else?"

"Hate being another"—she tilted her head, a smile dancing on her pink lips—"Love being another again. So first," she said, drawing my attention back to her and her lesson, "you need to really want to be invisible. Just like all your Phaetyn abilities, your desire will make the power much stronger."

I nodded, thinking back to how I'd wanted Tyrrik to be healed after being impaled. Desire . . . Yep, yep. Got it. Definitely wanted to be invisible from the Druman.

"Then you need to envision the power to make it happen. Think of it like a shield or covering."

I thought of the gold net over Zivost, the thin filaments like what I'd seen covering the forest when we'd first arrived. I closed my eyes and willed the golden magic to cover me and make me invisible. I took several deep breaths, firmly fixing the image in my mind.

I opened my eyes.

Nothing. No golden magic, no net-like mesh covering my body.

"Why didn't it work?" I asked, furrowing my brow. I brushed my hand in the empty air, trying to feel where my magic should be happening but wasn't.

Lani shook her head. "I don't know. Try it again."

I chewed on my bottom lip. "Okay, but can you cover your ears?"

The Phaetyn arched a brow and obliged.

Closing my eyes again, I took a deep breath, muttering, "Golden net of hair and twine, hide me, let your tendrils shine." I cracked an eye open and sagged. Nothing. I glared at Lani, whose shoulders were shaking. "You weren't meant to be listening!"

"Hard not to when you're shouting by the end."

Several attempts later, I growled, throwing my hands up in the air. "Show me again."

Lani did, covering herself in the golden net, and I glowered at her. I refused to believe I wasn't capable. I had crazy strong Phaetyn mojo. I'd healed Tyrrik, surprising Kamoi and his stupid parents with my power. I could do this. I thought of him lying in his black blood and me closing the wound and then burning out the golden droplets of Phaetyn poison.

"I got this," I said, straightening with my epiphany. My Phaetyn magic wasn't gold for starters. I envisioned a moss-green net, shimmering and iridescent, and pulled my Phaetyn power over me. I thought of the energy masking me from all eyes, making any who glanced my way blind to my presence.

"Whoa," Lani exclaimed. "How did you do that?"

I opened my eyes. The vibrant threads of power were the color of moss, cast out around my body like a coat of forest leaves. I glanced behind and saw I wasn't the only thing inside the net.

"That's odd," Lani said. "The pumpkin has disappeared too."

So I was a little protective of the remains of my pumpkin.

"What can you see?" I asked.

"Nothing. There's a huge hole, like someone scooped out that entire area. Your Phaetyn powers don't work like mine for some reason. But you can't do it that way, Ryn, or anybody who looks into the air will see a black space and know something is up."

"Anybody?" I glanced around the garden and saw someone lurking, pretending to pull weeds. "Ask that man what he sees."

The lazy gardner told Lani there was nothing there, but the Phaetyn queen insisted I try again.

"You don't want to be invisible to just humans, Ryn. That's not who we're worried about."

True. Maybe it had something to do with my mixed heritage. I thought of my net, this time pulling it in tighter to me and my body, and then I thought of how it should reflect the light and appear like I wasn't there but preserve the rest of the space around me.

"Nice," Lani clapped her hands. "If you can do that, we should be plenty safe all the way to Zivost, and you'll be safe on the way back. Just remember, this power takes energy. Like strengthening a muscle, it will get easier the more you do it, but the first few times are challenging. Or at least they were for me."

Having the added protection of the veil *did* make me feel safer, but there was someone else who I knew would appreciate the extra security when I left in a few hours.

4

I hefted my pack higher on my shoulders and peeked around the corner into the foyer of the grand entrance of the Gemondian Kingdom. I hadn't been back down here since arriving with an unconscious Tyrrik in my claws. The high-ceiled chamber around the corner made what I was about to do real in a way nothing else had. I was leaving Gemond, Tyrrik, and Dyter to protect Lani on the journey to save the Phaetyn. She was relying on me. And I wasn't relying on anyone but myself.

I shifted the pack again and straightened, squaring my shoulders as I set my face into hard lines. I could do this. I *would* do this. Not just for Lani or the Phaetyn. This was for me, and Tyrrik. For Dyter and the empire. It wasn't the first step in the rebellion, but it sure felt like mine.

Behind me, Lani's step was the lightest of anyone in the chamber but only because of her child size. The Phaetyn would-be-queen's grasp on the battles being waged showed just how mature she was.

"Hold on, I want to do something," I told her without turning.

Tyrrik could hear what I was saying, and I knew he could feel my presence around the corner because *I* could feel him. I closed my eyes, envisioning my net, and then pulled Lani under it with me.

"You'll tire yourself before we leave," she scolded.

"I'm practicing," I replied. "And it will make Tyrrik feel better."

Once sure I had everything tucked in right, I took hold of Lani's hand and strode beside her around the corner.

King Zakai and his son were talking to Dyter and Tyrrik. None of them stopped the conversation, and I grinned with my success. Crazy-strong Phaetyn mojo for the win.

Until.

Tyrrik frowned. And then grimaced, blinking to clear his vision. "Ryn? You're fuzzy. And why can't you hear me?"

The first time, I hadn't felt any drain from creating the veil, but as I dropped it a second time, relief trickled through my muscles and down my spine. I stood still, ignoring the startled yells of the others as my knees shook for a moment. Tyrrik yelled my name through the bond, and I winced.

Please stop yelling.

Lani leaned in as I regained my footing.

"Told you," she whispered.

"Would you like to walk to the forest?" I asked sweetly, but my enthusiasm waned with my new-found knowledge. This wasn't going to be as easy as I'd anticipated.

Her response was to show all her teeth in what could've been a smile, on a very bad day, in a very inhospitable place. Or maybe her expression was meant to bolster me due to its creepy ferocity.

Tyrrik's fading alarm still seared through the bond, and I jolted as the image of me, or rather what I had looked like to him, struck me. My body looked like an apparition, completely transparent, but oddly still *here*.

That was . . . new. I'd never gotten an image from Tyrrik before. *It's okay, I just had the veil on,* I told him. To Lani, I said, "How could he see me?"

She lifted a shoulder before dropping it. "Maybe it has to do with the mate bond."

I really hoped that was the case and not a sign all Drae could see me.

Tyrrik's emotions swung from panic to relief to pride. Whoa.

Time for goodbyes. My throat suddenly clogged with emotion, and I strode to Dyter first. Approaching my oldest friend, I fell into his one-armed embrace, patting him awkwardly when he wouldn't let go. "Love you, Dyter."

"Yes, well," he said gruffly. "Don't forget to . . ."

He apparently forgot whatever it was I wasn't meant to forget. I smiled at him through the allergies burning my eyes that were *certainly* the reason for the tears on my face. "I won't."

Prince Zared was next, which was easier. I shook his hand and then turned to his father.

"A safe journey, Most Powerful Drae," the king said with a wink.

I grinned, my heart warming even more to the aged ruler of Gemond. "Thank you, Zakai. Here's hoping for no turbulence."

My joke fell flat, and with no small amount of unrelated dread, I turned to the last man in the room.

Dyter drew the others away toward the door, and I waited until there was nothing more I could wait for. A vice clenched my chest, and my steadfast resolve nearly crumbled when I met Tyrrik's gaze. His eyes were inky black, but I could feel the emotions storming within.

"Make sure you use the veil while you're in your Drae form until Lani puts the barrier up again," he said in a low voice. "And use it all the way back, right up until you're inside Gemond. All the way inside."

I rested a hand on his arm. "I know, Tyrrik. I'll take care of myself. I promise."

He shuddered at my touch and onyx scales erupted on his chest, peeking out from his aketon and spreading up his neck. His voice deepened, turning part Drae when he spoke again. "I trust you, *Khosana*. It's everyone else I don't trust." *Be careful.*

Uncaring that the others would see, I wrapped my arms around his torso and lay my head on his chest. "We can trust Lani. I know we can."

"Lani, yes."

Standing at the doorway with the others, Lani called out dryly, "I'm so glad. Can we go now?"

I was going for a reason, I reminded myself. And even though those reasons didn't seem so urgent, now—proximity to Tyrrik made it hard to reason at all—if I stayed, I'd regret it.

Mum didn't raise no quitter.

I lifted onto tiptoes and planted a firm kiss on my Drae's hard cheek. "Al'right, I'm off. See you soon, Tyrrik."

The brusque farewell might have worked if my voice hadn't caught on every other word, but I turned and strode away, holding it in like a big girl though it occurred to me that bigger girls probably just had bigger tears.

King Zakai gestured for the guards to open the gates, and I'd nearly reached Lani when Tyrrik's fingers wrapped around my wrist, halting me.

I let him tug me back around and remained completely still as he grimaced, trying to control his Drae. He closed his eyes and pressed his face into the crook of my neck. His forest pine and smoke scent wrapped around me, and he trembled as he pressed his lips to our mate mark.

I felt a sharp pinch as his fangs lengthened, and I gasped.

"Lord Tyrrik," Dyter called, breaking the stupor around us. "You'll need to go with the guards to exit from the other side of the mountain."

Tyrrik pulled back, and I was nearly overwhelmed with the urge to announce I wasn't leaving. He broke our contact with a pained grunt, and the compulsion lessened.

Give me five minutes to draw them away, then you can leave, he thought through our bond. At my stupefied nod, he left the room so quickly *I* barely saw him move.

"So much sexual tension," Lani murmured.

I wrinkled my nose and noticed Dyter with his eyes closed. Poor guy never seemed to be in the right place at the right time.

"Okay," I said, only a slight tremor remaining in my voice as my determination and expression hardened once more. "Let's go save Phaetynville."

I BEAT my wings down with powerful strokes, catapulting us high into the azure sky over the central ranges of the Gemondian Kingdom. Even after at least eight hours, the lift under my wings and the stretching of my back felt wondrous.

Lani gasped and clutched one of the spines on my back as she shouted over the wind, "Was that necessary?"

Necessary? No. But gone was the time when I'd only do what was necessary. Life was more than survival, something I'd learned somewhere between dungeons and torture rooms and multiple kingdoms. I extended my lapis wings, stretching them as far as they'd go, and reveled in the joy of flying, one of the things that reminded me why I needed to fight.

"When are we going to stop?" Lani shouted. "The sun is going down."

I wasn't sure why she kept asking questions; I couldn't answer her in this form. In truth, though I could have flown for hours more, the moss-green power fueling the veil over us had grown steadily weaker over the day. While Lani could hide us if we continued, we'd agreed she'd save her energy to cloak the Forest. After today, I wasn't sure how she'd be able to cloak Phaetynville, but I knew she'd need all the strength she had to accomplish that.

I arched my long Drae neck to give Lani an awkward nod and then began my descent. I'd long since passed the summit where Druman had overrun Dyter, Tyrrik, and me a few weeks ago. Camping there overnight seemed to be tempting fate, but I spotted a similar peak which would do just fine.

I kept the angle of my descent shallow, circling in looping sweeps until I landed gently on the flattest part of the mountain peak. I inhaled long and hard in each direction, using my keen Drae senses to study the sky and the surrounding terrain. After that, I closed my eyes and strained my ears to listen for any pinprick of human or Druman noise within miles. Lani was in my care, Ryn the Protector wasn't taking any risks.

Satisfied we were alone but for the harmless critters scuttling about, I lowered onto my haunches and turned my mind to shifting. Achieving my Phaetyn form was like sitting down after standing for hours. I groaned in relief as the air shimmered around my Drae form, and I welcomed the now familiar shift of bones as I shrunk to Phaetyn size, the moss-green veil beginning to dissipate.

"You can get off now," I muttered from where I knelt with my face bent to the ground.

Lani stayed put on my back. "I don't know. I'm pretty comfortable."

"Off." An unsettling feeling tugged beneath my ribs, and I grimaced. Tyrrik hadn't been kidding when he said I'd miss him. The separation was not pleasant. The nagging sensation set me further on edge, and I clamped my arms to my sides to keep from extraditing the little queen.

The Phaetyn snorted and swung a leg over. "You're a grump."

"Finally," I groaned.

I let go of the last strand of moss but wasn't prepared for the backlash from holding the veil for so long. Pain whipped across my forehead, and I rolled onto my side, gasping.

"Make sure to let go of the veil slowly," Lani said.

I dug the heels of my palms into my eyes. "Thanks. That's super helpful."

I gasped and clutched at my chest as the tugging feeling sharpened into an acute ache for Tyrrik. It'd been how many hours since I'd left Gemond?

Khosana?

The presence of Tyrrik in my mind was the equivalent of slipping into a warm bath even if all I could feel was his panic. I wanted to hightail it back to Gemond right now, or maybe after a little kip. I blinked and slowed my breathing, focusing on releasing the tightness in my chest. *I'm okay,* I replied in a strangled voice. *Just tired.*

Whoa, the veil was nothing compared to this raw hollowness. I really should listen to Tyrrik a bit more.

I see . . . Want to talk? he asked.

My lips twitched. *Sure, but let me eat first.*

Go eat. When you're ready, the password is: Lord Tyrrik is the Most Brilliant Drae.

What? *I'm not saying*—Before I could finish, Tyrrik closed the mental door on me. I blinked up at Lani and said, "He's gone."

She paused part way through unpacking our dinner. "Right."

"Head talk," I explained, pointing at my temple.

"So soon? You mustn't have given him a proper send off," she replied, waggling her silver brows.

I flushed as Lani's meaning sank in. I wasn't sure how Phaetyn did their send offs, but *that* wasn't how I said my goodbyes.

"You'd both probably feel better if you had," Lani said matter-of-factly as if she could read my mind. Then her brow furrowed, and she tilted her head, examining me. "You've had sex with him, right?"

Holy pancakes. Was I really having this conversation with a fake adult? I shook my head, staring at my pack as though it could save me from the entire situation. I could just crawl inside it and live there. "I'm not sleeping with anyone. I'm not ready to. How do you even know about . . ." I waved my hand and mumbled, "stuff?"

"I'm over fifty years old."

"Look like eight."

"*Fifteen*," she insisted, nostrils flaring. "And we're not talking about *my* sex life."

Young Phaetyn got prickly about their slow aging. Kamini, Lani's younger sister, was like that too. "We're not talking about mine either."

I wrenched open the drawstring of my deer hide pack and rummaged for some water. I uncorked the skin and guzzled the contents.

"Well, maybe we should. Sex isn't something to be embarrassed about."

I choked and spat water all over my pack. Not embarrassing? I could think of a bajillion different reasons I didn't want to talk about maypoles and the potential dancing of them, number one being that I was tired and hungry, and rectifying those two things required my full and immediate attention.

"You've accepted him as your mate." Lani took the skin and looked at me pointedly. "Mating is part of nature. Just the same as a plant growing."

I rolled my eyes as she drank. "Yeah, thanks for that."

"You do understand how it works, right? Do you need someone to explain where the parts go?"

"No," I said in a strangled voice. "Please, no. I know where the parts go. My mother explained it all to me. Can we not talk about this?"

Lani said nothing, and as the minutes passed, I slowly relaxed.

Then she went and cleared her throat. "No, sorry, Ryn. I don't feel right leaving the matter alone. Dyter was hinting at it the other day, but he doesn't seem comfortable tackling it head on. Who would you prefer to talk to? Dyter or me?"

When she put it like that . . . At least Lani would be far away in a forest. "Kill me now. Okay, get on with it then," I huffed. "I've got things to do."

Lani peered around the empty mountain top but didn't call me out on my comment. "Have you had a boyfriend?"

I thought of Tyr, but he—

"Before you found your mate, I mean. Let's not include him quite yet."

The only other friend I'd had was Arnik, and he was more friend, not boyfriend. "Kind of?" That was such a lie, but I didn't want to seem uncool in front of the maybe-Phaetyn queen.

"He was at least a friend, right?"

I nodded.

"Great. Now, think about how you kept the friendship healthy and strong."

I shook my head. "I didn't really do anything. We hung out. Played pranks together."

"Did you ever give him a gift?"

I tipped back my head and pondered a moment. "On his birthday, sure. Otherwise, not really. We were a little poor for gifts. I gave him an autumn leaf I'd pressed flat in my mother's cookbook once." I grinned and added with a touch of sarcasm, "Took me ages."

But there were gifts, small things, like him walking with me to deliver soap. Sometimes, he'd find a pretty pebble and give it to me, and I'd saved plenty of honey-cakes for him over the years.

"Good relationships take effort to keep them healthy, and sex is a natural part of a mate-bond."

Heat crept into my cheeks. "I knew that." *Kind of.*

She studied me and nodded. "Good. Relationships take effort and time, and if you value the relationship, you'll give him both. You'll both change over time. That's just life, so make sure you're investing in your relationship so that distance doesn't grow between you. Because make no mistake, though you are mates and cannot bear to be physically apart, you can still grow distant in other ways."

I snorted and, in my best teasing voice, said, "I'm surprised you're such a relationship expert."

I knew the words were a mistake as soon as they left my mouth.

Her smile dropped, and her features took on a haunted look.

"I was just kidding," I rushed to amend the offense. "I mean I'm surprised. My mother never had a partner. There were hardly any males around in Verald."

I frowned. Was that why I was finding it difficult to fully accept Tyrrik's presence in my life?

She patted my leg and said, "When you're alone, you have a lot of time to think. And to regret. I want you to be aware of what can happen if you don't nurture your relationships, mate and otherwise. From what I've observed, what you and Tyrrik have is pretty amazing."

I hadn't had this I realized—another female to talk to. Childlike creepiness aside, I didn't *dislike* talking to Lani. I peeked up at her through my lashes, a smile curving my lips against my will. "You really think that?"

"I do." She smiled back at me before shoving dried meat and bread into my hands. "Now, eat before you headtalk your mate. I'll keep first watch. You need to recover your strength for tomorrow."

I wolfed dinner down double time and guzzled the rest of one of our waterskins. My muscles felt wrung out from the drain on my Phaetyn powers, but my mind kept replaying the conversation with Lani. I'd spent far more time pushing Tyrrik away than pulling him close. And sure, I'd had my reasons for a while. But I didn't want distance between us. I just truly, deep down, feared trusting him.

I feared he may not always be around—whether that came from my mother never having a partner, the fact there hadn't been many males in Verald growing up, or King Irdelron's brutality, which taught me to fear losing those I loved—and I was allowing my fear to rule my actions. Nope, not okay with that. I determined not to let fear affect what I might have with Tyrrik. What I did *have* with Tyrrik.

"Mate." I tried out the word, and the hairs on the back of my neck stood on end. Maybe it took a bit.

Closing my eyes, I leaned back on a rock, doing my best to be comfortable because I was not moving. *Tyrrik?*

And waited. *Tyrrik?*

Was he serious? I waited another minute and then sighed long and hard. *Lord Tyrrik is the Most Brilliant Drae.*

His presence flooded my body, filling me with warmth.
You called?

A short laugh burst from my lips. *You're an idiot. And I didn't mean it. My fingers were crossed.* I quickly crossed them.
You just crossed them. I felt it.

What? Sheesh, this bond is getting Strong with a capital S. I thought we could only see images from each other when our emotions are high. Is it the same with feeling how my body feels? I suddenly realized the implications of just what he might feel during future kissing meetings.

My father would check on my mother by using her vision. He was attuned to her heart rate as well.

I rolled my eyes. *Please tell me this isn't another 'males can do it but females can't' thing.*

His lips curved, and I gasped at the purring rumble behind the gesture. *I just felt you smile!*

There's the answer to your question then, he thought back. *My mother would use the connection to judge when to send my father energy on long flights and in battle.*

Tyrrik hadn't talked much about his parents. He'd been taken from them when he was nine. But I couldn't sense any hesitation or bitterness as he remembered them. I guess one hundred years was a long time to heal wounds. *During our fight with the Druman, I just looked at the strength of your tendrils, but paying attention to how drained you feel will be better. I'm going to practice.*

Don't overextend yourself. I can feel how tired you are from keeping up the veil all day.

A jagged piece of rock was digging into my back, and I shifted over a few inches. Tired was an understatement. *So,* I drew out, *what's your favorite color?*

We're asking each other questions? His amusement radiated through the bond, and my heart swelled with the warmth of his laughter. *Black,* he answered. *What about yours, love?*

Of course it was. I arched a brow. *Golden brown.*

Like your mother's honey syrup?

I smiled and slid down the side of the rock, cradling my hands under my head to get comfy. I closed my eyes. *Yes. What's your . . . favorite animal?*

Desert panther tastes the best.

Not to eat! I chuckled sleepily. *To have as a pet. Do you ever think about the things we can have when the empire isn't starving and people can do more than survive? I think I'd like a dog. One I didn't have to consider eating.*

I focused and was rewarded with an image from Tyrrik. He was out on one of the top balconies in the Gemond Kingdom, looking out to where I lay. I knew he couldn't see me from there, but it was comforting to know he was looking out for me.

I think I'd like a dog I wouldn't eat too, he finally answered. *Our dog.*

Who said Drae and human traditions couldn't see eye-to-eye?

"RYN," Lani whisper-shouted, shaking me. "Wake up."

I peeled an eyelid open and, noting the darkness around me, grumbled, "Leave me alone. It's not morning yet."

I closed my eyes again, curling up on the not-at-all-comfortable jagged stone, determined to get every last second of sleep I could before I took off. The Phaetyn invisibility power was great, but Lani was right; it took effort to keep it up. Normally, I healed super-fast, but the idea of having to resume that cloaking-cover made me even more determined to get some extra Zs.

A roar boomed overhead, ricocheting off the rocks around us, and I sat up with a gasp, scrambling for a hold as the entire mountain shook. Blood whooshed in my ears as my body stilled, and my mouth dried. There was a Drae . . . here.

Collecting myself, I crouched beside Lani, blinking rapidly to adjust to the darkness. The roar cut off abruptly, and the tremors stilled. *Everything* stilled, hushing in the presence of the sheer power of the beast above us. I swallowed and peered up into the night sky and then to my companion, my eyes wide, as the sound of beating wings tickled my ears.

Tyrrik? I shouted through our bond.

White fire streamed across the velvet night sky.

Tyrrik's fire was blue. Which meant that Drae wasn't Tyrrik, and there was only one other option. Terror pounded against my ribs as I contemplated what it would mean if Draedyn found me. I couldn't be locked away again. I grabbed my chest, gasping for breath.

Ryn? Tyrrik's voice was laced with panic. *What's the matter?*

An image of our bedroom in Gemond flashed through our bond. I could feel his alarm as he hurried out of the room, not bothering to get dressed. My thoughts derailed for a moment until he skidded to a halt in the hallway and repeated, *What's the matter?*

Lani whispered in my ear, "We're good, Ryn. We'll be safe under my veil. Tell Tyrrik. Now."

My mind raced, and I reached for the frayed threads of reason to form a coherent sentence.

If you don't tell me what's going on right now, I'm coming to find you. I can feel your fear, Khosana, and I need—

My fear evaporated, and a deep yearning hit me, as if the roar weren't a threat but an invitation. If I flew into the sky, I'd be able to meet my father. Yes, I'd been told my whole life he was terrible, but the truth was he'd risked everything to keep me alive because he wanted me. He had always wanted me, and even now he wanted—

Lani clapped her hand over my mouth, and in a blink her gold net of Phaetyn power cast over the two of us. I frowned and shook my head. What just happened?

"You had a bad dream," Lani whispered. "Tell him that. Make something up, Ryn, because he can't come."

I glared at Lani, tempted to tell her to shut her child mouth. Actually, I wanted both of them to shut up so I could process what I needed to do. "Let me talk to him," I whispered. "Pull the net away from my head, just for a minute."

She nodded, and the gold net inched away from me. *I'm al'right. Bad dream, and Lani freaked me out on top of it.*

Then why is your heart rate still elevated?

Because she's still pissing me off.

Lani jerked her head toward a large boulder, and I followed her toward the rock, glancing around the midnight sky for any hint of the emperor.

Tyrrik's doubt through the bond was so strong it was like he was standing in front of me holding a sign that said 'liar liar aketon of fire.' If I told him about the Drae in the sky, he'd shift and probably try to come to my rescue. But that would be pointless. And I needed him there in case the Druman attacked Gemond or Draedyn showed up. I could still feel Tyrrik's presence in my mind, almost like we were both debating what to say to the other.

Lani's going to put up the veil for a bit so I can sleep. I'll—

Are you safe?

No. Yes. Guilt hit me. *Mostly. Can you still feel me with the net up?*

I can tell you're alive, but that's it. Should I come—

No.

Lani pointed to the sky again as Draedyn released another jet of white fire, this one only two valleys to our right.

I've got to go. Lani's tapping her foot. She was inching the golden net up over my chin, in fact. *I'll check in as soon as I'm up.*

Instead of feeling his emotions quicken, I felt Tyrrik's determination and resolve. *I understand, Khosana—*

Lani closed the veil over us, cutting off his last words.

6

The terror of being caught and imprisoned bubbled inside me, and I continued to battle to keep it in the locked stone box where it belonged as the emperor lit up the sky with molten fire. The idea that my father was out there, *up there*, in his Drae form and hunting me, made me simultaneously want to shrink into a ball and go up there and slash his eyeballs out with my talons —but more of the former, like a one hundred to one ratio. I wasn't stupid enough to start that fight, especially with the Phaetyn queen at my side. No, hiding was smarter.

While I didn't know how effective my barrier was against Drae, with Tyrrik being able to see me through it, clearly Lani's golden veil was doing the trick.

Both Lani and I were huddled close under her Phaetyn shield, doing our best to breathe silently. A loud roar reverberated through the range, and we both flinched.

"Your father sucks," Lani hissed.

I glared at her. "Dyter is the only father I've ever known."

The next bolt of fire came from farther away, back in the direction of Gemond, and the tightness in my chest lessened along with my panic. Dawn kissed the horizon, breaking over the eastern sky. The sun's rays lightened the dark of night to a beautiful rich cerulean, just enough for me to see the tiniest sliver of white flame in the distance. A moment later, my remaining fear disappeared over the horizon.

Next to me, I felt Lani relax too. She took her hand off my arm and stood, releasing the veil. Bending and twisting, she stretched and then, as she marched off, mumbled, "Drak."

Is he gone? Tyrrik asked, voice weary.

I yelped, startled by his immediate presence and got another glimpse of him sitting with his back to the stone wall, head bowed in his hands. He heaved a long sigh and lifted his face, his features ravaged with emotion.

You . . . Did you know Draedyn was here the whole time?

There is very little that frightens you to that extent, my love. I'm intimately familiar with your nightmares. And only one person possesses the power to lock you away now.

I swallowed, pushing down the lump of emotion forming at the base of my throat. He'd known but let me pretend . . .

There was nothing more I could do.

Does this mean you're coming? Part of me wanted him here, but if he showed up, did that make me a failure?

Not necessarily, he answered. *But I'll need to discuss it with the rest of the council. Please don't try and deceive me again, Ryn. Next time, I might misunderstand your fear.*

I'm sorry. I felt like the biggest hypocrite. After all my tirades on his lack of honesty, I'd done the same thing. *I just didn't want you to come here and protect me when you didn't need to. I . . . I wasn't sure you'd be able to put your instincts aside.* He had stunned me because it meant he'd been listening to my fears about our mating bond. He really loved me, I realized, staring at my hands. He was going against his instincts for me. But was I willing to? Could I go against my instincts?

It wasn't easy, trust me. But . . . I also know you can protect yourself even if the concept of you needing to do so is foreign. At least to me.

Did he have any idea what effect his words had? Here he was, changing himself for me, and I couldn't even tell the truth. *Tyrrik . . . Thank you. You have no idea what it means to hear that.*

Now, go get Lani to Phaetynville. I'll go wake up the others and let them know Draedyn is not in his lands like we'd thought.

He stood and stretched, much like Lani had done a few minutes ago, only I was way more distracted by his lack of aketon and skimpy undergarments. His promise to show me what love felt like unfurled low in my belly, a languid desire. Even away from him I couldn't escape my attraction. Actually, that Ryn seemed less reasonable now than when I'd left, which was super great. Not.

I'm leaving here in less than twenty-four hours so I can meet you outside the forest tomorrow night. He stopped mid-stretch, corded arms extended to the ceiling. His chest twitched, and I focused on the muscles. *I can't wait to see you too.*

Hot potato, what a view, but I rolled my eyes. *I never said that. And are you looking at yourself to give me a peep show?*

I felt his grin widen, and my heart tried to race its way across Gemond to him. I stood like I was making to leave, but I couldn't help stretching up as if that would allow me to get a better peek at him.

I'm going to bathe. Too bad you're not here to join me. But I can give you a peep show for that, too, if you like?

My jaw dropped.

"Ryn!"

I squealed, my attention on Tyrrik destroyed by Lani's shouting. I turned beet red as I spun toward her.

She stood two feet away, waving her arms in the air as she jumped up and down on a rock, yelling my name.

"I'd like to go," she said when she had my attention. "I've only been waiting to find my people for fifty years, but feel free to continue your conversation."

I brushed off my hands and then my butt. "Yeah, Tyrrik and I were just discussing the . . . the plan. He suggested the same."

Lani raised her eyebrows and said, "Right. Sure he did." She shook her head. "Don't insult my intelligence. You were not discussing 'the plan' unless it was a plan for what he's going to do to you when the two of you finally hook up."

I felt Tyrrik's laughter as our connection faded, and I huffed at Lani but didn't bother denying anything. What was the point? Instead, I pushed past her to our bags and guzzled a waterskin of nectar before packing everything up.

Lani said nothing as she packed her stuff and ate breakfast. "I'll be right back," she said after she finished. "I need to go to the new and improved bathroom."

Huh? It was then that I noticed the scraggly spot we'd used for our toilet last night was no longer scraggly or small.

A verdant copse of evergreens rose high into the sky. Bright purple blackberries hung heavy on thick stalks of the thorny plants. The grassy undergrowth was almost waist-high, and several bushes filled the spaces between the trees. The lush growth melted into the surrounding area, and I stared in awe at what would surely be a beacon from the sky. We were so lucky that hadn't sprouted during Draedyn's fly by.

My mouth dropped open, and as Lani marched toward the area, I pointed at the thick growth. "Did you do that?"

I was used to seeing some change in growth at the places Tyrrik, Dyter, and I had stopped at on our way to Gemond—let's just say *all* Phaetyn fluids did the trick—but nothing like this. The trees were huge, like at least thirty or more feet into the air. And those blackberries were the size of Lani's fist. "Is everything still growing? What's in your pee?"

Lani said nothing as she marched into the copse of trees and foliage. A few minutes later, she returned, stopping to pick a blackberry that, yep, was way bigger than her fist. She took a bite, and its purple juice dripped down her chin.

"Your turn," she said cheerily.

She was eating her pee blackberries. *Yuck.* "Is that because of you? Or is that because there are double powers here?" My mouth hung ajar as I scanned the bounty before me, torn between disturbed and amazed. "Holy Pancakes, I can't believe—"

Lani started with a giggle, but the small chortle quickly turned to big guffaws, too much for her frame to handle. She shook as tears streamed down her face.

"You set me up?" I asked, incredulous. "You set me up! You sent power into the ground. Jeez! I thought we had some super magical pee going on."

She was seriously twisted. But then I thought about my ginormous pumpkin. Maybe there was something wrong with the Phaetyn who had ancestral powers. Did we all get a kick out of big? Maybe we were all really competitive.

"You're sick," I said as I walked into the trees. I couldn't help the grin.

"Yeah, you too."

A few minutes later, with our bellies full of fruit, I took off with Lani on my back for the Zivost Forest.

Did you fly all day and stay up all night? Tyrrik asked, interrupting my thoughts.

What? I asked. I'd flexed my Phaetyn mojo on and off all morning, alternately talking with Tyrrik.

You're still tired. Normally, your Phaetyn side heals you, but I can feel your exhaustion. He paused a moment before continuing. *Is the barrier that difficult to hold? I thought if you had the ancestral powers, it was supposed to be easy.*

You're not telling me anything I haven't already thought. I asked Lani about it, and she said it was like a muscle. Apparently, I don't do enough Phaetyn mojo sit ups.

Tyrrik chuckled, and I sensed him sitting against the stone wall in our room.

Where are you? How much farther do you have?

Tyrrik's questions drew me away from my musings. I calculated how much time we'd flown and the number of hours Lani had said at the outset. *Another hour. Maybe two. Why?*

Just wondering. I love you, Ryn. The council is sending me to get you now that we know Draedyn is hunting you. I'll leave tomorrow at first light, and when we get back from dealing with the pointy-ears, I want to show you what love feels like.

Whhaa—? My attention snapped to my mate, and I blushed, grateful for the cloak of Drae scales, but I still had to right myself in the air.

"Stop talking to him," Lani yelled from my back.

Instead, I altered the course of our conversation slightly. *I'd like that if we ever have time to just be together. Everything gets in the way.*

You're being pulled in a lot of directions, Khosana, but you need to remember to take the time for the things that matter most and do what it takes to protect them. I want you to know you're the most important person to me. The most important thing in my life. I want to show you that too.

My stomach flipped harder than pancakes made of rocks, and I couldn't help the slow smile tugging at my lips. I was giddy and immensely grateful to have found Tyrrik—or to have been found *by* him. A deep, glowing warmth for my mate unfurled in my chest. *You're pretty al'right yourself.*

He chuckled again. *I forgot to tell you, I found the most beautiful vein of lapis lazuli yesterday with Zakai's men. I had them pull a piece out so I could polish it for you tomorrow.*

I forced my emotional attention to my mate while keeping both eyes on the sky. *You know . . . you never told me how big your hoard of treasure is. And where you keep it. Is it in your lair in Verald?*

Our hoard, he corrected. *And I promise no Drae has ever had one as big.*

My heart sputtered, and I dipped in the air again. I couldn't help the satisfaction that pulsed through me with that bit of information. *Where is it?*

I won't tell you where. I want to show it to you. He laughed, and the emotion pulsed to me through the bond. *It's a package deal, Ryn, me and my treasure. But I'll tell you this; you could hide in the mound of treasure, in your Drae form, and be completely covered.*

My mouth dropped, and I plunged downward.

"Stop doing that," Lani shouted, pounding me with her fists.

7

By the time the sun was a quarter of the way through the sky, I landed in the familiar clearing outside of the Zivost forest. I took a deep breath as I surveyed the rock spikes I knew were covered in Phaetyn blood. The early morning sun bathed the rocky valley in golden light, and it seemed like an omen of the golden barrier that would soon follow.

I jolted as the stone spikes surrounding Zivost shifted. The ground seemed to liquify as the jutting rocks sunk into the dirt, disappearing from view.

"Ryn," Kamoi yelled, waving at me from the other side, just outside the tree line. His face was alight with excitement, and he grinned when our gazes locked.

Other Phaetyn were there with the prince, but I couldn't spot Kamini. The group edged farther out of the trees, their eager expressions filled with hope as they looked to the young woman with me.

Yikes. I still hadn't told the queen the name of her kingdom. "Uh, Lani? Remember how I called this place Phaetynville?"

She didn't deign to look my way, her gaze riveted on her people. "I know it's not called Phaetynville."

I sagged with relief. "Who told you?"

"Dyter," she whispered, her attention still on the dozens of Phaetyn before her.

Of course he did. I studied Lani's face, empathy for the Phaetyn queen spreading through my chest. I would never truly understand how she felt seeing her people for the first time, knowing that she wasn't alone anymore. I'd felt some awe the first time I'd been here, too, but at that point I'd known what I was for three months, not fifty years. I'd had my mum and Arnik and Dyter before that. What I'd felt must be a mere shadow of what Lani was going through right now.

I took Lani's hand and squeezed it tight before tugging her toward the forest.

The crowd surged as we did so, and Kamoi raced out, his lavender eyes bright with joy. He didn't slow as we met in the middle but crashed into me and crushed my body to his. Drak, he was excited. I froze as he stroked my hair, and then he lowered his face.

"Whoa—" I said, pulling back before he could kiss me. Hot indignation pulsed through me, and I raised my hand to slap his face.

Only I didn't. I couldn't. I needed the Phaetyn to accept Lani, and if I pissed them off now, I might ruin that.

What just happened? Tyrrik asked, confusion lacing his voice. *Are you okay?*

La la la. I forced myself to clear my mind before I showed or told Tyrrik anything. I thought of Mum's lavender syrup on sweet potato pancakes, Dyter throwing wet dish rags at me late at night while cleaning up The Crane's Nest, Arnik giving me a birthday present of an entire cluster of grapes—

That's not helping me feel better, Tyrrik growled after the last image. *Something happened; I can feel it, Ryn. I thought we'd discussed this.*

Right, we had. I deflated. *I'm safe. Kamoi's an ass.*

Tyrrik snorted. *Tell me something I don't know.*

I cringed, but I needed to be present right now, not conversing with Tyrrik. *Later. I'll tell you later.*

"Don't ever do that again," I snapped in a low voice at the Phaetyn prince, plastering a smile on my face for the benefit of those watching. I narrowed my eyes as I patted his face in what I hoped could be interpreted as a kind gesture to the Phaetyn around us but was definitely as hard as I dared with the watching crowd. I trusted the fake-smile and glare would communicate with him just how upset I was.

"I—"

"Ever," I said and then stepped to the side, still smiling as I glanced over our audience. Still no Kamini.

"Where's Princess Kamini?" I asked.

His smile faltered for a moment as he looked at Lani for the first time. "She's at her castle."

"We need to speak with her." I pointed at Lani and said, "Guess who I found."

THE UNEASE KAMOI'S greeting caused faded during the traipse through the forest into the center. The energy of Zivost filled me, and I smiled, reveling in the successful return of the Phaetyn queen. But when we followed the path to the Rose Castle I'd demolished not too long ago, we found it wasn't destroyed any longer. I studied the entrance of the newly erected rose quartz house, thinking *castle* definitely may be a better term. Though still under the tree line, the castle possessed at least two towers I could see.

Alani's ash tree was gone, and a huge courtyard spanned the meadow where the civil war had taken place, a tiered fountain splashing where the queen's tree had been. Kamini certainly hadn't held back. Nice to see she'd been focusing on the essentials of keeping Phaetynville safe. I shook my head.

"Ryn," Lani said low in my ear. "Are you okay?"

Was I al'right? Last time I was here I'd squished the queen and killed the king. *Last time*, I'd felt threatened from the get go, like a rope tugged between two opponents. I'd set out from Verald hoping to find answers

47

and a balm to my aching heart, and the Phaetyn here certainly hadn't delivered. But much had changed since that time. Alani and Kaelan were dead and gone for one, and I'd only seen the people smiling on my way in. I liked Kamini—even Kamoi when he wasn't being a freakin' prat. I took a deep breath and *tried* not to jump to conclusions.

"I'm fine," I said. "Just some lingering juju." *I hope.*

Juju, Lani mouthed, but she didn't bother asking aloud. She squared her shoulders and glided, appearing to float over the grass, to join Kamoi, who waited in the entrance of the Rose Castle.

I trusted Lani; that's why I was here. Despite what had happened with the previous Phaetyn queen and king, the power within the forest and the people had to be saved, for their good and the good of the empire. Their healing powers would be invaluable in a war, but if we won, Draeconia would still be a land leeched of its ability to grow. We needed the Phaetyn to beat my father and ensure the fight wasn't for nothing.

"You are a scary Drae with long teeth and pointy-eared mojo," I said under my breath. Nothing like a pep talk to calm the nerves. "You can do this."

I strode over to join the others, noting the way Kamoi was staring at me like I was a juicy peach and he was starving. If he didn't stop, I was going to burn his stew. In a sharp voice, I reminded him, "We're here to talk with Kamini. Stop being a tool."

His violet-eyed gaze flew to mine, his mouth curving in a wry half-smile. "Sorry, I can't help it. I've always been captivated by you."

If he continued, pretty soon I wouldn't be able to help shoving my foot up his butt.

Lani rested a hand on his forearm, and Kamoi jolted. His gaze dropped to where her hand was, and he furrowed his brow.

"It is imperative I speak with you and Kamini," Lani said to him. When he looked up, her gaze didn't waver, and her tone remained firm and commanding. "We must protect the people and the forest as our first priority. There is much happening in the world outside, and the Phaetyn cannot hide from it." Her features softened slightly, and she added, "And then I hope to start making up for all the time I lost with you and Kamini."

A small smile spread over the prince's face. He took Lani's hand in both of his and turned on the full intensity of his charm. "I would like nothing more."

My shoulders relaxed somewhat. Tyrrik had never liked the prince—though I suspected jealousy was a big factor. Even so, I couldn't dismiss the unsettled vibe I got or the way Kamoi wouldn't respect my boundaries. He seemed overly used to his position as prince, too used to getting what he wanted. Out of him and Kamini, I'd been least sure of his response to Lani's arrival, so his enthusiasm was a relief.

Probably more lingering juju.

I kept up with the others through the quartz passages, glancing side to side as we passed the open double doors of a ballroom, four sitting areas, and what *appeared* to be an inside waterfall . . . *not superfluous or ostentatious whatsoever.*

Kamoi broke off conversation with Lani when we reached a heavy door with a tangled vine carved into the rich wood. Before he could knock, the door was wrenched open.

A slightly younger appearing version of Lani stood in the entrance, dressed in silver robes with only a plain crown to mark her as leader of the Phaetyn.

Kamini's mouth dropped open, and her eyes widened. Together, the two looked really similar, but little differences, like the shape of their nose and the way Kamini's face was filled out, made them unique, too.

Lani's face lit up with joy I'd never seen.

The younger Phaetyn stared for a long moment and whispered, "Sister?"

I stepped back as the surrounding area seemed to hold its breath. A lump rose in my throat as Lani stepped forward and clasped her sister's forearms.

"Kamini," Lani answered, her voice breaking on her sibling's name. "I'm Lani"—she tilted her head back in my direction—"Ryn found me."

The prince was currently lost for words, so I cleared my throat and said, "Princess Kamini, this is your sister, Lani. She—"

"Queen Kamini," Kamoi said in a strangled voice.

The words settled like a heavy blanket, a heavy, *itchy, uncomfortable* blanket. Lani glanced at me, eyes wide. Kamini opened her mouth to speak, but nothing came out. Kamoi's slack expression made it clear he was reeling although how he could be so stupid to make such a comment was beyond me. He'd asked I find her in the first place. Regardless, I'd come too far to remain silent. I was grumpy without Tyrrik, and we had no time to mince words. I'd been embroiled in their stupid war once; I was not dealing with more Phaetyn lunacy. Success didn't include this horseplop.

"Yes, she *was*." I smiled at Kamini in the way a panther might smile at a chicken. "Kamini, you stepped up when the Phaetyn needed you, and I'm not lessening the magnitude of that. I'm sure the Phaetyn are grateful and all"—she held her hands up in surrender, and I rounded on Kamoi for my attack—"but I believe it was *you* who said leadership is passed to the female with ancestral powers. You asked me to stay because I had them, and you were the one who encouraged me to find Lani. And now, here she is with the ancestral powers you need."

Kamoi's brows lowered, and I raised a finger.

"Don't waste my time, Prince Kamoi." I glanced at the princess and nearly-queen. "We don't have the luxury to waste time."

Kamini nodded frantically though her gaze slid to check on her cousin in a way that told me she didn't want to hurt his feelings.

Lani stepped back, chin raised. "I have come to cloak the Zivost Forest once more so our people are safe."

"*Our people,*" the prince muttered, his expression dark.

"Kamoi," I said, my voice dangerously low. "My ears may not be pointy, but I can hear just fine, even better than a Phaetyn in case you've forgotten." The smile I offered when he met my gaze was hard. "I owe you a debt for saving my life the last time I was here, but I won't let you insult your future queen. You have *no idea* what she's been through or how she's longed to find her people," I snapped, my fangs elongating with my heightened emotion. "Pull your freakin' head out of your butt, or I'll do it for you."

Khosana? Tyrrik's voice reached into my mind.

I kept my gaze fixed on Kamoi, my jaw set while mentally answering my mate. *Just laying down the law.*

Good for you, love.

My lips twitched, and if I had to venture a guess from the way the prince paled, I'd say the gesture looked borderline psychotic. *I'm on a roll.*

I felt Tyrrik chuckle but kept my attention on the Phaetyn prince.

He held my gaze, nevertheless, his shoulders suddenly sagged, and he dropped his eyes. The prince turned and bowed to Lani. "I apologize most sincerely, Lani. The last few weeks has us all on edge, and I'm afraid stress got the better of me. Please don't feel unwelcome here. Both Kamini and I are overjoyed with your return home." He flashed her an apologetic smile I was all too familiar with. "Even if I'm doing a poor job of showing it."

Kudos to Lani; she didn't ease up for a second.

"Hmm," she said, observing him through narrowed eyes. "Your apology is accepted, cousin. However, considering your stress levels may impede the coming discussions, perhaps the next hours are better served resting while Kamini and I decide what is to be done."

Her voice was laced with steel, and Kamoi looked like he'd dropped his plate of syrup-covered honey cakes.

Don't laugh in Kamoi's face. Don't laugh in his face. A small, wheezing noise escaped my lips, but I kept my expression smooth as I covered my mouth and cleared my throat.

The prince glanced at Kamini, but the younger Phaetyn only had eyes for her sister. He bowed again, back stiff, and his tone was flat when he replied. "Of course. You are very wise, cousin. I will take this opportunity to rest."

I withheld my snort. *Tyrrik*, I thought. *Lani totally gave Kamoi a verbal beatdown.*

Good. About time. If you want to slice his head off, I wouldn't be opposed.

Not a fan of the Phaetyn prince. Nothing surprising there, and funnily enough, I was siding more and more with my mate. An image flashed through our bond, a Drae-eyed view of the Gemond mountains, and I smiled, realizing Tyrrik was on his way. *Where are you?*

Only a few hours from Gemond.

Fly safe. Remember—

Remember the emperor was around last night? he asked, amusement floating through our connection. *Funny enough, that completely slipped my mind.*

I sniffed. *Sarcasm is very unbecoming.*

I find it sexy.

Umm . . . A thread of heat shot through me, and my mind blanked.

Why did your heart rate just increase? Why is your body warmer?

I'm . . . running. Holy Drae-babies, he could sense my reaction to him from a bajillion miles away?

Yes, I know, he said with a growl. *You're running from me. But I will catch you eventually. You're mine, mate.*

The deep rumble of his thought radiated through me, and I caught a glimpse of the two of us locked in an embrace. Was that a daydream?

"Uh . . . Ryn?" Lani shook my arm.

I squeaked, face flaming. "Yes?" I pulled my thoughts back to the Phaetyn in front of me, blinking as I noticed only Lani remained. "How can I help you?"

8

Kamini pulled together two upholstered chairs inside the large conference room in the Rose Castle. A glance over Lani's head told me the room held a huge desk, several chairs, and what appeared to be a trickling stream to the right of an ash bar with small wine glasses set out across its top to the left.

Lani lowered her voice and jerked her head toward the doorway. "Are you coming in with me?"

"Come in with you," I repeated, thickly. The lingering haze of my discussion with Tyrrik burned away, and I shook my head. "Right, Uh . . ." I wasn't going to be there to hold Lani's hand forever, and really, she didn't *need* me to. The gal was fifty, and now that Kamoi was gone, I'd lost the urgency for moral support. Lani and I were on the same page. Kamini was plenty smart, and honestly, I was hungry for something more than dried meat and day-old bread.

"No," I said, reaching forward to squeeze her hand. I gave her a smile I hoped would be encouraging and added, "I trust you. Kamini's smart, but you're smarter, and you've got the perspective to make wise decisions. You'll do great."

Her face softened, and her mouth curved when my stomach growled. She arched a brow and laughed. "You're going to eat, aren't you?"

"Well, yes. I plan to partake in a bite or three. But I still trust you." My stomach rumbled again because I really was hungry.

Lani's laughter faded, and she stepped toward the doorway, heading after Kamini, but the Phaetyn queen turned back on the threshold, violet eyes shining. "Thank you for sticking up for me with Kamoi."

I winked at her. "That's what friends do."

"JUST A BITE OR TWO?" someone asked from above.

I recognized Lani's voice and didn't bother to open my eyes. The heat filtering through the trees combined with a slight breeze had me at the perfect snoozing temperature. The pale-green leaves of Queen Luna's elm tree shaded my eyes, and the sweet smell of honeysuckle surrounded me. "What do you mean?"

"I mean you're cradling your stomach like you're pregnant."

So I'd eaten more than a bite. The Phaetyn had chocolate, and I might've dipped fruit into the concoction for the better part of an hour. "I'm recovering my strength," I lied, opening my eyes now that my peace was ruined. I sighed and looked at my Phaetyn friend. "Drae tend to eat a lot after flights."

Lani raised her eyebrows, letting me know she wasn't convinced, and then her gaze went to the tree trunk behind me. "This was my mother's tree."

"Yep." I gazed up at the shriveled leaves. "It's seen better days. When I was here last time, it was green and vibrant."

"What happened?"

"With the tree?" I asked and then shook my head. "I have no idea."

The Phaetyn stared at it, and I recalled the deep pull I'd had to touch Luna's elm when I first saw it. A hint of fear entered Lani's eyes, and she tore her gaze away, giving me her full attention again.

"You should touch it and find out." I studied her as I reached back overhead to pat the thick bark. Was she scared of what she'd find if she touched it? Her memories of her mother had to be dim; she should be clamoring to touch the tree. But Lani and I hadn't really talked about Luna much. Maybe there was a reason. Or was she feeling nervous about the results of her talk with Kamini? "So . . ." I said, breaking the awkward silence. "What's the verdict?"

Her face brightened, and the tightness in my chest loosened.

"Tonight, I'll be crowned Queen, and I'll put the Veil back up." She flashed me a smile, her pulse feathering. "They're already setting the tables up for the feast."

I continued to hold my stomach with one hand, propping myself up on an elbow. "You nervous?"

"If a tree falls and no one hears it, does it make a sound?"

"Um . . . I'm not sure what—"

"Yes," she interrupted. "Yes, I'm nervous. Not about the barrier so much. It might require all my strength and focus to get it in place, but I know I can do that."

"You're worried they won't accept you?" I asked softly.

The fifty-year-old child swallowed. I'd seriously never get past that. "Lani," I said. "You're funny and clever and strong. You've hidden from the emperor your entire life while helping people outside the forest. There's no way these people won't see what I see. And guess what?" I asked, a growl entering my voice. "You're not really here to be liked; you're here to save them from the emperor. If they know what's good for them, they'll follow you into his lair ten times over."

Lani tipped her head back and sighed. "You're right. I know you're right, but I do want them to like me too." She shrugged, looking very much like an insecure fifteen-year-old. "So, I have a few last minute jitters."

I stood, my stomach emitting a groan. "That was my stomach. I swear. And you have zero need for jitters. I'd tell you if you did. Plus," I said, "I'll be there to have your back. If you want me to shift and scare the turd-twats, just tell me, and I'm on it."

She eyed my middle. "Will I need to roll you in?"

"I *told* you it's a Drae thing. You think I wanted to eat so much?

No, but I can't deny the call of my instincts can I?" Hypocritical, considering I was attempting to do just that.

The Phaetyn choked on her laugh. "No, Ryn. Don't ever do that."

"I won't," I said, dusting the leafy debris from my butt. "Now, come here and touch your mother's tree."

Her eyes widened as I reached for her, and she stepped back.

"You'll feel better for it," I continued, waving her to me.

Lani raised her hands, warding me off. "It's not that I don't want to. It's that I . . ."

I quirked my brows, totally not buying it. She was as scared as a scaredy thing in Scaredyville. "Yes?"

Her shoulders sagged. "I have an image in my head of what my mother was like. What if I've made her more than she was?"

She didn't want to be disappointed. I closed my eyes, thinking of my mother. She'd almost seemed to dance when cooking or ladling my Phaetyn water into containers, and she was always smiling. I remembered how her brown eyes gained an amber glint whenever she teased me. She'd loved me so much she sacrificed everything for me. From what I knew about Luna, she was just as kind and loving. "You don't have to look, Lani. But speaking for myself, I'd give almost anything to have a tree that could help me see my mother again." I blinked back the burning in my eyes and continued hoarsely, "And I've seen your mother. There's no way you'll be disappointed. She was a beautiful . . . amazing person."

Lani searched my face, her chest rising and falling in rapid succession until she took a deep breath. "You're right. The tree is a gift."

I nodded, unable to say anything else without crying, probably even ugly-bawling. As Lani approached the tree, I turned to leave.

"Ryn?" she called before I could get more than a few steps.

I paused, still fighting the emotion clogging my throat and blurring my vision.

"Could you stay?"

I nodded again and took a seat once more. The silence lulled me, and after blinking away my tears, I reached out. *Tyrrik?*

Mate.

Where are you? The urge to see him was making me nauseous—though that could also have been the fifth peach I ate.

I'll be stopping in another hour. Nearly halfway to you.

Hurry, I sighed, rubbing my chest. The tightness had lessened but not resolved. Not all of the pressure around my heart was related to the tension here in Zivost.

His dark amusement pushed through our bond. *You miss me.*

Did I miss him? *If a tree falls in the woods and no one hears it, does it make a sound?*

Yes. But I wasn't asking. I know you miss me.

I frowned. How come he knew the answer? And how could he be so confident? I sighed because I realized I didn't care. He could be confident that I missed him; we weren't being coy. *Right. Well, I know you miss me too.*

I can't wait to have you back in my arms, he confessed.

I bent my head forward so my hair covered my wide smile from anyone passing by. *I can't wait to be back in them.* Taking a breath, I focused on the bursting sensation in my chest, the huge knot there from missing Tyrrik, and pushed the overwhelming emotion through our bond.

Tyrrik's possessive growl ricocheted back in reply. *Now I really can't wait.*

A thud sounded behind me, and I glanced back to see Lani on her knees, her forehead pressed against the tree. That was about the reaction I'd had a month ago. Watching the Phaetyn have her emotional crisis reminded me of the talk I'd had with her on the journey here. Tyrrik would arrive late tomorrow, and not to be Avoidance-Agatha, but I wanted to start this particular conversation without him physically near.

I projected my next thought, *Should we talk about sex?*

Tyrrik stopped flying.

His complete and utter shock hit me like a slap. I recovered first and shot to my feet. *Flap your wings, Tyrrik!*

He wrenched out of his free fall, but his mind was still a reeling buzz.

My heart beat pounded in my ears, and I wasn't sure what else to say now.

You want to talk . . . dirty? he asked hesitantly. *Are you ready for that?*

Oh. My. Moons. That was not what I'd meant. I covered my face, squeezing my eyes shut.

No, I mean talk about it. Like about, I searched for a term from Lani's speech, *about the . . .* I couldn't remember any of her speech. I frowned as I mentally studied him. *Are you flying harder now?* He totally was.

He ignored my last question. *There are no expectations, Khosana. There is just me and you and hopefully a lot of time to explore each other.*

Well *that* made my heart want to burst into a million happy pieces. I took a deep breath and mentally blurted, *What I'm saying is I'd like to have sex with you at some point when all this is over.* I gripped the sides of my face as he plummeted again, only this time he corrected himself before I could say anything. *Mistress Moons, you're giving me a heart attack.*

The feeling is mutual, he shot back.

I closed my eyes and let my energy flow to him through our bond, feeling his uncertainty and concern flow back to me.

After a moment, he asked, *How long have you wanted this?*

I frowned. Tyrrik's pure masculinity and raw sex appeal was undisputable. I'd always wanted to touch his body, but would I have ever acted on that without understanding my feelings? No. Not unless Dyter's brew was involved. *I don't know. When did I first meet you?*

He laughed. *Again, the feeling is mutual, but then why have you been running?*

There was no accusation in his voice, which was probably why I didn't feel defensive. I had been running from him and *us*. From what my body told me I should do. However, being away from him wasn't better or easier. It kinda sucked.

His next words came through our bond just over a whisper. *Is it because I'm both older and more . . . experienced?*

A snarl tore from my lips, and I snapped my fangs. A group of Phaetyn passing by screamed and ran off.

Ryn? Are you al'right?

Drak. I blinked in the wake of my intense reaction. Where had that come from? Was that . . . jealousy over Tyrrik's past. Wave after possessive wave pulsed through me, and I reeled from the intensity. I did not want to become like that crazy girl in my cell, losing who I was because of my feelings for Tyrrik. *Uh, is it normal to be . . . possessive?*

I wasn't sure how much of my freakiness I wanted to share with him. At least not yet.

You don't need to explain, love. I struggle with that too. Often.

I let out a shaking breath. *How often?*

Right now, when Kamoi is probably panting after you? Every second. I'd like nothing more than to shove him over one of those jagged rocks, right through the spleen.

My brows lifted, but considering my reaction only a moment ago, I'd say that was pretty close to how I felt. *That's . . . pretty violent.*

Mates fight for each other. Our bond is the most valued relationship we could ever have; in truth, you complete me.

My fears melted away with his words. I tucked my silver hair behind my ear. *That's why you have me.* I stilled as the truth resonated through me.

Yes, my mate, he said in a whisper. *That is why I have you.*

"Are you serious? Ryn!" Lani shouted in my ear.

I jerked back to the present, arms flailing as I clutched my ear. Spinning to her, I grumbled, "What?"

"You'll see him tomorrow," she huffed, crossing her arms over her chest.

"I know, and ouch," I complained, rubbing my ear. Then I remembered what she'd been doing. *Talk later,* I shot at Tyrrik.

I'll wait for you, he purred.

9

"*A*l'right, I'm yours. So?" I nudged Lani. "How'd you do?"

The Phaetyn peered up at the elm tree, and I followed her gaze.

"Holy pancakes," I exclaimed. The sickly green color of the elm tree's leaves had morphed into a vibrant grasshopper green. The deep rivets in the gray-brown bark were filled out, and the trunk had swelled to half again its size. I blew a breath out. "You give it a little juice?"

Lani pursed her lips. "I couldn't help it. The tree is mine now. It's the ancestral tree."

The rich warmth in her voice had my heart expanding, and I understood the implication—it could've been my tree had I stayed. Maybe that's why the leaves had shriveled after I left. "I'm so glad for you. And Queen Luna?"

"You were right," she answered. "My mother was a beautiful person. I hope to achieve half as much as she did in my time."

We stared up at the tree. No matter what my reservations regarding the Phaetyn had been, looking at the elm tree, I was certain that with Lani's guidance, they would find their way. And whatever doubts she'd had about her capabilities, it appeared as though a trip down memory lane had refocused her determination.

I grimaced, rubbing my stomach. No one should be allowed to eat that many strawberries dipped in chocolate or that many peaches. "I'm going to go lie down. I think veiling for so long made me sick."

Lani snorted. "I'm sure that's what caused it. But no. There'll be no lying down until I'm done with you. I've taught you to focus your energy and how to veil, but our time is limited, and I still have a few more things I need to show you."

"I thought the rest of the Phaetyn mojo was instinctual," I countered. "I'll just pick it up as I go."

"You don't want to get a jump start on ancestral tricks it took me fifty years to figure out?"

The Phaetyn queen could negotiate; I'd give her that, so I hedged. "What kind of tricks?"

"How about I show you how to spear Druman with roots?"

I promptly forgot my aching stomach and leaned toward Lani. "Where do I start?"

I SPENT the rest of the afternoon with Lani. During my last trip to Phaetynville, I'd noticed a golden path, and apparently the path led to Queen Luna's castle. Or so Lani was telling me after her mother-tree encounter—no, *queen* tree.

I followed the lustrous path beside her, and we eventually stopped in front of Luna's empty home. *Home* was an understatement. Different than the Rose Castle, Luna's abode was ginormous, and the milky green stone slabs it was constructed from contrasted with beautiful gold inlays.

Good thing Tyrrik had a hoard of treasure for me. Us . . . I meant *us*. "What kind of stone is that?" I asked as we approached the steps to go inside. "It looks smooth, almost buttery."

Three steps led to a raised courtyard of the milky green stone. Leaves were grouped on the ground in bunches, indicating someone had maintained the massive space. A knee-high wall of the same rock bordered the square, and on the other side of the raised patio was the entrance to the castle—massive dark wood doors, each at least six feet wide and fifteen feet tall. The double doors appeared to be the only entrance into the structure although there were dozens of windows facing the clearing. The castle was at least as big as Caltevyn's in Verald.

Lani snorted in response to my question. "If you chip off any of the jade, I'll find a way to take your favorite gold trinket," she said as she stepped off the path toward her mother's house. "In fact, I'll find a way to take away a dozen of them."

I don't have a dozen. Yet. I narrowed my eyes at the Phaetyn queen. "You do realize threatening a Drae about their treasure is akin to . . ." *threatening their first born.* I couldn't say that to her, not after how rough things had been for her growing up. I cleared my throat and said, "You shouldn't do it. It's really bad."

"And you shouldn't steal from the Phaetyn queen." Lani threw the words over her shoulder as she bounced up the steps, never taking her gaze from the castle.

I rolled my eyes and hurried to catch up to her. "Don't be so dramatic. And you're not queen for another few hours."

The leaves crunched underfoot as we walked, and the air smelled of earth and mulch. With the sun filtering through the treetops, the creamy green stone was darkened in patches by the shadows of the trees, giving the walls a mottled appearance.

Lani went straight to the door, stopping to grab the trunk of the topiary tree to the left. With both hands, she pulled the entire plant out of its pot and dropped it with a grunt.

"What the—"

She bent over the now empty pot and a moment later emerged brushing the dirt off a key. Two strands of green stone looped around each other, the loops constricting at intervals to form the right cuts for the door before tapering into the tip. I narrowed my eyes and asked, "Did your mom's tree show you that key?"

"Partly," Lani said. She slid the key into the lock, and with a heavy groan, the door swung open. The smell of stale air exhaled through the now open orifice, and the Phaetyn glanced my way with a nervous smile. "Will you come in with me?"

I shifted my weight, but there wasn't really anything to consider. I was dying of curiosity. "Of course. I'll totally protect you although I can't imagine there's anything in your mother's home that could harm you."

She gave me a withering glare. "I'm not afraid of physical pain, Ryn."

Right. There were worse things than physical pain for sure. "If you want," I said with a wink as I led us into the house, "I'll hold your hand."

Filtered light illuminated the foyer. From the ceiling hung a glittering chandelier, the large drops of crystal sparkling and casting rainbows onto the surrounding stone walls. On the top of a large, gray wooden table sat a dried floral arrangement, bigger than me, as tall as it was wide. But the dry, brittle foliage was leached of color.

Behind the dead flowers, a floating staircase led up to a landing from which hallways branched off into darkness.

"What did the tree show you, Lani?" I whispered. The air was not only stagnant but weighted as if whatever happened within the walls was burdened with sorrow.

The frown she wore echoed my own emotion. I'd never really thought about how Luna's life might've been, but if this oppressive ache was any indication . . . her life had sucked. I wiped my finger over the gray wood table, revealing a glossy, rich brown the color of chocolate under the thick layer of dust. There was beauty here, hidden and waiting for someone to clean off the betrayals of the past so it could be appreciated once more.

Lani cleared her throat, drawing my attention back to her. She stood at the foot of the staircase. "I need to go to her rooms. She has a special crown, and I need it for tonight."

We reached the landing, and I couldn't help turning to take in the haunting allure of the castle. The walls here were carved with intricate scenes of the Phaetyn and their trees. A woman resembling Lani laughed as she danced under a leafy canopy, a sliver of moon carved into the sky. The obvious joy Luna had was displayed here. As I peered at the painting, I recognized echoes of my mother's life and the easing pain of my own experiences. Weeeird.

Lani shook her head. "I'd like to spend a few days here and explore the castle as it deserves. But we have a feast to get ready for."

I looked at the memories etched into stone, pieces of Luna's life immortalized, and nodded. "I don't blame you. This is awesome. Weird but awesome."

Lani led the way through the castle. Her sure step made it obvious she'd been here in her head. A few minutes later, she opened the doors to a sitting room three times the size of my house in Verald.

She wound past the couches and cushioned chairs, past the table set for dinner, and into a bedroom. The canopied bed was draped in rich velvet and sheer organza, but Lani bypassed it and headed for a small paneled closet. Lani went straight to the wall covered with painted slats and, before I could ask, inserted the same looped key into a rivet in the wood undetectable to the naked eye.

Holy Phaetyn sneakiness.

Lani pulled the invisible door open, and I peered over her shoulder into the black space within.

"What else is in there?" The space was way too big for just a crown, and obviously, whatever was there had to be super important. Or powerful. Or both.

"It's dark in there," she said, stating the obvious.

I chuckled and stepped around her. "But I can see in the dark," I said, crouching to look her in the eyes. "Just tell me what I need to get."

She narrowed her eyes and studied me a moment before answering. "A wooden box about this big with rounded edges and a distinct grain"—she held her hands about two feet apart—"sealed with a golden lock."

I winked and turned toward what I could guess was Luna's treasure trove. Or the Phaetyn semblance of one. I doubted it would be as good as mine once I put some serious time into my collection.

I stepped into the space and blinked, letting my eyes shift and adjust.

Whoa!

I blinked again, and a slow grin spread across my face. Queen Luna was definitely my kind of Phaetyn. The closet was narrow and a dozen feet long, just wide enough for one person to maneuver through. Her obsession with shiny and sparkly rivaled a Drae; I was certain because it rivaled mine. Thin rods of gold were draped with necklaces and bracelets, and black velvet lined the shelves of brooches, rings, and earrings. There were crowns, *plural*, on more shelves, again lined in the rich black fabric. Contrary to what Lani had said earlier today, I could fight my instincts. I wouldn't touch the gems and jewelry hanging in this closet even though they were practically begging for attention.

There were no drawers here, and on the bottom shelf, only one box sat tucked in the corner. I grabbed the small chest and fought a second urge to pilfer . . . a little token. My expression must've given away my longing because when I stepped out of the closet, Lani's worried expression evaporated, and she laughed.

"You really didn't take anything?" she asked. "There's a lot of—"

I strode right past her and into the bedroom, setting the box on the bed. "I know. But I don't want you to steal from me, so I didn't, al'right?"

"You could've taken something. My mother wouldn't have cared. Those were just things she got from people in Gemond." She giggled. "Trinkets to say thanks when she helped them."

"Ryn?" Kamini's voice echoed from another area of the castle. "Lani?"

Lani scooted the box off the bed.

I grabbed a pillow and smacked her hard enough that she grunted. With a smile of satisfaction, I ran out of the room. I didn't need another trinket. Tyrrik had me covered.

"Kamini?" I called, racing down the stairs. It was gross how dusty everything was, not that there was anyone to blame. No one could've gotten into Luna's castle without the key, and the sneaky Phaetyn queen hid it well.

The Phaetyn princess emerged from a hallway as I leaped the last five steps and landed in a crouch.

"Hey." She smiled brightly. "Where's Lani—"

"Kamini!" Lani grinned at her sister. "You were right."

The pair started talking over the top of each other, laughing as they chattered about finding the key. I tuned out as their talk moved to ancestral powers and coronation.

"We need to get ready. You too, Ryn," Kamini said.

I tuned back, quirking a brow at her wicked grin.

"Kamoi is going to lose it when he sees you all dressed up again," she said.

I scrunched my nose and walked over to her, waiting while Lani locked the door. "I wish he wouldn't," I grumbled. "I'm perfectly happy with my mate."

Kamini blinked, and her smile softened. "Don't tell Kamoi, but I'm glad to hear that. If you bonded with Kamoi, it wouldn't be good for *Kanahele o keola* to have two with ancestral powers here. At least not until all of the Phaetyn are united."

I nodded at her wisdom, my mind replacing Phaetynville for the name of their city. It kind of sounded like can-a-he-lay oh something-something. I wasn't going to be staying here any longer than I had to, and beyond my urge to make this empire safe for all races, I had no interest in Phaetynville . . . except for Lani and Kamini.

While I didn't belong here, I did want to know this side of my power, and I was certain there was more I could learn from Lani. I wouldn't hesitate to visit my friends in the future if everything somehow worked out, so I needed to learn the right name. "Would you say that again? *Kanahele . . .*"

Lani snickered and repeated the name.

Can-a-he-lay oh key-oh-la. "*Kanahele o keola*. Right. Got it."

The festive scene was reminiscent of the night Kamoi's father tried to kill me. However, the feel in the courtyard clearing in front of the newly constructed Rose Castle was as different as night and day. I sat in the same seat, next to Kamoi *again*, but this time, on my other side, Lani sat in the middle with her sister.

And everything felt . . . right. There was no division, no glaring, no secret plans for mass murder. The trees hummed in the forest, and a glorious chocolate fountain was waiting for me to dunk strawberries in its rich goodness. I smiled, filled with joy. The Phaetyn were healed at last. Of course, my joy could be due to the fact I now knew how to shoot roots from the ground to spear my enemies. So far, just the ones who remained stationary, but I'd work on the speed until I got it just right.

I looked at Lani and Kamini, both dressed like me in a silver-and-green corset with a flowy skirt of panels shaped like leaves. Kamini still wore her plain crown of silver leaves, but next to her sat the box I'd pulled out of the Jade Castle, which held the golden crown Luna wore when she ruled *Kanahele o keola*. Yeah, I totally had that name memorized.

"You look stunning," Kamoi said, leaning toward me, offering a smile with his compliment.

How had I ever thought he was good looking? So strange. Last-month-Ryn must've been running hard because when Today-Ryn compared Tyrrik with Kamoi, there was no contest. Like, zero.

"Will you dance with me tonight?" he pressed, resting his hand on mine.

I was trying to be nice, but he wasn't making it easy. "No," I replied with a tight smile. When his face fell, I added, "I'm just barely feeling better after shielding here from Gemond, and I have to fly back tomorrow."

I glanced at the prince and saw his gaze heat as it dropped to my torso.

"I'm up here," I said, calling him out. "This is your last warning to stop gaping at me like I'm a piece of ripe fruit."

He swallowed and met my eyes with a blush and low chuckle. "I apologize." He laughed again and added, "For the thousandth time. I understand how you feel, and I can respect your boundaries. Your mate is a lucky . . . man."

Whatever, I'd heard him apologize so many times the words were meaningless from his lips. "Listen, I'm sure you'll have your pick from the Phaetyn. I wish you a happy life. But that's not with me. I love Tyrrik."

"I understand, and I'll do my best to make sure I stop making you uncomfortable." He scooted his chair back and stood. "Excuse me one moment."

"Of course." This time my smile was mostly sincere. I glanced down at my now-empty plate smeared with chocolate and fruit juice and wondered who had eaten all my food. I turned to Lani to ask if she'd sneaked some, but she had three empty plates in front of her. I'd really eaten everything already?

I glanced over the other Phaetyn and saw Kamoi at the chocolate fountain. He had two plates laden with berries and cake and was pouring chocolate into a bowl. I could make nice, and I was hungry. I leaned over to Lani and asked, "How much longer?"

She said something else to Kamini before facing me. "A few minutes," Lani replied, glancing at the sky. "The sun is about to set, and I think we'll all feel more comfortable if the barrier is in place before darkness falls."

The barrier should've gone up as soon as we got here, in my humble opinion.

"I'm going to grab a little more—"

Kamoi returned with his food and surprised me by setting one plate in front of Lani and one in front of me. "A peace offering. I've been an idiot today."

I was already facing Lani and Kamini which was the only reason I saw the younger sister's face fall. I stood and smiled at Kamoi. "Thanks, but I think Kamini should have this one." I pushed the plate at her, and when she opened her mouth to protest, I added, "That's a Phaetyn-size portion. I need a Drae-size portion."

Kamini and Lani laughed, Kamoi joining in a fraction of a second later. I excused myself, grabbing an empty platter from the middle to fill so I wouldn't have to get up again.

While I was busy loading up the plate with all the delectables to eat, I noticed Kamoi filling three tall glasses of lavender lemonade. "Hey Kamoi," I hollered. "Will you please get me a glass?"

He grinned boyishly. "Already got you covered."

Mistress Moons, this was going way better than I had anticipated. My lingering juju was clearly unfounded.

I returned to the table and fell into conversation with the royal Phaetyn. The four of us ate and laughed, and I sipped at the lemonade, but the beverage was excessively sweet for my taste. I placed the drink to the side, lifting my glass of water to my lips to take a few sips.

The sun kissed the top of the treeline, and I nudged Lani. "Isn't it time for you to work your Phaetyn mojo?"

She laughed, and the shrill sound grated on my ears. I reached over and scooted her lemonade just out of reach and said, "I don't know what's in that stuff, but I think you've had enough."

Lani, Kamini, and Kamoi all snickered, and it took me only a moment to realize how stuffy I sounded. "Fine. Fine. I'll relax, but you said yourself you wanted the barrier up before nightfall. And don't get drunk. On lemonade." I had no idea if they put something stronger in drinks at celebrations.

The Phaetyn in the crowd were also acting strange, like they'd had too much honey ale, and I wondered if there was a separate table of it. Not that I wanted to be drunk, but maybe a cup would help me not feel like such a stick in the mud.

"What's the matter, Ryn? Don't tell me you're having regrets about not being Queen?" Kamoi asked.

What a question to ask. I rolled my eyes and reached for my water glass, but it was now empty, so I grabbed my glass of lemonade and took several long draughts of the over-sweet concoction. Party Ryn was coming to *Kanahele o keola*. After a few gulps, I coughed on the sickening taste. "Seriously, what is in that horseplop?"

Kamini snickered. "It's my mother's special brew." She blushed and added, "I mean, Alani's."

Double yuck. That's why I didn't like it. Clearly.

I grabbed Lani's water glass and drained it in an attempt to get the funny taste out of my mouth.

Ryn? Tyrrik's voice in my head startled me a moment later. *Are you okay?*

I gazed out over the throng of Phaetyn and smiled. *Absolutely. Party Ryn is here.*

Kamini stood and held her mostly empty glass up, tapping it repeatedly with her fork. "My dear Phaetyn," she said, grinning. "We've come together tonight to celebrate the return of my elder sister, Lani, rightful heir to our throne."

The entire congregation of Phaetyn erupted in shouts and cheers. I whistled, clapped, and bellowed with them, reveling in their triumph.

"If my mother, Queen Luna, were here, she would rejoice with us as Lani embraces her right and responsibility to rule and protect our forest and our people." She leaned over and hefted the polished elm chest up onto the table. "Dearest Lani—"

An ear-splitting roar reverberated through Zivost forest. Shock blanketed the clearing in silence for a prolonged heartbeat that seemed to last an eternity. The confused gaze of the crowd fell back from the sky to Kamini, but the princess had frozen on the spot.

Panic seized my heart as I lifted my chin, dread forcing my eyes to the sky. The twilight was still streaked with the sun's setting rays, but the sky was otherwise empty.

Please just be in my head. My mouth dried.

What? Tyrrik asked, and I got a glimpse of him jetting over the mountains.

It took only a moment to process that he was flying and not setting up camp for the night. He'd told me he'd soon be stopping, but the image of the mountain ranges told me he was not the one roaring above the Zivost.

Lani stood, gripping the edge of the table, her eyes wide, immobilized by the same terror I felt. She gasped for breath, her gaze darting around the clearing and into the sky.

"You have to put up the golden barrier," I said, struggling to regain my wits. These people would be looking to us to guide them. "You have to put it up right now."

She nodded and closed her eyes. The golden threads appeared around her body. The tendrils slowly stretched toward the sky.

Khosana!

I shook my head, dazed. *Drak.* Whatever was in that lemonade was potent, way more potent than Dyter's honey ale. *How many times have you yelled my name?* I asked Tyrrik. *I think I had too much to drink. I don't feel right.*

What's going on, Ryn?

A deafening roar obliterated Tyrrik's voice from my mind as effective as a bucket of cold water to the face.

Chaos exploded around me with hundreds of Phaetyn screaming, pushing, and shoving one another. I looked at Lani and then back into the sky, but the golden net meant to protect the Phaetyn was not even a tenth of the way over Zivost.

The heavy beating of wings pounded high above. Another deafening roar blasted through the clearing. My jaw dropped, my chest tightening as I stared at the massive emerald Drae circling over the forest. Horror rooted me in place as he opened the talons of his foreclaw and dropped a dozen Druman.

They fell through the air and landed one after the other in the courtyard.

Through the lingering effects of the brew, I understood this was no longer a matter of protection by simply putting up a shield. We had to defend the forest and the queen.

"Kamini," I slurred. "Get Lani to safety. Kamoi mobilize your warriors. Remember, the Druman will die easier if you infect them with Phaetyn blood first." I glanced around. "Kamoi?"

He was already calling the guards to him. Right, he didn't need me to tell him how to do his job.

Ryn! Tyrrik sounded on the verge of hysteria.

Not now. I needed all my strength and focus to deal with the Druman. And I sincerely hoped Lani's shield would be enough to deal with the emperor because I could feel the overwhelming menace of his power, and I wasn't sure I stood a chance against that.

I grabbed a knife off the table and then a second, pushing down the clawing fear inside my chest. These Druman were like the others we'd fought in the mountains, barely more than animals with matted hair and filthy clothes. Their stench wafted on the breeze, and my heart begged me to flee. Even though I *wanted* to, I wouldn't. I could do this. I'd done it before, more than once, and while I still had fear, there was nothing paralyzing me from dealing with these monsters.

Ryn! Tyrrik yelled through our bond again. He was pumping his wings as fast as he could, the darkening sky blurring as he sped toward me. He would feel my fear, and there was nothing I could do about it. My mind was too fuzzy from the lemonade for me to focus enough to block him. With everything else going on around me, I probably wouldn't be able to do that and fight the Druman.

I could feel Lani next to me, and I turned to yell at the two sisters, but Kamini had dropped to the ground, her head lolling to the side. Lani remained rooted, her eyes closed as she tried to push the net over Zivost.

"This can't be happening now," I muttered under my breath. Not when we were so close. I grabbed Lani's wrist to get her attention. I raised my voice and shouted over the horrible melee, "You've got to get out of here."

The Phaetyn queen startled, and her gaze locked on mine. "What's happening?"

I shook my head and pointed at Kamini. "Watch Kamini. She's fainted. No matter what happens, stay here until Tyrrik comes. Do you hear me? Even if I have to fight."

Lani nodded, eyes focused on her small golden net above.

Bloody drak. Clearly, she'd had too much to drink too.

I ran forward, scanning the crowd, relieved to see Kamoi leading a group of his guard toward the Druman, their spears dripping with fresh blood.

The massive emerald Drae had disappeared, and I shouted at Lani to put the net up, hoping we could shield from further attack.

My stomach roiled as one of the Druman sliced through a Phaetyn guard. I roared in protest and rounded the table as blue scales crawled over my skin. I ran forward, and in a pulse of blue light, I shifted into my Drae form, tail lashing in fury.

I bellowed at the mutant bastards as I charged forward, stopping to whip in a circle to swing my spiked tail at a group of them charging me.

Several of the Druman growled and grunted, and two of the creatures flew through the air, their bodies broken and mangled. I turned back and roared again, slicing through one and then another with my talons. Black blood spilled to the ground, and I scooped up a mutilated torso, launching it back at the remaining monsters.

I glanced up at the skies, my heart in my throat as I saw the golden net wavering, still not even a quarter of the way across the forest. What was wrong with Lani? What was taking so long?

Another roar thundered from above, and the emerald Drae, my *father,* appeared above me. He spewed fire into the forest as he descended into the clearing.

11

*P*haetyn's screams filled the courtyard outside the Rose Castle as white-hot flames enveloped them, burning them alive. Those lucky enough to avoid the fire unscathed turned to flee.

The emerald Drae landed, the ground shaking with the force, and he towered over me.

My knees shook as I instinctively tried to sag and make myself smaller in some pitiful attempt to escape the emperor's notice. How was he here? For all our plans to kill him, I hadn't been prepared for this moment.

My daughter, he crowed.

His pride filled me until it was all I could fathom.

Draedyn was bigger than Tyrrik. My father's scales were a deep emerald, but several areas of his body lacked the jeweled-like armor as if the pieces had been plucked or carved away. His eyes were a glowing green, the same color as his scales, but despite the vibrant color, there was no life within their depths.

You are magnificent, he said. *I've been searching for you, and here you are, my most incredible triumph.*

Satisfaction thrummed through me. How I'd craved my father's

75

approval. I yearned to make him proud. To be a daughter he could trust.

I have longed for our meeting. Dreaming of the time we would be reunited. Whatever lies you have heard of me, I hope you will grant me the opportunity to prove my paternal love for you.

I could feel the honesty of his words, his sincerity. I thought of how, as a child, I'd wished for my father, and here he was. But if my wish had come true, why did it feel wrong? No, he just wanted a chance. Confusion swirled in my mind, and I wrestled to hold onto what I knew.

You must come with me to my castle and be the princess you were meant to be. Let Draeconia know of your greatness so they can worship you at my side.

I lifted a claw in his direction, the trickling of his excitement spreading to the tips of my talons and down my ridged spine.

I could feel how much he wanted this, and I wanted it too. This would fill the healing hole inside once and for all. This was the answer to my problems. *Yes.*

Before we go . . .

The emerald tendrils of his power pulsed against my mind, forcing my Drae powers to part and let him inside. Excitement turned to fear, and he clearly felt the shift within me. His presence flooded into me, shattering the natural Drae barrier encasing my mind, to take up residence, gripping my will in his own.

I couldn't move. Why couldn't I move? I still had my mind, but an oily emerald-green power, my father's power, was disconnecting me from controlling myself.

Bring me the Phaetyn.

An image of Kamini, her silver hair up in an intricate updo, wearing her plain crown, filled my mind, and I struggled to control my body. No. Not Kamini.

I pivoted, unable to refuse my father's bidding. My body walked toward the princess, under his complete control.

My mind screamed, but I stepped toward the table where Lani and Kamini were hidden. My insides twisted, splintering, and my heart broke as I batted the table away and exposed Lani, an unconscious Kamini, and a half-dozen other cowering Phaetyn.

I flicked Lani away with a talon, mentally begging her forgiveness for what I was about to do. And then I plucked Kamini up.

Ryn! Tyrrik screamed my name, and I regained partial use of my vocal chords, releasing a strangled noise. I tried to break from the emperor's hold, but I couldn't respond to my mate. The brief reprieve was over, my voice was gone, my control was void. The only piece of Ryn left was my awareness, but I had no way to enact my will. Even the choice to do nothing had been ripped from me, I couldn't access my Drae powers at all.

Lani screamed, and Kamini was still in her faint in my claw. I turned back to my father, carrying my friend to him.

You are everything I'd hoped you be. And because of that, I have left you with your mind as reward for pleasing me, daughter. Remember, I could have taken that, too, but I chose to be merciful.

Disgust surged from within, but I crossed the clearing toward the green Drae.

I'm coming, Tyrrik called to me.

I could feel him drawing near, and a tear slipped down my cheek.

Tyrrik, I managed to get through, jerking when Draedyn tried to take possession of me again. I stumbled, and poor Kamini slipped through my talons to the bloodied ground.

Don't let him take her, Tyrrik threw at me.

Draedyn lunged forward, his claw scooping up the dirt beneath Kamini as he grabbed her.

I bellowed in outrage, and the alpha's hold on me lessened as Tyrrik's proximity gave me strength. *Hurry!*

Lani leapt from behind the toppled table, and I shifted to block her, immediately grasping the emperor's mistake. He thought Kamini was the queen because she wore the crown.

Kamoi ran out from within the trees, several other Phaetyn with him, screaming as he raised his spear on behalf of his cousin.

Draedyn didn't even flinch. He extended on his hind legs and, with his talon's extended, severed the heads of two guards. He snatched up Kamoi and two other Phaetyn in his claw, Kamini dangling from his other. With another bellow, the emperor glanced my way.

I rule through fear, daughter. Always fear. But I believe there will be love for us after the fear has passed.

With a snap that had white lights exploding across my vision, he released me. His oily powers slipped away and allowed my blue Drae tendrils to reconnect with my mind.

My body shifted, and I dropped to my knees and screamed as he took off into the twilight sky.

"Ryn," Tyrrik said hoarsely, crouching beside me to wrap me in his strong embrace.

Phaetyn still cried. The acrid scent of burning flesh filled my nostrils, but the chaos blurred around me as I sobbed into his chest, my shoulders shaking. "He made me give Kamini over. I couldn't control myself, Tyrrik," I wailed. The pitch of my voice grew, my words slipping together. "I-I couldn't stop."

"Ryn," he said firmly. He pushed me back, and caught my chin, forcing me to meet his gaze.

My eyes widened, and I hovered on the edge of hysteria.

"I know what happened," he said. "I felt it. It's *not* your fault."

I tore my gaze from his, staring back at the ground. Pieces of broken dishes mixed with the food they'd once held, bits of napkin, a broken wine glass, dark fluid I wanted to think was lemonade littered the courtyard . . . *It's my fault.*

No, my love, Tyrrik said, his voice unrelenting in my mind. *It wasn't your fault. It was mine.*

He picked me up, my body shaking, and as he sped us into the Rose Castle in a blur, the putrid scent of smoke lessened. Setting me in a pile on the ground, he said aloud, "I'm going to get the Phaetyn together and find Lani."

Relief, shame, and fear found me with his words. The Phaetyn needed a leader right now, someone to show them what to do in the wake of Draedyn's attack. As the bridge between the races, that should be me—ideally, by Lani's side. For all I knew, she was out there trying to do the job while I cowered in here. And yet, even knowing Tyrrik was needed elsewhere, I didn't want him to leave. I choked on the words, forcing them out. "Hurry back."

At least I had that much self-control.

"I'll be back soon." Tyrrik stroked my hair softly before disappearing outside once more.

I stared at the hemp weave of the golden rug, curling into a ball. My braid fell forward over my shoulder, hitting me with the saturated stench of the bitter smoke from outside. I shoved my silver braid back with a trembling hand and sat up, hugging my knees to my chest.

What just happened? What had I done?

Draedyn attacked. Dropped his Druman and set the forest aflame and killed countless Phaetyn. How many I couldn't possibly know. How much had been lost in the anarchy? I didn't even want to guess.

A sob caught in my chest as I recalled the look on Lani's face when I'd kicked back the table and taken Kamini in my grasp. The burning shame collected behind my eyes, and a tear spilled over the edge and slid down my cheek. Lani had just found her family, and now both Kamoi and Kamini were in Draedyn's possession. *My fault.*

They could already be dead.

I handed her over.

I stared at the weave, unblinking, and picked at the fringe. I didn't even bother to look up when Tyrrik re-entered the room.

"We've gathered everyone in the ballroom. The injured are already being healed," Tyrrik said.

The injured. But what about the dead?

Someone else strode in after him but stopped at the threshold to the room.

A heavy weight sank in my stomach as I slowly lifted my gaze to Lani's. Queen Luna's crown dangling in her hand.

Fat tears hovered on the edge of her bottom eyelids. Her violet eyes were rimmed red from the smoke and crying. The rise and fall of her chest became increasingly rapid as she held my gaze.

I didn't close my eyes to her pain but etched my mind with her shock and terror so that I would always remember. More tears fell from my eyes, and I croaked, "I'm sorry, Lani. I'm so—" My voice broke, and my body shook as guilt wracked my very soul. *My fault.*

And worse yet, I could feel Tyrrik's heart breaking through our bond alongside mine.

"I couldn't get the barrier up," Lani said, staring at the crown in her hands. Her tears dripped to the floor, and she released a strangled sob.

Wait. She thought this was her fault? I struggled to my feet, and Tyrrik hurried over to help me. He slid his arm around my waist and remained at my side.

"Lani," I said, shaking my head. "This isn't your fault. You saw what I—" I swallowed hard. "You *saw* what I did."

"But you know, Draedyn is Ryn's father," Tyrrik said darkly. "He was controlling her actions."

Lani swallowed. The Phaetyn queen scrubbed her tears away and crossed to a cushioned futon, perching on the gilded edge. "I knew Ryn would never hand Kamini over of her own volition. But"—her gaze went from Tyrrik to me—"How was he able to do that?"

I tilted my head back to look up at my mate. I didn't want to voice my guess out loud.

He avoided my gaze, and I frowned at the uncharacteristic gesture, recalling his comment about the attack being his fault.

"Draedyn is the alpha of our kind," he answered. "This makes Drae susceptible to his will. But Ryn also shares a familial bond with him. Influencing her"—a low growl slipped through Tyrrik's lengthening teeth as he fought to control his Drae—"*controlling* her will be easier because of this bond."

"That would've been nice to know beforehand," snapped Lani.

I blinked at her uncharacteristic outburst, but my mind replayed Tyrrik's words.

The Phaetyn sighed, rubbing her temples. "I'm sorry. I know that's not helping."

"No, you're right," I said, chest tightening again. "I-I knew he'd be able to impose his will. Tyrrik had told me. I just didn't realize his control could overpower my *own*. I should have taken it more seriously." But what could I have done against him, really? How could I possibly fight against such power?

"We'll work on your defenses," Tyrrik said, squeezing my waist.

I stared around the glistening quartz room. The chamber appeared to have everything, but really it was empty aside from the few bits of furniture which made it functional. The room and I had a lot in common.

"I felt something similar in Gemond," I said, straightening. "When Draedyn was flying overhead. I had this weird moment where I wanted him to find us."

"Really?" Lani dropped her hands. "Why didn't you say anything?"

"I didn't think anything of it," I said numbly. "I didn't realize the thoughts weren't mine; in the same way I don't notice I'm breathing all day. It just happened, and then it was gone right when you put up your gold veil. It must have kept him out."

"You were in your Phaetyn form too," she replied. "Maybe that helped."

"And I was closer to Tyrrik," I added. The events of the night played over in my mind again. "I regained slightly more control as Tyrrik drew near. The closer he got to the forest tonight . . ." The truth hit me, and I looked at my mate and said, "My resistance to Draedyn is stronger when you're close."

A heavy silence followed my words, and Tyrrik cleared his throat, breaking the stupor. He turned his attention to the Phaetyn, an impassive mask falling over his features, leaving me chilled.

"Queen Lani," he said. "Your people need direction. You need to pull yourself together."

My people, she mouthed, and then she exploded. "On my first night of rule, I get so drunk I can't complete the barrier, and Draedyn slaughters fifty of my people, taking the prince and princess and at least two more." Her eyes shifted to me. "I come to 'my people' with a Phaetyn-Drae who gives the princess over to our enemy."

I froze, anguish slamming into me.

Lani rushed to add. "That's merely what the Phaetyn are thinking, Ryn. You must see how they'll mistrust you even when I explain what happened. You both must see how wary this will make them."

Knowing her words were true did nothing to lessen the hurt as she spoke them.

A menacing rumble filled Tyrrik's chest, and I could feel his ire rising on my behalf. "Watch what you say, Phaetyn."

"Do not forget yourself," Lani whipped back with a glare, shooting to her feet.

A menacing smile curved his lips, and his skin rippled as scales climbed up his neck. "And do not make the mistake of forgetting who *I* am."

"You're right," I whispered, releasing my pride. Tyrrik's arm tightened around my waist, and I held up my hand wearily before he could reassure me. "No, I'm serious. This isn't a pity party. This isn't a blame game. I screwed up. I should've been working harder on my defenses. Maybe I should've realized what the emperor was doing or what he was capable of, but now that I know . . . I'll shovel dung uphill to work on overcoming that weakness." *No one controls me.*

I met Lani's eyes across the room. "And you need to get the barrier up. Then we need to save Kamini and Kamoi—"

"How do you know they're even alive?" Lani asked harshly, her grip tightening on the crown she still held. "How do you know he hasn't killed them?"

Tyrrik answered, "Why would he kill them when they are the perfect hostages?"

A glint of hope entered the Phaetyn's violet eyes, but she deflated again as her gaze fell on the crown. She curled into herself and bowed her head. "I can't put up the barrier. I'm not strong enough." She sucked in a strangled breath and added, "I couldn't even do it as my people burned." She dropped the crown to the quartz floor, watching the ornate circlet rattle around and eventually settle. "I'm not Queen."

She was wrong. My certainty solidified as well as my intentions as I thought of what would come next.

My love, Tyrrik spoke in my head. *You know what this will mean?*

I glanced up at him. *Yes. I know.* I probably didn't, but I knew enough. And Draedyn needed to be dethroned. *I'm ready to fight in this war, mate. To the end.*

The air caught in his throat, and his eyes burned as he changed the subject. *You have accepted the M word?*

How could I have ever doubted? *Yes, I have. Next time I decide we need distance . . .*

I'll lock you in a room and never let you out.

My brows lifted at his tone. I'd been joking, but Tyrrik sounded almost angry as he replied.

Stepping free of his embrace, I approached the hunched Phaetyn and then crouched by her side. She didn't lift her head even when I reached for her crown.

The intricate circle of metal leaves was surprisingly light, weighing far less than a golden object of its size should. Warm power trickled from the crown, soothing my frayed nerves and minutely stoking my energy. One minute later, and Lani would've had the crown on her head and everything could've worked out so much differently. She could've put up the barrier. Fifty Phaetyn may still be alive.

But thinking that way was pointless now.

I took a deep breath and whispered, "You are the Phaetyn queen, Lani." I brushed back her silver hair. "And you *will* wear this crown and be who you need to be, despite what you feel. You'll do this because your family is in danger and because your people need you."

She looked up at me, her eyes glistening with tears.

"And you need them," I added. With that, I gently placed the crown on her head.

Golden light erupted around her, enveloping her small frame. The room jerked and spun, and I gaped to orientate myself as a vice clenched my abdomen. I glanced down and realized Tyrrik held me, his arm around my middle, and my back was against his chest. I glanced over at Lani.

The Phaetyn queen stared at her glowing hands, eyes wide as she rotated her palms.

The air around her body radiated a luminescent gold so bright my eyes began to water. I tried to step out of my mate's embrace and glanced down.

"Tyrrik," I said, patting his arm. My feet weren't touching the ground, and I was dangling like a doll clutched in a child's arms.

He set me on my feet. "Sorry," he muttered. "Little bit on edge."

Obviously. And as soon as we were alone, I'd be making sure he knew none of what happened was his fault.

Lani stood abruptly, and I eyed her askance. She better not go Phaetyn-hate-Drae on us.

"You seem . . ."

"I'm stronger," she said, still turning her hands over.

Tyrrik stepped close again and asked, "How?"

Lani took a breath and removed the crown. The glow disappeared like blowing out a candle's light. "When the crown's on, it's like I'm touching my tree."

I walked to her side and peered at the pale-green stone set in the looping golden crown. That's what had been in the box hidden in Luna's castle. No wonder she'd kept it locked away. "Do you think there's a bit of your tree inside?"

Lani placed the crown on her head, and I lifted an arm to shield my eyes from the glare.

"There has to be," Lani said breathlessly. She closed her eyes, and several seconds passed before she opened them again. In a voice full of awe, she said, "I can talk to the forest through this. They're welcoming me. Ryn"—her voice tightened—"I'm stronger with the crown. Much stronger."

"Now you'll be able to erect the barrier," Tyrrik said from behind us.

A soft smile spread over her shining face. "Yes. I definitely will."

Zivost Forest would be protected, and so would the Phaetyn.

Lani frowned. "But how are we going to save Kamini and Kamoi?" she asked, removing the crown once more. "Putting up the barrier doesn't help us get them back. If Draedyn has them hostage, they'll be in his empire."

"Yes," I agreed. I glanced over my shoulder at Tyrrik. *You sure you're ready for this?*

I am. Draedyn's rule must end.

His conviction joined with my own, and my face firmed as I took Lani's hand. "We will go to save your family and people," I said. "It's time to end the emperor's reign of terror."

Lani's eyes met mine, and her jaw dropped.

I continued, a growl slipping into my words, "We're going to war."

At Lani's request, I'd kept to my chamber inside the Rose Castle for the last two days as she regained control of her people. But the time hadn't been the relaxing reprieve I craved. My mind felt bruised from Tyrrik's repeated attacks, but he was adamant that if I was able to keep him out, I'd be able to keep my father out too.

So far, Tyrrik had strolled into my mind every single time. No problem. Gone was the time of pulling my energy back into myself to erect a barrier. Our mate bond kept us linked, despite my best efforts to keep him out. Yep, everything was on the up and up.

I lay on the spongey grass underneath Lani's elm and stared up at the dark sky, the twin moons hidden beneath a canopy of clouds.

The golden barrier shimmered high above the forest, ensuring my father could not attack here again. Although, knowing how easily he'd seized control of my body had me tossing and turning every night.

With a sigh, I spoke to the night, asking my deepest fear, "Are we rushing into this war?"

The night answered me in his silken voice. "No."

I sat up, smiling at Tyrrik as he slid behind me, his arms encircling my torso just under my breasts, and I leaned my head back against his chest, breathing in the pine and steel scent of him.

The darkness wrapped us in its embrace, and I continued to bare my fears aloud. "The Gemondians are still recovering though they're healthier than they were. Verald has had longer, but it's been weeks since we last saw Calvetyn. The Phaetyn are terrified after the attack. And we have yet to contact Azule—"

Tyrrik didn't reply immediately, but I waited, listening as he drew a long breath.

"There never seems to be a right time to fight back."

I twisted in his arms, placing my hands on his forearms as I looked up into his inky gaze. "But?"

"When I was enslaved to Irdelron, there were many moments I fought his control, despite knowing I couldn't break the blood oath. When the possibility came to break his power over me, when I found you, the time still didn't feel right. But then, it wasn't because of certain failure; it was for fear of failure. Because then I had someone to lose."

After the dungeon, I thought I'd lost just about everything that mattered. Not true. And despite my legitimate concerns of the rebellion's readiness, maybe Tyrrik was right. Was this weight on my chest fear? The heaviness grew as I thought of losing those I had left—Dyter, Lani . . . my mate.

I searched Tyrrik's face, my heart in my throat, and asked, "Do you think we can do it?"

"I think," he said, and his brows furrowed as he stared up at the sky, "the stronger we get, the stronger Draedyn will become. Waiting five, ten, or twenty years will make no difference; it won't give us the certainty of success we all crave." He pursed his lips, and his jaw set. He scooted back just enough so when he tilted his head, he met my gaze. "But to win, we must fight while the people of Draeconia can look at their bodies and see the evidence of how he starved them while the dirt is still soft on the graves of their husbands and fathers, and while the land is yellow and dead, leached of life by its diseased and evil ruler. He might hold Draeconia by the throat now, but if we rise together, we will disembowel his reign and then execute him for his abuse."

As he spoke, my breath quickened, and I rose onto my knees. I'd missed exactly when I'd tightened my grip on his forearms, but I was ready to leap into action. "Wow," I said, easing my grip, exhaling my energy. "You need to write that down."

He snorted.

"No, seriously," I said, nodding. "I could actually do battle right now and win."

His lips quirked, and he wrapped an arm around my neck, bending down to press a kiss against our mate mark on my neck. I shivered, and my thoughts of battle derailed. I scooted closer. That kiss was fine, good even, but Tyrrik's tongue was for more than just talking. I wet my lips as I glanced up at him through my lashes. "Mate," I said plainly, my lips lifting into a smile at the sound of the title. "Mate."

Tyrrik shook as he chuckled low in his throat. "Getting practice in?"

My eyes narrowed.

"You were practicing the real name for Phaetynville in exactly the same tone."

"*Kanahele o keola*," I said then smiled sheepishly. "Okay, I might be practicing a *little*. It just . . . still feels strange. Good strange though."

Whatever you need, my love.

I snuggled into his chest, and our bodies swayed gently underneath the elm tree and black sky.

"Hey, Tyrrik?"

He hummed in the back of his throat as he ran his hand up and down my back.

I opened my eyes, remaining pressed against him. "You know the attack wasn't your fault, right?"

He only froze for a second, but the brief reaction was all I needed to confirm my theory.

"You think it was," I accused, pulling back. "Why? How was Draedyn taking over my mind possibly your fault?"

He pulled the darkness to him, shadowing his face above the neckline of his black aketon. "How is it you blame yourself for how easily your father was able to penetrate your mind?"

"Nuh-uh," I said, standing as I blinked away his cloaking power. "Don't turn this interrogation around. I'm asking you, Tyrrik. Don't deflect, and don't you dare try and hide."

He rose, taking a step back into the inky shadows, his eyes flooding black as he took me in. His nostrils flared, and he tore his gaze from me and began to pace in jerky strides.

"Tell me," I said quietly, staying right where I was. "It wasn't your fault, Tyrrik."

"It was," he said, halting before me. "I went against my instincts."
What?

He continued, "My every instinct said I should not allow you to leave alone; I should be by your side to fight with you, *for* you. To protect you as I should. I overrode those instincts, and you were attacked. I didn't make it to your side in time, and you were hurt."

I blinked at him, struggling to understand the emotions assailing me through our bond. But this made no sense, the guilt he felt. "I asked you to remain behind."

"And I knew better," he growled, clenching his hands. "I should have followed you."

I took a step closer, needing to soothe him. I shook my head, protesting his supposition. "Then you would have gone against my wishes."

"Then so be it," he snarled, tilting his face to the night sky. "I would rather you hated me again than to feel your helplessness when Draedyn controlled you."

My mouth opened. And closed. My mind stuttering as it processed his words. "I . . . I thought we were getting better at this."

He shuddered and hunched away from me, scales climbing the sides of his neck. His emotional turmoil wracked him, and I ached to make it go away, but what could I say? I kept still as he controlled the instinct to shift.

Tyrrik stopped shaking but didn't turn back. When he spoke, his voice was weary. "Ryn, you know I have tried. And I don't plan to stop trying."

I waited. There was a definite *but* on the end of his sentence.

He blurred forward and took my hands. "Please, my love. Promise me you will never ask me to be parted from you again. You know I would move the world itself to make you happy. But please, *please* do not ask me to leave you unprotected again."

My heart lodged in my throat. My Drae, my mate, was begging. A man who had held strong through one hundred years of enslavement was now pleading. And yet, though my heart ached as his heart ached, and my soul burned as his soul burned, could I lie to both of us and grant his request?

We were immortal. To promise such a thing for one year, for two, seemed honest. To promise to *never* be out of reach of my mate for eternity didn't seem possible.

I understood his fear was raw. I understood he'd been terrified. Hadn't we both been clinging to each other for strength a moment before?

But I couldn't lie. Not to him, and not to myself.

"Tyrrik," I whispered. "I promise to never leave your side . . . unless I believe I have to. Unless it's life or death."

His harsh exhales were accusations in the silky darkness. "But you *would* leave my side again?" he asked, his condemning gaze drilling into mine. "After I have begged you not to, you still would go?"

I swallowed. Did he think I wanted to? "You can't protect me from everything, Tyrrik. That is not a burden I want you to carry. No one should have to."

"It is who I am!" he roared. "I am a Drae. You are mine to protect. It is my privilege and my purpose."

"I am yours," I said, drawing myself up. "Just as you are mine." I reached for him, waving him to come back to me, and my voice dropped to an earnest whisper. "But I will not lie to you, and I will not let you take responsibility for my actions. I'm not going to abandon you, but I—"

Tyrrik brushed away my reaching hands.

"Tyrrik," I said. "Please understand." My heart ached to make this right, but I had no idea how. I couldn't compromise on what I knew was right. "I won't ask permission for everything I do."

He'd turned to leave but stopped, looking over his shoulder. His profile showed his fangs had lengthened, and scales covered his arms and neck. "I understand you will do what you believe to be right."

I sighed in relief.

"Just as I will do what I believe to be right," he finished.

I stayed rooted to the spot, as Tyrrik stalked away from the elm without another backward glance.

I AWOKE EARLY. Even curled against Tyrrik, my sleep had been restless. Not just because our argument hung heavy between us, but today the Phaetyn would start their march toward Gemond.

"*Khosana*," Tyrrik murmured, pulling my back against the length of his body.

The warmth of his presence only made my heart hurt more. I rested my head against his arm, reviewing the words I'd rehearsed in the dark. "I'm sorry I hurt your feelings last night."

I held my breath, waiting for his answer.

"And I am sorry to have hurt yours." He pressed his lips on top of my hair.

What we hadn't said seemed to speak louder—but I refused to retract what I'd said.

Yet I loved him. There was so much chaos surrounding us that having contention between us didn't seem right. I rolled to face him, seeing my conflict reflected in his gaze as we stared, unspeaking, at each other. We didn't have to agree on everything to be together. I knew that. And he knew that. Searching his face, I wiggled my arm free and rested my hand against his cheek. His whiskers were rough on my skin, and his heat trickled into me. Biting my lip, I leaned forward and pressed my lips to his.

Searing heat pulsed between us, and the urge for more thrummed through me. Tyrrik growled, nipping at my lip, and his hands gripped my waist and pulled me closer. Our tongues brushed against each other, and I arched, instinctively pressing my body tighter to his, gasping when he trailed hot kisses down my neck, stopping to suck the sensitive skin. Our bodies were tugged closer together as though a rope had been jerked tight about our middles. My feet found purchase on his calves, pushing me up on their own accord. My thoughts clouded with want, and I pressed harder into Tyrrik, aching for more. Tyrrik's hands seemed to be everywhere, my waist, my thigh, then higher on my torso, his thumb grazing the underside of my breast.

"Mate."

The deep rumble of the single word vibrated in the walls. I shivered as his possessive claim swept through me, my head falling back as he pressed hot kisses down my neck and just above my collarbone. His teeth rested against the base of my neck, and my eyes widened, my breath halting as he held his lengthened fangs over our mark. For some reason, I knew a bite there would be significant. He'd done it too often for me to miss the gesture.

I remained still as his breath warmed my skin, my heart galloping wildly. As his lips drew over his fangs. He kissed the spot, whisper-soft, and slid a hand behind my head to draw my face to his and crush his mouth against mine.

"Tyrrik," I moaned into his mouth, energy coursing through me.

We grabbed and pulled, kneaded and stroked, our hands frenzied. My mind was everywhere at once and yet wholly consumed with this man, my mate. I needed more. "Please."

Our teeth gnashed together, but neither one of us relented.

My fingernails lengthened, clawing down the front of his aketon, leaving no blemish in his smooth, bronze skin because he was mine and I was his. I pushed my hands over the ridges of his muscular chest, gripping his shoulders.

He rolled above me, and his hands bunched in the front of my nightgown, his eyes wild. His intention clear.

"Yes," I panted. I wanted the cumbersome garment gone. I needed him closer.

The fabric tore slightly, my heart, mind, and body all ready for more.

"Lord Tyrrik and Lady Ryn," a voice interrupted, muffled by the door to the chamber. The staccato pounding barely registered. "Is everything all right in there?"

The words made no sense as I lay panting with Tyrrik above me.

Something else was said, but my mind barely registered the sound.

I blinked, and Tyrrik was gone. The groan of shearing metal and splintering wood pierced through my foggy mind, and then the chamber door was ripped from its hinges as my mate slammed a Phaetyn against the far wall of the passage.

That doused what was left of my passion, and I leapt off the bed, yelling, "Tyrrik! Don't kill him!"

I rushed to his side, the quartz walls blurring with my speed, and gripped his wrist, pushing my body between the two. Tyrrik's hand was wrapped around the throat of a Phaetyn guard.

"Tyrrik," I said. "Hey. He's no threat. He's a guard. He thought . . ." I had no idea what he thought, and I threw out, "He thought we were hurt."

The Drae's eyes were inky and wide, his fangs well past his chin. I continued to talk to him, touching my hand to his skin, calling his name, and slowly my words seemed to penetrate the bucket of desire *his* head was in. The black receded from his eyes, and he blinked at the man, releasing him without warning. The guard crumpled on the ground.

"Ah . . . Sorry," I called after the Phaetyn as he scrambled away from us and sprinted down the hall. I scratched my chin, certain the incident wouldn't do anything to help endear us to the Phaetyn. Though it was a blip to what else I'd done.

Tyrrik turned in the now empty passage and tugged me to him. He kissed the top of my head and whispered, "Holy pancakes."

I threw my head back and laughed. "You did not just say that."

He smiled dryly, eyeing the mangled wooden door to our chamber lying in the passageway with us. "I might've briefly forgotten myself."

I laughed again, gasping for air between my chortling. When I'd reigned in my laughter, I managed to say, "You just strangled someone because he knocked on the door."

There I went, showing off my brilliance. I shook my head in disbelief. Was this really my life now? I'd been a Drae for just over a month, and I'd known I was Phaetyn for longer, but if any moment hammered in how strange I could expect my future to be, if we survived this war, it was now.

"Well, that was some kiss," Tyrrik announced before moving to pick up the door.

A kiss I'd like to continue, I shot at him. Really, I wanted to hear him saying holy pancakes again. My new goal in life. I smoothed the front of my rumpled nightgown, eying the tear that exposed my collarbone. I looked up to see Tyrrik watching me. I raised my eyebrows in question but decided to ask something else instead. "Do you think that guard was meant to deliver a message?"

Tyrrik sighed, dropping his head back to stare at the ceiling. "We should probably go and find out."

I looked at him, Lord Broody-Drae. He was totally sulking. Not that I could blame him. Honestly, I kind of wanted to after the way our handsy wake up could've gone.

Leaving the door, which didn't fit in the doorway anymore, we walked toward Lani's meeting room, the same room Kamini had been in when we first arrived.

Just as we reached the entrance, Tyrrik touched my elbow, drawing my attention back to him.

I quirked a brow and waited.

"I'm glad we were interrupted," he said.

"You sure look glad," I said, quirking a brow. I pointed to his shredded aketon. "And we probably should've taken a moment to get dressed."

He lifted a shoulder, expression wry. He closed the distance between us and folded one torn flap of my nightgown over the other. "I'm a Drae who has found his mate. The urge to bed you is nearly as strong as the urge to protect you." He ran his fingertips over my lips and said, "But I do mean it. Your first time shouldn't be like that."

"I don't think my ticker will continue ticking if there's too much more than that before the aketons come off," I said truthfully.

Tyrrik's eyes heated and he crowded me, pushing my back into the wall as his hand slipped over my collarbone.

The door to Lani's office opened with a creak.

I jumped and spun, my hands going to my torn gown.

Lani stood in the doorway, glowering. A peek past her revealed the guard Tyrrik had strangled . . . a little. I hadn't done anything wrong, so why did I feel like I'd been caught with my face in the honey syrup jar?

I cleared my throat, attempting to sound stern. "What's the news?"

Lani threw me an exasperated look. "Are you kidding me? You'd know if your rampant hormones weren't tearing the castle apart."

Graphic, but accurate.

One glance at Tyrrik showed he wasn't bothered by the queen's reaction. Of course not.

"So—" I drew the word out until she spoke.

"So, my people are nearly ready to go," she said, lifting her head enough to include Tyrrik in her scowl.

The elderly and children had departed yesterday at first light for Verald, escorted by a guard of fifty. The rest of the Phaetyn, the vast majority, would march under Lani's barrier toward Gemond. Tyrrik and I would fly ahead to alert King Zakai.

The morning light had chased away the largest of my doubts.

There was so much I had no control over, but Dyter and Cal had been planning this for years. When we got back, a group of us would push on to Azule and rally them to our side. It wouldn't matter that I had no experience in a war of this magnitude; I was surrounded by those whose *only* thoughts for *years* were of tearing down Draedyn. I wasn't in this alone, and I had to remember that in the days ahead.

"Have you got everything you need?" Tyrrik asked Lani.

She shrugged. "We won't want for food, and I'll cloak us the entire way. We have plenty of weapons coated in our blood." Her face twisted. "I sincerely hope we come across some Druman on the way."

I wasn't the only one who wanted revenge, and I suspected Lani's urge was motivated even more by the need to prove herself to her people.

Me? I needed to make things right. I'd accepted blame for what happened, even if it was because I hadn't done enough practice and not put enough stock in Tyrrik's warning of what the emperor could do. I still had to make things right and get Kamoi and Kamini back. If anything happened to them, I'd never forgive myself.

"When do you leave?" I asked, dragging my focus back to the queen as the guard edged around Tyrrik and escaped the room.

"One hour." Her voice was firm, but there was a wild look in her eyes as if she couldn't believe what was happening.

I understood. None of this felt real even though the evidence was all around us. "Al'right," I said, glancing between Tyrrik and the Phaetyn queen. I took a deep breath. "Let's go."

The Phaetyn queen lifted her chin, the ghost of a smile softening her lips. She arched a brow and said, "You might want to get dressed first."

*H*alfway to Gemond, the sharp, acrid smell of ash settled on the tip of my sensitive tongue. I exhaled, hoping the scent would diminish as we flew—perhaps the smoke was just a fire from one of the settlements of Gemond elders. Maybe they were burning their useless huts and making their way back to the hub of the kingdom now that the land was healing.

The darkness of night did nothing to obstruct my vision in this form, but the jutting peaks of the mountain ranges hid the valleys ahead, and the low-hanging clouds concealed the rising trail of the smoke.

Do you smell that?

I swallowed before answering. *I'd hoped it was just me.*

No. Definitely not just you.

The strain in Tyrrik's voice was palpable through our mental bond. When he increased his speed, I knew something was wrong.

What is it? I narrowed my eyes. *Don't tell me you can see through clouds. Because that would not be fair.*

What clouds? he asked, glancing up at the sky. *Ryn . . .*

I swiveled my long neck to glance up, and the stars winked at me. Peering back the way we'd come, I saw the velvet stretch of night to Zivost was blemished only by celestial lights. I faced

Gemond again, flattening my Drae form to cut through the air, and Tyrrik's sympathy hit me.

I stared at the haze as the smell of smoke got stronger and stronger. We were still quite a way from Gemond . . .

What was on fire? Something huge to cause this much smoke. My heart fell, and a crushing weight forced the air from my lungs. My vision blurred, but the murkiness covering the tops of the mountains didn't fade. *Mistress Moons.* Where was it coming from? I pumped my wings harder, sucking in the pungent air, the stench growing with every mile, and my certainty of the smoke's origin growing with it.

The smoke hung over the main center of the Gemond kingdom. Tyrrik pushed us higher into the clean air, but the closer we got, the higher we were forced to go to escape the pollution.

The sun rose, and with the light of day, the gray haze hung over the entire Gemond valley. When we finally descended into the kingdom proper, my mind blanked as I surveyed the destruction.

The homes of the Gemondians were gone as were the barns, the market buildings, shops, storehouses . . . *every* single structure was destroyed. The scorched ground extended as far as I could see. Only three charred walls, the remains of the buildings, jutted out of the blackened earth like broken, crumbling teeth. The closer we got to the mountain where Zakai's castle resided, the heavier my heart became until I was swallowing back nausea.

There were no pieces of the past, no evidence of the people who'd once resided in this land. There was only the befouled ground, the deathly white ash, and the noxious smoke rising in the air.

It is not your fault.

I couldn't respond. How could he say that? He'd only left Gemond to protect me because Draedyn . . . Draedyn had exposed our weaknesses and capitalized on them. Tyrrik had responded to my fear. If it wasn't my fault, then whose fault was it? Certainly not Zakai's or Zarad's or the other people of Gemond who willingly sent their quotas and their sons to the emperor. None of them had plotted to rebel, not until we landed in their kingdom a couple weeks ago.

Do you think anyone is still alive?

Hopefully they're safe in the mountain.

Tyrrik's words felt flat, and his attempt at reassurance did nothing to soothe my fear or guilt. The entire kingdom couldn't fit in Zakai's castle. There was no way most of the people outside would've had enough warning to get in there. How many had died? How many would we have left to fight?

Would Zakai still want to fight?

We should have been here. I should have dropped Lani and come straight back. Then I wouldn't have been around for Draedyn to take over my mind and force me to hand Kamini over. And our absence wouldn't have left our friends open to harm.

We can't possibly be everywhere at once. They'll understand this. Let's go to the back. Tyrrik led the way to the other side of the mountain.

I expected him to fly deeper into the valley, but as we descended, the smoke clogged my throat, and I struggled to draw breath. Could anyone have survived? Yes, I told myself firmly. I refused to believe Dyter could be gone.

Zakai is smart, Tyrrik said. *I'm sure they have contingency plans for attacks.* He tucked his wings and angled down and then disappeared into the trees on the northern side of the mountains where he'd acted as a decoy to my departure to the Zivost not so long ago.

Trees!

I fed the spark of hope, focusing on the organic evidence that not all was burned to ash, and followed my mate. I flew between the scraggly pines, eyes scanning for any movement, uncertain if I should be relieved or devastated when there was none. No Gemondians, but also no Druman. Was that a good thing? I clung to hope until I reached the base of the mountain behind my mate. Relief flooded me when I saw Tyrrik already shifting to his human form, standing on a short ledge . . . next to Dyter.

I roared in joy and sped toward my friend. I'd never shifted midflight, but I'd seen Tyrrik do it several times. I belatedly realized

Tyrrik made a lot of things look easy that weren't. Tearing through the air like a Phaetyn projectile, I crashed into Dyter.

Tyrrik's Drae reflexes stopped us from hurtling into the rocks. Instead, Tyrrik absorbed the impact of us, and of course, he was the first one on his feet. He offered Dyter a hand, letting me get up on my own. Perhaps put off by my scowl in response to his twitching lips.

"You're okay," I said, the tightness in my chest lessening as I buried myself in Dyter's one-armed embrace.

"My girl," Dyter said, choking on the words. He clung to me, patting my head, my back, and my hair.

I wasn't sure if it was his body or mine that shook, but after the second drip of moisture hit my head, I realized Dyter was crying. A lump clogged my throat and I wiped away my own tears, pulling away just enough so I could see him.

"You're a gruesome sight," I said, my voice thick.

His skin was filthy with soot, the tracks from his tears leaving streaks down his grizzly face. His dark-blue aketon was torn and singed on the bottom hem. His stump was red and raw, but he grinned as if welcoming me to work at The Crane's Nest back in Verald.

"I'm glad to see you're al'right." He glanced at Tyrrik and added, "Both of you."

My eyes welled again, and I pulled tight for another hug. "I'm so glad you're safe."

I couldn't lose him. Not ever.

King Zakai appeared in the shadowed entrance of a doorway I hadn't noticed until that moment. A closer look showed me how the heavy stone door seemed to meld with the mountainside.

Zakai's complexion was wane, his thick brows drawn over shadow-rimmed eyes. But when his gaze met mine, his shoulders relaxed and his eyes sparked.

"Most Powerful Drae," he said, the corners of his lips softening from their frown. "Welcome back to Gemond. We're immensely relieved to see you."

I felt Tyrrik's pride through our bond and was grateful he had the decency to not say told-you-so.

There are some things too sacred to make light of.

Zakai gestured us inside, and as Dyter and I neared the threshold into the mountain, I noticed the numerous archers lining the wall, backs to the mountain, scanning the outside landscape, bows and filled quivers nearby. More gold-plated guards stood at attention, their bodies pressed to the wall as they gazed through tiny murder holes.

Dyter wrapped his arm around my shoulders, and I leaned over and asked, "Were they going to shoot us?"

My old friend grunted. "They're like the young pups in Seven. At least they have a few wise, old men who can count and tell the difference between blue, black, and green."

Right. Good thing that.

Zakai led us farther into the mountain, but we were angling upward instead of returning to the areas I was familiar with. I didn't want to ask, but for some morbid reason, I had to know . . . "Did Gemond lose many?"

Zakai stopped. In two weeks, he'd healed a lot; his once sunken features weren't plump, but he no longer danced on the verge of death. His wiry gray hair was shorn close to his scalp and his beard trimmed tight to his square jaw. His clothing no longer hung on an emaciated frame although he was still thin. But right now, his haunted and ravaged features reminded me of when we'd first arrived. He pressed his lips together as if contemplating his words.

He stepped toward me, and Dyter's grip tightened around my shoulders.

The king said, "Each person we lost was one too many. But you are no more to blame for the evil of your father than Zarad is for my stupidity." He offered a small smile. "After Tyrrik left and we knew we were vulnerable, we offered shelter to as many as we could. Criers warned those in the outskirts to flee into the hills. I hope many heeded the warning and the damage was limited."

My eyes burned, knowing what he did not. I'd seen the damage as we flew in and knew his hopes would not be met.

"Hesitation will not win battles or wars," Tyrrik stated. "But Ryn and I deliver you hope. The Phaetyn are marching to join your force on the border of Azule and Gemond. How many men are under the mountain?"

Zakai straightened and tilted his head toward the long hallway leading farther into the fortress. "Let us confer with Zarad and Gairome. My son and his first have been strategizing with me. We will want to discuss our next step with them."

We traveled farther into the caves, and I stared at the evidence of hurried departures scattered throughout: a dropped doll, a harried and dirty mother scolding her child in a shrill voice, a disgruntled man complaining about not enough to drink.

We passed one couple deep in conversation, and as I walked by, I heard her say, "I'm just so tired of pumpkin everything. Why couldn't she grow strawberries or cherries or something sweet?"

I'd make time to visit the gardens as soon as we were done talking about the army.

Make sure you replenish the soil, too, so their crops will continue to thrive after we're gone. Whatever you grow won't keep forever.

My pumpkin is holding up pretty well.

Tyrrik snorted. *I never liked pumpkin.*

I gasped and turned, Dyter's arm falling from my shoulders as I faced my mate, mouth opened and ready to deliver a scathing reply.

I froze when I saw Tyrrik's wide grin.

His black aketon was dusty with ash, his face sported a couple days of growth, and his dark eyes were smoldering heat—for me.

My irritation evaporated, and an answering heat rushed in to take its place in my chest. His well-timed quip effectively distracted me from my wallowing. I tried to suppress the smile and likely looked like I was having a seizure. *You better love my pumpkins and potatoes and cherries and anything else I decide to grow.*

I promise I will love anything you grow, mate.

Desire sparked low in my belly with the low rumbling embers of his voice as he claimed me as his.

Dyter tugged my sleeve and said, "Come on, Rynnie. Zakai is waiting." He slung his arm back over my shoulder and whispered, "You two better spend some time alone before we leave —"

Mistress Moons, Dyter was *not* telling me to have sex.

"—talk a little or play cards together so you're not distracted as we march. Focus is important in battle, both yours and his."

My relief about Dyter's meaning was so heartfelt that Tyrrik, feeling it also, let out a strangled laugh behind me. I blushed. I'd been caught staring like a love-sick pup, but my head was totally in the gutter.

Tyrrik and I had been dancing around our intimacy for too long. I was going to play cards with him.

"We've amassed what supplies we could since your arrival. But I'm afraid almost no one harvested their Phaetyn blood crops before we raced into the stronghold." Gairome was taller than Zakai and built like an ox.

I stared at his muscular build, wondering how he'd grown so big on a meager diet, and noticed he was missing his hand and the lower portion of his arm, almost all the way up to his elbow —like Dyter.

Fifteen people, a mixture of female and male Gemondians as well as Dyter, Tyrrik, and me, stood around a table. It wasn't just any table but shaped to mimic Draeconia. A map was carved into the surface, showing the three kingdoms, the southern desert, and the empire. Mountains, forests, and rivers were detailed on the Drae-shaped table. The intricate table was a treasure. I loved it. I wanted it.

You shall have one, Tyrrik promised me.

Do you think I'm spoiled? I asked him.

He didn't reply.

"If we don't have enough food—" Gairome started.

"Food won't be a problem," I said, cutting him off. "If you have seeds, we'll be fine." I faced Zakai. "The Phaetyn have started their march; they'll be at Azule in less than two weeks. According to Dyter, it'll take you ten days to get to Azule, and that's if nothing goes wrong."

"Something always goes wrong," Dyter muttered.

I tipped my head at the old coot but kept my gaze on Zakai. "Like he said, you'd better plan on something going wrong, which means you need to be out of here tomorrow, day after at the latest."

"Someone needs to alert King Caltevyn," Dyter added.

"Already done," Tyrrik said, his low voice causing several of the men to cast sideways glances at the Drae. "Lani sent her elderly and children with a guard of fifty to Verald. They're carrying a message to your king."

Zakai looked at his son and the other Gemondian leaders. "Then circulate the notice: we leave at daybreak."

Several of the men and women filed out, and I glanced at Tyrrik. The Drae was listening to Dyter and Zakai—or at least looking at them intently.

Are you coming? I asked.

Go do your . . . mojo in the garden; you'll feel better after it's done, and I should fill Zakai and Dyter in on everything that happened in Phaetynville.

I snorted. *You know, it has a name. A real name.*

Yes, love. Go grow the people some food. You need to leave everyone who will remain enough to survive until we return.

Even after pouring my green Phaetyn powers into the veggie patches of the royal gardens for several hours, I wasn't satisfied with the result. The elderly and children were going to have a hard time if the war was ongoing. Who knew how long we'd be away.

I sighed heavily. I needed to go outside and reverse as much of the damage there as possible. *That* was the root of my discontent.

I stopped at the gardens, gathering two bags of huge pumpkin seeds as well as other fruits, vegetables, and even a few dozen nuts. It wasn't enough to fill the land, but it would get them started.

My heart fell as I strode through the kingdom doors and saw the damage. I'd expected the gray haze to still be masking the ruin, but the rain had poured through the smoke from the sky while I was inside, catching the haze in its droplets and forcing it to the ground.

Everything was black and charred. No life remained here.

This is something I can fix.

I shifted and carefully took both bags in my front talons. Launching this way was harder than usual, but minutes later, I soared over the blackened earth, scattering the seeds into the ash.

I purposely left my Phaetyn veil off, knowing Draedyn would feel I was back. I wanted him to know there were Drae here who would fight against him for the people of Gemond. When I returned to the entrance, I sat outside the doors and did as I had in Verald before leaving, pumping my Phaetyn energy into the ground, willing the land to heal and the seeds to grow.

I thought of big pumpkins, large enough for Tyrrik to stand in, and potatoes the size of goats. I willed the fruit trees to blossom, hoping we weren't too late in the year for the bees to pollinate them, but what did I know? I spent a lot of time on the nut trees. And then the grapes, pinot gris, like the ones Arnik spent hours working with—because we'd need wine to celebrate when we won the war.

I felt the sun warm my skin. The rain had stopped, but I didn't bother moving. The rays filtered through the canopy above, and I breathed in the verdant smell of a late summer afternoon after heavy rain.

"Are you done?" Tyrrik asked.

I'd felt his presence draw closer, and I smiled, my eyes still closed. I patted the ground next to me as I sat up, and unable to resist looking at my mate, I opened my eyes.

"Holy Pancakes!" I gasped.

Tyrrik stood before me, his hand extended, admiration in his dark eyes. Behind him was an oasis of flourishing growth, stretching out into the valley almost as far as I could see. I took his hand, but my gaze was riveted on the flora. "I think that's your pumpkin," I whispered in awe as I pointed at a squash the size of my old house in Verald. "Right there."

Tyrrik glanced over his shoulder. "I said I like your potatoes better."

I nodded, my gaze sweeping over the growth, and pointed at the leaves of a potato plant. "You can dig a couple up over here then."

I grinned with deep satisfaction. I was no longer the soap queen. I was Ryn, Potato Queen, destined to feed thousands. I was moving up in the world.

I lay back down as Tyrrik dug up two potatoes. He dusted off his hands after fifteen minutes. Yep, they were totally bigger than goats.

The sun disappeared over the mountaintops, and I sighed, feeling guilty for having fun and for feeling joy while Kamini and Kamoi were in danger because of me and while a battle loomed on the horizon.

"There's always a reason to enjoy what life gives you," Tyrrik said.

He lowered the two boulder-sized potatoes speared on his talons and then retracted his natural weapons before pulling me into his arms.

"Let's have dinner," he said, nuzzling my neck. "With candles."

"Will you light the candles with your Drae fire?" I asked.

His tongue traced my feathering pulse, the warmth and moisture shooting trembling pleasure low in my stomach. He kissed my ear, tracing the outer part first before sucking my lobe into his mouth, his teeth grazing the soft skin.

"And then," he whispered, guiding me backward until I was sandwiched between him and the mountain, "I want to be the reason for your joy."

He pressed his body into mine, making me gasp as his hips molded against mine. A heavy ache for him had me instinctively pushing back.

"I want to be all you think about," he said, trailing kisses down my neck. He pulled the neck of my aketon open and brushed his stubble along my collarbone, trailing his nose up my neck on the other side, inhaling deeply.

I moaned and leaned closer, my hands gripping his waist as I circled my hips against him.

"I want to be one with you, both body and mind. I want you to know how much I love you."

My mind, hazy once again, thought only of him as the rest of the world fell away.

"Tyrrik," I begged. *Mate.*

A loud grating sound made me freeze, and a moment later I heard a man calling, "Lord Tyrrik? Lady Ryn?"

yrrik growled in response to the interruption, but this time *I'd* had enough. I grabbed Tyrrik's hand and yanked him toward the door. As we brushed by the guard, I snapped, "There's plenty of food out there. Lord Tyrrik even dug up some potatoes for supper."

I stopped and took two steps back to the wide-eyed man. "Tell whoever you have to that Lord Tyrrik and I are done dealing with everyone and anything else for the night. Al'right? As in: Do. Not. Disturb"—I poked my finger into the man's chest—"the Drae. Unless someone is dying." I pulled up short, grabbed a fistful of his aketon, and narrowed my partially shifted eyes at him. "Is someone dying or dead?"

The guard shook his head.

"Excellent." I patted his chest lightly where I'd poked a moment before. "Good fellow, we're on the up and up. Right." I raised my hand to my eye level and pointed at him. "Do not disturb. Understood?"

He nodded.

What a brilliant communicator. Someone should give him a medal. "As you were, soldier."

I rotated to my mate with a grin, reaching for his hand. "We have some unfinished business."

Tyrrik raised his eyebrows but said nothing, accepting my hand. When I stepped forward, he stayed rooted to the floor, making me stumble back.

"Where are we going?" he asked.

I shrugged. I didn't care where we went. There was a giant pumpkin right behind us that was good to go—

The guard cleared his throat.

"Excuse me," he said, taking a tentative step forward. He held out a golden key with a smooth oval of polished lapis lazuli. "King Zakai sent me to show you to your chamber. Down this hall, take the first right, and it's the first door on the left."

I flashed the guard a smile as I plucked the key from his fingers, my expression turning cheeky when I met Tyrrik's gaze. "I've always liked King Zakai."

"So you've said," he replied. He lifted his gaze to the man and said, "Thank you. Please convey our gratitude to your sovereign."

Oops. "Yes, thanks." Guilt made me turn back and add, "Sorry about . . . earlier. You took me by surprise, and I might've overreacted a little. Or a lot. Oh, and there are potatoes out there; you might want to pick them up or have someone help you. They'd be good for dinner."

Tyrrik slid his arm around my waist, and I stopped talking. The guard picked up the Drae's cue and hurried away.

I groaned when Tyrrik opened the door to our room. There was a sitting area with a full table of food, including a tureen of pumpkin soup, and beyond that sat a bed the size of Tyrrik's one back in Verald. A gilded entranceway graced the opposite wall of the chamber, leading to what I assumed was a bathroom.

I couldn't help stroking the walls, the *lapis* walls. Lovely. That Zakai was fabulous.

My mouth dried as realization hit me. This was it. I was in this room with Tyrrik, and while there was no doubt I wanted to be here

. . . I was. And I was about to claim my mate, and he would claim me.

"Nervous?" Tyrrik asked, wrapping his arms around my midsection.

A bajillion butterflies unfurled their wings in my belly, competing for the limited space. "No." Yes.

I smiled shyly, resting my hands on his arms as I leaned against him and told the truth. *Yes.*

Come with me. He slid his hand into mine and led me through the room.

I eyed the food as we passed, noticing a whole chicken and a plate of fluffy white rolls. Seriously, Zakai needed a raise. We walked to the bed, the thick posts of the canopied frame carved into intricate designs and inlaid with gold. The silken blankets were a pale shade of the same lapis lazuli color as the stone walls.

Tyrrik led me past the beautiful clean bed and toward the open double doors of the bathroom.

My heart thudded, and my hands were clammy in a fraction of a second. It wasn't that I didn't want this—I *really* did. But the weirdness of knowing that was where we were headed *right now*, plus his experience . . . My tummy flipped as I recalled that gem. *Experience.* "Uhh . . ."

"Do you want to play a game?" he asked, stopping inside the doorway, his inky gaze dipping to my lips.

I swallowed, still caught up on the experience part. "Is this a game you've played before?"

A slow smile started at his lips and radiated into his gaze. "I promise I've never played this game with anyone else."

I narrowed my eyes. "Then how do you know about it?"

He chuckled, a low throaty sound, and closed the distance between us. "Because I remember how my father revered my mother."

I grimaced. Uhh. "I'm not sure I want to play a game your father taught you. Like, just at this moment."

Experienced, but clearly lacking in the pillow talk vicinity.

Tyrrik dipped so he was looking me in the eye. "Oh, the game's all mine. If you don't like anything, you tell me, and we'll stop. I promise." He brushed his thumb over my lips, and his voice was husky when he added, "Please?"

What do we do? I couldn't believe I was agreeing because kissing seemed to be a way better idea. One I wasn't going to deny myself. I stepped closer to Tyrrik and brushed my fingertips over his lips before I rose to my tiptoes.

Tyrrik indulged me with a tender kiss before pulling away. "All you have to do is tell me if you like this?"

"Like what?"

He trailed his fingers down my neck to the fold of my purple aketon, pulling the thick fabric open enough so he could trace first above and then below my collarbone. "Do you like this?"

I sucked in a sharp breath. "Yea—"

His fingers dipped lower, tracing the swell of my breast, and air hitched in my throat. Holy-Drae-babies.

"Do you like this?" he asked, stopping to look me in the eye.

His touch was fire, and I nodded, swaying closer.

"What about this?" he asked, guiding me back with his body until I was sandwiched between him and the wall.

His hand went to the tie at my waist, and he pulled the knot loose.

I wore a chemise to bed most nights, so it was stupid to feel shy about him exposing my underclothes, but the concentration with which he did it sent a deep flush into my cheeks.

He undid the tie on the other end and pushed the outer garment off my shoulders.

"You're getting rid of our clothes?" I asked.

He didn't answer, but two could play at this game.

I pulled the tie at his waist on one side and then the other. Pushing my hands up the smooth planes of his chest, I asked, quirking a brow, "Do you like?"

"Yes," he growled, and the warm embers of his voice called to me.

He pushed his body into mine, dipping his head to my neck

111

where he pressed his lips to my pulse. And then to our mate mark. I stilled as Tyrrik groaned deep in the back of his throat and applied more pressure to the mark than ever before.

I gasped, heat flooding through me at the small, dominating nip.

"Do you like this?" he asked. Before I could answer, he gripped my waist, kneading his way to my hips. "What about this?"

Is that even a question? I moaned and pushed my hips to his in response. He dipped his hand under the gathered fabric of my chemise and asked, "Do you like this?"

I swallowed, and my voice was thick when I answered, "Yes."

He pushed his calloused hand up the side of my body, lifting the chemise over my head. "This?"

My breaths were shallow, and I nodded as Tyrrik dragged his eyes over my mostly naked body. His low, throaty growl reverberated from him to me. Aching want tugged deep in my stomach, and I moved toward him in a blur.

You are ethereal. Tyrrik traced his fingers down between my breasts, only the barest of *essentials* still covered with my bralette. "Come," he said, his voice rumbling between us. "Let me warm your bath."

"Bath?" We were stopping for a bath?

He lowered his head, his lips hovering just above my mouth, and then brushing my lips, he said, "Tell me if you like this."

Tyrrik kissed me, nipping my bottom lip, and I opened my mouth to him. His tongue stroked mine and his hands caressed me, his touch my entire world. When he put distance between us, I whispered his name. A plea.

He stood me at the edge of the bath, dropped his undergarments, and glanced back as he got in. "You've still got clothes on."

Problem solved. I followed him into the bath.

Steam rose from the water, swirling around us. Tyrrik's onyx power seeped through the room. My lapis energy danced and dipped, and as the two powers met, they tangled around each other and flared, the sudden glow bursting through the bathroom.

Tyrrik continued the pretense of his game, asking question after question, driving me steadily insane until there was no me or him, no separate bodies, no separate powers.

There was only us. Tender touches, the silken stroke of fingers, whisper-soft caresses, and soul-deep sighs.

We pushed each other to places of aching desperation. And when the stars and moons exploded, lights burst behind my eyelids.

Our lives intertwined, indiscernible as mine or his.

Tyrrik was mine.

And I was his.

"TYRRYN?" Tyrrik asked, tracing his finger down my face.

I groaned, batting his hand away, too lacking in sleep after our love-making to want to be up this early.

"Tyrryn," he growled. "Mate."

Then I processed what he'd said and sat up holding the sheet to my chest.

"Tear-Ryn?" I scrunched my nose at the name on my lips. It sounded . . . odd. Not that I was opposed to our mate-bond, but I wasn't so sure I wanted to be Tyrryn, tearin' through the sky. Tearin' to the gems.

"Tearing through the sky?" he asked, faint amusement in his voice.

But underneath the forced humor, I could feel his confusion and hurt. Whoa. The bond-thing was legitimately stronger.

"I don't understand," Tyrrik said, his brow furrowing. "You don't like my name?"

Okay, that might've sounded a bit . . . rude. Tyrrik leaned over me, and heaviness settled in my chest as I peered up at him. "I've only ever been Ryn, and my mom was Ryhl. The r-y is kinda the only thing I have left from my mother, Tyrrik. It'd be like me asking you to be Ryrik. I'm just not sure . . ."

He searched my face, his expression serious, not even going for the Ryrik-bait. He nodded and asked, "What would you like to do?"

"I could still be Ryn, and you could still be Tyrrik?" I said weakly. "We're mates. Officially, if we have to write it down somewhere, I'm from the house of Tyr. I'm one hundred percent team Tyr. But everyday . . . I'm just going to be Ryn. Maybe we dispense with that part of human tradition?"

Amusement flooded his eyes. "And where do you think that human tradition came from?"

A moment passed before I got it. "Really?" I asked pointing at him. "It's a Drae thing? So, does that mean I would've been Draeryn because the emperor is Draedyn?" And I thought *Tyrryn* was odd. "I like Ryn."

His features smoothed, and I grasped his thoughts just a fraction before he spoke them aloud. "If I compromise on this, will you promise to remain by my side?"

"Like conjoined twins?" I asked glibly.

"No, just within the vicinity," he said, throwing his hands in the air. "I want to be able to get to you quickly if someone tries to hurt you. *That's* what I mean. If you're days away, I can't protect you."

His words hung heavy in the air. I frowned, struggling to separate my wants from his. A part of me desperately wanted to never be without him, but swearing to always being that close was a big issue. *Always* left no room for freedom. "Are we starting that again? After what we shared last night?"

"No, my mate," he said, kissing away my frown. "I would not have that."

But the sad ache of his forlornness at my answer echoed through me, battling against my resolve. This bond might take some getting used to.

"Tyrrik?" I said, reaching up to loop my hands around the back of his neck as I let the sheet go.

"Yes, my Ryn?"

I took a deep, happy breath. "I love you. So very much."

A rumble, almost akin to a purr, filled the space between us, and his joy swelled within me.

I stared at him, my heart full, and realized I'd never said the words before. I'd mated with him, mentally and physically, and yet never acknowledged what that meant out loud.

His eyes shined as he lowered his head to place a tender kiss on my forehead. "I love you more than life itself, my mate. I hope you enjoyed last night."

I nodded, smoothing my face though I couldn't conceal the way my heart leaped. "It was pretty good." I pulled him closer and whispered in his ear, "I think we should play cards again tonight."

"Play cards?" He laughed when I blushed, his body shaking me and the space around us. But he shook his head. "No, you'll be sore from last night."

Ha! "That might be true if I were human or just Drae. But us Phaetyn? We've got all the skills." I tightened my embrace and grinned impishly before licking his ear. "Come on," I whispered, my heart pounding. "Play cards with me."

"What have I started?" he replied.

Honestly, I was wondering that too.

A slow smile spread across his face, and I let out a squeal of delight as he knelt upright and ripped away the blankets between us. His handsome face and boyish grin was all I could see as my Drae reached for me.

*H*unger drove us out of the lapis chamber, and my stomach growled as we walked through the empty corridor. I was going to eat an entire boulder-sized potato. Mmm. Roasted with rosemary and salt. *Maybe Tyrrik can breathe fire on one.* I snickered.

Tyrrik and I held hands as we wound up through the kingdom, and by the time we reached the level of our old rooms, I pulled him to a stop as the silence settled in. I grimaced up at Tyrrik and asked, "Where is everyone?"

"My thoughts exactly," he murmured.

That had been his thought? Had I mistaken it for my own? I blinked several times, trying to untangle him from me.

It was your own.

I narrowed my eyes at the amusement in his mind voice. "Yes, I know," I huffed, even though I knew he'd *know* I was lying. "But when I start thinking about it all, my mind gets weird and twisty."

Your human notions are getting in the way.

I snorted and tugged him forward. "Whatever, *Ryrik*."

He growled, and I smirked. Definitely needed to remember that quip.

Two golden-guards clattered down the gem-encrusted passage toward us.

They bowed, and the smaller one said, "Lord Tyrrik, Lady Tyrryn."

Whoa, whoa, whoa! Why were they calling me Tyrryn? My eyes rounded. *Drak*, they knew we'd mated? My cheeks flushed. How did they know?

"Where is everyone?" Tyrrik asked, ignoring my imagination of rocks crashing and Drae roaring.

Please tell me that didn't really happen.

At the same time, the guard rotated his attention to Tyrrik. "The army left five hours ago, my lord. King Zakai instructed you to be left alone until . . ."

I fixed the man with a cool glare. He better not go there.

He never even glanced my way but still blanched and wisely didn't finish the sentence. Maybe Tyrrik had shown some fang.

"They expected you'd be able to catch up," the second guard said.

Right, we had wings. Pretty safe assumption.

"Indeed. Thank you," Tyrrik said. Grabbing my hand, he led me around the guards.

Do you think everyone knows we were playing cards? I asked.

He didn't even glance my way, but a blind man could've seen Tyrrik's huge grin. *In one word? Yes. What we did is nothing to be ashamed of, my love. I'd imagine everyone else wishes they were doing the same.*

I wrinkled my nose then tried to un-judge my judgment of everyone judging us. Sex was a pretty natural thing; every person, human, Phaetyn, and Drae was the result of *playing cards*. "Well, I'm not confirming any rumors, regardless of how natural spawning is."

His grip tightened on my hand. "I plan to become intimately familiar with you." *And no one will see you like that but me.*

An image flashed in my mind. Walls? "Wait," I said, stopping outside the doorway to the kitchen. "Did you just find a human thing you liked?"

"Perhaps walls have their uses."

Trust him to pick the most possessive human thing he could.

He pushed the door open and the scents of yeast, potatoes, and roasted meat wafted in the air. My stomach rumbled, and I grinned in anticipation. We were in the kitchen. Food.

I inhaled, trying to eat the smells, and all-but ran to a flat tray of steaming potato wedges just out of the oven. My mouth watered, and I hovered on the verge of tipping the whole tray in my mouth before recalling those left behind would be waiting for food.

I took four and stood back as Tyrrik took four also. He totally needed more, and so I reached forward and grabbed a handful for him. "I'll grow a few more potatoes on my way out, but you better get enough to eat."

He raised his eyebrows and grabbed another handful then held them out for me. "You too."

Our hunger abated; we left the rest of the food for the others, knowing we could hunt on the way.

"Excuse me." I addressed the closest cook, a rail-thin man who didn't sample enough of his creations. "Would you know where I could find some seed stores? I need carrots, beans, squash, tomatoes. Small seeds for vegetables and fruits, nothing that grows on a tree or needs more than one season to grow, preferably."

"I will send someone to collect some for you." He waved at one of the kitchen maids.

I stared at his scrawny arm. The woman who joined him was just as thin. "Thank you. A bag the size of my fist should do. And some potato and beetroots too. Could you ask them to meet us at the northern exit?"

The cook nodded and told the woman where to go to get the seeds, and then she hurried over to a teenage girl, hushing instructions in her ear.

We walked through the mountain halls, winding to the back entrance where we'd arrived early yesterday morning. Had only one day seriously passed? I felt changed, grown, at peace. Sliding my gaze to Tyrrik, I didn't have to puzzle over the reason.

My mate completed me. His contentment was my contentment.

After everything we'd gone through, separate and together, I'd do it all over again, knowing this was the end result.

Potato wedges long gone, I planted the other potatoes and beets, throwing some vibrant Phaetyn-mojo at them, and told the young girl to wait a quarter of an hour and then get some help digging up the root vegetables.

Tyrrik shifted just outside the Gemond Kingdom, and I joined him after stretching my moss-green veil over my Drae form to keep my presence cloaked from Draedyn. We wanted to keep our plans from him for as long as possible. I rose into the air just above the treetops to join my mate in his onyx Drae form and then extended my veil until it covered us both. The air was now clean of smoke and ash, and I grinned as we started northward to join our friends.

So, Tyrrik said casually, drawing my attention from the ground. *Spawning.*

My wings froze for half a second before they resumed their rhythmic beating. *Yes?*

You mentioned spawning?

I'd mentioned the word errantly, and so my reply was flippant. *I like practicing.*

I could feel through the mate bond how much my answer meant to him, so I considered my words before answering further. He was over one hundred years old; he might've wanted Drae babies for longer than I'd been alive.

I want to have Drae babies with you, I said. *But I'm also younger than you. I feel . . . I feel I'm getting better, stronger, and a bit wiser. But I don't know if I'm ready for little Tyrriks yet. We have time though, right?* If we lost the war, my answer was pointless anyway. I closed my eyes, refusing to think of what might happen to Tyrrik if we lost.

We have time, he replied. *And experience and wisdom will be good for you and them.*

Good. Besides, I want to get my treasure stash all set up too.

He swept his great head to look at me. *Of course. That's a given. I'll extend my trove into a cavern beautiful enough for my mate—*

I was glad we were on the same page about babies and the privacy thing.

You will store your treasures there and then have our babies throughout the ages.

At least I thought we were on the same page. It bothered me we hadn't come to a compromise on the 'don't leave my side' issue. Maybe I shouldn't have brushed him off earlier, but I hadn't wanted to ruin the mood.

Before long, the trailing members of King Zakai's army were visible dots moving on the stoney ground far below. As we descended, I shivered with how easy it would be for the emperor to spot them. He could unleash a jet of fire upon the army and kill them all without even landing.

Good thing Tyrrik and I were here now. But still . . . *Hey, can you attack my mind for a bit? I need some practice.*

I instantly turned my attention inward, knowing he wouldn't delay. I imagined my mind as a ball and then drew the blue tendrils of my Drae power away from my mate, ignoring the hollowness in my chest as I did so. I wound the tendrils of power around my mind, thread by thread in a sort of turban-like shield. Working as fast as I mentally could, I thickened the glowing blue strands creating a shiny defense to outside attack.

Tyrrik's mental blow hit my forehead with the force of a battering ram. I roared, feeling the buffer around my mind dissolve instantly, the power rebounding back to coil with Tyrrik's black tendrils.

Drak! I snapped my fangs in frustration. *Why can't I get it? I've actually gotten worse. I didn't even hold you out for a single second this time.*

We are fully mated now. Keeping me out will be much harder.

Great, I grumbled. Not that I wanted to keep him out. I was long past that. But if I couldn't keep Tyrrik out, would I be able to keep my father out?

Try again, my queen. You are creating a barrier. Why don't you try making the barrier harder or thicker?

Al'right. I wound my tendrils around my head again, coiling them tight, and then imagined the individual tendrils merging into one thick shell as though my spiked tail was wrapped around my mind. I knew Tyrrik was giving me too much time, time the emperor wouldn't give me, but I focused on hardening the Drae shield, making it an impenetrable diamond.

I nodded, not breaking my concentration. And Tyrrik attacked.

The battering ram struck me just as hard, and I clung to my wall. *Diamond, diamond, diamo—*

My blue power shattered like glass sugar, the shards blasting inward, and pain stabbed my temples. I reached for the pieces, straining to catch them and form a shield. But once again, the blue energy was drawn back to Tyrrik's power.

I opened my eyes and sighed, the sound coming out my Drae mouth as a weary groan.

That was better, Tyrrik said. *You kept me out for a few seconds, and even then, I couldn't immediately seize control.*

I felt like I'd played my first game of hopscotch and Tyrrik was telling me I wouldn't fall and scrape my knee next time. *Thanks. Perhaps it's like my Phaetyn veil, and I just need to strengthen the muscle.*

We'll keep trying. We have weeks, maybe even a couple of months before we'll reach the heart of the empire.

That didn't mean Draedyn wouldn't find us first. My thoughts stirred uneasily as I scanned the ground again. We were nearing the front of the procession and descended side-by-side. Soon after, we shifted and strode back through the first ten rows of gold-plated soldiers to reach Zakai and Dyter.

"Hey," I said, pretending the entire army hadn't left the Gemond Mountains and neither Tyrrik nor I noticed because we'd had our clothes off.

King Zakai nodded, graciously playing along. "I'm glad to see familiar faces. The sky had been worrying me. I'm afraid we are easy targets out here."

They are, Tyrrik said.

I hummed in agreement. "You are vulnerable from the sky.

Tyrrik and I can help if the emperor attacks, but I don't want to rely on that."

Phaetyn veil.

I wasn't sure if the thought was mine or my mate's—it didn't matter.

The army was huge, not as big as Zivost, but I'd need to create a veil, larger than any I'd made before, and definitely larger than I was capable of holding for any length of time. Just more mind-muscle work.

"You have a solution?" Zakai asked, rubbing a hand over his shorn scalp. He looked younger without the long, stringy hair he'd had when I first met him.

"Your Phaetyn veil?" Dyter said, joining us. He was quick on the uptake as always.

Walking beside the king, I replied, "I'm not making promises, but I should be able to cover some of the army if we're attacked by Druman or Draedyn."

"What if the army could converge into a smaller space if we're attacked from above?" Tyrrik asked. I watched him, noticing he took one stride for every two of mine.

Zakai glanced over his shoulder at his son and Gairome who were listening. "What do you think?"

Zarad pursed his lips. "It could be done, of course. In an orderly fashion. My only worry is if our army sees the emperor, they'll panic and hurt each other." He paused. "I shall run drills on this when we stop for the night." He glanced up at Tyrrik and asked, "My Lord Drae, would you be willing to help?"

Tyrrik consented, and Zakai smiled at his son. I felt a pang as I thought of my mother's smiles.

"I'll get practicing on that veil then." *I can do this*, I decided. Maybe only a quarter of the army to start. But I could do this for Gemond. If I didn't try, I'd be the one to blame for any life I could've saved.

I glanced back at the army behind us and blinked as I encountered the burning gaze of the young man who'd hurled accusations at me yesterday before I grew the potatoes. His anger made me frown and face forward, marching in time with the Gemondians. What had happened to their kingdom was horrible, and yes, I felt some responsibility. That I should shoulder *more* of the burden for what happened to them hadn't occurred to me until the soldier behind me shocked me with his vitriolic opinion.

No matter what I thought about myself, those around me saw me as a Phaetyn-Drae, someone with enough power to change the outcome of this war and this world. They didn't see *me* but rather a person capable of things they could never do.

As much as I had shied away from taking responsibility for the kingdom's future since learning of my powers, I now saw I shouldn't be shirking away from taking any burden either. I was a Drae and a Phaetyn; hadn't Mum talked about power and responsibility?

Protecting the Gemondian army was one of those responsibilities I needed to pick up. I'd do for them what Lani was doing for her people. And when Verald and Azule joined us, I'd work harder again to protect them all. I had great power, and I guess that came with great—and mostly unwanted—responsibility. But now, I was done running. I had to step up.

I'm going to be working on my veil until we stop, I informed Tyrrik.

Ignoring the smiles of the others, he bent down to plant a kiss on my lips. *And I will keep to the skies to scout ahead. I'll alert you to anything significant.*

Let me know how far my Phaetyn veil reaches too? He'd be able to see where the army blurred and didn't. As my mate, Tyrrik could see through my Phaetyn veil. Although I was unsure if last night had obliterated the effectiveness of any barrier against him.

"I guess we'll find out," he replied aloud, drawing the confused gazes of those around us.

With an amused look on his weathered face, King Zakai asked Dyter. "Do they do that a lot?"

Dyter released a pent up breath and rolled his eyes. "You have no idea, Your Majesty. And I suspect it'll only get worse."

16

Be on your guard, Tyrrik spoke to me from high in the darkening sky. The last streaks of sunlight melting into the rich twilight. *There's a squirrel to the east with an evil look in its eye.*

I snorted, waving a hand at Zarad when he looked at me strangely. *The squirrel only has one eye?*

Before, Tyrrik wasn't able to talk to me through the veil, but now he could. I'd been right, completing our mating bond changed the effectiveness of the wall against my Drae. Not that I minded.

"It's like I'm listening to one-twentieth of a conversation," King Zakai muttered. "How incredibly frustrating."

I believe he lost it while killing a Drae.

I whistled low and grinned at the Gemondian king. *That's one fearsome squirrel.*

Do not fear, mate. I will keep you safe.

Chuckling, I said to the king, "We're in the clear."

Then I tuned them out and focused on stretching the moss-green power farther behind us. I could see the edge of my Phaetyn wall ahead; the power tucked around the ten rows of Gemondians in front of the army. I'd spent the last five hours extending the veil to the men behind me.

A trickle of sweat rolled down my neck, despite the evening air, and I knew when I dropped the veil I'd need some serious nectar. On the positive side, holding the power steady was much easier in my Phaetyn form. I supposed my Phaetyn side still preferred light and my Drae side still preferred darkness. Unfortunately, that meant to prevent unnecessary fatigue, I was on the ground while Tyrrik was in the air, scouting. *How much am I covering now?*

I got an image from his mind's eye and smiled at the aerial view of my work. Oh yeah, I was getting better. I whooped aloud and said, "One third."

"One third?" the Gemondian king asked, his brows knitting together. His tone was sharper than I'd ever heard. "One third of what?"

Yikes. I guess the partial conversations were really getting to him. I met his weary gaze and explained, "I'm covering one third of your army with my Phaetyn powers. With it up, Draedyn won't be able to see your men."

I had no idea how effective the Phaetyn mojo was against the alpha's fire. I couldn't only go on what happened at *Kanahele o keola* and the journey there. Draedyn couldn't enter the Phaetyn veil when it was up, and Draedyn's first attempt to take over my mind had cut off when Lani's veil went up, so I assumed Draedyn's physical powers couldn't penetrate a Phaetyn veil either. But even with ancestral powers, I didn't have a magic crown. I shouldn't rely on the veil being impenetrable, especially because I shared a bond with the psycho-ruler I was attempting to hide us from.

I'd had so little time to explore my powers, yet everything seemed to hinge on me figuring them out.

Now that my father had broken in and controlled me once, would he be able to do it again with ease? What about when I was in my Phaetyn form, could he do it then? Or even when I had my veil up because he was related to me? I swallowed back the churning insecurity and doubt.

"Once you're able to cover the whole army," mused Dyter, walking beside me, "we should practice keeping the veil up in battle.

Draedyn isn't going to just sit quietly while you assemble your defenses. You need to be able to fight *and* keep the veil in place."

He'd spent most of the afternoon pulling me back into line. When I concentrated on my Phaetyn powers, I *occasionally* forgot to pay attention to where I was walking.

"Yeah, about that. I think I should try to juggle, too, all at the same time. Maybe even while riding a horse."

Dyter grimaced. "Perhaps something more like avoiding punches and swinging a sword?"

He was so easy to bait these days. I hummed. "We should do all of the above." I nodded. "Excellent. Thanks for the advice, Dyter."

Zakai cleared his throat. "Gairome, this seems a good area to stop our march for the day. Night is falling fast, and I'm certain the men need what's left of the light to set up camp."

I can't wait to drop this thing, I admitted to Tyrrik as the call went out for the army to halt.

He hurtled toward the ground, and I could feel my eagerness echoed in his impatience.

The last time I'd released the veil, I practically collapsed, so I waited until he'd shifted and was approaching before slowly letting go.

I groaned under my breath with the release. Seriously, if someone was rubbing warm stones up my back, the relief would only be half as good.

I exhaled as the moss-green power shrunk, and then when only Tyrrik and I were covered, I let go of the Phaetyn veil completely. My knees shook, and although letting go of the veil felt amazing, my muscles trembled with exhaustion.

Tyrrik leaned over and scooped me into his arms.

"Hey," I accused, half-heartedly narrowing my eyes at him. "You landed inside my veil."

"You can't keep me out now that we've fully mated," he said with a smirk.

I laughed at the burst of male pride radiating through our bond. "That comment would be super creepy if it weren't true." Now, I had no defenses against Tyrrik, not that I even wanted or *needed* any defenses against him. I nestled to his chest. I mean who'd want to keep out a handsome hunk of Drae like Tyrrik, except for past-Ryn who couldn't see clearly. Maybe past-Ryn could've done with a few wakeup slaps.

His features softened, and he added, "You look tired."

"Lord Tyrrik, Lady Tyrryn."

Mistress Moons. What was with the guards? I listened to Tyrrik's quiet snicker, making a mental note to inform Zakai my name was, and would always be, Ryn. There was far too much pun potential with Tyrryn. Tyrryn down walls. Tyrryn toward danger. The world couldn't handle all the puns I would make if they continued to call me Tyrryn.

I eyed the man, surprised my eyelids still worked because my body had checked out for the foreseeable future.

"Your tent is set up this way." The guard bowed.

What did I say about liking Zakai? I yawned.

I'd much rather stare at the stars, Tyrrik answered.

Privacy.

I didn't have to say more. Tyrrik picked up his pace, following the guard through the pine trees to the middle of the encampment.

Good, if the army was camped around us, I'd be able to cover more of them if we received a night visit. Though I'm not sure how I'd do after holding the veil up all day.

. . . Drak.

I was exhausted. My stomach churned uneasily as I thought of our camp exposed all night because I'd overextended myself with practice during the day.

"Do you require anything else?" the guard asked, gaze shifting to where other soldiers were trailing out of the trees, back to the main valley.

"What's happening?" I mumbled, too tired to even properly fume over my mistake. I couldn't wear myself out to this extent again. The potential weakness in the veil due to my familial bond with Draedyn was one thing, but if I couldn't put the defense up *at all*—

or couldn't hold it because I was spent—we were all goners. *I've got to do better.*

You will, my love, Tyrrik answered.

I shot him a weak smile.

"Prince Zarad is running a drill," the guard said. "If the emperor attacks, the prince wants us close together so it's easier to spread your power of invisibility over the group." The man's eyes were round with awe.

Tyrrik coughed.

Power of invisibility, huh? I liked it. I nodded sagely. "Practice hard, soldier."

He bowed low, and Tyrrik coughed again, not speaking until the guard had joined the line leaving the forest.

"You're going to call your veil that from now on, aren't you?" Tyrrik asked. He ducked us into our tent.

"Hmm, what?" I asked as he set me on top of a blanket, and I lolled there like a blob. "What are you talking about?"

"The power of invisibility."

"Oh that," I said casually. "Maybe. I hadn't really thought about it."

Eyes narrowed, he stared at me until I couldn't hold my grin in. He snorted and dropped from his stooped position to sit by my side. I wasn't sure who'd carried our tent and set it up, but I was glad for it. Really glad. Like, I would maybe show the person something from my hoard in return. Except I'd hidden it back in Gemond, so it would have to be an *IOU one glimpse at my hoard* kind of thing.

The tent ceiling was low, only to the middle of Tyrrik's chest, and the tent appeared to be made of a quilted material. Whoever put it up had strung it between two trees and then stretched out either side before lining the interior with soft cushions and two thick blankets.

There were perks to being a Drae-Phaetyn with the power of invisibility.

"Aren't you tired?" I asked Tyrrik, who was staring out the entrance to the tent.

"After my battle with the one-eyed squirrel? Exhausted."

He blinked and picked up my legs, removing my boots. I groaned as he rubbed my calves.

"Sweet potato pancakes," I mumbled. "Please don't ever stop doing that."

"I'm not inclined to when you make sounds like that." He kneaded the muscles down, rotating my ankles before moving onto my feet.

At this rate, I'd be asleep in the next few minutes, but there was one thing I needed to do first. I handed Tyrrik the pouch of seeds and said, "Would you go scatter some of these outside. We're going to need to eat tomorrow."

I pulled up the two thick blankets covering the ground and pressed my palm atop the dried pine needles beneath.

"Are you sure that's wise, my love? You've expended a lot of energy today already."

I yawned and shooed him toward the door. "I'm no use against Draedyn tonight anyway, and growing stuff doesn't take much energy. But food will keep the army's strength up so they can fight."

Does this help? Tyrrik stared at me, and a moment later, the tendrils of his onyx power extended toward me. He pushed the tendrils into me, his energy seeping through the warmth of the power swirling around me. I sighed as the black threads settled back with mine into our normal intertwining bond.

"Better?" he asked.

"A bit, yes. How . . . Did you know that would work?"

I didn't feel great, but he'd definitely restored some of my energy levels. I felt stronger.

He shrugged. "I didn't know. But if you can strengthen me, it makes sense I could return the favor."

Wow. How progressive. In Drae culture, the male was the strength and the female the peace-maker. She tempered his violence, and he protected her above all else. For Tyrrik to strengthen me spoke volumes, almost more than anything else he'd done. And if I had to keep a veil up for a long period of time, reversing the power boost could come in useful.

My heart swelled with emotion, but I swallowed my reaction, not wanting to embarrass him. "Thank you, my mate. I love you."

He paused, his fingers still where he'd been massaging the front of my thighs, and whispered, "And I love you."

Leaning forward, he plucked the seeds from my hand and stooped to exit the tent. I listened to him scatter the seeds around the clearing. He returned and replaced the packet in my aketon.

Boosted somewhat by his energy, I focused on my palm, shooting green Phaetyn energy into the ground. I kept up a steady trickle, stopping far before I usually would. *Perhaps pumpkins don't always need to be the size of a Drae.*

With a fraction of my mind determined to understand my power and most of my attention on Tyrrik's hands, I sunk into slumber.

———

The smell of damp dirt and leafy growth made me shiver and whimper. A heavy weight pressed on my mind because I knew what that smell meant. I opened my eyes, and horror's vice-like grip forced the air from my lungs. I gasped, shallow breaths, trying greedily to take what I needed to remain calm.

But it wasn't enough.

Tall sunflowers surrounded me, fully blossomed, their vibrant-yellow petals mocking me, taking me back in time, holding me prisoner there. I leapt from my bed, pushing the blankets to the ground, and reached for the nearest stalk, knowing time was running out. No one could see these flowers! The hairs of the spiky stems dug into my palms, but I ignored the discomfort and frantically yanked.

The soil released the shallow roots, and the sunflower pulled free. *One down.* I rotated, grabbing stems in each hand as I tried to clear my cell. One, two, five, twenty. Faster and faster.

If Jotun saw the growth, he would know what I was. He'd turn me into King Irdelron, and I would forever be a slave. They could hurt everyone I cared about. And if they knew I feared these things, they would use that knowledge against me.

My heart pounded as I ripped up bloom after bloom, twisting and snapping the thick stalks, my fear squeezing from my eyes and dripping into the rich dirt. I glanced behind, and a dismayed moan left my lips. Where I'd pulled out the sunflowers, more had grown, a lot more, at least two to three times as many, but bruised petals and broken stalks littered the ground too. Jotun would know I'd tried to hide the sunflowers.

They'd know what I feared.

The outer door clicked open, and I stilled at the sound of a blade on Ty's bars. No, not a blade. A *talon*.

Lord Irrik was here to play his sick games once again. Only now I knew what would hurt him. I knew his weakness to Phaetyn power. I could exact my revenge.

I threw the flowers to the dank dungeon floor and gritted my teeth. Crossing my arms over my chest, I stood defiantly and waited. But confusion nagged at me, and I frowned. Why did I feel that Lord Irrik was . . . misunderstood?

I shook my head as the wisp of uncertainty was dragged away, and purpose infused me.

Lord Irrik crossed to my cell's bars, the sleek and powerful lines of his frame gliding forward like liquid darkness. Jotun trailed behind with a cruel smile contorting his features.

"Take her to the torture room," Lord Irrik said, his voice licking my soul with its warm embers. "Show her what we do to traitors."

My stomach roiled, and the hatred I held for the Drae and his cruelty burned through my chest, stretching out to my extremities. He would pay for what he did to me and my mum. Shaking my head again, the doubt returned. This wasn't right. Something wasn't right. I was missing something about the Lord Drae. I glanced at the still-smirking Jotun. He was the enemy. I . . .

Bending forward, I clutched my head.

"Ryn?" Irrik said.

I jerked violently. Somehow, he'd gotten into my cell without opening my door. How was that possible? He loomed over me, his fingers tracing from my temple to my chin, his touch liquid fire. He nudged me, tilting my chin high, and then buried his face in my neck. His lips trailed kisses down my pulsing vein, and I gasped at the fire coursing through me.

The desire was forced away, and darkness replaced the fire.

This was Irrik's game. The poisonous kiss of a Drae, meant to control me and force me to do his bidding. He was evil, wicked, his touch poison.

He needed to die.

I screamed, striking him with my Phaetyn power, throwing him into the sunflowers surrounding us. I was sick of doing only what was necessary. I refused to live in fear any longer. Yet fear was driving me as I clenched my fist, bringing the yellow blooms and their long stems tight to his body, wrapping him in their growth to bind him to the ground. No one would enslave me again. No one would hurt the people I loved.

I grinned in glee at the shock on his face. Yet my grin faded as I looked beyond Lord Irrik to Jotun. The Druman was blurring and fading—the sunflowers, bars, and dungeons dissipating as though sucked from the surrounding air.

The darkness and fear in my chest was replaced with a sense of panic and fury, emotions distant enough I knew they weren't mine.

"Ryn!" someone shouted from far away.

Bright light exploded in my mind, my vision of the world around me obliterated with the force, and then all was dark.

$\mathcal{I}$ blinked, staring up at Tyrrik in a daze. Shredded pieces of plants littered the space of our tent, covering most of the blankets and pillows in green bits. I was standing. *When did that happen?*

The quilted fabric of our tent hung askew, pulled off its supports by the upright Drae. He stood, watching me, his eyes wide. His chest, where I'd fallen asleep earlier, was wound with vines—not vines, *long sunflower stalks.*

I fell to my knees on the fragments of plants and pressed my hands to my temples.

"What happened?" I asked weakly.

"Are you . . . you?" Tyrrik asked, pulling pieces of stem and vine from him.

I sucked in a slow breath and nodded, though even *I* didn't believe myself right now. "What was that?"

I'd never had a nightmare that real before. Was it even a nightmare? It was like I'd been fighting against my own mind. As though someone was trying to . . . to remember things in a different way. That *someone* had wanted me to hurt Tyrrik.

There was only one person besides Tyrrik who had access to my mind. "That was my father."

The shock sucker-punched me, and my tongue stuck to the roof of my mouth. My voice was gone, but I forced the next question out, despite dreading the answer. *He can do that?*

Tyrrik's glower spoke louder than if he'd shouted actual words. He reached out for me, but I pulled back. I needed a moment to collect myself, to remind myself I was here with Tyrrik, not in the dungeons with Irrik. The simple fact Irrik had featured instead of Jotun proved my mind wasn't driving the nightmare.

How can he do that? Never once in my time in the dungeon had someone taken my mind. That's how I'd survived, by finding my corner. My father had seized control of me once already in the forest. But *this?* He'd warned me; he ruled through fear first. He'd even said leaving me with control of my mind had been a reward. But to not even realize I was being manipulated as I slept? He'd accessed my fears and used them against me. I remembered the way the nightmare blurred at the end. *Did you pull me out of that?*

Yes, once I realized what was happening, Tyrrik answered.

I'd thought what happened in the Zivost forest was as bad as it could get. I'd been wrong. I shook uncontrollably. There was nothing more frightening than what just happened. Ever. He'd plunged me into my most haunting memories. He made me hurt Tyrrik.

I turned to my mate. *Was it because I'm more vulnerable asleep? Is that how he got inside my head?* Draedyn was only able to get in at all because of the familial bond, but . . .

I thought I was protected against Draedyn with you near.

The silence stretched between us.

Tyrrik's eyes were flooded, and his mental voice faltered. He sat still, but his jaw was clenched, and his fisted hands trembled. *Ryn, I need to touch you.*

I nodded, exhaling slowly, and he pulled me into his arms, his body shuddering as his tension waned.

Tyrrik squeezed me, burying his nose in my silver hair. He kissed my head then let go to straighten the tent above us. He brushed the greenery out of our small space while I sat and watched, waiting for him to regain enough control to speak.

I was so shaken, I hadn't even process that there were horrible lashes across his chest from where I'd bound him to the ground with the sunflowers. I'd attacked him in my sleep. Worst mate ever. *I'm so sorry, Tyrrik.*

Tyrrik's movements were short and sharp, and his jaw clenched as he moved about the small space, setting it back to how it was, or close to it. *Don't be. It wasn't your fault. Neither of us could've predicted that.*

And yet I couldn't help but feel it *was* my fault. Fear burgeoned my chest, and I forced myself to say the words out loud. In a voice just over a whisper, I choked, "Are you worried it will happen again?"

He froze, pillow in hand. A moment passed, and he tossed the pillow to the ground, now covered with shorn stalks. *Now that I know what to expect, I'll be better prepared. I won't let him do that to you again.*

He was not taking the burden for this. *How did you get him out?* Maybe if I understood that, I could understand how to keep him out myself.

We are mates. Our bond is stronger than any familial bond you share with Draedyn. In the forest, he was able to attack you because we hadn't mated and I was too far away.

I glanced up at him. *You think that's why?*

The males of my kind occasionally would leave their mates behind to go and fight, knowing their bond would not diminish over distance, nor the ability to send energy to the male in battle.

But you've always said we're stronger together, I countered. *And what about now? Do you think our bond still weakens with distance?*

Yes, we are stronger together, he agreed. *And I'm not referring to our bond or the sending of energy between us. I think your mental barrier against your father is stronger when I'm near. When I'm away, it's easier to shatter. He is not only your father but the alpha of our kind. Tonight, I was able to push his presence away when I realized what was happening.*

He'd cut you off from me somehow. It was only when you started attacking me that I noticed.

So he can affect you. I wrapped my arms around myself and thought about how I could've attacked Tyrrik. *What did you see?*

No, he can only affect me through you. I'm a male Drae, not sworn to him, and no relation. And I saw an emerald-green coating the blue strands of your Drae power.

Could Draedyn do this from anywhere? I had to sleep sometime. I shivered, looking out the tent flap at the dozens more tents housing slumbering Gemondians. What could've happened if Tyrrik wasn't sleeping next to me tonight? How many could Draedyn have made me kill? The entire army? I stared at the lash wounds on Tyrrik's chest again. They'd healed into thin red lines already, but my chest squeezed.

I wish I remembered more. His thoughts were laced with frustration. *Male Drae would never have left their mates if they knew their female would be left vulnerable.*

Maybe they didn't know. How many ancient alpha Drae are there to force their way into their daughter's heads? And weren't the Drae supposed to be the protectors of the realm?

Tyrrik's eyes gleamed in the dark as he watched me. *True on both counts.*

He faced me, crouched in the tent, and held out a hand. "Come on. Let's go back to bed."

I closed my eyes, bowing my head in defeat. *I can't keep him out. I'm not going to go back to sleep.*

He sighed, his chest rising and falling. *I'll watch over you, my love. I know what to look for now, and I won't let anything else happen to you.*

He'd stay awake so I could sleep? Because *that* made me want to sink into a dreamless slumber. I could feel how much he wanted his promise to be true, however, and I realized he felt just as much guilt for what happened.

I crawled across the tent and tapped on his leg. "Come down here with me."

He joined me on the blankets and pillows. Our lapis and onyx threads wound together, and I opened my heart to him, uncaring which emotions were mine and which were his. Our bond and emotions merged, unidentifiable as belonging to each of us, and I rested both of my hands on his chest, using my restored Phaetyn power to remove the physical evidence of the pain I'd just caused him.

"I'm so sorry," I whispered, speaking for both of us. "And I'm so afraid."

If I stay awake, I can keep him out. We'll just have to rotate our sleep schedule.

I'm not sure how I feel about that. I raised my eyebrows in an attempt to lighten the mood as I wound my arms up over Tyrrik's shoulders. He rewarded me with a smile, albeit a tight one.

We need to keep you safe, first and foremost.

First-shmirst. I pressed my lips to his. *I love you. No matter what Draedyn made me do, my feelings for you haven't changed. At all.*

That was never in question.

I chuckled, my shoulders relaxing a tiny amount. *Glad to see the sunflowers didn't injure your confidence.*

Tyrrik deepened our kiss, splaying his hand over my neck. *Not much can.*

I broke off our kiss, staring at him in false shock. *You don't say? Is that a Drae thing or a Tyrrik thing?*

He lowered his mouth to mine again, saying, *A Tyrrik thing. Would you like me to show you?*

TWO SOLDIERS STOOD BARRING our tent entrance when I awoke the next morning. I patted the blankets next to me. Tyrrik was gone, long gone judging by the lack of warmth under my fingers. Closing my eyes, I concentrated on my ears, growling in irritation. Not just Tyrrik, the entire army was gone.

I stared at the width of the two men. They wore golden chain-mail, and their physique resembled that of a tree trunk: thick, wide, solid. Some of the Gemodians must have fed their young well before sending them off to die.

I shook my head. After last night, I was feeling acutely morbid and heart sick. Though with my father taking over my mind and forcing me to attack my mate, I was probably allowed to be disheartened for a day, especially because he could do it again.

What, my love? Tyrrik asked.

Where are you? I closed my eyes and saw the army through Tyrrik's mind, and then he shifted his gaze to the surrounding mountains. *How long have you been gone?*

Since sun up.

I pursed my lips at his non-helpful answer. "Excuse me?" I called out to my babysitters.

Both young men turned to face me.

"How long ago did the army leave?"

I looked at the two young men, both of whom were surveying me as though measuring my worth. Was it written on my forehead or something? They were close to eighteen, if not already there, and curly hair the color of dry dirt stuck out in thick waves around their square faces. They were neither handsome nor ugly, and their eyes were pretty close to the same color as their hair. I'd heard of identical twins, but I'd never seen two people who looked *exactly* the same.

The young man on the right tossed an empty corn cob away. "Five hours, give or take."

Five hours?

"Lord Tyrrik insisted you sleep as late as you wanted," the other said, his eyes shifting to me.

"That sounds about right," I said, turning my attention to the rumpled blankets.

The two young men stepped away from the tent a couple of yards and sat down in front of a pile of green husks.

I took the privacy they'd offered and threw off the blankets, running my fingers through my long silver tresses. They were silent as I pulled my aketon and a pair of hose out from under the blankets. I patted down the bedding, unsuccessfully trying to find . . . *Where are my shoes?*

Just outside the tent. On the left.

I huffed. *I can't believe you left me.*

I can see the tent from here, I could burn both of them to a crisp in seconds, and I'm watching our bond. Draedyn won't sneak past. You know I'd never abandon you. Besides, you're invincible, remember?

Oh yeah, I forget that sometimes. An evil emperor taking over my mind helped with that forgetfulness. A lot.

Just be careful with the boys. Zakai and Zarad said they're the best they have.

I looked at the two young men. One was grinning as he murmured something to the other. They both chuckled as they sat on the ground, shucking corn. The grinning one caught me staring and held out an ear of corn, the husk already removed. "Do you want some?" He wiggled the vegetable at me. "Best corn I ever ate."

Beyond the guards, where the clearing had been, was a garden. A vegetable garden, with no rhyme or reason to the plants' order, fruits of my labor before sleeping last night.

I couldn't stop the curiosity bursting inside. What had I grown? Was there enough for everyone? Honestly, it wasn't my biggest work . . .

Quality over quantity, that was my new motto. At least until the war was over.

I stepped out of the tent and slipped my feet into my boots. And stared.

Vines surrounded the tent—no, they were grasses, only they were mutant forms of the mountainous vegetation. The thick blades were over an inch in circumference, and at least ten feet in length. Two sunflowers lay on the ground, their stalks as thick as my wrist, the blooms three feet in diameter.

"Lord Tyrrik said you'd want to see," one of the twins said, his voice softer than the one who'd offered me the corn.

I nodded my thanks, not grateful at all as I stared at the growth I'd created, knowing at least some of it was grown with the intention to kill Tyrrik. The back of my throat burned with shame, and I swallowed it down, disgusted not only with my father but myself.

I was too weak to keep Draedyn out of my head again. That made it twice by my count. And both times, someone got hurt. I had to figure this out.

I accepted the corn from the smiling twin and sat next to the not-smiling twin. Corn, zucchini, and tomatoes had all been picked over, and many of the plants trampled underfoot. In the back of the clearing, a pumpkin sat, untouched. Hmm. Should I take offense to that? Did they think everyone could make pumpkins grow overnight? It wasn't the small size putting them off, was it?

Grumbling a little, I bit into the corn, sweet and crisp, but the normal thrumming of joy and pride in my chest after growing something amazing remained absent as I looked over the patch of food.

"Lord Tyrrik said you could shoot those vines straight through a Druman's guts," Smiley said.

Smiley had a morbid streak. I glanced at him and held his gaze. "What's your name?"

"Niemoj," he said, raising his brows.

I shifted on the grass, blinked, and took another bite of my corn. I wasn't really sure how to make small talk right now. What I wanted to do was crawl in a corner and hide. If I couldn't protect my mind from Draedyn, I wasn't an asset to our army. I was a liability. If I could turn against my mate, I could easily turn on the others fighting for us. Tyrrik was strong enough to withstand an attack. I couldn't hurt him, really. But what if I'd attacked one of the guards last night? Dyter? The king or prince? I might've killed someone.

Maybe I shouldn't be heading into this battle. Maybe I should listen to my fear and hide.

The silence extended way past the awkward stage.

Niemoj said, "My name means *not mine*. My brother"—he pointed at his twin—"is Nielub. It means *unloved*."

I blinked at them in disbelief. "You're kidding. That's . . ." *Awful.*

No, wait. Manners. I scratched my eyebrow and said, "That's . . . unique."

Niemoj laughed, throwing his head back, and even Nielub the non-smiler grinned.

"My mother's family was from the Slav range on the northern border of Azule. Their tradition was to give their babies a substitute name for the first decade of life. If children lived past ten, then they received a different name."

I realized my mouth was open and closed it, but I couldn't help staring at him, completely dumbfounded. All I knew of Azule was that they were the fishing community and the kingdom closest to the empire.

I asked the only question that made sense. "They lost a lot of babies to illness?"

He pursed his lips, eyes squinting as he considered my question. "Perhaps. Probably not any more than most areas though."

"Then why . . ." I didn't even know how to ask. The practice seemed cruel.

"Because the community was on the border of Azule and Gemond," Niemoj said as if that were explanation enough. When I raised my eyebrows, he added, "Emperor Draedyn has a different relationship with those of Azule, or at least he did in the stories my mother told us."

Really, I needed to know more about the other two kingdoms. If I'd asked more questions before we went to *Kanahele o keola*, I would've been more prepared for the insanity we encountered. And if I'd asked more about Gemond, I might not have made assumptions about Zakai being evil. Though I'd been a bit anti-all-rulers there for a while. Right now, my ignorance about the ins and outs of my powers and the familial bond with Draedyn was threatening to overwhelm me. There wasn't space for anything else.

Yet there had to be.

I nodded to let Niemoj know I was listening.

"There was some belief that you could trick the evil ones, that those who stole children in the middle of the night only wanted the best children. If parents loved their child, then those were the children to take."

That was some twisted logic. That was like saying your pancakes tasted bad just so no one else would want any. "So if you were unloved, the emperor and his Druman wouldn't steal you?"

Niemoj looked at his brother.

In a softer tone, Nielub said, "Our father, Andrik, meaning brave, died before we were born. He was taken to war by the emperor. My mother's father, Jedrik, meaning strong, was taken just before her brother, Milos, was born."

"Let me guess, Milos means loved?"

Nielub shook his head and stripped the husk off another ear of corn. "It means most favored."

"And he went to serve in the war?" I asked. These people had some seriously sad family history.

"Maybe. He was taken when he was ten. The Druman swept through Wojslav and took a dozen boys and a dozen girls. Our mother was spared because one of the neighbors said she was worthless."

"So your mother named you after what she believed would save you?" I felt like I was barely grasping the edges of their stories. Not that I didn't understand the words, but the paradigm of their childhood sounded more like . . . like the whispered stories I'd heard as a kid and always thought were just tales from the emperor meant to scare us into submission.

Niemoj chuckled. "When you love someone, don't you do everything in your power to save them?"

Well, of course. It was why my mother fled, why she'd kept the Phaetyn power a secret for so long. It was because of motherly love that Luna Nuloa gave me her ancestral powers . . . I possessed the strongest traits of both of these women. My mother's Drae powers, and Luna's—

Whoa. I blinked with the epiphany. I had *two* powers. Which I knew—being a Phaetyn-Drae, but . . . I'd missed something huge.

I'm only using one to protect myself from Draedyn. I groaned, earning a curious look from the twins.

Tyrrik? I sighed.

Yes, my love?

I've been using the Phaetyn sheild to protect the army, but why haven't I been using it to protect my mind from Draedyn too?

J felt Tyrrik drop, the shock hitting him the same way it had me. He pulled his wings down hard repeatedly to climb back into the air.

Using both your powers at once doesn't work, he said immediately. *I was able to attack your mind yesterday on the way to catch up with the army.*

No, I replied. *You didn't attack me through the veil; you were inside it already.*

I waited as he processed that, feeling the way his mind turned over the problem, studying it from all angles.

You're right, he said. *And that is so obvious.*

I grimaced with him. The Phaetyn had protected their forest from Draedyn for decades with a veil. *If anyone asks, we knew it the entire time.*

Tyrrik's lips curved.

I inhaled, determination settling in my bones. Maybe Draedyn would've had a harder time entering my mind if I hadn't exhausted myself yesterday. I wouldn't make the same mistake twice. *I'll see you soon, mate.*

I peered at Niemoj and Nielub. "How old are you?"

Their matching grins were so wide and gleaming I drew back. I'd just woken up; I didn't want to see that many teeth right now.

"Twenty-one."

I shook my head because no way did I hear that right. The only man I'd met of that age was Calvetyn, and I was pretty sure he *had* gone to war and then escaped. "Did you serve in Draedyn's army?"

"We lived out in the mountains because Zakai would not risk his kingdom by harboring the emperor's enemy, and the rebels didn't want to risk their base by having Draedyn swarm through Gemond. But after word was spread of your visit and your intent, the rebels came to Rostisek, the center of Gemond. We gathered here in hopes of being able to free our loved ones."

That was what we all wanted, myself included. Kill Draedyn, bring the men home from the emperor's ridiculous war of expansion, and we could . . . just live instead of merely surviving.

"And what's your role? Are you my new body guards?"

They are not, Tyrrik snapped, gnashing his fangs.

It was a joke, Mr. Confident!

"We do whatever Zakai tells us to: fetch people, deliver messages, kill people," Nielub said.

And at the same time his brother, Niemoj said, "We're assassins."

I studied them again, whistling low. Yes, undoubtedly big, but could they sneak? Maybe being that big meant they didn't have to sneak. "How many Druman have you killed?"

Nielub shrugged. "We stopped counting after the first couple hundred."

If Arnik had said the words, they would've seemed like boasting, but Nielub delivered them casually.

Holy-flippin'-Drae.

Tea-time is over, Ryn. King Zakai wants to strategize while the army rests for lunch.

I stretched tall to get the blood flowing after sitting for so long. "Well," I said, taking a deep breath before continuing, "It's nice to meet you. I hope you assassins aren't afraid of heights."

"Nope," Niemoj said. "Though I don't want you to grow a pumpkin around me ever."

I narrowed my eyes. "That was you?"

Nielub laughed. "He loves that story."

I waited until we'd exited the forest and were in the rocky valley to shift.

I tilted my chin up, my hair tickling my lower back, and pushed my Phaetyn veil over my body. Then I let my Drae take over. My bones shifted and expanded, my skin stretching to form the membranes of my wings, and scales rippled across my body into my Drae armor.

Soon, I stretched my wings out, arching my long neck in bliss.

Being in my Drae form felt so right.

I tucked my wings close to my sides and cast my slitted-eyed gaze at my passengers. They stood a respectable distance back, near the tree line, and couldn't currently see me under my invisibility cloak. I pushed my moss-green veil out until the two assassins were underneath it. Smiley was smiling, non-smiley wasn't smiling, but both of their eyes widened as they looked upon my lapis Drae. Totally impressed.

I jerked my head to the spikes at my back and lowered my left shoulder to the ground, tucking my wing in tight.

Niemoj's grin faltered.

Definitely impressed. I felt somewhat redeemed after the small pumpkin fiasco.

I held still as the twins boarded, and then I glanced back as a silent kind of *hold-on-tight-or-you'll-die* warning. I took a deep breath and bounded forward into a run, pumping my wings.

Hard.

I launched into the air, dipping and swaying as I adjusted to the extra weight. What the heck were these guys made of? Seriously, I'd carried Lani, Dyter, and Tyrrik, but they were nothing compared to the density of the two rebels on my back. They probably killed people by sitting on them I realized, connecting the logical dots in the rebel-assassin training regime. That's why they wore gold chain mail. Their clothing was probably made of ground-down rock to help, too, and they put bricks in the base of their boots.

I chuffed at my own joke, chortling harder as Nielub whispered. "I think she's going to eat us."

I quit laughing, wondering if I could actually snap rocks with my fangs. *Tyrrik?*

Yes, you can.

My lips stretched back into a smile, exposing all my fangs to the cool wind. *How do you know that?*

Because I was twelve years old once. Even under the blood oath.

I harrumphed and squinted at the sky ahead. Tyrrik was swooping in lazy circles over the Gemond army, the beating sunlight reflecting off his onyx scales and reminding me of the graphite interior of the cave where I first transformed.

I didn't land immediately though I could hear the way one of the assassin's breath was catching in short, shallow bursts. We were on Drae time now, not assassin time. I wanted to see my mate.

When's the meeting? I asked, sweeping underneath him and up the other side.

One of the assassins gagged, and I quickly stabilized. The thought of him vomiting on my back or wings, and where the vomit would be when I transformed back to my Phaetyn form, made me do my best to hold steady.

We were waiting for you to catch up before we met, Tyrrik said. *I'll land with you.*

I craned my neck to where he flew slightly above me. *You could have woken me, you know?* I wasn't entirely happy the whole army managed to leave camp without me noticing.

You were exhausted; better for you to sleep while you can. We'll have to take shifts remember?

I sighed, the sound coming out as a deep rumble in this form. I caught myself mid-sigh and forced a controlled exhale. *I know. But what if this war goes on for years? We can't rely on sleep shifts forever.*

No, but we'll work on that. Tyrrik banked slightly to meet my gaze. *We'll get there, Ryn, I promise. One thing at a time.*

That's a fine thing to say if we actually had time. I grumbled but kept my body as stable as possible. Draedyn could attack at any moment—or his Druman. My father could make *me* attack anyone unless I had my veil and shield up or was right next to Tyrrik *and* one of us was awake.

We'll be okay, my love. I'll make it okay. And there is some good news.

Yeah? You defeated the one-eyed squirrel as I slept? I quipped.

Tyrrik's joy at my humor radiated through our bond. *No,* he said solemnly. *He still runs rampant, leading a life of debauchery. Worse, he's inspiring others to join his band of nefarious villainy.*

Did I think that one day I'd be flying next to Lord Nightmare listening to his jokes about squirrels? Not for a second. Obviously, it was the little things for him. *We're heading the wrong way then. He's the real enemy.*

I agree, but in the meantime—Tyrrik swung his head forward and raised his chin—*there is the first sign of Azule.*

Really? I swiveled to see and grunted. I had to strain to make it out, but in the blurry limits of my vision, the mountain ranges stopped and the edges of a cobalt ocean shimmered on the horizon. Azule, as close to my father as we'd safely get. Though he'd shown physical distance wasn't really a factor in controlling me, so maybe that didn't matter as much as I thought.

I wonder what the plan is, I pondered through the mate bond.

No doubt they'll fill us in.

I felt the stirring of determination and realized it wasn't all coming from me and my ambition to fight this war the right way. *You're planning something?*

Not so much planning, but with you involved and how far we've come . . . I'm not content to just go along with their plans.

So what you're saying, to be clear, up until now you've been passively agreeing to everything? I snorted. Pretty sure Tyrrik wasn't going along with anything. I didn't even give him time to answer. *Because I'm pretty sure I remember you've told every ruler you'd kill them if they didn't do the right thing.*

He chuffed, and I heard one of my passengers squeak. Tyrrik

banked left, and I followed, still being careful of my sensitive cargo even if I did want one of them to be taken down a peg or six.

What I saw and what I can be bothered doing are different things. I'm invested now. I should've been a long time ago. The Drae are meant to be guardians of this land. I've been remiss in my duties.

The blood oath didn't exactly give you the freedom to help people.

No. Now I am free to help though, and I believe I must make up ground.

I frowned at his words and turned my attention to the army. I spotted Dyter, his bald, shining head a beacon, and Zakai near him. Several soldiers unloaded stacks of neatly folded canvas, and dozens more converged to help. *You want to help. You're not doing that because you feel guilty, right?*

Yes and no. I want the world to be safe for you, and . . . to some extent I feel a sense of responsibility to make reparation for the things I did under oath to Irdelron.

Tyrrik had nothing to apologize to me for, but I knew from experience he'd need to heal in his own way and in his own time.

Then let's hop to it, I said brightly, increasing the angle of my descent.

My love, there's no need to act happy when you feel sadness, not on my behalf.

Bloody bond. *That's not sadness,* I lied, knowing I wasn't fooling anyone. *It's indigestion. I ate too much . . . raw corn.*

His amusement trickled through our bond, and we fell silent as we swooped down to land.

19

yrrik was already back to his two-legged version that made my knees weak and my insides all melty. I waited for my two passengers to disembark before shifting back and dropping the veil.

"Have fun?" I asked the twins.

Neither of them was smiling now.

"Not the word that comes to mind," one answered. Niemoj, I assumed.

Tyrrik took my hand and, leaving the twins behind, we weaved through the army side-by-side, making our way toward a big tent. The Gemondians around us sat and ate, but I noticed many of them shiver or draw away from me and Tyrrik as we strode through their midst. They were human, mortal. And as surely as their ways were once my ways, to them we were predators, powerful and otherly, the most feared creatures in the realm.

I'd changed somewhere. Obviously I was a Phaetyn and a Drae now, yet my mind had changed too. Despite my best intentions to cling to the human life I'd had, my perception had altered. I didn't see, think, or feel like a human any longer. I'd never thought like a Phaetyn though I did understand that part of me more now, thanks

to Lani. And I still didn't think entirely like a Drae. I was somewhere between.

And I was okay with that. *Mistress Moons.* Actually, having
control of my own mind seemed like a good day at this point.

"There they are," Tyrrik murmured, dropping his arm from my
shoulders only to take my hand.

The Drae part of me got it. After a few hours without him, I was
craving his physical touch as well. I squeezed his hand as we got to
the clearing where the large tent stood. *I'm glad I have you.*

Tyrrik drew back the tent flap. *And I, you.*

All that canvas had been erected into a large dome just for the
purpose of our strategy session. Seemed overkill for a meeting over a
lunch break, especially because we were all on the same team. Not sure
who they were keeping secrets from, but golden guards had cleared a
wide space, surrounding the perimeter so no one would overhear.

"Nice sleep-in?" Dyter asked when I ducked in under Tyrrik's
arm.

"Mmm," I answered noncommittally. Was that a dig at me? Not
characteristic of Dyter, but maybe he was stressed. Or was he giving
me a heads up? Did the Gemondians think I was slacking off? *Do
they know about last night?*

Tyrrik's unease seeped through to me before he answered.

*I was waiting to confer with you. General knowledge of Draedyn's
control over you may do more harm than good.*

*I'm not so worried about the Gemondians turning against me. Not the
majority of them anyway,* I added. I hadn't been there to protect them
as I should have, but I had also done a lot for them. *The Phaetyn are
already afraid of me, and they might not take the news of Draedyn's
control over me very well, but it might affect our strategy.*

We should inform the leaders, Tyrrik replied.

I agree.

"So." King Zakai drew out the word, his eyebrows raised. "Are
you joining us now?"

His son, Zarad, and his first, Gairome, were there with Dyter and Zakai, as well as the four women and men who made up Zakai's command team, including the two assassins, Nielub and Niemoj. All eight of them stood around a slab of wood balanced atop a thick chest.

Tyrrik and I stepped up to the makeshift table. A map of the Draecon Empire had been tacked to the wooden slab, and several more pins were scattered in clusters in different areas. I brushed my fingertips over the green pins just outside of Verald and took a deep breath.

"Before we start," I said, keeping my head down, "Draedyn attacked my mind in my sleep last night. Tyrrik and I will be rotating our sleep schedules until I learn to keep him out." I raised my head and glanced at Dyter. "We thought you should be aware of the development."

Prince Zarad straightened. "When you say attacked your mind . . ."

"She means he seized control and forced her to attack me," Tyrrik growled. "I was able to break through, but my delay in responding was because I hadn't anticipated the possibility."

All attention turned to me, and I met each of their gazes in turn.

"You are actively working on . . . keeping the emperor out of your mind?" King Zakai asked.

"I am," I said, inclining my head.

"I don't like it," one of the female Gemondians said. "We have a Drae in our camp that the emperor can control. He can turn her into a weapon at anytime, and we're supposed to be okay with that?"

Tyrrik's lips curved. "With all due respect to your station, whatever that may be—"

"Commander Smurt, Gemond's second battalion," the woman snapped.

"Hmm," Tyrrik mused, the curve of his smile widening. "Well, Commander, with respect to whatever qualification your role or title indicates in human affairs, you, and every single one of you in here, know nothing about the complexities of this subject."

The woman flushed red and clenched her jaw. She glared at

Tyrrik and opened her mouth to respond, but Tyrrik didn't give her an opportunity.

"If Ryn is awake, she'll have her veil up, and Draedyn cannot get through. If she's asleep, I'll be awake. If I'm awake, Draedyn will not be able to control her." His lip curled, and his fangs lengthened just below his lips in a chilling snarl. "The point is Draedyn will not get through again."

The woman might have a secret death wish. She leaned over the table, meeting Tyrrik's glare with one of her own. "Do you have any idea what she could do if you slip up?"

Tyrrik's eyes shifted to ink-black slits. I rested a hand on his arm and, noticing his talons were extending, sent him a jolt of my energy.

"I do," I said to the woman. "I understand."

She opened her mouth again, and Zakai interjected. "Would you rather the two Drae leave our army, Dilowa?"

She shut her mouth and eventually shook her head. "No, My Liege. Just thinking of the safety of my battalion."

The king inclined his head at the older brunette. "For which I am most thankful." He shifted his gaze to me and asked, "Lady Ryn, could you please keep us informed on your progress?"

"I can," I answered, removing my hand from Tyrrik's arm now that his onyx energy wasn't glowing violently. Seriously, Smurt must mean death-wish.

"I wish you luck," Zakai added. "Not just for our sake but yours as well. I can't imagine any circumstance in which I'd want the emperor in my head. Most unpleasant."

Like I needed a reminder. I threw him a tight smile. "Most definitely unpleasant."

Gairome cleared his throat in the wake of awkward silence. "Back on track then. In eight days, we'll reach the borders of Azule. The arrival of the Phaetyn *should* coincide with our own. Verald's force will lag two days, four at the most. Our force when we arrive at the fishing kingdom should be two thousand five hundred strong."

You okay now? I asked Tyrrik, only half-listening to the numbers of our army.

Mmm. Yes. More than okay. He accompanied his answer with a jolt of white-hot lust that had me gasping out loud.

The voices around us faltered, and I stared back at eight pairs of wide eyes while I tried to gather my thoughts . . . out of Tyrrik's aketon.

Tyrrik wasn't nearly so stunned since he was the one causing the disruption. He spoke silkily, "Carry on."

Once the discussion resumed, he thought at me, *That's the first time you've sent me energy when I wasn't dying.*

I arched a brow, attempting to appear nonchalant, but my heart continued to throw itself against my ribs, desperately wanting to dance the maypole with Tyrrik. Clearly, my power must've made him feel all kinds of turned on, and he wanted to return the favor. *Bad timing*, I shot at him, and his laughter echoed in my mind. *Seriously, since combusting in the tent and card playing are out right now, I'm going to focus on the conversation.*

They're talking about the potential alliance with Azule. Once we cross the border, we'll still have a full day's journey to the center of the country where the king or queen lives.

How are you—I tuned him out and focused on Zarad.

"While we enter into talks with Azule's leader, we'll also be awaiting the arrival of King Calvetyn and the Veraldians," the prince said.

I butted in. "Who rules Azule?"

"By our last report, Queen Mily held power, but Azulis have been known to change their ruler frequently. The queen was reported to be . . . eager. If luck is with us, she still holds the throne."

I'd already gotten the sense of rural Azule as a harsh, rugged kingdom from the twins, and Zarad's vague information was confusing, but I wouldn't pass judgment until I'd met the queen myself. Even so, I didn't assume she'd be sending out a welcome party. I slid my gaze to where Zakai now sat on a wooden stool, studiously attending his son's words.

"When Caltevyn arrives, he'll want to negotiate the terms of the plan I spoke of last week. But I think it would be wise to introduce the possibility before his arrival if we can lay the groundwork," Dyter said.

Hold up.

"What plan?" Tyrrik beat me to the question.

Dyter glanced at us. "Using Azule's fleet to bring back the young men from the emperor's war overseas. Our numbers would be greatly increased by doing so."

I stared at him, my eyes narrowing the more I heard. Finally, I snapped. Doing my best to control my frustration, I asked, "How long has this been Calvetyn's plan?"

The tent hushed, and the tension ratcheted up a bajillion notches. Dyter looked at me, and I looked right back.

The man who had always been my mentor and protector scanned my face, no doubt picking up on the unstated accusation and my irritation for being kept out of the loop.

Dyter squared his shoulders and said, "Since Calvetyn was sent to the frontline by his father. To die. He ended up meeting several key people, and the army has been ready to return and fight with us. It is *why* the rebellion first accepted Calvetyn into their midst. He merely required the means to bring the army back, but Azule has more than enough boats to achieve this. Our army could be increased within a few days, doubled within a month if the plan is undertaken immediately."

I clenched my jaw, holding Dyter's gaze. At what point was he going to tell me all of this? He'd found time to tell the Gemondian's. He'd obviously known Cal's plan before leaving Verald. Dyter had travelled for months with me, with the specific intention of opening negotiations with Azule for this very purpose.

I was a part of this. Not to toot my own horn, but I was a big part of it. By the end of the war, I'd either be slave to my father or finally free. I was investing my powers, my life, and my *mind* to the cause, risking every single one of them. At one point, months ago, I hadn't wanted to know anything, but that time was long gone, and *I* knew Dyter knew that.

"I don't appreciate being kept in the dark," I said, in what I believed to be a mostly calm voice.

No one else spoke.

"There's hardly been time," Dyter countered.

One minute in the last three weeks. That's all it would have taken to say: Oh, and Calvetyn-will-be-asking-Azule-to-send-their-boats-and-retrieve-the-overseas-army. I pursed my lips, wanting to call Dyter out on it, but I wouldn't embarrass him in front of the other rulers. He was worthy of more respect than that. I just needed him to acknowledge I was no longer the same oblivious-Ryn who'd worked for him in the tavern all that time ago. I tilted my head and asked, "Do I look the same as the girl in The Crane's Nest?"

He sighed, unsurprisingly understanding my unspoken context. He scrubbed his palm down his face and then said, "You don't, Ryn. And I apologize. It was remiss of me not to ensure you knew of the plan."

I searched his gaze, seeing only the same Dyter I'd always known. His sincerity rang true, and his eyes were filled with love as they always had been for me and my mum. I decided to take him at face value, literally. I nodded and admitted, "We have been busy."

Tyrrik leaned forward, tapping a black talon on the wood. "Is there anything else Ryn and I haven't been informed about that you would like to tell us now?" He looked at Zakai, Zarad, and then Dyter. No one spoke, and Tyrrik nodded. "Let's make sure we all act in good faith moving forward."

"How will Azule react when an army shows up on their doorstep?" I asked. "Do we know how Queen Mily thinks? What she will do?"

The tension in the tent lowered somewhat, the Gemondians talking over the top of each other about how little information we had about the Azulis.

Was I overreacting? I seized the lull to ask Tyrrik.

No, Tyrrik responded immediately. *But you're not the only one who needs to accustom themselves to the changes in you. I believe Dyter just saw that. And those who knew you before you went to the forest.*

I exhaled slowly and studied the group.

"I had planned to send an envoy ahead of the army," Zakai replied.

Because I was watching the group, I saw the woman who'd challenged me flinch. I crossed my arms and asked, "You don't agree with that, Commander?"

She jerked in her seat, her attention jumping to me, and then she darted a look at Zakai and wet her lips. "Not exactly. I mean, no. I believe arriving with the army might come across threatening, but to send in a single emissary is just a different risk. We don't know how an envoy will be received any more than the army." She shrugged. "How could a message convey what we need to say? How can we be certain of Azule's allegiance or whether they'll trick us? I think it wiser to see their eyes when brokering for the freedom of nations."

"What are you proposing, Commander?' the prince asked. "You want to send in how many?"

Tyrrik shook his head. "She doesn't want to send in a group of messengers; she's proposing we go ourselves." He grinned. "I like it."

"We don't send an envoy. We send a small show of power," Dilowa added. "Not enough to threaten but enough to make them pause if they are considering foul play."

"I like it too," I said. "I'm going." There's no way I wasn't meeting the Azule leader to get the measure of her. Or him.

"As am I," Tyrrik said. "If we wait to leave until the army is within a day's walk of Azule, Ryn and I can be here in a couple of hours or so if Draedyn attacks."

"I'd like to represent Verald," Dyter said.

King Zakai glanced at his son. "Zarad will represent Gemond, and I would like Commander-General Gairome and Commander Dilowa to accompany him."

"Someone will represent the Phaetyn," I hastily threw in. "I'd like to convince Queen Lani to remain behind if she'll agree, in case

Draedyn attacks. She'll be able to veil the entire army. I'll go scout for her before we leave. She can't be far away."

Dyter blew out a breath as those in the tent quieted, each of us staring at the map. "Decades of blood, sweat, and hunger," he said. "We've waited a long time for this to come together."

I thought of the Penny Wheel where I grew up. How normal hunger had been for me and starvation for most everyone else. I thought of the meetings Dyter held in his tavern and Arnik's blazing ideas of rebellion that had ended too abruptly. The assassins I'd met this morning had dedicated their lives to better the world. Every person in this tent, every person in this realm, had lost something to the emperor.

My gaze traced the ink lines of the Azule kingdom on the map, northwest of our current position. Dyter was right: every person in this room had paid their taxes to Emperor Draedyn in blood, sweat, and hunger.

We're getting closer, Tyrrik said, staring at the same spot on the map.

Yes. I took a deep breath. *We are.*

20

"*Khosana*," Tyrrik murmured, shaking my shoulder.

I groaned, rolling onto my back as I considered, possibly, maybe, opening my eyes. The sleeping roster was a pain in my Most-Important-Drae butt. This was the worst, when I'd only caught a few hours because of staying up all day.

"Sleep longer," Tyrrik said, removing his hand.

I groaned again. Tyrrik was at least as exhausted as me and still offering to keep watch. He'd let me sleep the entire night. Again.

I dragged my eyelids apart and blinked up at him through bleary eyes. "No, I'm awake." I scrubbed my face with both hands. "I'm awake. I'm awake."

He lay down beside me and pulled me to him, my back to his chest, and kept his arm wrapped around my waist.

"Anything interesting?" I mumbled.

He stretched the collar of my chemise and kissed my shoulder. "Nothing."

I sighed and turned to kiss him, threading my hands through his black hair. He pulled me close, the blankets tangling between us. The worst thing about the sleeping roster was that it didn't allow time for playing cards or dancing the maypole. And Romantic-Ryn definitely wanted a repeat of our game-time in Gemond.

Although, perhaps not in a tent in the middle of an army.

I brushed my tongue against Tyrrik's one last time and then pulled away to breathe. Because that was important and oddly easy to forget when I was kissing my mate.

I peeled back the blankets and got on my hands and knees. Focusing, I slowed my breathing and concentrated. I blinked as my eyes narrowed to slits and the objects in the dark tent gained definition.

Using my Drae eyes, I quickly located my aketon and hose.

"You're getting faster," Tyrrik said, followed by a yawn.

At least I was getting better at something because that something certainly didn't feel like my Phaetyn veil and Drae shield. I was still too slow at getting them in place if they were down, and still I had to focus to keep them up. "Thanks."

Tyrrik's eyes were already closed when I ducked out of our tent. I kept my night vision going and focused on my sense of smell. I'd always found scent easiest to engage; something about it felt more instinctive to my Drae form. Tyrrik said the nose and ears were most instinctive, followed by the eyes. My fangs came and went as they liked, usually in response to anger or the deep yearning low in my stomach I now knew meant I wanted to practice making Drae babies.

I *was* getting the hang of the eyes now, so next up was talons. I'd wait until the perfect moment then flick out a blue blade. Maybe opening a letter in a meeting. Or chopping up a chicken roast. I had plans. Big plans.

I followed my Drae sense of smell, picking up Tyrrik's pine and smoke scent immediately. We were camped at the base of a mountain, still within the Gemond ranges. We hadn't encountered another forest since that first night, just small copses of trees here and there, but I preferred the open space. It meant I could see everyone at once, and when our food supplies ran low, there was still a coating of dirt on the valley floor to grow vegetables.

I traced Tyrrik's scent to a rock a short way up the mountain, which put me at eye level with the tent tops. Tyrrik always found the best spots. I smiled when I saw the blanket he'd left out for me.

Sitting cross-legged on the flat rock, I scanned the sleeping army, spotting the sentries in their usual places around the perimeter while some of them stood guard part way up the mountainside as I did.

I took a deep breath and closed my eyes. Flexing my mind muscles, I cast my Phaetyn power outward. With my next breath, I opened my eyes and directed the moss-green veil over the tents beneath me, stretching it all the way across the valley. Right. Good. Our tent was central, so I pushed the veil out to the right first, stopping at intervals when my mind felt strained. I kept at it, propelling the blanket-of-invisibility until it reached the outskirts of the right flank.

I paused to catch my breath. What did the sentries think when they peered up and found half of their comrades gone? I mean, we'd warned them after the first time, but still, seeing it had to be strange.

"Okay, Ryn," I grunted, wiping away the sweat trickling down the side of my forehead.

Keeping the right side of the veil where it was, I took a mental hold on the other side, still in the middle of the encampment, and began to nudge it toward the left. I'd been covering more and more of the army each night. But when they were like this, all in one neat and *much* smaller spot, covering them seemed almost achievable. Half an hour to concentrate? I could get almost eighty or ninety percent. No problem.

Zarad was drilling the army daily, forcing them to congregate into a small space in case Draedyn attacked. I was the limiting factor because I wouldn't have thirty minutes to erect my defense.

I panted, my nudges to the veil much more like shoves by now—out, out, out.

I trained my eyes on the glistening edge to the left. This invisibility cloak felt like it was about to snap and was still short of covering the army. *Nope. It's all good. Just hold it here for a bit.* I could usually push it a little more after that—like leaning down to stretch the backs of my thighs.

I breathed in and out, focusing on the veil.

When the tension dissipated slightly, I shimmied the power to cover more of the left flank and held it there again, shifting the veil out another few feet when it relaxed. On the next hold, the tension didn't dissipate. At all.

I rolled my neck and told myself I should try again. Maybe at the end of the night. I brought the veil inward until I was the only thing inside its protection and then glanced over the army. I was getting better. I'd have to find a way to practice while we left the mountains. Our small envoy party would be leaving in the morning for Azule.

Al'right. Next.

Placing both hands on the ground, I focused on a tiny shrub wedged between two boulders before me. Building the pressure like water held back by a dam, I let the moss-green Phaetyn power accumulate inside my hands without release, staring at the shrub. The dam burst, and the power exploded from my fingertips. I grinned as a thick, pointed root as tall as Tyrrik shot out from the ground like a spear.

Druman-killing-root-practice done. Cracking my knuckles, I shifted my butt on the rock and then adjusted my blanket. Think fast, Ryn. I held my Phaetyn veil in place, reached for my blue Drae tendrils of power, and whipped them around my head until I'd coiled them into a solid covering. *Diamond shell, diamond shell, diamond shell.* I could practically feel my power getting tougher.

With my Phaetyn cloak and diamond helmet, I was invisible to everyone and everything. And I was thankful for that invisibility because my helmet and cloak had to look absolutely, freakin' ridiculous.

I continued to focus on my powers, on keeping them solid and tuning out everything else around me: soft sighs, not-so-soft snores, the scrape of boots on stone as the sentries moved about, the fluttering of the tent flaps.

Then I dropped all of it, the cloak and the helmet.

And repeated.

Again and again and again.

Because one day, *this* would have to be enough.

THE CRISP MOUNTAIN air did nothing to cool my anxiety; it crawled over my skin and, even in my Drae form, made my stomach churn. The plan was to leave for Azule today, but Lani and the Phaetyn were still nowhere to be seen. This was my third flight in search of her gold veil, and it would have to be my last. *Our last.* Keeping my Drae shield wrapped around my mind and my Phaetyn veil in place were easier now, but we were running out of time to beat the army to Azule.

I'm going to land.

Why? Do you see them? Tyrrik asked, swinging his head toward me.

No. But see those trees over there? I tilted my chin toward the small copse of evergreens. *Maybe the trees out here will talk to me like they did in Zivost.*

Gone were the days where I would consider talking to trees the height of crazy.

Clever. Tyrrik followed my lead, and we banked hard within the moss-green confines of my Phaetyn veil, dropping altitude fast due to the limited flat area on the slope where we intended to land. I touched down on the gray shale, Tyrrik landing behind me. The mountain side plateau where we'd perched was just large enough to contain us. In front, the level space was bordered with a dozen tall evergreens clustered together.

The area felt bigger as soon as we shifted—for obvious reasons.

With Tyrrik still by my side, I strode forward, wove my way to the base of the trunk of the tallest tree, and put my hands to the rough bark, kindly asking to speak with Lani.

163

I frowned and glanced at Tyrrik. "Nothing," I said. "It's not working."

Tyrrik grimaced. "Have you ever tried to talk to the trees outside of Zivost?"

"No. But Lani said it didn't matter as long as I was in my Phaetyn form."

"Try covering the tree with your Phaetyn-mojo," he said with a cheeky grin.

You're hysterical. I actually thought the word mojo on his lips was pretty funny.

I tuned into my duo powers. The last three days, I'd done my best to keep the Phaetyn veil and Drae shield up as much as possible while awake. By the time I went to bed, I'd crash, but I *was* better at maintaining both simultaneously.

I expanded the moss-green veil to cover the tree and tried to converse with it again. "Nope."

Was Lani wrong about how this worked? Was she okay? Had something happened to the Phaetyn? We needed them, especially if Zakai's numbers regarding Druman were correct. Good ole Pops had fathered a lot of mules, and we couldn't take them Druman-to-human. Not without the Phaetyn's help.

"Maybe we should wait another day," I said uneasily.

Tyrrik's smile disappeared, and he shook his head. "We can't afford to put off our trip to Azule any longer. We have to get there before the army arrives to smooth the way, and every day we wait is another day for Draedyn to plan. We need to get those boats in the water and bring the human warriors back. Time is everything if we want to be on the offense in this war."

I sat down and scooted close to the trunk, the pine needles poking and scratching my legs and knees. I placed my hands on the trunk and then rested my head on the rough bark. "Tell me, tell me, tree of pine, tell me, tell me how to find . . . Lani?"

Tyrrik snorted.

"Not my best rhyme," I grumbled. Desperation obviously didn't make me brilliant. I closed my eyes, burning with fatigue, and felt my Drae shield slip as my energy sought Tyrrik's. As soon as the shield around my mind fell, I caught an image of the Phaetyn army marching. "Whoa!"

I straightened and grinned at Tyrrik. "Phaetyn powers and Drae powers don't mix."

He raised his eyebrows. "I'm fairly certain every Drae and Phaetyn know that, my love."

Shifting my butt on the gray stone, I glared up at him. "No, I mean they don't mix, and I'm mixing them. Stay close by. I'm going to have to let my Drae shield down to talk to the trees." I bit my lip as nerves twisted my stomach. I didn't like the thought of dropping my Drae barrier, but Tyrrik was here.

I relaxed the tendrils of my Drae power from where they'd been wrapped around my mind, letting them crawl and wind with Tyrrik's onyx energy. With a deep breath, I placed my hands back onto the rigid bark of the tall evergreen.

Hundreds of Phaetyn were marching through the Gemond mountains with Queen Lani, their expressions concentrated and serious as if they each understood the task they'd chosen to undertake.

The tightness in my chest unfurled and I sighed, my shoulders relaxing. I had no idea if the Phaetyn had passed this way or were yet to come, but the healers from Zivost were, in fact, coming to join us.

I withdrew my hands, and my skin brushed the pine needles closer to the surface. A new vision filled my mind's eye.

This tree, this copse of trees swayed in the wind. The Phaetyn passed by, and there near the edge of the trees, stalks of tiny pale bluish-purple flowers sprouted through the rocks.

I blinked, and my vision cleared. I glanced over the cliff edge at the flowers and then met Tyrrik's gaze with a grin of triumph.

"How long ago?"

"Not long." I pointed at the cluster of blooms swaying in the breeze. "Those flowers were fresh in the tree's vision, just like they are today. I don't know how long these bloom for, but they looked the same."

"Leave your Drae shield down while we fly and only your Phaetyn veil up. Maybe then you'll see her gold power."

"Stay close," I said, knowing he would understand my nervousness. There was no way I wanted to lead my father to the Phaetyn.

The mountains blurred beneath us, but just like the trees had said, eventually on the horizon ahead, I saw shimmering gold.

There it is. I sent Tyrrik an image so he could see the Phaetyn power himself. I was counting on my ancestral power to get us both through Lani's barrier while in our Drae form.

We descended and landed just inside Lani's golden ancestral veil without a hitch. Five Phaetyn froze, their mouths gaping as they stared at the two Drae in their midst.

Could be worse, I decided, considering we were their natural enemy.

One of them crumpled to the ground, and I frowned. Maybe that Phaetyn was prone to fainting attacks?

Tyrrik and I shifted back to our other forms, and three of the remaining group of Phaetyn screamed and ran. I sighed. The Phaetyn were definitely terrified of us after Draedyn's attack and my role in handing Kamini over.

One stood rooted in place, blinking, trembling, his fists clenched to his sides.

"That's your fault," I said to Tyrrik. *They probably think you're the emperor.* I waved at the single Phaetyn and said, "Hey there, friend. Is Lani around?"

His shoulders relaxed, and he closed his eyes. "You"—his voice trembled as he spoke, but he held my gaze—"sh-shouldn't b-be allowed t-t-to d-d-do that."

Tyrrik slid his arm around my waist, and his irritation flashed through me before he spoke. "I always believed the Phaetyn would have incredible distinction for color. The idea that they can confuse black and emerald green makes me question their intelligence."

I snickered to let the Phaetyn know Tyrrik was joking, or rather he should've been joking. We both knew the Phaetyn were necessary even if there was no love lost between our races. Plus, as long as they could tell the difference between an injured person and not, I was happy.

"If you can't help, friend, that's al'right," I said to the guy.

Why do you keep saying friend, my love?

Shh, it's working.

We both turned toward the sweating and shaking Phaetyn.

See? Looking away from the terrified man, I squeezed Tyrrik's waist and, tilting my head toward the crowd, said, "Let's go and find Lani."

We didn't have to in the end. Lani marched through her people, silver robes billowing behind her.

"What took you so long?" she asked when she stood directly in front of me. "I expected you days ago."

I stepped away from Tyrrik to draw the Phaetyn queen in for a tight hug. "I was getting worried too."

Pulling back to look her in the eyes, I noticed a tightness around her lavender orbs. "There have been some developments. Let's fly far enough away so we can talk."

"I can't," she said with a tilt of her head at her people, her hand immediately going to her head to keep her silver crown in place. "I'm just now starting to feel confident in the trust I'm striving to build with my people. If I leave now, it will derail all my efforts."

She grimaced, and I felt a twinge of pity for her. A big twinge, actually, because her people could be *really* vicious. Healers . . . and brutal murderers. Oxymorons, the lot of them.

As if reading my mind, the queen said, "I need their trust, and so do you."

Ouch.

That trust isn't going to last if they find out Draedyn is invading your mind, Tyrrik said.

He wasn't telling me anything I didn't already know. I shook my head, trying to convey to her how weighty said development was. "It's *my* secret."

A breeze lifted her hair and ruffled everyone's aketons and robes. The air caressed my skin, and Lani offered me a sad smile.

"Ryn, what happened back in the forest with your father wasn't your fault, but I know you understand the consequences of being forced to hand my sister over, unfair or not. If you want to earn their trust after what they saw, you're going to have to be vulnerable enough to earn it. They're uncomfortable, and you'll have to show them they can trust you if you want to change their perception."

I simultaneously saw her point and didn't. Deep down I resented the assumption that because of my power, I was expected to do more than everyone around me. Yet again, I was being asked to give another piece of myself away. Even knowing she had a valid point, I didn't like it. And yet, I'd already given away so much. Why stop now? I heaved a sigh. "Fine. Do you want to erect a platform so I can announce it to all of them? Then I only have to do this once."

Lani crossed her arms over her chest and snapped, "Grow up. You've been a victim. Don't let it define you."

"Hold up," I retorted. "Did you even think about what you're asking me to do, Lani? Would you like a whole race of people to know the ins and outs of your power?" I challenged. "Would you be willing to detail all of your strengths and weaknesses not only to King Calvetyn but all of Verald?"

We glared at one another, and she finally broke the stare-down. Waving at someone in her entourage, she said, "Makau, help Osofi."

169

She pointed at the Phaetyn who had fainted and then at me and Tyrrik. "Let's confer with my counsel then."

Lani led us toward a blue canvas pavilion, much like the one King Zakai had used for his council meetings. Maybe there was a handbook for new rulers or something in their genetics that drove them to have these canvas structures created with their ascension to the throne, or maybe they were passed down from ruler to ruler. Stupid canvas tent of doom. I showed *my* massive maturity level by not saying anything . . . out loud.

I hate them too. I had to shift in one once, and the tent lines got tangled in my talons.

The visual cheered me up as he'd intended no doubt. *Thanks for that,* I said, snuggling closer. *You're the bestest.*

Mmm-hmm. I know. His jaw hardened as we drew closer to the pavilion.

Kamoi's guard, now wearing aketons the color of the mountain stone, stood around the tent, spears in hand. Most kept their attention fixed outward, but my gaze collided with a couple of the men, and their eyes narrowed. One guard tightened his grip on his weapon in a way that didn't seem to scream *welcome.*

"They're not going to try and attack, right?" I asked. Not that anything they did could harm me, but I wasn't going to be forgiving if I had to burn gold Phaetyn blood out of Tyrrik again. Ever. Or if they upset Lani's trust plans. I rolled my eyes at the thought, realizing *I* was upsetting her trust plans.

"My guards are loyal, and they are well aware of who the enemy is, Ryn," Lani said. "You have nothing to fear."

Right. Their distrust rolled off them in waves. Not that I could blame them after recent events, but still. *Stay on your toes.*

Already on them, he replied, stepping forward to hold the tent flap open for me. *I can count on a single talon the number of people I trust.*

After what had happened with Dyter, I was kind of feeling the same. I knew the old coot would do anything for me, but Tyrrik would cease to breathe without me. That took the trust thing to a whole new level.

The light was muted inside the canvas structure, but the temperature was warmer. Ten Phaetyn sat cross-legged on folded blankets, obviously awaiting our arrival. Three more cushioned seats made of pale silvery-blue fabric were unoccupied.

I settled on my cushion, and Lani took the one beside me.

Tyrrik stared at the remaining cushion and rumbled. "I'll stand behind my mate."

I felt his flash of irritation and glanced behind at him. His eyes had flooded black, but he was making an active effort to not partially shift and intimidate them. I understood his vigilance and distrust. Some of these Phaetyn might've been in collusion with the ones who'd been poisoning him while they sliced him to ribbons.

I studied each silver-haired member of her cabinet. Most of their faces were unfamiliar, and unsurprisingly, most frowned at my attention before looking away. I recognized the nice older man I'd met that could do water magic as well as the antagonistic Ertha. How had she gotten in here? I turned my attention to the older man, racking my brain for his name, and asked, "Fabir, wasn't it?"

His smile lit his eyes, and he nodded. "Beautiful child, it is nice to see you again."

Someone grumbled, probably Ertha although it could've been any of them. I seriously didn't like her; something about the way she'd called me an abomination just didn't sit right.

Probably because it was an insult, my love.

I snorted silently at Tyrrik but kept my gaze on the serene Fabir. "You too. I'm glad you're on the council. I'm sure your wisdom will shed a lot of great perspective."

What I wanted to say, but couldn't without for-sure offending the lot of them, was: they'd better get their heads out of their butts if they wanted to win this war and be part of this realm. But I bit my tongue. Maturity at its finest.

"You all remember Ryn and Tyrrik. The Gemond army is—" She looked at me expectantly with a wave of her hand.

I blinked, and before I could formulate my response, Tyrrik

spoke. "Just over the next ridge. One day if you march quickly, two if you dawdle."

Lani pursed her lips, probably at Tyrrik's lack of diplomacy. Clearly by his tone, he'd expected them to have caught up to the Gemondian army by now.

Lani continued to stare at me and then asked, "And what of these new developments?"

"A small convoy from each kingdom will leave in the morning for Azule. We hope to ascertain the mood of the people and find out if their ruler will join our side in the war. We need boats to bring the men back from the emperor's war, and Azule has boats."

"And?" Lani asked, raising her eyebrows.

You don't have to tell her.

The Phaetyn may decide to upset Lani's rule, but it wouldn't come from me. *Anyway . . . If any of the Phaetyn find out, and we didn't tell them, we'll lose their trust. Possibly forever.*

Not sure that matters to me.

It does; you just don't want to admit it. We need them. You know we do. "Draedyn invaded my mind again, a few nights ago."

Several Phaetyn gasped, and I raised my voice and rushed through the rest of my explanation. "Tyrrik blasted him out within seconds. He hasn't gotten through since, but we wanted you to know. Full transparency in the *alliance* and all."

"How do you know you're keeping him out? How do you know if he's even tried again?" Lani shot back. I knew she was just showing the others here that she was responsible, and so I didn't take offense.

I shrugged. "I've given you the only assurance I can. We know Tyrrik can blast Draedyn out if he gets in. Tyrrik can sense when he's in my mind too. What you decide to do now is up to you." I held Lani's gaze and said, "You wanted me to be vulnerable, so I was. Draedyn is getting into my mind, and I hate it as much as you do, *more* because it's happening to me."

I shifted on my cushion and forced myself to look at each of the other eleven Phaetyn in the circle. "I'll not have you accuse me of deliberately hiding something from you. I know I've caused problems, but any harm was unintentional. None of us are perfect. At least, I've never pretended to be. I've also done a heck of a lot to help your race in recent weeks," I said, pointing at Lani. "Don't forget that."

Fabir nodded. "Well said, young one."

I really liked that guy. Tyrrik growled, but I ignored him. He wasn't really jealous, and we both knew it. Fabir was, like, ancient.

Probably hundreds and hundreds of years old, Tyrrik thought to me. Always one to help me stay the course of monogamy.

"How long before you leave?" Lani asked. "We will confer on who to send with you."

The sun would set in less than two hours, and it would take us close to that long to get back. Assuming we pushed hard.

"We'll fly out in five minutes," I said, standing. Several of the council grumbled, but there was nothing I could do about it. "Sorry, Lani, even that is cutting sunset close."

I took Tyrrik's hand, and we edged out of the tent. "Let's go make some nectar while we wait."

A young Phaetyn fetched us two full canteens, and we drank our fill after doing our Drae-mojo for each other.

Lani soon emerged from the discussion tent, her people filing out behind her.

She smiled when she saw Tyrrik talking to the young Phaetyn who had fetched the canteens.

"You'll take him," she said aside to me. "Tiago is my best guard."

I raised my eyebrows, not sure that I believed a sixteen- or-seventeen-year-old would be the best. I was an anomaly, wise beyond my years.

"He's eighty-five," she said flatly, somehow guessing my thought process. "And he has a great mind."

Turning toward Tiago, I studied the Phaetyn. "I'm sure it's a nice perk that he's easy on the eyes. You know he's like, thirty years older than you, right?"

She snorted. "You're one to talk with a Drae mate watching over you who always wears tight-fitting black and growls when old men pay you compliments."

True. "Al'right. Let me know if you need a sex talk," I said, doing my best to keep a straight face. "If he's your best guard, you want to keep that relationship healthy."

She snorted and shoved me lightly. "If I speak to every other person in this realm and I'm still confused, I might consider asking you."

"You'd reconsider if you knew how good I was at playing cards. I've got maypole dancing skills."

She fought against a grin and lost.

"But seriously, please look after yourself, Lani," I said to her as Tyrrik wrapped up his conversation.

Lani rested a hand on my forearm. "You know I will. And you can rest easy knowing I'll keep the Gemondians safe in your stead. You worry about Azule. I'll handle protecting the army until we meet again."

22

*O*ur scouting party was enroute, and good things were coming. I wasn't sure if the feelings were mine or Tyrrik's or both, but the prospect of uniting the three kingdoms and Phaetyn against Draedyn was a monumental step in the end of his rule. I was certain that if—no, *when*—Azule joined us, we would have enough strength to end his tyranny.

Have you been to Azule before? The sparkling water appeared turquoise today, and I wanted to soar closer to the liquid gem. Or maybe I was getting some serious treasure withdrawals after Gemond.

No. Irdelron didn't allow much vacation time. His flippant tone and words indicated he was kidding, but memories surfaced through our bond as Tyrrik struggled to block the horrific visions of torture and cruelty from me. His next words were somber. *He ruled with fear.*

I was all too familiar with what that meant. Fear stole freedom. And yet looking back, I could see that Irdelron had *only* ruled with fear. That had made him predictable. Draedyn ruled with fear first, according to his words. If fear was first, what else was he capable of?

The choices he made aren't a reflection on you, I said.

No. But mine are, Tyrrik said. The image of him yelling at me in a

175

dark alley flitted through his mind, and his regret leaked through our bond.

I was only receiving a fraction of what he felt, but there was nothing familiar about the memory.

I don't remember that, I told him. *If you're going to feel guilty about something, at least reflect on a time when you actually did something wrong.*

The memory expanded, and I recognized the first time I'd seen Tyrrik in the courtyard inside Zone Seven when he yelled at me to get out of Verald.

You were trying to save me. How funny. I'd never been upset because he'd yelled at me that night. I had lots of my own regrets and painful memories, but seeing his had only made me want to comfort him.

I'm sorry. I'm not sure if I've ever told you. His voice throbbed with sincerity. *I've owed you an apology for a long time.*

I caught a memory of Dyter saying something about love and apologies, only it was Tyrrik's memory, so Dyter and I sat side-by-side while Tyrrik watched from behind us. I had my own version of this one.

I remember that night. I remembered looking up at our twin moons, hoping they weren't going to crap on me anymore. Dyter's advice also opened my eyes to how Tyrrik treated me. *And even though you hadn't said words, your actions showed your sincerity. I've forgiven you, Tyrrik. All of it was worth it because I got you.*

Tyrrik hummed, a warm purr that made my insides curl, and I thought of other things I could do to make him purr.

Maybe we could take a few minutes, I thought at him, glancing at a copse of trees on the mountainside.

Funny, Ryn. Let's get safely to Azule and drop off the humans first. He chuckled, but his interest wasn't any less than mine. Maybe more and only mitigated by the openness of the terrain . . . and the small audience on our backs.

The mountains melted into rolling hills as we approached the border. The foliage changed too. The lower altitude deciduous trees were shorter and fuller than the mountainous pines and cedars. There was no line separating the kingdoms, but after flying for a few hours, I knew we'd arrived in the Azule kingdom.

Buildings dotted the land before us, the rolling hills smoothing into flat grasslands and vibrant fields bursting with a red, yellow, and orange autumn bounty of which I'd never seen. The exclamations of surprise from my back and those echoing in Tyrrik's mind let me know I wasn't alone.

In the distance, the structures were far more concentrated, and an unfamiliar tang rolled in the air, tickling my sensitive nostrils. The smell felt wrong, and I wanted to turn back for the clean mountain air.

The people ambled around far below, talking and laughing with each other, in no hurry to find cover. They weren't even glancing up at the sky for the emperor every five seconds like the Gemondian army.

They aren't afraid, Tyrrik mused.

Sinking dread pulled at my chest because that could only mean one thing.

They aren't worried about Draedyn, he said louder.

The twins said he treats Azule different than the rest of the realm, I said. I scanned the ground again, noting the homes weren't in disrepair like in Verald, not even here in the outskirts of the kingdom, and the people, the Azulis looked different too.

Their hair ranged from gold to orange, red, and brown, like the autumn leaves around them, and their skin ranged from creamy white to rich mahogany. What set them apart, *distinctly* apart, from the rest of the Draconian Empire were their frames; their healthy, well-fed bodies looked nothing like Verald's people, even the wealthy Veraldians, and the contrast of the Azulis' bodies to the Gemondians was far starker than that.

I remembered the three Druman in Dyrell's tavern and said to Tyrrik, *Maybe it's the fish. They live close to the ocean, so all they have to do . . .*

I had no idea what it took to catch fish—not that it mattered.

The lush vegetation of the fields contradicted my ridiculous statement. Access to fish wasn't the only reason Azulis looked different.

The castle is there, Tyrrik said, nodding toward a massive structure on the horizon. *Do you think they'll want to stick to the original plan or reconvene first?*

I honestly didn't know, but unless Dyter was keeping things from us again, I had to imagine everyone else was reeling too. *I think we should talk first. I'm not sure 'join our cause for freedom' is going to resonate as well with them.*

Or resonate at all.

Agreed.

Tyrrik and I circled back out toward the foothills, landing far enough away from civilization that there was no risk of someone stumbling upon us.

"Why are we here?" Tiago asked Tyrrik though he was still Drae. "I thought we were going straight to the castle?"

As soon as the rest of the passengers were off our backs, Tyrrik and I shifted. Dyter's pinched expression was enough for me to know he hadn't known about Azule's prosperity. Neither had Zarad by the look on his face though his features were pinched with rage. Neither Gairome nor Dilowa seemed shocked, only disappointed. And the twins wore matching somber expressions but displayed no surprise whatsoever.

Zarad turned to the assassin twins with a frown twisting his lips. "Did you know? How long has this been happening? Their land isn't dying. They have access to Phaetyn blood."

Nielub glanced at his unsmiling brother before speaking. "We tried to tell your father that Draedyn was supplying Azulis with blood. I don't think he believed us. Or believed that Azule wouldn't send aid if they could afford to."

I wasn't sure if I would've believed them either. The idea seemed so preposterous. And yet Zakai had traveled many times to Zivost to beg for aid. Had he known deep down that the Azulis were not on our side? I would've appreciated a heads up if so.

"Azule is the gateway kingdom to the emperor's personal lands,"

Nielub said. "He keeps them as allies, likely so they act as a buffer between him and the other two kingdoms."

Preposterous but a simple and brilliant tactic.

"Are they as ignorant of the rest of the realm?" Dyter asked, absently rubbing on the stump of his arm. "Perhaps we can still appeal to their sense of justice."

A cacophony of exclamations exploded in the tall golden grass, the opinions clashing, each mortal expressing their view louder than the person standing next to him or her. We'd brought a whole heap of leaders with us and not enough listeners though I knew what we'd seen had upset everyone. The rantings were pointless. We didn't have any options.

Go ahead and shift. We'll have to take our chances. Without waiting, Tyrrik bellowed, "Stop."

With my shield and veil firmly fixed, I close my eyes and released my Drae.

"Do you know anything else?" Tyrrik asked Dilowa and Gairome then jerked his head at the assassins. "You four are the only ones unsurprised by the state of Azule."

I rotated, fixing my violet eyes on the mortals as I gnashed my teeth. Nothing like a little fear to loosen the tongue.

Dilowa shook her head. "I'd only heard rumors. I used to patrol one of the border towns. Two decades ago, we had a swarm of Druman entering Gemond. Occasionally, they had a human with them. The emperor's Druman don't stop to gossip, but mortals do."

"Azule was always different. Even prior to the Druman swarming in," Nielub said. "We still have to try and win them to our side."

"If not, we'll lose many of our men wading through Azule. Even if their army is abysmal, they're well fed and will defend their country. Any advantage we might've had will disappear."

Dyter scratched his chin. "We'll have to get the boats. No matter what, we have to bring our soldiers back."

"Al'right. Everybody understand? Let's go." Tyrrik stepped away from the group and shifted into the massive onyx Drae he held within.

The rest of our party settled into heavy silence. The humans clambered on our backs, and Tyrrik and I checked the air.

I maintained the veil and my shield as we soared over the prosperous Azule. The buildings were well cared for, many boasting fresh milk paint from earlier in the year. People bustled to and fro, many snacking on fresh fruit, apples, and pears. My mouth watered. My Drae would probably prefer an entire deer right now, but it could settle for fruit.

We approached a majestic structure of smoky glass that didn't quite fit the description for a *castle*. The palace was situated on the edge of the white-sand shore in the bay, its spires rising high into the air. The shore extended in front of the palace, turquoise waters lapping the sand, and the briny smell of the ocean overpowered almost all other scents. The afternoon sun hung lazily in the blue sky, lighting up portions of the opaque structure and creating a beautiful picture so foreign I struggled to remember these people had prospered where none other had.

How is that opaque material possible?

Tyrrik chuffed beside me, the sound of disgust. *If you melt sand, it will turn to glass.*

Did they do that? Or was it Draedyn? If the Azulis had done this, it must have taken them decades.

Keep yourself veiled and shielded, Tyrrik said. *There's no reason for anyone in Azule to know you're here. In fact, while you're at it, keep me and Tiago veiled as well. Too much could go wrong.*

The logistics of landing and delivering everyone into the castle in a way that seemed normal eluded me for only a brief moment before I grasped how to implement his plan. *Got it.*

A courtyard sat below. A platform was pushed to one side of the sectioned off area, and on the other side of the wooden railing, a large crowd of people milled around. We descended into a mostly empty portion of the courtyard railed off from the rest just outside the smoky castle.

I kept the veil around our party and allowed Tyrrik to land first. He waited for the others to disembark before he shifted and held his finger to his lips.

"Dyter, don't tell the king or queen about the Phaetyn," he said. "Be as vague as you can with the plan, parceling out the details only as necessary. Ryn will keep me, Tiago, and herself veiled while you discuss an alliance." He glanced at the rest of the group, directing his instructions more broadly. "If we need to leave urgently, Ryn will veil everyone, so if you suddenly see us appear, it means Ryn pulled you back into the veil or she's dropped it entirely. Either way, you'll need to move fast. If Dyter or Dilowa"—Tyrrik studied the party—"or either of you assassins can tell negotiations are headed in the wrong direction, use the keyword Ryhl, and we'll get out."

By the time he was done talking, I'd shifted into my Phaetyn form, keeping my veil around everyone. As a group, we climbed over the railing of the empty portion of the courtyard and into the crowd.

Why do you think there's a platform there?

I have no idea, Ryn. But I don't like it.

I stared at the beautiful Azulis, listening, and tried to decipher their language. I hadn't expected them to speak another language, really. The Phaetyn and Gemonds all spoke the same as the place I'd been raised. It took me several moments to realize they were speaking in the same language I'd heard all my life, just the accent and some words were unfamiliar.

"Och, what a tzimmes! You'd 'ave thought she done it on purpose," a man said, frowning when he bumped into me, only to see nothing there. "Oye, I've tipped too much tonight, thought something was there, but no . . ."

We pushed through the crowd, jostling our way across in single-file until we reached the other side of the courtyard. I pulled the shield off the assassins first and then Dilowa.

Drop it now, one at a time.

I'm already on it, mate. I squeezed Tyrrik's hand and pulled the

Phaetyn shield off Zarad and Gairome and finally Dyter but keeping me, Tyrrik, and Tiago covered.

Dyter wasted no time approaching the guards at the castle doors to request an audience with the ruler of Azule. Before, we'd been excited about the queen ruling . . . but it didn't seem to matter who ruled the kingdom any longer. We were all on edge, and I was surprised when the Azuli guard greeted Dyter with a smile and waved us inside.

Tyrrik, Tiago, and I followed behind the group, sticking close together under my veil as the Azuli guard led our party within the castle. A cool breeze rolled off the ocean and drifted in the windows, wafting through the busy halls.

The courtiers wore pale linen aketons, some thin enough that the garment bordered on sheer. The women wore their hair in curls and braids, some piled high on their heads and others cascading over their shoulders. Many wore gems in their hair, around their necks, wrists, and fingers. The farther into the castle we got, the more jewelry the women wore; some had small stones embedded in their ears or the fleshy part of their nose.

Why are their lips so red? The woman I was staring at had lips the color of the rubies around her neck, and the lids of her eyes were painted gold and orange with a black line extending from the corner of her eyes, making her appear almost feline. Her fingernails were long, at least half an inch and painted in a vibrant orange. She was engaged in conversation with someone, but she held my attention until we'd passed. *What is it with these people?*

It's a status of wealth I'd assume, Tyrrik said.

It makes them look . . . unnatural. I grimaced. I couldn't even fathom how much time it would take to do something like that. And why? *Are all wealthy people crazy?*

Maybe, he replied. He threaded his fingers through mine so we could walk side-by-side. *You're wealthy. Are you crazy?*

I'm not going there, I replied primly, squaring my shoulders. *Besides, if I'm crazy, you most definitely are. And I'm not wealthy yet. Not until I get our hoard. Right now, I'm just a thief people won't tell off because they're afraid I'll eat their bones—or something.*

We approached another group of individuals, and only Tyrrik's movement propelling me forward stopped me from gaping. These four wore shimmery aketons that were completely sheer. They all wore a fitted garment around their parts, and the two women had their breasts mostly covered, or were those jewels?

What is that? I pointed at the group as we strode past and turned my head to continue to study the nobles. *They put jewels on their bodies? And why wear anything if your garment is completely sheer?*

You can study their culture later—

I faced forward again, my gaze snagging on yet another group. Their robes were no different than others we'd seen, but dark paint covered their skin instead of jewels. Unease skittered down my spine.

I tore my attention away from the Azulis and focused on my mate, whose attention was fixed on . . . Dyter's head. *Why are you staring at Dyter's head?*

If you don't mind, I'd rather stare at his head.

Tyrrik was barely maintaining control over his simmering emotion. I shrugged, trying to make him relax. I glanced at Tiago who was also staring at Dyter's head. Poor Dyter. I hoped they didn't burn a hole through his cranium.

We followed our party through an arched doorway beyond which was a large room, easily the size of Irdelron's throne room, maybe even bigger. The din of raucous laughter, the clink of glass, and multiple conversations reminded me of the banquet in *Kanahele o keola*, not a link I wanted to make here, considering how both feasts ended.

Dyter and the rest of our group were stopped just inside the room, forcing Tyrrik, Tiago, and me to stand in the middle of the arch, invisible under the veil but still blocking the entrance. Were Tyrrik and Dyter having the same trepidation? My heart beat wildly.

"Dyter of Verald and Zarad of Gemond," a tattooed and sheer-robed man bellowed. "The party seeks a Royal audience, Your Majesty. A matter of urgency."

I watched his butt jiggle, unable to look away for some morbid, better left alone reason. Apparently the richer the Azuli, the more naked the Azuli.

The crowd hushed, and Dyter stepped forward, the rest of our party following. By the time Tyrrik, Tiago, and I stepped farther into the room, the noise of the melee had returned to its previous volume.

Mistress Moons. I blinked, stunned at the scene before me. The chandeliers were the size of Tyrrik in his Drae form, a large golden orb made of loops and swirls of the precious metal with crystals. *Drak,* I hoped they weren't real gems because there was no way I'd be able to resist rolling one of those orbs right out the palace doors. The shiny spheres dangled in a way that refracted the light into vibrant rainbows all over the room. I narrowed my eyes, sharpening my gaze to see inside the orb and—squeezed my eyes shut with a gasp.

There's no way that's happening up there, I thought at Tyrrik, blushing furiously.

What—Oh. Ohhh?

His mental voice sounded strangled and slightly interested, which was plenty confirmation that people were, in fact, dancing the maypole inside the golden chandeliers.

Focusing on ground level seemed like a great thing to do.

The occupants inside the room made the people I'd thought

were the top courtiers in the halls look . . . shabby. Their clothing seemed paradoxical: shimmering fabric and *completely see-through*, a canvas for their wealthy display. Numerous jewels were stitched into the iridescent garments, accentuating and concealing in a titillating display. The men wore aketons, and the women shifts resembling a chemise, but in neither case did the clothing cover anything.

I'd initially skimmed over the servants until my gaze snagged on a silver tray. I stared at the person carrying it, trying to reconcile what I'd already assumed to the new reality presented before me. The servants were dressed much like the wealthy, but they were the ones with their bodies painted in swirling black patterns. I stared in shock as a man fondled the woman holding the tray. She dropped the platter of bite-sized something, and then the two of them—

I dropped my gaze to the floor. I was just going to look at the floor for a while.

Just look at the back of Dyter's head, Tyrrik said, his voice still strangled. *You can't be staring at the ground, Ryn; you need to keep the veil up. They've taken us through here to purposely unsettle us.*

I wasn't so sure. No one seemed to be trying anything; most Azulis weren't even paying any attention to us. These people were . . . different. Utterly different. They had different worries, different priorities. I couldn't relate to them on any level. I didn't understand how they could be like this with what was happening outside their kingdom.

Were they aware of the troubles? If they were, this party was completely depraved. Yet, though I was baffled and disturbed by the goings on around me, I couldn't detect true malice.

We followed in the wake of Dyter, Dilowa, Gairome, and Zarad. I glanced away to search for the assassins and immediately averted my gaze back to the front.

There was something *really* wrong with these people.

Dyter approached the dais, his bald head glowing with embarrassment. He'd caught me and Tyrrik kissing and been mortified. I was surprised the old coot wasn't yelling about his eyes right now.

A stunning redheaded young woman sat upon a gem-encrusted

throne, her face alight with excitement. She wore a shimmery green dress with emeralds circling her breasts and dipping in a V toward her lady bits like an arrow showing everyone the way. She clapped her hands and squealed, and the jiggle was *real*. "I am Queen Mily. Have you come for a visit? All the way from Berald?"

No. Way. Was she serious?

"Verald," Dyter corrected her, raising his voice to be heard over the din.

She bounced in her seat, her breasts springing in and out of view. I leaned forward, squinting at the emeralds. How had she stuck those on?

"Berald sounds so romantic," the woman said. "The story about that girl in the dungeon who is really a princess?" She sighed and clasped her hands to her chest. "I hope she gets her prince."

This lady had to be kidding? She clearly knew something of the outside world if she'd heard about my stint in the dungeons. The queen was either stupid or a very good actor, and I really didn't trust either option.

"We've come to see if we could use your boats, Your Majesty," Dyter continued, not wasting any time, perhaps flustered by her gem-encrusted chest.

"Of course you can," the young woman said. "I would do anything for Berald and that sweet girl."

Sweet girl? Tyrrik's sardonic implication was clear.

Whatever. I'm totally sweet.

"How soon would you be willing to let us—"

The stunning redhead straightened in the throne and wiggled her shoulders, adjusting her legs.

My gaze lowered, and my brows rose. *I've never seen nudity flaunted so much before.*

Tyrrik snorted quietly. *There's a bead of sweat running down the back of Dyter's neck.*

Sounds interesting.

It's the most interesting thing I'm willing to look at right now. Unless it's you.

"Sir Lamar!" The queen grimaced as a man crossed in front of her. When he stopped and her eyes lit with recognition, her frown flipped into a smile. "Ah, Sir Lamar. Will you please let the boatmaster know that . . . Dretems here"—she pointed at Dyter—"is going to use some of the boats tomorrow?"

Seriously? Just like that? That seemed . . . too easy. If she was genuine, then I had to believe this kingdom really was as frivolous and out of touch with reality as they appeared. Yet *that* was hard to swallow too. I wasn't even sure I could forgive that level of stupidity. But she'd also called Dyter Dretems, which I planned to make the most of later.

"Of course, Queen Mily," the dark-haired man said with a nod. "Did you want me to find him now or in the morning?"

The queen leaned over and asked, "What do you think? Is he at the party?"

Sir Lamar nodded. "Yes, but I could find him if you'd like."

An icy chill brushed over my skin, and I glanced away from the queen to see a tall dark-haired man with vibrant-green eyes staring at her.

She must've felt his gaze on her too, for she looked away from the man she was giving orders to, and when she saw the green-eyed man, she waved away Sir Lamar saying, "Today, tomorrow. Whichever is fine." She glanced at Dyter and said, "Enjoy the party. Tomorrow morning you can do whatever you need with the boats." She stood and, as she descended the steps, said, "Please excuse me."

Uh-uh, what had just happened? She sidled up to the green-eyed man and wrapped around him like a vine—whoa, yeah. I did not want to see any more of Queen Mily's body. Ever.

Dyter turned to Sir Lamar, but the man's gaze had gone steely, and he said, "You'll want to be at the docks in the morning. Feel free to enjoy Queen Mily's birthday party in the meantime."

He turned and strode through the crowd.

"What do we do?" Dilowa asked as her attention darted left.

I looked and saw a young man, easily half Dilowa's age, beckoning her suggestively.

"We should leave," Dyter said, looking first at Zarad and then at the rest of our limited group. "There are a lot of distractions here—"

Zarad and Gairome nodded, although both were eyeing different women. A few minutes later, a gong sounded, and the chandeliers began to lower.

"Did you want a turn in there?" a guard asked Dyter. "There are plenty of slaves to go around."

A growl slipped between my teeth. As soon as we won this war, that would be the first thing to go.

Dyter shook his head. "No. Will you show us to our rooms, please?"

The guard burst into laughter. "The party lasts all night; everyone will be staying here now. The doors are closed."

Was that a command? I glanced back at the archway we'd entered and noticed the doors were, in fact, closed.

"Now what?" I asked, frowning.

"Keep the veil up on you and Tiago, but let me out. I can still see and hear you, regardless," Tyrrik said. "Let me talk with Dyter."

I slipped Tyrrik out from under the veil, my attention rooted to my mate.

"What's the plan?" Tyrrik asked, yanking back Gairome as he stepped toward a beckoning beauty.

Another servant passed by with fingerfood on her tray, and Zared stopped her. She held the tray out with a pancake stuffed with cabbage and diced tomatoes.

"What is it?" Zared asked.

"Fish packets. It has a cilantro crema. They're my favorite," she said, her gaze raking over our group, and then she shook her head, expression full of pity. "Here. Try one."

Zared reached for one, and Dyter grabbed the prince's wrist. "What if they're poisoned?"

The woman replied, "It's the queen's birthday party. She's all about good things. There's no way she's poisoning anyone." She grabbed a folded pancake and bit into it. "See?"

Holding Zared back, Dyter studied the woman, his scar

blanching the longer he stared at her. "How long have you been here in Azule?"

Why was he so fixated by her? I shifted my attention from him to her, examining her features beyond the black tattoos. I recoiled, filled with disapprobation as awareness settled in my mind.

She dropped her chin toward her chest and said, "Five years." Her lower lip trembled. "I heard Cal was Irdelron's son. And the crops are growing again."

Dyter nodded. "Which Zone?"

"Eight. House of Dar." Her eyes filled with tears as she spoke.

She was from Verald? Had she chosen to leave, or did someone take her? Both options were equally awful.

She held the tray out toward Dyter, her hands shaking enough that the silver platter trembled. "Here, take them all. You'll feel better if you eat."

Dyter glanced at the food. He had to be starving—we all were—but he pushed the tray away. "We can't take any chances—"

"I promise," she said, pushing the tray closer. "I swear on the house of Dar that the food and drink aren't poisoned. I've been to four of Mily's parties this year. She doesn't poison anyone."

"I'm not eating that," I said to Tyrrik, shaking my head.

"No thank you," he said to Dyter.

I could see the condemnation in the firm set of Dyter's mouth. He was practically screaming *she's from Verald; have a heart.*

I had a heart, but her tray could remain full, in my humble opinion.

The Azule kingdom was creepy, too creepy to eat their fish-pancake thingies. Nothing about this place made any sense.

Queen-Bouncy had agreed to send ships to collect the men at war, and I felt suspicious and oddly deflated. *Did that seem too easy for your liking?*

Dyter accepted one of the packets, smiling at the Veraldian woman with the sad eyes before taking a bite. I watched him closely, but he swallowed and remained unchanged as he continued to talk with the servant.

Maybe, Tyrrik answered. *I'm trying to decide. Maybe it's a reflection of their general ignorance to hardship. The queen didn't give any of the tells I've seen in liars, and she doesn't seem old, or wise enough to fake sincerity.*

I hummed and nodded, trusting in Tyrrik's perceptiveness. All of the general weirdness could account for the warning stir inside. *Let's keep our guard up anyway.*

Glancing at Dyter again, I saw he'd moved closer to the servant. Or she to him. And her smile wasn't sad anymore, *at all.* Dyter drew closer to her, and I wrinkled my nose, leaned in to Tyrrik, and whispered, "Dyter's not acting that way because of what he ate, right?"

"Why don't you go ask him?"

I raised my eyebrows and leveled my mate with a flat look that made him grin.

"Will you please go and check?" I asked, avoiding further glances in Dyter's direction. That woman had been eyeing Dyter the way I looked at Tyrrik, and considering the activity around us . . . "Please?"

Tyrrik cleared his throat with a suspicious twitch of the lips. His eyes were still fixed on Dyter's head, and I didn't dare turn to look as my mate side-stepped me to go and talk to Dyter.

I tried to locate our group. Five women had clustered around the twins, and the entire group was now occupied in leisurely pursuits involving taking their aketons off. Dilowa was busy not-speaking to the man who'd distracted her before, and he was frisking her . . . maybe for hidden weapons. I felt like the floor rolled under my feet. How had our entire party lost their minds? And Zarad . . . I threw my head back with frustration, and my gaze snagged—

My jaw dropped, and I squeezed my eyes shut. No way. *No* way. That was too much.

Dyter wants to be where he is.

My discomfort with the current situation simmered close to anger. *Are you kidding me? Did you ask him properly?*

I breathed in his face and asked him. So, yes.

I huffed with frustration, but I couldn't argue with that.

191

Dyter glanced over at Tyrrik and offered a half-smile. "Don't do anything stupid."

"That's it?" I asked.

Almost as if he could hear me, Dyter continued, "I guess we're here for the night, so enjoy a little time off. Meet under the arch if things go awry or tomorrow at first light."

I dropped the veil and hollered after Dyter, "Is that . . . wise?"

Only Tyrrik remained. I hadn't even noticed Tiago disappear. I groaned. Was I the only one freaked out by this spawn show?

Ugh, what are we going to do to kill time? Seems like everyone else is playing cards. I stepped closer to Tyrrik as a scantily clad Azuli male brushed my side. *I don't want to leave them here in case something is afoot. Am I seriously the only one who thinks this is weird? Do you really believe we can't leave until morning?*

There are guards at the doors. The queen agreed to help, and there's a lot of stimuli. Tyrrik dragged his finger down the back of my aketon and then tugged me closer. His heat radiated into the space between us, and like a moth to the flame, I inched back a little further. *Want to find a corner?*

I lifted my brows even though he couldn't see. The crowd of people continued to writhe in their frenzied orgy, and I worried my eyes were going to pop out of my head. A lot of *stimuli* was an understatement. I took another step back until my body was flush with Tyrrik's. Wiggling my butt I asked, *A corner to do what?*

He stilled behind me. *To watch the room.*

I pursed my lips, a little disappointed in his response. *Oh yeah, that's what I was thinking too. Or maybe play cards. Or dance the maypole. Everyone else is doing it so we should, too, right?*

Tyrrik spun me to face him with his hands on my shoulders, and I tilted my head to peek up at him through my lashes. I grinned at his heated gaze. I rose up on my tiptoes, bringing my mouth closer to his, and asked, "Are you okay?"

No.

I brushed my lips down his jaw. *Has anyone ever mentioned you become monosyllabic when you're turned on?*

He kneaded my back and nestled closer to me. *It's because all the blood leaves my head.*

I snorted and then suppressed a laugh. I needed to stop playing cards, or I wouldn't want to stop, and neither would Tyrrik. I wrenched myself back and rotated away from Tyrrik's face, hearing him groan behind me. Risking my mental health, I stole a glance to Dyter and the Veraldian servant. And froze. My mouth dried, and panic thundered in my chest.

"Where's Dyter?" I asked, spinning back to Tyrrik.

yrrik blinked as though trying to see through a fog, and then shook his head, the focus returning to his eyes in a moment. He glanced over the crowd, a much easier task for someone of his height, and frowned.

"Well?" I demanded, still scouring the throng of Azulis myself. "They said no one leaves until morning."

I can't see him, Tyrrik said. *But have you considered that he's gone to find a corner somewhere? Maybe he wanted privacy?*

I don't care. He doesn't get to do things like that. And he wouldn't. Not when we're in a new place with dodgy people.

I sniffed the food, Ryn. There was nothing wrong with it. And she was from Verald. Maybe they're just catching up on old times.

"Like how Irdelron was the spawn of evil?" I snapped. "Sorry, but nope. I don't care if I see Dyter's hairy butt," I decided after chewing on my bottom lip. "I need to know he's okay. He can play cards where I can see him if that's what he wants to be doing."

I glanced around the room at the rest of our party again and sighed. If we went to find Dyter, the others would be left unattended, and they were definitely *not* being responsible. Crazy sex-show or not, I was done. I growled, "Let's round the others up."

"You go and get Dilowa," Tyrrik said. "I'll handle the others."

"You mean you don't want me to look at the naked male bodies of our group," I grumbled, secretly relieved. Or not so secretly I supposed, thanks to the mate-bond. *Bonded life.*

Not waiting for his reply, I pushed into the throng, weaving my way through the pulsating and sweaty gathering toward Dilowa. Reaching out, I snagged what I hoped was her wrist.

She turned to me, cheeks flushed and eyes heavy with lust. Slurring, she said, "Lady Ryn?"

"Hey." I drew the word out, doing my best to avoid looking at her partner, though they did appear to have most of their clothes on, unlike pretty much everyone else in the room. *Drak*, I hadn't thought of an excuse for my interruption.

"Bathroom break?" I offered, jabbing my thumb behind me.

Her now-clear eyes narrowed. "Okay."

"Woohoo," I said and then pulled her away from her partner and into the crowd. I made it five feet before realizing how much resistance she was giving me, and I glanced back to see I was all-but dragging the commander along the ground. *Yikes.* "Sorry, my Drae is a little on edge right now."

Releasing her wrist, I waited as she regained her footing and then averted my eyes as she adjusted her aketon.

Meet where we were before, I thought to Tyrrik.

"What's actually happening?" Dilowa asked, now standing next to me. "I thought we were going to have the night to work the room?"

Is that what she called it? Okaay.

"Who was that?" I asked, jerking my head back at the guy she'd been with.

She arched a brow and moved in close, whispering in my ear, "Prince Marb, Queen Mily's brother. He's responsible for security."

My eyes rounded. Either Dilowa knew how to pick 'em, or she was incredibly lucky. "No way."

"Way."

"Can he get us out of here?" I asked as Tyrrik arrived with the rest of our team.

Zarad was shrugging back into his aketon, and an image of his butt flashed in my mind. I hoped I wouldn't have to relive that memory too many more times.

"What's the matter?" Zarad asked, his eyes flashing with frustration. The others in the group seemed to be hiding their frustration better if they were feeling it.

"Dyter's missing," I said to our group, lowering my voice, still untrusting of the clamor within the huge hall. Several of our group gave me a blank stare, and I huddled forward until they all did the same and repeated, "Dyter's missing."

"You don't need us to find him," one of the assassins said, straightening.

"Yes," I snapped. "I do. I'm not leaving any of our group here in this strangeness." I glared at Nielub and said sharply, "We came here for a reason, and it wasn't just to have a good time. Or have you all forgotten that?"

Seriously, I was how old, and they were *how* old?

Tyrrik came to stand behind me. "We're searching for Dyter now. Everyone is helping. Pair up, and canvas the room. Meet back here in ten minutes."

Neilub cast a longing look back into the crowd and then groaned. "Fine."

He spun away toward the archway to our right. It was the closest doorway to where Dyter and the woman had been. Perhaps the assassin had been paying more attention than I thought, but then he started toward the door, and I rolled my eyes.

Ten minutes later, we were all back at the same place without Dyter. I was officially done. *He's not here,* I told Tyrrik. *Which means it's possible to get out. If I have to fly out the window—*

"But what are you all doing?" Queen Mily asked, appearing out of freakin' nowhere. "Are you not enjoying the party?"

She was doing my head in, creative use of emeralds aside. Did anyone really want to see that much of her anatomy? Neimoj's eyes were huge, so I guess someone was enjoying her peep-show.

Should we ask her about Dyter?

Do you think she would even know if something else was going on?

Maybe. Probably not. But still . . . Will you breathe on her and ask?

Tyrrik leaned over me and blew a breath at the queen.

Her eyes widened, and she smiled dreamily at Tyrrik as she swayed forward.

"Do you know where Dyter is?" he asked, straightening. He pulled me in front of him so I would buffer the queen.

She shook her head. "No, but he's going to use my boats in the morning. You could meet him at the docks then." She shimmied, shaking, well everything, and said, "Will you lie with me and let me bear your children?"

Someone coughed, and I elbowed Tyrrik for using so much of his Drae breath on her. I actually didn't like that he was using it at all.

I turned to the Azuli queen and, channeling my best inner Dyter, said, "Nope. We're weary after our travels, Queen Mily. Have one of your servants show us to a chamber to rest, please?"

"No, you must—"

I growled, my Drae canine's lengthening as I narrowed my eyes. Now I was done. Tired, worried, and completely over watching the bizarre and sick sex show. Not to mention her hitting on my mate. Dyter could be pissed at me later. "I must what?"

Her eyes widened, and her smile faded. Her shoulders sagged, and even her breasts seemed to droop a little. She dipped her head with the first serious expression I'd seen on her face yet. She looked at Tyrrik longingly. "I apologize. I wasn't thinking. Of course, you must be weary after your journey. Tonte!" She waved to a man who approached her and bowed. "Take our guests to our finest chambers. Get them anything they need. I'm holding you personally responsible to ensure they're comfortable."

The servant bowed, and I returned the queen's nod, still aware she'd be sending boats to collect enough men to double our current army. "Thank you, Queen Mily. I hope you have a happy birthday."

Several members of our group snickered, but Tyrrik was smarter and swept my hand up in his as we followed the servant out of the sex-fest. As we moved farther away from the party chamber, fewer people graced the halls, and fewer giggles reached my ears from the dark nooks.

We turned down an empty corridor, and Tyrrik and I shared a glance.

He looks smarter than his queen.

Yep, I replied. *Definitely.*

Tyrrik blurred forward to the servant. The man reared back into the wall, but Tyrrik followed him, blowing a long breath into the servant's face and then held him against the smoky glass. When the man's eyes glazed over, Tyrrik asked, "A man who was with our party left the hall. Where is he?"

The servant smiled and swayed toward Tyrrik, puckering for a kiss.

The assassin twins shared a grin, but I couldn't reply in kind, having been on the receiving end of Tyrrik's breath before. I didn't relish taking away this servant's will, but Dyter trumped anyone and anything.

Did that make us like my father? He'd taken my will away only weeks before, and I shuddered, feeling nauseated with the comparison. Where was the line? How far was too far? When did the ends no longer justify the means? My father clearly had reasons to take over my mind. Why did I feel our reasons were okay but his weren't? Guilt twisted my insides, and I grimaced.

"Dyter," Tyrrik said firmly to the servant, evading his mouth with an expert dodge that attested to how many times he'd had to do it.

The man nodded, a sloppy grin plastered on his face as he stroked Tyrrik's cheek. The servant then pivoted on one heel and marched back the way we'd come.

"Someone needs to go in ahead of me," I whispered to the group.

"Don't want to see Dyter doing it?" Nielub asked.

"Oddly enough, no," I replied, shivering. "Would you want to see your mom playing cards?"

Niemoj frowned. "Playing cards?"

"What are you—" Nielub started to ask but cut off when Tyrrik glared at him.

The servant veered to the right, down a hallway less than half the size of where we'd been. The distance between torches more than doubled, and our group was forced into pairs in the narrow space.

"Anyone notice this hall seemed dark and generally foreboding?" Dilowa asked.

Yep, I silently agreed. But I'd learned there were worse things in life—like well-lit rooms full of naked people.

The servant took a left and then opened an opaque glass door flush to the wall that blended perfectly with the glass of the palace.

Niemoj held the door open, and I glanced back at Tyrrik who was just behind me and then pointed at the rickety stairs leading up. There was only enough room for us to go up in single file.

I don't like it, Tyrrik said. *Something feels off.*

Obviously. There was nothing about Azule I liked, and everything felt off. *But the servant is under your breath mojo.*

I'm well aware. But Dyter wouldn't have entered a place like this.

Not in his right mind. But I also never thought he'd disappear to do the horizontal jig, so I was officially floundering in new territory. *I'm genuinely worried about him, Tyrrik,* I admitted. Where was Dyter?

I'm going to check first. Please stay here.

I didn't even have time to formulate a reply. Before I could open my mental mouth, he was gone, far beyond the servant who had only just ascended the first step, still under Tyrrik's influence.

"Where did Lord Tyrrik go?" Dilowa asked, her gaze darting back the way we'd come.

"To check if it's a trap," I said with a sigh.

Feeling Tyrrik's approach, I crossed my arms over my chest and pursed my lips. I was *not* happy about his chauvinistic *check for danger* attitude.

I blinked as he appeared, knowing he could feel my seething frustration, and snapped, "Well —"

He blew a lungful of breath in my face, his panic pulsing through our bond.

"What was that for?" I asked, waving the air away. His breath wouldn't control me now, so what was he . . . My fingertips began to buzz, and I dropped my gaze to them. *What did you just do?*

A monstrous weight wrapped around my head, and I fought against the urge to close my eyes. I peered up at my mate with dawning horror. That weight . . . The blackness . . . That was his power.

The emperor is here, he spoke softly in my mind. *I'm sorry, my love.*

He flooded his power through our bond, and heavy lethargy spread down my shoulders, into my torso and down my legs. My knees trembled as I fought his control. *Tyrrik,* I slurred. *Please don't!*

I have to, my love. Your Phaetyn veil has been down. His regret and sorrow pulsed into me as he pulled me toward unconsciousness. *Sleep.*

Even knowing it was my fault I'd dropped the veil in the orgy room, even knowing he could only control me if it was a life and death situation, I was angry. He'd said we were stronger together. My own failure was exacerbated by his betrayal. My knees buckled, and Tyrrik pulled me close, my forehead bouncing against his chest. I opened my mouth to scream at him, but darkness swallowed me whole.

The last thing I heard as I drifted out was Tyrrik's choked voice whispering, *Sleep.*

J woke up livid. My fists were clenched almost as tight as my jaw, and I knew I wanted to hit someone. At first, I thought I'd been rudely awoken, but then the memory of my *mate* compelling me resurfaced, much like a slap to the face.

And my anger turned white-hot, building to don't-touch-me-or-I'll-kill-you-*rage.*

Knowing how much I hated what my father was doing to me, how much I'd trained to prevent the vile manipulation from the emperor, Tyrrik still thought he was somehow justified? The emperor had been up those stairs, and Tyrrik had reacted by taking me out of the equation? I was Ryn, the most . . . the *freakin'* most powerful Drae-Phaetyn. What part of plan put-Ryn-to-sleep made the smallest amount of sense? Because my veil had been down? What did that matter if Tyrrik was near?

I opened my eyes and stared into darkness. With fury pulsing through me, partial shifting was just a blink away, and the darkness melted away with my Drae eyes.

Oh, no he didn't. I looked at the small space, a broom and buckets and rags were shoved in the narrow closet. He'd chucked me in a closet. A cleaning closet. My chest rose and fell rapidly as my emotions climbed, and in a blur I was on my feet. My fingernails extended and tapered into deadly talons. I was going to throw him—

Ryn?

I paused, my hand poised at the door, ready to demolish, but his panicked voice made me pause.

You controlled me! You could've just had me—

Put your veil on!

Drak. I pulled the mossy-green Phaetyn power over me, still too angry to feel foolish for it not being the first thing I thought of since waking. *Why did you do that? Where are you? I'm coming—*

I'm sorry. Truly, I am. I thought you'd stay asleep longer—

Longer? I snarled. He still wanted me unconscious? *Don't you dare do that again. Ever.*

The moment of hesitation between my demand and Tyrrik's answer was enough to make my anger slip. I focused inward, gasping as I saw my vibrant-blue energy almost completely alone. He'd withdrawn most of his onyx tendrils from my powers; only threads of black lined my blue. I focused, harder, and felt a twinge of discomfort I knew wasn't my own. He was there, but then why had he drawn his powers in?

I can't put you under again. It would take too much energy from here. And we're trying to find Dyter.

Guilt stung me, and my talons retracted an inch. *Did you find him?*

No. Not yet.

There was a moment of silence so profound I wondered if Tyrrik was still there. *What are you doing—*

Will you . . .

I waited, but he said nothing more. And now, with my fury interrupted, I couldn't quite get the emotional vehemence back. Especially considering the reason for Tyrrik's manipulation. Despite what I'd been through and my angry words, I'd let myself be controlled ten times over if Dyter's safety was in the balance. The emperor was here, or had been, and might still be around. I wasn't about to step out of the door without some precautions. I listened, letting my Drae senses pick up smells and sounds on the other side of the closet door: the clatter of dishes, the murmur of anxious speech, hurried footsteps. The briny smell of ocean was still heavy in the air. I was still in the Azule palace. With my next breath, I extended my moss-green Phaetyn veil just over the door.

Then I annihilated the wooden barrier.

Standing in the splintered remains of the cleaning supply closet, I panted and retracted my talons, feeling a little less hostile after a bit of exercise.

Will you please stay there until I can come for you?

Uhh, I've got my veil on. He can't see me.

What? Ryn. Panic pulsed through the bond, and I got a glimpse of Tyrrik, Nielub, and Niemoj arguing with Gairome and Zarad. *Where are you?*

Focusing on Tyrrik's location through our bond, I took off at a run. *I'm coming to you.*

No!

I could feel him mentally scrambling, but he blocked me from his thoughts, so all I could feel was his anxiety. I sent him a pulse of my energy as I ran toward him, following the wisps of our connection. I rounded the corner and skidded to a stop when I arrived at the same passage as before. But then I hesitated, focusing hard because my mind was telling me Tyrrik was straight ahead . . . through the solid stone wall.

I glanced at the irregular opaque glass on the door to my right which I knew concealed a stairway. I tapped on the wall, but where I could feel him sounded solid, the glass as thick as a normal stone wall. Had they gone into the stairwell and then dropped down somehow? Or did one of the adjacent passages have an entrance to the room beyond?

I examined the entire stretch of wall, but there was only the one door. I gently opened it and listened hard. Nothing.

My jaw was still clenched as I closed my eyes at the base of the stairs. I imagined my Phaetyn veil as strong as diamond. Not sure if that would help, but while I was imagining, I wrapped my Drae tendrils around my mind, thicker, thicker until the weight of the veil and shield *felt* mentally heavy. After all that practice, surely the emperor wouldn't be able to get through. The Drae powers alone, maybe. Phaetyn powers, no way. Together, I was invincible.

Ryn. You need to get out of here.

I can help you. I've got my veil going strong. I'm good. I wanted to yell at him. Tyrrik should be here with me, by my side, or me with him. But he'd left me behind like a coward. *He* had patronized me for months with platitudes about us being stronger together. And even though I'd seen the panic in his eyes and felt it as he breathed into my face, that didn't excuse his action.

I could guess at the reason behind his choice to take my will, but I needed Tyrrik to know that he *couldn't* do that to me if we were going to be together. Because what he'd done? That wasn't love even if I could understand the fear that had driven him to act in such a way.

Inhaling the scent of dust and wood and man, I opened my eyes, tilted my head up, and began up the stairs, flinching when the wood creaked underfoot. Someone needed to oil these—or whatever people did to stop stairs from creaking.

The closer I moved to the top of the stairs, the more I could feel power, and I assumed that meant my father was still here. But wouldn't he have felt me while I was asleep? If he knew I was here, why wait to take control? I hadn't had my veil on while I was sleeping, but he hadn't attacked. Nearing the top, I stopped again, realizing I hadn't thought this through, entirely.

Ryn—

Because now I was certain the emperor was still here. I could . . . feel his power on the other side of the door at the top of the stairs, the oiliness of it, just like when he'd coated my mind. The dark power left a sour taste in my mouth.

Tyrrik's control disappeared, and his energy whipped through me. I heard Nielub tell Zarad to not be a fool through Tyrrik, and then I was hit by my mate's overwhelming drive to protect me. He growled low.

Tyrrik, I'm fine.

I glanced behind me, straining my ears again, but the only sounds of activity were the clamor at the other end of the castle. Uneasiness tightened my chest, and I didn't shift from my position four steps from the top.

If my father was up there, wouldn't there be some kind of noise? I concentrated on my connection with Tyrrik and asked, *How do I get to you?*

I wasn't a fool. I had no intention of taking on my father alone. I had my veil up, but I could sense Draedyn's powers from here. I didn't want to risk him sensing me somehow—even if it was by smell or sound.

You can't right now. You would have to come into the throne room.

Is there another way?

I don't know, Ryn. Please . . . I need you to be safe. His body trembled as he fought the urge to dart out of his hiding place and come to me. Which meant he was hiding very close to danger. And I could guess that meant he was near the emperor.

If the emperor had been able to sense me lurking in the stairwell, I'd already be in his clutches. I'd check another way first, some place my father's power wasn't looming. Turning, I lowered my foot to the step but froze as the door opened below. *Please be a breeze . . . in the middle of the palace.*

What?

Voices rose from the foyer, followed by the creaking of weight on the stairs. My heart pounded, and with nowhere else to go, I tiptoed up the remaining steps and twisted the door knob with my sweaty hand. My insides churned, my heart pumping out dread with every beat. Easing the door open a crack, I peeked through, relief washing through me when I saw the space was empty. I slipped into the room and closed the door behind me.

Hidey, hidey, hidey.

The space was an alcove, sparsely furnished with an old rickety table and chair and several rows of bookshelves. The opposite wall was not really a wall. The waist-high structure was made up of ornamental balusters of twisted glass with a thick and wide handrail. Across the distance were similar rooms with half-walls and balusters. The makeshift desk was empty except for the scuffs and nicks from years of use. The balcony opened over a larger space, but before I could look, I heard the men talking on the landing just outside.

My mouth dried as the door opened, and I spun in the middle of the space as two Azulis walked through the entry. I waited for one of them to gasp or shout when they noticed me, and I morphed my talons in anticipation. I was so consumed in the moment I couldn't even hear Tyrrik. I could do this. I could do this.

But their conversation didn't even falter.

Relief, both mine and Tyrrik's, flooded me. I nearly snorted aloud but settled for a shake of my head. *Phaetyn veil*—I wasn't sure if the thought was mine or Tyrrik's, but neither of us cared.

I side-stepped to let them pass by and then trailed in their wake as they crossed the space to the shelves and then disappeared. I sank into a crouch.

I was close enough to the edge to see that the room was a veiling balcony, and a thin path ran either way, giving access to the bookshelves lining the walls around the room's perimeter. The space below had a glass ceiling. I peeked around the corner of the bookshelves and saw the two Azulis men walking down a small, spiraling stairwell, and I grinned.

I think I found my way to you.

Tyrrik's attention was fixed on the Gemondian prince. Zarad and Gairome were arguing about visiting the harbormaster while they had the chance. Nielub, Niemoj, Tyrrik, and Dilowa were trying to explain why the idea was *unwise*.

Feeling a little sheepish because what I was doing might be called that, I duck walked—still in my crouch—to the balustrade of the balcony and pressed my face between two of the pillars to glance down.

The balcony looked down upon a room below, circular like the rest of the area, but a thick layer of glass covered the space underneath the balcony where I huddled. Whoa. That's why I hadn't heard anything. The muffled murmurs were only *just* discernible now.

I frowned, shifting my position to see more. Lots of people down there, Azulis judging by the fabric they wore. From my current angle, I couldn't make out more.

I swallowed, debating my next move. But I could feel Tyrrik now, and he was closer, so I slowly stood, torn between wondering if I was moronic, courageous, or *hopefully* safe with my Phaeytn veil on. Maybe a mixture. I gripped the edge of the balustrade and, with only as much of my head showing as necessary, peeked over the side.

26

Queen Mily was in the room below as was another woman who looked vaguely familiar, probably one of the many courtiers I wished I could scrub from my memory. I grimaced, trying to make sense because the other courtier held the crown and then leaned over the queen and laughed. Queen Mily, still in her party dress, had her hands cuffed behind her back. Several other Azuli's were lined up too. I could feel Draedyn's power and mentally added several additional layers to my veil. I panned my vision back from the two women and saw *him*.

I stared at my father, never having seen him in his human form. His hair was dark brown, almost black, but the sunlight picked up the burnt umber's reddish hue. His face was angular and skin pale, probably from living in a cave. He had to be hundreds if not thousands of years old, and yet he appeared only a few years older than Tyrrik. The Azulis around him fidgeted incessantly as if subconsciously they knew. Prey had a natural instinct to run from their predators, and Draedyn was all predator. They were nothing, and deep down, they knew it. He sat, one leg crossed over the other, in an everyday wooden seat. He didn't wear an aketon. He wore no trousers or boots, no hose or belt. He wore a misshapen, unadorned knee-length and sleeveless tunic. To call the garb a tunic was even a stretch. The garment was at odds with his angular and sharp appearance, and I couldn't understand the intentional juxtaposition of it. He thrived on power. He'd killed thousands, maybe even hundreds of thousands over the millennia. Why was he dressed like a pauper? Wouldn't he want sleek clothes to match his cruel heart? Not look as though he'd crawled out of a cave?

I tore my gaze from the conundrum and massive threat of my father, and I choked back a gasp.

Kamini!

I leaned farther over the railing, inching my hand to cover my mouth. Kamoi was down there, too, standing in front of the two other Phaetyn who'd been taken. They were corralled at the far end of the room, near the base of another spiral stairwell.

Pulling back, I huddled behind the pillars of the railing once more, mind working frantically.

Mistress Moons. Lani's family was down there. I lifted my head. Could I save them? I had my Phaetyn veil on, but the emperor was there. Was an attempt to rescue them now too risky? Yes. There were too many down there for the disappearance of four Phaetyn prisoners to go unnoticed. And how would I get them out? We could still be caught though invisible.

I shook my head, realizing the effort at this point was futile.

Someone screamed below, and I jumped and then huddled over the banister again. My stomach clenched as I saw several Azulis fighting Druman captors. The mules rounded up dozens of the scantily clad humans, herding them into a corner, and then drew large swords.

Shock seized me, rendering me immobile, and I gasped, screaming silently as the Druman slaughtered the Azulis. Blood sprayed, and I closed my eyes, bile burning the back of my throat. In my mind's eye, I heard Arnik screaming my name. Nightmares from that past moment solidified in my mind and left me momentarily reeling.

Ryn. Tyrrik trembled to avoid shifting and was only vaguely aware of Gairome and Zarad leaving, but through Tyrrik's eyes, I saw the prince and his first storm off.

I'm coming to you, Tyrrik said, moving in a blur.

Only then did I realize he, and the few remaining members of our party, were tucked around a corner from the room below.

No, I gasped. *I'm safe. Don't.* If he did, he'd risk exposing them all. I felt his control slipping and sent him a pulse of comfort and love. *Really. I'm okay.*

A lie but a necessary one. The power must've helped because I felt his control tighten.

Queen Mily was on her knees, her head bowed. The courtier stood over her, speaking, and the stunning redhead brought her hands to her face. The other woman kicked the queen, the *former* queen, I realized. No matter what she'd been a few hours ago, it didn't look like she was the ruler any longer.

Draedyn approached her.

My heart thundered against my ribs, my limbs begging to shift or fly or run. I watched, filled with terror as Draedyn's hand shifted. His emerald talons slid out, and he crouched in front of Mily. His face was impassive as if speaking about the weather, and then his eyes flooded.

The emperor of Draeconia slid the tip of his talon into the abdomen of the young woman.

Mily jerked her head up, her eyes wide and her mouth opened to scream. Only nothing came out. Her hands went to Draedyn's wrist, and she clawed and tugged, uselessly, to free herself.

Draedyn leaned over, grabbed her hair, and yanked her head back. In one fluid movement, he pulled the embedded talon upward and then straightened and stepped back.

Mily's hands went to her stomach a moment too late. Her entrails spilled out in front of her. Grayish pink bowel fell to the ground, sliding out on the glass in front of her. She leaned forward, hands grabbing her insides as she scrambled to gather them back to her.

My mind blanked, and I turned away and retched, my stomach heaving at the gruesome sight.

Ryn!

Tyrrik. I closed my eyes, opening them again immediately when the scene repeated in my mind. *He has Kamoi and Kamini.*

I know. We're waiting for a chance to save them.

I waited. *I can help. I can veil you.*

Tyrrik said nothing, and I was still reeling enough to glance around, and my gaze snagged on my father. Draedyn was standing. He said something to the new queen, who was wiping her mouth, and then he addressed the room. Scales rippled on his skin, crawling up his arms, and I blinked, trying to make sense as to why he, of all Drae, would have a difficult time controlling his shift.

And then he was moving. He was moving! The muscles in my thighs tightened as I tensed to run. Downstairs. Draedyn was gone. He'd disappeared past the staircase and out of my sight. Which meant we needed to strike.

Ryn! Tyrrik bellowed in my head, his voice filled with terror.

What? I snapped. *Draedyn just left. We need to—*

Your veil and shield are down. Why is your veil down?

I blinked, stunned as realization pummeled me. I'd been so shocked by Draedyn's presence and the brutality—

Black spots flashed across my vision as pain bludgeoned my head and then my chest. Bright-green slithering power coated my mind before I even had time to close my eyes against the lancing hurt in my skull. Draedyn's power.

I sunk to the ground, clutching my head, neck muscles taut with silent agony. But before I could fall, liquid fire cooled me, pouring down from the crown of my head into every searing facet of my mind, calming my fear. A flood of Tyrrik's power pushed away Draedyn's attack, filling me until there was no room for anything or anyone else.

I'm sorry, he said. *So sorry.*

Only this time, I wasn't mad. He'd saved me. There was a difference between helping me fight and knocking me out against my will.

You need to get your veil back up, Tyrrik said, his voice strained. *Veil first, shield second. Hurry.*

I took a deep breath, doing my best to settle my mind and my racing heart so I could concentrate. I forced my attention to my energy and worked at stretching my Phaetyn veil over me. No problem there. I added a few extra layers of the mossy-green web and then focused on my Drae shield, wrapping the blue around my head like a helmet.

All that practice, and my defenses had crumbled in a matter of minutes. I couldn't let that happen again. Draedyn had attacked me, which meant he now knew where I was. He could be upon me any second. Actually, it was surprising he wasn't here already with how fast Drae could move. Tears burned my eyes, and I hurried back the way I'd come. *I don't know how I dropped it.*

But I did. We both knew I was still haunted by my time in the dungeons. We both were. I'd lost my concentration, and I was furious at myself.

Are you okay? I asked him, wrapping my arms around him when he suddenly appeared. I would never forgive myself if harm befell my mate, and that's what I'd nearly caused.

I'm fine. I'm just relieved you're okay. He kissed my head. *Veil me?*

I pulled the mossy net around him, clearly not thinking straight even now. *I'm sorry.*

Not all your fault. Now let's get out of here.

Wait, I said, pulling him to a stop in the middle of the hall. *What about . . . everyone else? What about the boats? What about getting the soldiers back? Tyrrik, we have to do something. If we leave them like this, the rebellion will lose.*

Tyrrik closed his eyes, his shoulders sagging in defeat. *We've already lost. The boats are gone. They left this morning.*

My mind reeled again. How many more blows could we take? *We have to go after them. We can fly—*

But could I? If I went and Draedyn followed . . . would I be an asset or a liability? *You should go. It's the only way. You go take the rest of the team, and I'll let Lani and Zakai know what happened here. Maybe they can hold their attack until you get back.*

I was wrong. He dipped his forehead to mine. *I should've never controlled you like that. I thought if you were unconscious with my power, we would be done here in Azule and gone before you awoke. It was a foolish, cowardly decision, my love. I'm so sorry.*

My chest filled with love for him, and I pressed my lips to his, opening my heart so he could feel the truth of my words. *I forgive you. Now, let's get out of this mess. You go get . . . anyone left, and I'm going to—*

I love you, Ryn. Be safe. He disappeared as quickly as he'd come.

His determination drove me forward, and I scurried down the next flight of stairs, slid out into the hall, and sprinted through the passageway.

I've got the assassins, Tyrrik said. *How are you?*

I'm good now. On the up and up. I turned my head right and left, searching for a way out.

Tyrrik's power ebbed, slowly draining out of me and receding back into him. *Are you out of the castle yet?*

No. Almost. I turned the corner and frowned. Everything looked the same: smoky glass and arched doorways. I looked around for the courtesans, servants, or slaves, but the hallways here were empty, the loudest sounds of humanity coming from the other side of the castle.

Bad sign. I ducked into an arched doorway of a small bedroom, the bedding rumpled and unmade. I had no idea if and when the occupants would be back.

I felt Tyrrik gathering his black tendrils into himself and froze. *Wait! Please . . . Please don't totally withdraw again.* I could feel his hesitation and wondered . . . *Why don't you trust me to be part of you right now?*

My love, I do trust you. I also know you. Your time in Irdelron's dungeons still affects you, and I don't want what I'm seeing to hurt you. Or distract either of us from doing what needs to be done now.

213

Okay, that was kind of thoughtful—and maybe necessary considering I'd dropped my Phaetyn veil by accident for that very reason. But wherever he went, whatever trouble he got into, I wanted to be there by his side, to help in every way I could. If that meant the tendrils had to be connecting us, then I'd have to handle anything I saw through his eyes. *You said we were stronger together.*

Yes, we are. The bond is still there, Ryn. I can't sever it. It actually takes effort to block you, but Draedyn isn't done in Azule, and I want you out of here. I'll leave a few more tendrils out so it's easier to connect. But when we talk and feel each other, images can seep through.

The problem wasn't whether he trusted me; it was if I was willing to trust him. Was I willing to not just give orders but take some too?

What about Dyter? Have you found him? I asked.

Not yet.

I thudded my head on the wall, inhaling slowly through my fear for Dyter. Where was he?

We'll find him, Ryn. You know Dyter can handle himself.

I could feel Tyrrik talking with someone, but he was blocking me from whatever was happening. His weariness seeped through our bond, and I shoved a wave of energy toward him.

I need you out of here, he said. Probably for the thousandth time.

I poked my head into the hallway and drew back in as quickly and silently as I could. No good. Two Druman down at the far end, headed this way. I looked at the window and tried to convince myself the idea fluttering through my mind was a good one.

How far up are you?

Ugh, he'd already caught me. I crossed the room and looked out the window, squinting to make out any details of the people below. *I'm in one of the spires.*

The window was nothing like the massive balcony in Tyrrik's room in Verald. I heard grunting behind me, and the rancid stench of wet leather and unwashed bodies wafted through the room. Druman. *Time to go.*

I pushed myself off the smoky glass ledge and launched into the air. My stomach jumped into my throat, and I clung to the green net of my Phaetyn veil first and foremost which showed just how crazy my life had become in recent months. The flow of the air seemed so natural now. My confidence that my Drae form would save me made plummeting to my death almost fun.

Shift, Ryn, Tyrrik growled.

Geez, let a woman have her fun. But the primal timbre of his voice called my Drae to the surface. Roaring wasn't entirely advisable with my father around, so I only let a quarter of it out, but knowing Tyrrik's ears, Draedyn had probably heard me shift. Why wasn't he coming after me? Was the noise of the party covering my escape?

He wouldn't just let me go, would he?

27

The sun was well on its way to the evening horizon as I pumped my wings and headed toward the mountains of Gemond. The briny scent of the ocean faded with the setting sun. The first half-hour's uneventfulness brought no peace. I spent just as much time looking behind me as I did in front. When memories surfaced, and my panic simmered past boiling, Tyrrik pushed calming energy through our bond. By the end of the first hour, my heart no longer raced, and the fresh mountain air beckoned me.

True to my word, I hadn't asked Tyrrik for any details the entire time, leaving him to concentrate on rounding any others he could find. I scouted the ground, looking for hints of shimmering gold to find Lani, and remembered I'd need to drop my Drae shield to be able to see her. *Drak.*

Tyrrik?

My concern must've leaked through our bond because his reply was immediate. *Are you okay?*

I'm getting close, but I'll need to drop my Drae shield to be able to see Lani's veil.

Bloody drak. I'll do my best to protect you, Ryn, but we don't know how far that part of our mate bond travels.

Right. He'd already said that. I'd flown over an hour by now, but being fully mated had to help our bonds stretch. Giving voice to my itching curiosity, I added casually, *How are things there?*

Wet. An image flashed through my bond. Dark water rippled as far as I could see. Tyrrik raised his head, and in the distance, at least a dozen boats sailed, clustered together in the water appearing black with the backlight of the dying sun.

My jaw dropped open. *You've almost caught up to them? I thought it would take more time to collect the others before you could leave.*

Promise you won't turn around?

I snorted with disgust, the sound coming out of my Drae snout as a chuffing noise. *Yes, I promise to not turn around. Lani and Zakai need to be informed, too. I'm not going to abandon them.*

We lost Dilowa and Gairome. Zarad's gone, too, but I think he's still alive.

What? I replied dully. *Lost, how?*

They're dead, my love.

Images flashed through his mind, memories of earlier in the day. Dilowa whispering an idea to the group about the man she'd met the night before. The twin assassins and Tyrrik arguing with Zarad, and the prince storming off with Gairome. I'd seen that happen.

The boats left at dawn. The twins found out about an hour before you awoke. The vessels are carrying young men from Verald and Gemond. The boats were about a quarter full. Zarad and Gairome wanted to talk with the harbormaster themselves. They thought with the emperor in the throne room, they could move around undetected, but they didn't come back.

Dilowa?

She left to talk with Prince Marb, Mily's brother, but didn't come back. Nielub, Niemoj, and I got out of the castle just after you. Do you remember that platform outside?

He showed me a mental picture of the courtyard and the raised platform near where we'd landed on arrival. Before he could block it, another image seeped through. Not just an image, a memory.

The distance was significant, and I could only see the details because Tyrrik had partially shifted to use his Drae eyes. A crowd of Azulis surrounded the platform, dressed in clothes not quite sheer.

This group reminded me of the people in the outer corridors leading up to the wild orgy.

Queen Mily stood on the platform, wide-eyed and whole, her insides still in, although her dress was shredded and saturated with blood. Marb, Dilowa, and half a dozen other people stood near the former queen.

Draedyn flapped his wings overhead, the massive Drae shifting in the air to land on the platform in his coarse tunic. The afternoon sun bathed the entire courtyard in golden hues, but the prisoners paled.

Mily shook so hard as Draedyn approached that she appeared to be having a seizure. She fell to her knees before him, her head bowed.

My heart pounded with dread as my mind reeled with confusion. I watched my father disembowel her this morning. How was she still alive? And whole?

Draedyn's angular features didn't change. He wasn't smiling or frowning, but his narrowed eyes gleamed. He brought his arm back as if he was about to slap the queen, but his digits shifted as he moved, and the razor-sharp talon sliced through her neck. Her eyes widened and mouth opened as her head fell to the platform's edge and bounced into the crowd.

Tyrrik had looked up then because I saw Draedyn smile and bring his talon to his lips.

My stomach heaved again, and I begged my mate, *No more.*

Tyrrik broke my connection to his memories just as Draedyn approached Marb. *I'm sorry.*

Was it that fast for all of them?

No. He forced Kamini to heal Marb and Dilowa several times before he finally ended it for them.

Draedyn must've had Kamini heal Mily, too. My heart ached for my Phaetyn friend. *I'm not sure I can tell Lani.*

Don't. It's not your trauma to share. Lani isn't ignorant of Draedyn's cruelty.

I wasn't so sure, but I wasn't going to worry about it right now.

A weight tugged at my heart and pressed on my shoulders. They'd all been alive this morning. So much could change in the blink of an eye. *What if we don't win, Tyrrik?*

We'd gone into Azule anticipating their allegiance for the final battle against Draedyn. First the weird party, and then Draedyn's presence and waking in the closet. Kamini and Kamoi had been with him, and I didn't pay enough attention to defending myself. Now, the Azule kingdom had a different ruler, set on the throne by Draedyn, and more than half of the group we'd gone with was dead. *We should have never entered that place.*

My throat was tight with sadness and bitterness choking me. I'd had a bad feeling from the get go. The Azulis' insanity, Dyter's disappearance. Why hadn't I listened to my instincts and never gone inside? Or forced everyone to leave when we all saw what the people of the Azule kingdom were like? People of that level of baseness, so comfortable in Draedyn's realm, couldn't be trusted.

It's not your fault, Ryn.

He was flying over a freakin' ocean and reassuring me.

I could have done more, I said. *I should've done more.*

You are doing more.

I didn't reply. He had a point, and that made me feel marginally better. But then Boyra's words reared in my memory, telling me I was only doing more to try and lessen the guilt I had for killing more people. I forced the doubt away; I had a job to do. Feeling guilty was a luxury I didn't have time for. The army should be close. *I'll work on this end.*

Tyrrik mentally *tsked. Good, and I need to focus on the boats.*

Okay, I'm going to drop my shield so I can find Lani. Are you ready?

I love you, Ryn.

I love you too. Words failed me except those that were honest. I wanted to laugh, to somehow make a joke. I'd always joked, even in the dungeons of Verald, but my humor had apparently fled.

I took a deep breath, double checked my Phaetyn veil, and then relaxed the blue bands of my Drae shield from around my mind.

The sun dipped below the horizon, the sky's hue deepening from cerulean to indigo. My Drae vision was still fine, but my anxiety increased every time the shade in the sky darkened. Normally, I loved the night. Back when I lived in Verald, I went through a romantic phase where I believed the darkness called to me like a lover. Now, I was fairly certain most of those emotions were my Drae transformation building within me. I still liked the darkness, a lot even, especially if it meant I got to be in bed with my mate. But flying in the night sky with Draedyn on the loose made my Drae skin crawl. Even with my Phaetyn veil firmly in place.

A roar from behind me shattered my thought, cutting through my attention to Tyrrik. Fear spiked through my spine, raising the hairs on the back of my neck. My heart raced, but I didn't even have time to turn before a heavy weight crashed into me.

Sharp talons pierced my scales, and I shrieked in pain.

Tyrrik!

My mind blanked for a moment amidst my panic. Then I was reaching for the azure bands of my Drae power. I pulled them close, tossing them in loops around my mind. Faster, faster. I needed my shield; I knew what this was . . .

An explosion of emerald detonated in my mind. My chin dropped, and I blinked to clear the blurriness from my eyes. I pumped my wings, weaving in the sky as I grabbed for the threads of my power, but the lapis lazuli strands evaporated faster than I could grab them. Every time I snagged a bit of my power, deep-green ropes wound around the blue and pulled them away, swallowing them whole.

Dark, oily power poured over me, pushing through the shattered blue bands, cracking the remains of my shield as the emerald force flooded into my head.

Ryn—

I latched onto Tyrrik's voice, screaming his name. My panic spiked and then waned as the Drae-energy of my alpha father swamped me, coating my insides.

My connection to Tyrrik disappeared, followed by my fight. I had a fleeting concern about the hunger behind Draedyn's determination to own me, followed by a passing thought, now no more than curiosity, about how my father would've found me. The darkness of the emperor's strength swallowed me and my entire world. My sole focus became the will of my alpha.

I was my father's daughter, and I only wanted to serve him. I *needed* to. I had to make up for all the problems I'd caused.

Come, my beautiful daughter, let's go home.

He thought I was beautiful. I bowed my head in reverence even as a quiet voice in the back of my mind screamed in protest. *Yes, Father.*

Cover us with your Phaetyn veil.

I pulled the mossy-green net over Draedyn, seeing for the first time that my father carried a passenger. The silvery-haired man sat astride my father between two of his spikes, facing away from me. *Hiding*, even. He was clearly a Phaetyn, our enemy. My father's disgust echoed through me. The Phaetyn had to die. All of them.

The traveler turned, and the shock at seeing his handsome face and stunning smile disconcerted me enough that I reared back in the sky . . . though I couldn't place why I did so.

Or how I knew the Phaetyn's name.

Kamoi.

28

I stretched out in bed, one of those long extensions with the arms above the head and the toes pointed. The morning movement was my favorite with muscles taut the length of my body; the occasional shuddering spasms were like kisses of life.

Except it didn't bring a smile to my face as it had in the past.

I threw my arms out, extending my hands to either side of me on the bed before opening my eyes. The sheets were coarse and cold, like burlap left out during a frost. Rough but unrumpled. *Unused.*

Something was off. My excitement for a new day, the pleasure of a stretch, even the knowledge that something was wrong only produced a mild, blunted emotion. My fingertips felt numb, and although I could move and *think*—

"You understand, of course, I had to remain in your mind. You're far too volatile, and until your will has melded with mine, I will be present, at least in some capacity, daughter."

I wrenched my eyes open and stared at the ceiling overhead. Matte-black graphite as though the room had been carved into the side of a cliff greeted me, the dull darkness disturbing. Dread rioted in my stomach as I propped my elbows up to sit in the bed, but my head felt stuffed with cotton. The coarse sheet fell down the front of my nightgown, and despite the fact Emperor Draedyn was definitely in the room, my gaze dropped to make sure I was decent.

My shoulders sagged at the plain black nightgown I'd been put in, which covered me from neck to wrist and—I shifted my feet to check—to my ankles. Emboldened by this and very little else, I lifted my gaze to peer across the room.

Draedyn sat semi-reclined, at ease on a black velvet couch. He had one arm propped on the cushioned side. Behind him, a red woven blanket draped across the back of the couch, the contrast like blood on a battlefield.

"Where is my mate?" I croaked, surprised to still have control of my voice. I forced myself to look at my father and tried to ignore the blood-red throw.

"What of me?" Draedyn asked. "You do not want to greet your father?"

He sent an emerald-green pulse out with his second question, and the wave of power swept through the large chamber with such force all reason fled from my mind for the space of two gasping breaths. I straightened—*when had I bowed?*—and said, "Can't say I do, really."

Draedyn grinned, his white teeth gleaming. His garb was as unassuming as the sack-like garments I'd seen him wear in Azule, maybe even the same. His eyes were solid inky black, and he met my gaze hungrily. He sat, unmoving, as I darted repeated glances his way, trying to measure my enemy. His power—I inhaled sharply again—I couldn't even sense the depth of it. To be so close to the source of this massive force was like falling through a dark cavern and not knowing *when* I'd eventually hit bottom.

"Can you hear my thoughts right now?" I asked, tersely. Where was Tyrrik? Had he reached the boats filled with men meant for the overseas war? I had no memory of how I came to be here. The last I could recall was Draedyn crashing into my side and then here.

Draedyn's finger twitched on the couch, and a slow smile touched the corners of his lips. "Your mate went after the boats."

A horrible suspicion entered my mind.

"Yes, he was meant to go after them," Draedyn answered before I had a chance to finish forming the words into a question.

A trap. I closed my eyes to block out the angular lines of his cruel face. Neither Tyrrik nor I had seen Draedyn coming. But I didn't care about that. I couldn't even care for myself or the situation I was in, not yet.

"He is alive, daughter. Your mate still lives."

I shuddered at the immeasurable control under the alpha Drae's leaden voice.

"Is he *well*?" I asked, stressing the last word. There was a big difference between being alive and being well.

I watched my father's expression carefully. His gaze and the hold of his mouth remained unchanged as we stared at each other.

"He is far from here," Draedyn said. "I've done nothing to harm him. There is no reason to; the extinction of our species has never been my design."

"Well, you're doing a *great* job of that," I said. Despite my sarcastic reply, my bottom lip trembled, and my hands shook. Thank the moons and stars and whoever else was looking over me. My mate was alive and free.

The emperor tilted his head, and his eyes narrowed.

"What?" I asked brusquely.

"Haven't you heard that to kill your mate would be to risk killing you?" he asked. "Why do you think I went to so much trouble to get you away from him?"

All at once I understood. He'd pulled our strings like a puppeteer. And we were as foolish and naive as children. How had we not put it together? That he was merely attempting to lure me away. As soon as we knew he was there, we should've run "Did you know I was watching when you cut Mily open?"

He shook his head. "I didn't know when you'd be watching, just that eventually you'd find me when the old human male went missing."

How did he know how important Dyter was to me? My stomach clenched as realization set in. He'd accessed my mind more than

224

once. He likely knew how much everyone meant to me. Could that mean Draedyn had him? He'd said 'went missing,' so I was inclined to assume not—or maybe that was desperation talking.

"Then why didn't you strike when you attacked my mind? Why not just take me then?" I asked.

"Because your mate could've broken it," he said plainly. "Just as he did."

As plain as his appearance. As plain as his power. As plain as his cruelty. None of them had trimmings. None were dressed up. Was that the point beside his lowly appearance?

He smiled suddenly. "Very good. There's no need for pretence."

I wouldn't roll my eyes. Not when I had to live for Tyrrik; my chest ached with the thought of him. "What happened after you took me?"

Draedyn stood, slowly, at human pace. "We flew here."

I screwed up my face, not bothering to move. Tyrrik could move faster than light, and Draedyn had to be faster. The only reason for his deliberately slow pace was because he didn't want me to know exactly how fast he could move. "Yeah, sure. *That's* why you cut the memories out."

He shrugged and stepped toward the bed. My chest tightened, and my heartrate picked up, an instinctive reaction to the destructive power infusing the chamber. "I wondered if we would have a chance for a fresh start, but you've recalled more than I anticipated. Somehow."

Daddykins didn't seem too happy about some of my memories filling in from the blackout of his control, so I latched onto his tidbit of displeasure like a lifeline.

"However"—he studied me like a prize piece of cattle—"to hear your thoughts is rather . . . fascinating. I've not shared a familial bond with another in a long time, and I find myself curious to hear your thoughts. Curious enough to permit you most of your mind and body . . . for the time being."

Hope leaped in my chest, and my eyes widened. I clutched my sheet and leaned forward with anticipation.

His face hardened. "Your mate is far away, Draeryn. My hold on you is absolute, regardless of these little freedoms I allow you. You're inside my empire, and not even a Drae could fight his way in."

Part of me sincerely hoped Tyrrik didn't attempt it, and another part of me expected him to arrive any second. I expected Draedyn to know more than I how hard a male Drae would fight to get to his mate. But maybe not. Maybe Draedyn had never had a mate. I really didn't know. There was so much I didn't know, and in this moment, if the news was bad, I didn't even *want* to know. I hoped Dyter, if he was even alive and with the army, would be able to talk reason into Tyrrik. With savage force, I turned my thoughts away from Dyter and back to Daddy-Draedyn.

"I'm in your lair?" I asked, glancing away from the emperor's intense perusal of me to take a better look at the room. My bed was the centrepiece of the space, the velvet couch with its blood-red throw and a leather-covered trunk at the end of the bed were the only adornments to the chamber. Like the emperor himself, his lair was plain, another testament to his faux-humility. Like anything material would distract from his power? How hard would it be to hang up a family portrait—ugh, no. Maybe a picture of his mother or a landscape or sunset? Black, black, black.

"I'm seeing a decorative theme here," I muttered. A door to my right offered a break in the dark graphite rock. Did that lead out to the rest of his lair?

"This is my *home*. Wild animals have lairs. My empire is all of Draeconia, from the front of the cliffs, extending out to the water on all sides, all the way down to your precious Verald. And yes, that door will lead you to the rest of my abode. Behind you is your private washroom, through the smaller doorway there."

I didn't even need to speak anymore to be answered. How convenient. I offered Daddy Draedyn a tight smile.

A foreboding darkness billowed out from him, the only response to my flippant thought. The creeping dark-green power crawled through the room toward me, and I had a minor freak out. He didn't expect me to watch my thoughts, did he? That was probably impossible for anyone.

The ominous pressure retracted like a knife pulled from a wound. I was drawn forward as though dragged by an invisible force.

"Very true, daughter," the emperor murmured, walking around the bed *away* from the door. "Our thoughts are the essence of what we are. As you think, you will become. Do you know what guides me?"

Ugh. Was he giving parental advice? Or trying to bond? When would he just go— *Oops.*

He turned to the black wall, hands clasped behind his back. He was huge although his choice of apparel made him seem smaller. As he drew closer, I better appreciated his height, maybe five or six inches taller than Tyrrik although thinner than my mate. To the outside observer, only years might've separated us, but in truth, Draedyn was hundreds or thousands of years old.

He'd killed my mother. Not directly, but he'd led her to a life of secrecy and fear. What life could my mother have had if not for being rounded up and carted off to him to be a brooding mare?

What the hay was he looking at the wall for? The meaning of life?

"Betrayal," the emperor said.

Maybe he was touched in the head—more than his utter ruthlessness and greediness for power suggested. I took a deep breath and, humoring him, repeated, "Betrayal?"

His shoulders tensed.

His mind-reading-thing was reducing the likelihood of my escape.

"Hundreds upon hundreds of years have gone by," he said, still speaking to the graphite wall. "And yet the strongest memories I have are those of betrayal. What it *felt* like: the twist in my stomach, the wrench in my heart, the fire in my belly. I used to get angry and frustrated with the inconvenience. I had to create plans to exact my revenge. I deserved recompense from those who dared to defy me, or worse, rise against me. I vowed never to forget a betrayal, and I didn't. Each time someone significant broke my trust, I pulled a scale from my Drae body. That way I had merely to look upon my true form and be taken back to the exact moment, the exact *feeling* I had."

That. Was. Messed. Up. Seriously.

That, right there, that was why he was crazy, with a capital K. Revenge? Recompense owed? Burn someone's pancakes, chop down a tree, or get a hammer and go bang some nails into a stump like a normal person. Better yet, go blow fire at the stars.

I cringed as the oily green power began to creep back. What a time to learn my mind liked to rattle one insult off after another. Actually, I might've known. Tyrrik hearing my thoughts and Draedyn hearing them weren't the same thing.

The emperor turned, hands still at his back, his facial features fixed in an impassive mask I was certain male Drae were born with. "I have spent my entire life serving this realm. I came from the Draekon desert with the goal to leave a legacy the Drae could be proud of. But the Drae began to rise against me. My own people denied the aid necessary to obliterate our mutual enemies. I was forced to look for a different route to success. I sent Irdelron and my Druman to give them a choice. There is no way to straddle a line when it comes to war. If you aren't for, then by default you are against, and the Drae refused to join me," Draedyn said, his neck tightening as he reigned in his emotions.

Ouch. They mustn't have liked him at all. No surprises there.

Draedyn's hands curled into fists.

He continued his history lesson. "Irdelron and the Druman were forced to slaughter them and bring me the female Drae. I took every precaution I could with those of my kind. I collected the Phaetyn, knowing the healers could help the females with child, but we lost so many. And then there was Draehl. I remember the reports of your mother's progressing pregnancy." His eyes flicked to mine and I stilled. "I visited her, felt you kick her belly. I watched over her. She was not my mate, but I felt the same protective draw to what she carried in her womb—to you. I was desperate for you. I forced Phaetyn after Phaetyn to heal you and her, but she continued to decline. I remember when the Phaeytn queen poured her vitality into your mother."

The creeping darkness, the color of rotting garbage, reached me, sucking the air from my lungs as it clawed up my body to my mind. I reached hands to my throat, but there was nothing there I could pull against, no way to free myself.

"I was told she died, just like the others, by the midwife. But I *remember*, weeks later, being informed of Draehl's betrayal." He straightened and inhaled through his nose, tipping his chin slightly. "Yes," he said, drawing out the word. "Years go by, but memories of betrayal remain, and recompense will be paid."

My eyes watered, and I whimpered from the lack of air.

He glanced at me, his eyes widened, and the creeping power fell away like water down a sluice on irrigation day.

I coughed, wheezing to fill my lungs.

He clicked his fingers, and the door swung open. "But I do not blame you. Which is why I would welcome you into my empire, heir-daughter, with a gift."

I drew my hand across my watering eyes to clear them. The dark power still lingered around the edges of the room, and I focused on it, forcing myself to stare until I was able to distinguish the dark-green power hovering over the floor like wet soot. Curious. I turned my thoughts inward and searched for my Drae tendrils of energy. The lapis lazuli threads were there, locked *outside* my mind by a shield of Draedyn's emerald powers. His shield looked just like a thick-cut gem wrapped around my head, separating my mind from the entirety of my Drae side. I tried to think about shifting, but there was no way to access, let alone wield my power.

A light tread outside the doorway announced someone's arrival.

I turned and scowled, my heart twisting with dislike and distrust as another piece of my missing memory came back.

"Kamoi," I greeted coolly. A tiny sliver of doubt, the thought that Kamoi might have been forced to do what he'd done, was all that kept me from launching off the bed and strangling the Phaetyn prince.

He'd been sitting on Draedyn's back when they captured me. And it was the reason he'd been there that had my fists curling into tight, white-knuckled balls. Phaetyn could see through my veil. When I'd been searching for Lani, I'd let my Drae shield lax in order to glimpse the gold of her veil around the army.

But I'd had the Phaetyn veil up.

Kamoi had been Draedyn's eyes. The Phaetyn guided the Drae straight to me. I was here because of the prince's failure. He either hadn't been able to lie well enough or *worse*. His only decent decision in their capture of me was he'd had the guts not to give up the entire army.

"Ryn," he said, his voice quivering as he shifted his violet gaze to the floor.

"Is Kamini al'right?" I asked, jaw clenched.

He dipped his head.

Barely. I deserved a mite more attention than that considering he freakin' gave me up! A growl slipped through my teeth, and my body trembled with rage.

"Yes, heir-daughter. This Phaetyn has proved *most* helpful. But you don't know the half of it," the emperor said, amusement lacing his voice. "Would you like to know *all* that he's done?"

Kamoi flinched horribly, his pale skin blanching beyond what could be normal, even for a Phaetyn.

I dragged my attention from his cowering frame to my father. Wariness snagged under my ribs, tugging on my chest in a way that made my skin crawl and my feet tingle with an urge to flee. I pushed off the scratchy burlap sheet, scooted to the edge of the bed, and with fluid ease that bespoke my father's permission, I stood on the opposite side of the bed to Draedyn and Kamoi, closest to the door.

"What do you mean?" I asked quietly, my gaze darting between them. My heart thudded an uneven rhythm, and the word betrayal rang in my ears. There had to be a point to Draedyn's little show, and my gut churned, a warning that what came next wouldn't be good.

Draedyn shifted, his body angled toward the Phaetyn prince, and arched an eyebrow. "The Phaetyn's service began when he first contacted me a month ago."

A month ago?

Kamoi stumbled back a step.

"I was in the Zivost forest a month ago," I blurted, frowning at Kamoi. Before I could put the pieces together, Draedyn continued his reveal.

"You'd just arrived," Draedyn said, not shifting his eyes from the prince. "You'd brought back their ruler, if I'm not mistaken, and this *prince* objected to your plan. Rather than protest publically or raise a rebellion, he reacted . . . sorely."

I frowned. My father was the emperor of understatement, but the odd deflection did little to ease my trepidation.

"Sore enough to leave the forest in pursuit of *me*, his alleged enemy"—Draedyn spread his arms wide like a benefactor expecting a hug—"to offer information in exchange for *you* and the Phaetyn throne."

I blinked. No. That couldn't be. I wouldn't believe Draedyn's lies—

"Tell her," the emperor ordered. "Tell her how you helped me, dissident."

Kamoi rotated, half-turned toward me, and stuttered, "I d-drugged the d-drink I gave you, Lani, and Kamini, so that none of you would be able to access your powers. Lani couldn't get the barrier up—"

"You," I whispered, the shock robbing me of my voice. "You let Draedyn in." I couldn't even believe my words. "The lemonade tasted strange. Lani was out of it. My head was foggy." My eyes rounded as I turned toward the possibility this wasn't all a lie. My chest tightened with Kamoi's betrayal. "*You* let Draedyn into Zivost forest."

"I let him in to make sure the throne went to those who had always held it, to someone who understood it," Kamoi replied loudly, his face going red. "You were supposed to take Lani, not Kamini. I let him in to protect my people—"

"You let him in for *yourself*," I shouted, stepping toward him with balled fists. I remembered the need to take the Phaetyn with the crown to Draedyn, and realized Lani was alive only because Kamini had been wearing her silver crown. "You let him in because you wanted power. You bastard!"

He licked his lips, and his gaze darted around the room. "Kamini would rule us—"

"You would rule behind her," I cut him off with my sarcastic retort. "You wanted someone you could control." I thought of all his untoward advances, all the times he tried to kiss me, and my stomach turned. "All this time?" I asked, sick with understanding. "Your pursuit of me . . . You wanted to rule so much"—bile rose in my throat, and I swallowed the sour revulsion down—"if not through your sister, then me through marriage."

He watched me now, his violet eyes fixed on me carefully. He had to be wise to the danger of an angry Drae, even if I was the lesser of the powers in the room.

"Since you came to Verald?" I pressed him. "Has the throne always been your objective?"

He quirked a silver brow, and I wondered how I hadn't seen the faux-charm oozing out of his pores and the silkiness dripping off his words clearly until this moment.

"Yes," he answered plainly. "I would see my people, the Phaetyn, restored to their former glory."

Former glory? The Phaetyn had been renowned healers, and I stared at Kamoi, my eyes narrowing as I thought of my time with him. I shook my head, recalling our journey from Verald into Gemond. Not once had he done *anything* to heal the land. Not once had he done anything to help anyone that wasn't also helping himself.

"Lani's still alive, you idiot." I growled. "Your 'people' stand at *her* back, not yours. They have never stood at yours, never once done anything by your order. Kamini led the rebellion against your parents, not you. You think the Phaetyn will *ever* allow you to remove Lani from power?" I crossed my arms. "You're power hungry and desperate, but you're a moron, Kamoi."

His eyes brightened, his lips pursing with anger. He strode toward me with a heavy stride.

My eyes flashed, shifting Drae, and I whipped my hand in front of me, feeling my fingertips grow into talons. I slashed at him, his perfect face hiding the ugliness within, marking him as a warning.

Kamoi gasped, flinching sideways as he covered his cheek with his hand. He pulled his extremity away and stared at the silver blood now staining his fingers and smeared on his face. Rivulets trickled down his neck as he turned to meet my gaze.

"Does Kamini know?" I asked after a heartbeat of silence.

He glared at me, clutching his cheek. "No. And she won't. Your father has promised me your hand."

My hand? I could guess our marriage was just a contingency

plan for if Kamini's rule didn't work out. Or maybe Kamoi planned to usurp her too. The idea of marriage was laughable. If Draedyn meant it, he could shove it. I was mated. I turned my back on them and stepped away. I'd go puke in the bathroom and crawl back into bed for a thousand years. No way was I ever going to be within inches of Kamoi—

A rushing sound crescendoed, a roar echoing in my ears, and I began to turn, to face the emperor, but halted as Kamoi stumbled forward with a gurgling strangled sound. He hunched over, coughing.

Silver blood.

I blinked, but the image didn't change.

Great mouthfuls of vibrant blood poured from the prince's mouth, saturating his silver robes, and splattering onto the dark floor between us. Warm droplets splashed onto my bare feet.

"Kamoi?" I whispered. My gaze dropped to his stomach as he glanced up to the shining, dripping talons exploding through his stomach. And the black droplets dripping off their tips. Draedyn had cut himself. The wound was lethal.

Kamoi was only upright because my father stood behind him, the force of his deadly talons up against the solid bones in Kamoi's torso. Clutching the Phaetyn's silver hair, my father yanked Kamoi's head up.

I stumbled away, crashing into the side of the bed and falling to the floor. I covered my mouth with both hands, and my vision tunneled. I gasped for air, dropping my head between my knees. One, two, three breaths later, I looked up, and my stomach roiled.

The emperor propped a hand between the prince's shoulder blades and pushed.

Kamoi slid off the talons spearing him from back to front and fell to the stone, landing in a pool of his own blood, splattering me and Draedyn with death.

I retched, bile burning my throat as blackness oozed up the Phaetyn's chest, streaks inching up over his face. The black spots widened and branched at a rapid pace until the prince was nearly covered with the stain of Drae-poison.

Kamoi's sputtering spasms slowed. He blinked, his gaze locking on me, and reached out as if I could help him now. He mouthed words I'd never hear. And then his eyes turned glassy.

And all was still.

I stared at the Phaetyn prince, watching the last of his blood pool beneath him.

"You killed him," I said dully, ears ringing. My feeling, my emotion disappeared. I couldn't deal with Draedyn and feel. I couldn't deal with death and hurt. I locked away my emotions, vowing to never let them out while I was in this black palace of evil. I couldn't respond with sentiment, not now, maybe not ever again.

"I betrayed a betrayer," Draedyn said simply. As simple as his clothing now stained with silver blood. As simple as the black stone floor which reflected the evidence of death. His power was simple, straightforward, easy to comprehend, and effortless. That was what this demonstration was about.

He shook his head, denying my conclusion. "There are dozens of other ways for me to demonstrate my power if I felt you needed further proof. I have merely killed your enemy, heir-daughter. Though," he said, using his sack tunic to wipe the silver from his huge emerald talons, "I'd expected you to kill him yourself as retribution."

I stared at the scratch I'd given the Phaetyn prince. Yes, he'd betrayed me and Lani and Kamini and the Phaetyn people. It might be easier to name those he *hadn't* betrayed. But dealing out his justice hadn't been my responsibility. That had been up to Lani. By betraying us, he'd nearly ruined Lani's rule before it began, but instead of ruining it, he'd united the Phaetyn behind her. His plan to marry me was bad, but it hadn't happened. Even in his betrayal of me to Draedyn, I was still alive. I could still do something.

The creeping emerald darkness reappeared, crawling toward me, and I gathered Draedyn wasn't impressed with my way of thinking.

"So that was my welcoming gift, huh?" I asked him, still dazed by the gory scene before me.

The emperor, my father, stepped over Kamoi's corpse and ambled to the doorway. We might've been discussing the weather if not for the stench of blood and sweat lingering in the air of my bedchamber.

"A gift," he said, turning back. His emerald gaze held mine. "Yes, you may think of it as a gift and a lesson."

I watched him disappear out the door, my stomach churning. I might have been young, but I wasn't a fool. That was no gift, and the only lesson was confirmation of his brutality.

I betrayed a betrayer.

I lie to the liars.

I kill those who kill.

His words were a warning to behave. A firsthand show of the way he ruled his empire—as *simply* as he seemed to do everything else. Direct and severe.

I gagged and covered my mouth as I looked upon Kamoi's body again.

My mind wasn't safe. My body was only on lease to me for the time being. But I'd been in places I couldn't get out of before. I'd had to bide my time, take risks, and probably take a beating or two.

But right now, I had no idea how I would ever escape this place.

Draedyn and I were both immortal, but then Irdelron had been immortal too.

30

I traipsed through the hallways of Draedyn's abode, following after two servants dressed in a sack-like tunic closely resembling my father's. The servants were dressed in black uniforms of a severe cut. As I stared at the servants' suits, I realized the material was the same as my couch. Nice. Apparently, Draedyn liked things to match: the servants to the furniture and father to daughter.

How quaint.

The entire residence was cut into the black graphite cliff. The passages were dark, and I shifted my eyes to see. How did his servants get around without constantly tripping? Maybe he kept them in the dark for sick reasons of his own.

The two servants stopped walking and took their places on either side of a low and open doorway.

Murmuring voices swept out of the room toward me, and I tugged at the bottom of my sack. The plain tunic covered me from the tips of my shoulders all the way to my knees. I was barefoot, but I'd torn off a bit of my black nightgown to tie my silver hair back into a ponytail to keep it out of my face. Maybe I'd get a chance to fight my way out today. Maybe my chest would stop aching for Tyrrik.

Both were equally unlikely; the first because Draedyn would know escape was my intention, and the second, well, same reason.

"I go in there?" I asked the sentries.

Neither of them even looked my way, so I ducked through the doorway, blinking in the bright light of day. That it was daytime was news to me, having come from my windowless pocket of the emperor's lair, er, *abode*.

The room was set with a long rustic table and two dozen plain wooden chairs, many of the seats already occupied. All of my attention was fixated on a wall of connecting doors that had been flung open. I inhaled the briny sea air, quelling the urge to throw myself from the balcony and flap my way to Tyrrik.

My feet took me in the direction of freedom regardless.

"Good morning, heir."

Just heir? Heh? Was daughter only confined to when we were in private? Was this game for me or the others here? Either way, I hated it.

"Draedyn," I answered shortly, not stopping on my way to the balcony.

There were others in the room. Their conversation dwindled to a stop as I passed. I spared a glance to either side, peering back at them, and inhaled subtly.

And stopped.

They were all Drae. Female Drae.

I glanced once more at the balcony. *Tyrrik.*

I had to try, even knowing the attempt was hopeless. If Tyrrik were close, he'd be trying to establish contact. I still wanted to jump off the balcony, but regardless of the manipulation, I now wanted to be here. With a sigh, I turned to the emperor who sat at the head of the rustic table.

"What is this?" I asked, circling my finger. Hopefully he understood that meant *why am I meeting the other Drae.*

Draedyn didn't stop buttering his toast. "*This* is the rest of our family. Well, most of them."

What? So these were the favorites in his harem? I narrowed my eyes at the other female Drae, staring at them suspiciously. Though they all ranged in height and posture, each of them had black hair and an athletic build. I had no idea how old they were, except they had to be over one hundred years old if they'd been rounded up when Tyrrik was placed under the blood oath.

They watched me, most with smoothed expressions, a couple with pity, one with thinly veiled mistrust. They wore similar sack-like tunics, sleeveless and undyed like mine. The one pursing her lips had a silvery scar climbing up the left side of her neck, and as soon as she caught me staring, I blushed and forced my gaze over the group, taking them in as a whole.

As I looked at them, studying them as they measured me, the oddest thing occurred. A sense of kinship swelled within me. They *were* family. I could feel something with each of them, a tether, a duty to protect them, a heritage that tied us together.

"Is that because they're Drae or because you're their alpha and I'm your spawn?" I asked, knowing Draedyn would be paying attention to my thoughts.

"Because you're Drae," he answered before taking a bite from his toast.

The other women and I continued staring as their rapist, my father, casually chewed on his toast. I hoped the bread stuck in his throat and killed him.

His growl rumbled through the room, and many of the women blanched or cowered.

I smiled, taking morose pleasure in his irritation. The horrors he'd inflicted on these women grossly overwhelmed my fear.

"I'm Ryhl's daughter," I announced. My anger rising swift and hard to her defense, I continued, "You know, the one who escaped the empire with the Phaetyn's help and evaded all attempts to find her for seventeen years?"

The shock on the women's faces was well worth the bravado comment. Even the one with the scar raised her eyebrows.

Draedyn cleared his throat. "Seventeen years is but the blink of an eye. Draehl could have had eternity *and* you too. Alas, now she is dead, her effort for naught, and you are back in my possession."

I hunched forward slightly. His words were akin to a physical blow. I managed to control my expression but not my mind. The sorrow of her death pierced my heart, and I couldn't help but wish things were different, that I still had her.

A cruel smirk crossed Draedyn's face as he listened to my silent lament for my mother.

But his callousness fed my anger, giving me strength. I straightened, smiling back at him. "Not all for naught, I think."

I glanced around the room as if taking it in as I continued my thoughts internally. If I'd grown up here, who knows what I might have become. *Ryhl* taught me more in seventeen years than I could learn in seventeen hundred years from this second-rate loser with wings.

His face contorted, but before I could continue to insult him, one of the female Drae stepped forward. She appeared a year or two older than me, and this close, I could see that her hair was dyed, the blond roots a sharp contrast to the black. Her skin was pale, and her eyes were a warm honey brown. She was maybe an inch taller than me but way curvier. Beautiful. She passed behind the other chairs until she stood before me. "I am named Draesi."

Indignation burned hot in my chest. That wasn't her real name. Draesi was her slave name.

Another growl, this one louder, slipped through Draedyn's teeth, and the women froze. One of them whimpered, and two of them exchanged fearful glances. Draesi smiled tightly.

I tried to appear unbothered. With the crushing force of emerald power in the room, that was no easy feat, but I took the extra moment his temper provided to engage my full senses and look at the energy of the Drae women. Unsurprisingly, most of them were drenched in the oily emerald green, but a few of them had other colors peeking through: gold, red, purple, and a rich royal blue.

"Nice to meet you," I replied, omitting her name from the end. It wasn't the first time I'd used this plot to undermine someone in secret, and it wouldn't be the last. Except I guess Draedyn was in my head, so the secret was missing the secret part.

The strange connection between the women and me intensified with Draesi closer. Acting on instinct, I reached out a hand and touched her. The smile fell from our faces as we stared into each other's eyes.

Scales rippled up my neck, and my shoulderblades ached with the need to allow my wings to burst forth. Fierce determination pulsed within, and I clenched my fists. No one would harm my kin.

"You've never met another Drae?" Draesi asked, her expression softening.

I inhaled deeply and pushed back the stunted start of transformation. "Not since coming into my powers. No one but my mate. He'd spoken about the kinship between Drae, but—"

I hadn't expected it to be so strong. I wanted to do whatever I needed to help them.

She flipped my hand over in a blur and squeezed it. "It is a beautiful feeling. I'm very glad to have met you."

One of the others stood, the scarred mistrustful one, although she was just as beautiful as Draesi, just in her own way. "You have a mate?"

I nodded, aware from Tyrrik that they would never find their mates because the emperor had Irdelron kill all male Drae.

"He must be going insane right now," the same woman said, her blue eyes narrowing.

I nodded. He would be going insane. *I* was going insane. My chest was going to explode from the ache. I was unreasonably glad that we *had* gone our separate ways a few times in the last month or I'd be freaking out right now.

"Heir," Draedyn said, rising, "Join me on the balcony." He dabbed at his mouth with a plain napkin, same bland color as all the other fabric in his lair, and then walked sedately to my side.

The balcony? There was no place I'd rather be, even if I had to suffer daddykin's presence.

I threw one last look to the female Drae, wondering how often I'd get to see them.

"As often as you like, heir," Draedyn answered.

"If I stay here, right?" I asked, rolling my eyes.

The female who'd first approached me lifted a hand in farewell before leading the others from the room. It was just me and the ruler of the realm, stepping out into the sunshine for a balcony chat. At least I was fairly certain we wouldn't get interrupted by Druman coming to beat me.

Up and up.

I dragged in a huge breath as soon as we were outside, but the briny smell made me wrinkle my nose. Draedyn and I stood on a jutting triangle of black graphite, no railing, just like Tyrrik's balcony in Verald. I lifted my gaze, and the uninterrupted view of Draedyn's realm was—I was loathe to admit—breathtaking.

These cliffs protruded into the middle of the realm's western most point, and the area in front of me, facing south, was a large flat plain until land met ocean. Low, white houses were arranged in neat rows covering most of the plain, leaving a wide berth as a barrier between Draedyn's palace and his people.

"Is it the same on the other side?" I asked.

The emperor nodded, not paying attention to me as he stared southeast.

"Are all your people Druman?"

"No," he replied flatly.

Obviously I wasn't going to get any more information from him, so I followed his gaze. I blinked; the edges of land around the Azule kingdom were blurry.

I sighed. "Can I have my Drae eyes for a sec?"

"I permit it," he answered. "Don't do anything foolish."

Oh great. That was so nice of him. And I wasn't that stupid. Yet.

I focused, and using a tiny gap in Draedyn's power around my mind, was able to draw my Drae eyes forward and look afresh. I gasped. "Smoke. There's smoke coming from the Azuli kingdom."

I moved to stand by Draedyn's side, barely able to contain my glee and then fear. I wanted to jump, shout, scream, and cheer. The army attacked. They were still doing what we'd set out to do. Except I wasn't there to help, and maybe they'd attacked too early. My friends were there, my family. I might not have kinship hoo-ha with them, but these were people I loved, who chose to love me, and I loved them too. They meant more to me than any of the female Drae I'd just met.

Draedyn half turned to me, his features pulled down in confusion. "You . . . love the humans?"

Was Tyrrik there fighting? Would they come to Draedyn's realm next? After they won? Azule wouldn't present a major barrier, especially with Lani and Tyrrik there. And their new queen seemed far cannier than Mily, but the people were the same.

I arched a brow at my father's callous question, ignoring the rapid beat of my heart. "You obviously don't."

"They are like cattle," Draedyn said after a beat. "Their existence is necessary. They serve a purpose. I even appreciate what they can do. But love? I do not love them; they are animals. Animals which need tending in order to do what I need them to do."

Un-freaking-believable. Draedyn's warmth and humanity clearly set him up to be beloved by all. He was a shepherd to a flock of none. A curved staff would complete the twisted image he'd put forward. And he wanted me to be his heir? Heir of what? Savagery and deceit? Had he always been so vicious? Sick-o.

"I grow weary of your rambling," the emperor said, his chin jutting forward.

I smiled sweetly. "Oh, pardon me. You don't like my thoughts? Then feel free to stop listening."

Through our bond I felt his irritation spike, and then oily darkness oozed from him to me. I lost my Drae vision immediately, and my adrenaline spiked, causing my mouth to go dry and my heart to race.

His demeanor shifted, no longer patient parent but ruthless ruler.

I reached for my tendrils on the other side of the emerald barrier in my mind, but it was futile. I couldn't reach my lapis Drae power. Turning, I studied the edge of the graphite platform with new awareness; if I fell here, I'd be utterly at the emperor's mercy during the fall.

"Yes, daughter," he said, stepping closer, a predator coming at his prey. "You are subject to my mercy, but it does not have to be that way. *Be* my heir, and I will relinquish my control."

"Never," I spat. I'd die first—except I was immortal. I'd had pain before, and while I would do almost anything to avoid sadistic torture, I would not bend my will to Draedyn's.

"Seventeen years is the blink of an eye, if you recall," he said, stepping back. "I expect you will change your mind one day. They all do."

I opened my mouth to protest, but his power flooded through the crevices in my mind.

I smiled widely at him, bowing in obsequiousness. "Anything to please you, Father."

31

"*D*oes he pull that a lot?" I asked the female Drae sitting across from me, the scarred one. I tried to remember her name but couldn't remember if she'd told me. I hadn't spoken since waking an hour ago in a room with five other female Drae.

He'd fully taken over again, and I'd been left with only a black hole between the end of our conversation on the balcony to waking. Yet as I'd sat in silence, pieces came back to me just like before when I'd remembered Kamoi's presence on Draedyn's back in Azule. I'd then turned my focus to the other black holes in my memories from his control. I couldn't remember everything I was certain, but I was getting glimpses of flying over Azule, of the smell of smoke and the distant screams of battling humans on the ground. I shook my head as a memory of a servant clasping me about the arm to lead me into this room flashed before my eyes. Was I supposed to be remembering this stuff? If not, why? He'd seemed displeased about that fact yesterday. Were my Phaetyn powers helping me out? It seemed the likeliest explanation.

Of one thing I was sure: next time Draedyn should just eat his toast and leave me alone.

"You sure have a mouth on you," one of the young women who

was probably a century old said. "I hope you can back it up when the time comes."

Time comes? Time comes for what?

"Hush, Draelys," Draesi said.

The Drae with the scar on her neck turned to me and smiled, though her shoulders and neck remained taut, accentuating the jagged blemish. "Would you like to visit the bath chamber, Draeryn?"

I pursed my lips before swallowing my automatic reply of *Just Ryn*. I wouldn't even take the start of Tyrrik's name, and he was my mate. Draedyn literally stood zero chance of smooshing with my name. But with the offer of a bath, I didn't care what they called me.

A slow smile spread across my face, warming my heart. "Yes, please."

I'd done the best I could to clean in my washroom, but the facilities were limited. Really limited. Like a chamber pot and basin of water. A few specks of Kamoi's blood dotted my legs and feet, only a few specks, but every time I splashed the remains of the bowl on me, I seemed to miss a few.

The one who'd offered me the bath asked the others if they'd like to come. Apparently, this wasn't a solo bath experience. All but three gave a reason to excuse themselves—thank the inventor of private bath chambers—five still seemed like a bit of a crowd for bath time.

As we walked down the hall, I darted covert looks at the other Drae. The one leading us looked familiar, and she walked next to the one who'd spoken of knowing my mother. How well had these women known Mum? They'd been with her anywhere from eighty to almost a hundred years, so I wanted to assume they knew everything about her. But then Irdelron hadn't known Tyrrik, and they'd been together a century. To know someone, both sides had to open up. What if my mother had never opened up to these women?

We zigzagged down into the base of the cliff, and warm, sulfurous air billowed out from a cavern. An entire cave in the mountain was dotted with hot spring-fed pools, over a dozen of them—some bigger than the throne room in Gemond, which was saying something. The heat and moisture greeted me, warming my skin, and I wanted to skip through the doorway despite the rotten egg smell. As soon as we were inside the cave, I shed my sack-tunic and dipped my toe into the nearest pool, sighing at the languid feel of the soft heat.

"Come back here," the scarred Drae said, waving me to the back of the cave. "These pools are used less often."

Less often? Like there wouldn't be witnesses if she drowned me? Or these pools are cleaner? If she was just a stranger, I would've taken off running, but I could hear the sincerity in her words, so I followed her back into the chamber and finally, *blissfully,* sank into the warm water.

Not gonna lie, sitting neck deep in hot water felt really good after the last two days. The heat drew the tension from my muscles like sucking venom from a bite, and with all the horror in Draedyn-land, I felt a bit of gratitude for the other captives, my only remaining kin, being nice enough to show me the ropes.

The Drae who'd invited me to the back sank into the water across from me. "Feels good, yes?"

I murmured *yes,* my gaze trailing over the room, stopping on the two Drae who'd remained by the door. "Are we watching for something?"

Her answering smile looked a lot like pity, and said, "We're always watching for *something.*"

"Is there more than him to watch for?" When the Drae shook her head, I returned to my initial question. "So, about earlier, does he do that mind control thing a lot?"

She ran her hands through her now wet black hair and studied me. "You mean imposing his will?"

I nodded. Every time it happened, I wanted to scrub my mind with strong-smelling and gritty soap, something to rid me of his omnipresence.

"Not usually, but then you're a lot like your mother, and he always had a hard time with her."

"A hard time?" I asked, perking up with pride. Heck yes, he did.

"Ryhl struggled to conform too."

I smiled at the compliment; intended or not, it was nice to know I was like my mother. I sagged at the tightness in my chest, a vice around my heart, gasping at the suddenness of the pain. The spasm lasted only a few seconds, but my heart pounded in the wake.

The scarred Drae watched me, her brows drawing together. "Does that hurt a lot? Is that from being separate from your mate?"

"Yes and yes." I rubbed my chest, but I wasn't talking about Tyrrik inside these walls, kinship or not. Instead of divulging anything else about my mate, I asked, "Will you tell me about my mother?"

"What would you like to know?" The woman dragged her hand through the top of the pool, sending ripples across the surface.

I shrugged and hiccuped, only then realizing I was crying. What the hay? I laughed at myself, frustrated with my inability to control my emotions about someone who was already dead. Or was that sadness doubling up with missing Tyrrik and the lingering fear from the blackouts? Regardless, the overwhelming emotion clogged my throat, and I croaked, "Everything. Anything. What was she like when she was here? What did you all do?"

These women had been with my mother here for over eighty years in Draedyn's company and likely longer before that. My desire to know more about my mother was insatiable. I wasn't foolish enough to believe Draedyn *wouldn't* find out or that there wouldn't be consequences, but it didn't matter. Whatever aftermath ensued would be worth it because right now in this very cavern, my mother and these women had spoken together, lived together, grieved together, just like we were now.

The three female Drae laughed at my stream of questions, and I held up my hand to stop them. "Wait. Before you start, before we go any further, will you tell me your names again? I recognize Draesi up there, and you're Draelys, right?"

When I first saw the Drae women, I'd thought they looked so similar; obviously, they were all kin to one another. But after a couple hours in their presence, my mistake was embarrassingly noticeable; both by appearance and personality, these women were not carbon copies of one another, regardless of what Draedyn had attempted to do.

"This is Draemyr, and that one over there with Draesi is Draenique."

My gaze darted back and forth several times, and, jerking my head to the last two Drae, I asked, "Are you two sisters?"

"No," Draemyr said, cracking a smile. "At least not by birth. Growing up together in this palace made us sisters, regardless of who our parents were."

Draelys perched on the edge of the pool and tugged her tunic up so she could slide her legs in beside me. "I don't remember my parents. I was four when Irdelron stole us."

Draemyr squinted and counted on her fingers for a moment. "I was five, almost six."

Holy pancakes. I didn't even have memories from when I was five, and that was only thirteen years ago. Crazy.

"How many of you were taken? Or how many of you made it here?"

The woman with the scar answered. "There were fifty-two of us taken. Forty-eight made it here to Draedyn's palace. Twenty-two died in childbirth before your mother had you, only one since then."

Twenty two! My mouth fell ajar. He'd killed nearly half of them through forcing them to bear his child unmated. I did the math in my head, but the numbers didn't gel. There weren't twenty-four anymore. "What happened to the others?"

The Drae ran her hand through the dark water again. "Several found ways to take their own life. There were Phaetyn in the palace after all. And Draedyn has used a few more of my sisters as . . . examples.

I didn't need to know what they were used as examples for. Clearly, being an example did not end well. No surprise there with *plain-ole'* eat toast and then control everyone Draedyn.

"I couldn't help noticing some of you have similar names. Why is that?" What I really wanted to ask was why did *Draedyn* and I have a similar name. The fact that his name was Drae with a –yn and my name was R-yn had not escaped my notice.

The leader leaned toward me in the water and whispered, "It's usually the firstborn child who gets the suffix –yn."

Which meant Tyrrik had an older sibling before being taken. My heart panged, and I rubbed my chest again. "So Draedyn was the first born?"

"No. He was not. He was the second child, and like many second children, he struggled to find his place in his brother's shadow."

That Draedyn had a complex shouldn't surprise anyone. "But he was the emperor, or rather, he *is* the Emperor."

"Yes, but his older brother was the alpha Drae."

"So Draedyn's brother was the one to refuse to help in the emperor's war?" Is that what he'd meant by the 'those who don't fight for me are against me rubbish?' I continued, "Draedyn had his own brother killed."

Power could make people do crazy things, like Kamoi. He'd barely flinched when his parents were killed, and his mother had basically killed her own sister for power. Yet with Draedyn, my gut told me there was something . . . *more.*

"No. When Draedyn's brother, Aedyn, disappeared, Draedyn, then known as Aerik, believed he should become the alpha, but the position of alpha male is not inherited within familial bonds. Aedyn chose his successor before he left, and it wasn't your father." She looked at me meaningfully. "Any guess who it was?"

How was I supposed to know? I shook my head, not wanting to interrupt her but also cataloging a question about the meaning of –rik later.

The female Drae continued, "Aedyn died as did his mate, and a new alpha male rose into power over the Drae, Baeyn. Aerik, your father before he was Draedyn, was already emperor over the humans. He declared war oversees and asked Baeyn for aid. The previous alpha had refused, so the new alpha did as well. Aerik changed his name to Draedyn, declaring he would one day rule all of the Draeconia and the Drae. This led to his movement against our kind through the Veraldian king."

I knew the rest from Tyrrik. "Yes," I said sadly. "I know of that day."

"We were corralled and brought here, but a young male Drae was found hidden in the bushes. Irdelron had him brought forth and tricked him into a blood oath."

Tyrrik.

The detail in her recount made me wonder. "You were old enough to remember all that?"

She nodded.

"I was sixteen when we were taken, one of the oldest."

"My mother's family name really was Ry? I'd wondered if she just made it up after her escape."

"It was your grandmother's pre-mated name. Ryhl reverted back to it once she was captured."

"What was it before?" I asked, curious.

The scarred Drae looked up at Draesi, who shrugged her shoulders. She stilled suddenly, peering back to the entrance. A heart beat passed before she relaxed and shook her head.

Something else was happening. "What's—"

"We are always biding our time," the Drae said with a hard stare and a finger to her lips.

Okay. That seemed both encouraging and terrifying considering Draedyn could hear everything in my mind. "Did you know my mother?" As I asked, I realized I still didn't know this woman's name. Had I been told before? I wracked my memory as she answered.

"Yes. Your mother was the third daughter in her family. She was the baby. Her parents adored her."

I'd adored her. I closed my eyes at the sharp pain under my ribs. "How old was she when she was taken?"

"Eight. But even then she was impertinent and headstrong. She was a fighter. Not always with her words and not always overtly, but she always said she would find a way to end this. Once we got here, she befriended the Phaetyn. She was the first among us to reach out to them, to be compassionate to their imprisonment and the draining of their blood. She would sneak down to their cells and take them food. It's no wonder the Phaetyn queen respected her so much."

My mother's kindness and generosity were what won the Verald peoples' loyalty too. That her nature had always been such didn't surprise me.

"Thank you," I said, my heart swelling. "There were times I thought my mom wasn't who or what she'd led me to believe. It does my heart good to know the truth from someone who knew her. I thank you." I frowned. If I'd been introduced to her, I'd forgotten this Drae's name. Or had she been deliberately obtuse? "What's your name?

Her eyes filled with tears. "–Yn means defender. It was the first-born's right to defend the family." She leaned forward and whispered in my ear, "My name is Ryn."

32

I blinked several times. My tongue was thick, my mouth dry, and I struggled to formulate a coherent question as I stared at the woman sitting across from me. "Wh-what?"

"Ryhl was my youngest sister." Ryn pulled back to look me in the eyes. "She was the one smart enough to change our names on the ride into the emperor's realm. Our sister, Ryli, was one of the first to die in childbirth."

This woman was my aunt? I could hardly believe it. I still had family?

A searing agony shoved at my mind, and my aunt flinched.

"Now!" Draesi yelled from the entrance.

I jumped, spinning in the pool to look for the danger, my mind fully clear for the first time since arriving in Draedyn's house.

Ryn leaned forward and spoke in a rushed whisper, "Our family name was Bae. You are the granddaughter of the last alpha. Now, listen: that pain you just felt was Draedyn's. You have a few seconds to act—"

As soon as she said the pain was my father's, I knew what I needed to do. My heart and mind were on the same page. I had to call Tyrrik. My instinct was to scream out for my mate. With his help, I could shatter Draedyn's hold on me and flee. But running wouldn't defeat this monster, and I *needed* to defeat him. For everyone I'd lost, for everyone I could lose if I didn't.

My heart thundered, and I turned my attention inward. I could see Draedyn's shield, but the normally solid emerald power blocking my Drae energy from my reach was fissured and cracked. Wherever he was, his rage was so consuming his loss of focus was affecting his shield, just as mine had in the Azule kingdom.

It wouldn't last.

Ryn continued whispering hurried instructions about contacting my mate, but I knew if I did this the wrong way, Draedyn would know. And if he knew, he would outmaneuver us again. We had to be smarter, trickier—like Tyrrik was when breaking the blood oath.

I reined back my instinct to scream to Tyrrik for help with a shaking inhale and coaxed a single, thin filament, the veriest bit of my Drae power I could entice away from the rest to thread through Draedyn's momentarily fissured shield. On impulse, as I pulled the vibrant-blue strand to me, I coated it in my moss-green Phaetyn veil, hoping my gut instinct would serve me.

"Need to hurry and call him." Ryn gripped my arm, shaking me.

"Shh," I hissed, pulling away from her. "I need you to be quiet so I can concentrate."

Someone else said something, and I did my best to ignore her. I needed a moment of peace to make this work. I took a deep breath and ducked under the water. The silence was immediate, and I strained to follow the thread of my Drae energy snaking through the emerald-green shield of Draedyn's power. He was distracted, but how wasn't he feeling this? Was it because I'd cloaked my tendril in my Phaetyn veil? It had to be. Honestly, I hadn't even reached for my Phaetyn powers because I'd been so focused on how to regain access to my Drae powers. But maybe I'd been looking at this wrong.

My wisp of power snaked free, and *then,* and only then, did I give over to instinct, throwing the wisp toward where I could sense Tyrrik. I sobbed aloud at the feel of him but pushed away all the panicked questions I wanted to ask him and focused on the single message I had to convey.

I could feel the exact millisecond I touched Tyrrik's onyx bond. Tears squeezed from my eyes at the exquisite torture of feeling him again. I focused on the task.

Shh. Don't yell. Just be quiet and let me show you, I told him. Love, like warm honey, coursed through my soul, and I pushed my love, my very soul back to Tyrrik as I continued. *I'm in Draedyn's palace, and he has a shield of power around my Drae energy. I'm concentrating right now, but I don't think this will last.*

I sent the images of how I saw Draedyn's power, and what I was attempting to keep Tyrrik and me connected. Knowing time was running out, I sent him images of Kamoi and Kamini, of the female Drae and Druman, of Draedyn looking toward Azule and tracking their actions.

I see it, Khosana. I won't try and contact you, but keep that thread covered by your Phaetyn veil all the time.

An image flashed to me, one of Tyrrik's trembling fingers pressed to his lips, of him on his hands and knees as he listened to me speak for the first time in days.

I will, I answered him. *Be careful. He's worse than Irdelron, one hundred times worse.* I suspected it was more like one thousand times. *I need to go.* I was blind to what was happening on the other side, to my physical body, but the pressure of holding my breath was starting to affect me. *I miss you. I love you.*

I love you. Be safe.

He pulled back, and it took everything I had to let him withdraw. But it was necessary.

I followed the thread of my Drae power outside of Draedyn's shield back inside his ring of control, and as soon as my awareness returned to my body, I wrapped the thin wisp of blue thick inside mossy green until I couldn't even see a bit of the lapis lazuli.

I broke through the surface of the pool, gasping for air. Chaos swirled around me in the darkness.

"Make her hurry," Draelys snapped.

"Ryn," Draenique yelled, "We're running out of time. Make her—"

"They can't distract him forever," Draemyr said, the r turning into a feral growl.

My aunt grabbed my arm and yanked me to her. "Did you reach your mate? Is he coming?" Her voice was laced with panic, and her warm hazel eyes were wide. "You need to hurry. If you yell to him now—"

I wiped the streaming water from my eyes and slicked my hair back. With a shake of my head I said, "No. It won't work."

A low ache blossomed deep in my belly, vice-like pain seizing the organs of my abdomen, making my stomach turn. I glanced at the other Drae women, blinking in surprise when I saw not only their individual bodies but flashes of color in their core. Whoa.

This was their Drae power coated in the emperor's emerald-green energy. Draelys, Draemyr, and Draesi, with pale violet, deep orange, and pale pink, respectively. The thick layer of emerald not only coated their power, but there were tendrils of the green seeping into the other colors.

Even if I could break them free in this moment, to do so would alert Draedyn and doom us all to failure.

The ache in my belly worsened. I grimaced with the pain, noticing the other Drae were also contorted. I sucked air in through my teeth and asked, "What is that pain?" While I really did want to know, I was also trying to change the subject.

Not a moment too soon either. The oily darkness of Draedyn's power slithered through me. I did my best to ignore the one fila-ment of hope covered in mossy webs, not knowing how easy the thought would be for Draedyn to pick up in my mind.

My aunt frowned, recovering from the agony a heartbeat after me, and then her eyes welled with tears. "You didn't yell to him. You didn't call to your mate?"

I forced my mind away from everything I wanted to tell her and pursed my lips, shaking my head. "I did not yell to him." She hadn't answered my question. Was the pain we'd all felt because Draedyn had been in pain? Because his power was inside our minds? Or was it something from the other female Drae?

Her beautiful face, similar to my mother's, contorted in rage. The scar on her neck darkened, and she leaned forward, getting into my personal space as she gripped my arm and seethed. "You fool. You selfish, *selfish* fool. You wasted our sacrifice: mine, Lyz, Lys, Nique, all of us." She flung my arm away and screamed, "All of it."

I flinched with her anger, wanting to reassure her but hopelessly unable to. "I couldn't *yell*." That's as close as I dared to go.

"Liar," she said. "You are your father's daughter."

Ouch. I flinched. That hurt.

The emerald power around my mind intensified, and on the same whim as moments before, knowing I was onto something important, I stretched the green webbing of my Phaetyn veil to block a little corner of my mind, stretching the veil from where it was attached to my Drae-blue messenger thread, making a little private bubble. Inexplicably, I knew this bubble, this internal Phaetyn veil, was safe. Light and dark did not mix, not until me anyway.

Maybe I could keep this little area for all those stray, super-inappropriate treasonous thoughts, and to protect what I'd just done. Not that I was going to follow Draedyn now, at least not on everything. He needed to believe any changes were sincere. Small changes, turning toward him, would lead to more freedom eventually. A sudden change of heart, especially now, would increase his suspicion and hence, keep his attention fixed upon me.

"I was wrong." Ryn climbed out of the water and grabbed her plane tunic, keeping her back to me the entire time. "You are nothing like your mother. She would be ashamed of you."

Even if the words weren't true, they stung. I sat in the water as Ryn gathered the rest of the female Drae together, whispering about my ineptitude and cowardice. Her cruel comments burned the back of my eyes.

"It's not a whisper if I can hear everything," I called to them.

You were right to refuse her, Draedyn said, his pride pulsing through our connection.

Get out of my head, I snapped. *I hate you. Now the women are all against me.*

I felt his chuckle at that, the greasy revolting pleasure he had in my pain and that of the other Drae. But I focused on my private bubble, holding my breath inside and out as I dipped under the surface to wash new tears from my face. Was it working? Surely the game would already be up if not.

"Ryn?" Draesi called from the doorway. "Come on. Your aunt will forgive you. We've all had a run-in with her over the last century. This place, our numbers, they are too small to hold grudges against one another."

Seemed to me people should count to ten before hurling hurtful comments then.

I dunked under the water again, rinsing the rest of my pain into the sulfurous liquid of the caverns. I steeled my heart. I needed to not feel, to *not* allow my emotions to rule my actions. I climbed out of the water and pulled my tunic over my wet body and dripping silver hair, fixing my face into an impassive mask.

"It's fine," I said to Draesi. "Her disappointment and frustration are her problems. I'm tired of having people, human, Druman, Drae, and Phaetyn, all try to use me to their ends. I will not be anyone's tool."

Except mine, Draedyn reminded me.

I rolled my eyes.

We crossed to the exit, and Draesi's shoulders dropped, along with the corners of her mouth. "I understand why you feel that way."

Well, that was a first. I appreciated that she didn't push.

Draesi led me out of the caverns and back to my room. I changed into a dry tunic and offered one from my closet to the other Drae. The beautiful blond-turned-black-haired woman brushed out my hair and plaited it. Before I could offer to do the same, she gathered her dyed hair with nimble fingers into a braid, drawing the long length forward over her left shoulder. I couldn't believe Draedyn made the women dye their hair to look the same. That was ten levels of sick. I wondered if he was trying to make them look like someone in particular.

"There now," she said. "Let's go have dinner. You hardly ate a thing at breakfast, and you slept through lunch."

What a nice way to say that Draedyn had taken over my being, and I'd passed out and then gone through a whole bunch of weirdness over a bath. My stomach rumbled, reminding me of a lesson from the dungeons of Irdelron's castle: hunger made even the smartest human or Drae foolish. I needed my wits about me.

We returned to the dining room where the other Drae sat around the rustic table, waiting. The scent of seared meat made my mouth water, and my father waved me to the head of the table, saying, "Thank you, Draesi, for your constancy. Heir, by me."

Maybe that was why he didn't call me by name, to avoid confusion. Nice. I trotted over to him like a good little daughter.

My father carved a large roast, the smells of garlic, rosemary, and fresh bread reinforcing my previous memory. As soon as the loaded plate was set in front of me, I reached for my knife and fork.

Someone sniffed, and I halted with the utensils in my hand, but the silverware was still touching the table.

With my head still down, I glanced left to see Draedyn now still, his hands frozen mid-slice of the thick cut of meat, and out to my right Draelys shook her head, her hands in her lap.

Seriously? I let the thought slip through. "Excuse me," I said tightly and returned my hands to my lap. The food would just get cold.

I waited for everyone to be served and then raised my attention from my clenched hands. The large glass plates were laden with food: a thick slice of the meat, still pink all the way through, was surrounded by roasted root vegetables. Seeded brown bread sat to the side, and a crock of butter was being passed around the table.

I watched carefully and mimicked what Draelys did opposite me, all the way down to the way they buttered their bread.

And still no one ate. What was this torture? Give me pain, take my will, but do *not* get between me and rosemary potatoes.

"In honor of your fidelity, heir, we are having beef," Draedyn announced. "Now, don't worry, unlike some of your precious cattle, you did not know this cow." His dark eyes gleamed.

"Was that meant to be a joke?" I gritted my teeth. Doubt about the origins of the meat in front of me held me back from the thick slice of steak. There was no reason for him not to hear my thoughts or feel my disgust, and I let my revulsion of his insinuation the meat was human flow freely to him.

A low growl rolled out from his lips across the table, making the glasses shake and the silverware rattle against the wood.

I straightened, squaring my shoulders. Even knowing he would feel the insincerity of my humility, I kept my gaze down.

"Yes," he said. "But even with the insincerity, your actions are moving in a more desirable direction. And, you misunderstand me, heir. I would not have us be enemies. *I* don't see any difference between humans and cattle. *You* have made your opinion on the matter quite clear."

"So you're saying this meat is cow; it's not human?"

"It is cow," he said simply. "Now eat it."

My distrust did not ease as my father sliced into the meat, bringing bite after bite to his lips. The rest of the Drae women followed his example, but still I couldn't bring myself to eat from the thick slice.

I ate the roasted potatoes, parsnips, and carrots. I added more butter to my bread and ate all of it, sipping on the wine and water by my plate. I kept my gaze fixated on the meat, cutting into it and then pushing the pieces aside for something else until it was the only thing remaining on my plate.

"You do not believe me?" he asked, his irritation pulsing through our bond. "Have I ever lied to you? Have I ever betrayed your trust?"

"What kind of question is that?" I replied. "You've stolen my will at least four times." I met his gaze and continued, slowly, convinced of the veracity of my accusations. "And you *would* lie and betray me if it served your purpose. I can feel it right now through our bond."

And through the bond, I could feel his surprise and then pride at my comment. I could also tell he was telling the truth about the meat. I picked up my knife and fork again and cut a large piece of meat and then stuck it in my mouth.

Just like my bond with Tyrrik, this bond with my father went both ways. Useful? Perhaps? I didn't need help seeing—

Stop thinking while you're ahead, Ryn, I reminded myself.

33

We finished our meal, and the emperor cleared his throat. I felt him gather up the energy of our bond, and I glanced inward, seeing the mossy power webbing still obscured my thread-like link to my Drae power. He wasn't completely gone, however I could still feel his sick anticipation.

Something awful was about to happen.

Druman filed into the room, surrounding the walls two layers deep. Their unwashed, disgusting presence extended out into the hall, dozens of them waiting to act on the will of their master.

The energy of the female Drae around the table shifted, going from mild content to anxious and tense trepidation.

Draedyn leaned forward, dark eyes bright. "I find our bond increasingly fascinating, heir. I've found when you become excessively emotional, your energy, thoughts, and feelings permeate my mind. While I know you could control and stop me seeing and feeling your thoughts if I give you access to your Drae powers, I'm not sure I will ever want to give this up. I've discovered so much through you."

"I don't know what you mean."

He licked his lips and pushed his chair back. "No, I don't suspect you do. Come," he said, standing. "Let's go out on the balcony. Draeryn and Draelyz, you will join us."

I whipped my head to look at my aunt. That wasn't a good sign. She and the female Drae across from her paled, and Druman pulled their chairs out from the table.

Draelyz stood, resting her hands on the table, and my aunt rushed around the foot of the table to help the other Drae forward. Frozen with fear? Yeah, I'd been there, done that.

"Did you know," Draedyn asked, linking his arm through mine.

What the hay? We were on linking arms terms now?

If the thought had reached him, he ignored it, saying, "The Drae women used to try to defy me all the time. Your mother was usually an instigator."

I yanked my arm from his and said, "That doesn't surprise me much."

He smiled, fangs elongating past his lips. "No, I don't suspect it does."

Druman herded the other two Drae out onto the balcony and then stood shoulder to shoulder to cut them off from the rest of the room.

The orange-and-red rays of the dying sun glistened over the water. Smoke still rose from within Azule in the distance but much less than yesterday. The tang of ash coated the air. I stepped past my father, yearning to reach out to Tyrrik, regardless of the danger and stupidity of doing so.

I took a deep breath and pivoted to the two female Drae.

Draeryn and Draelyz were on their knees although the fierce expression of insolence my aunt wore was eerily similar to how *my* eyes narrowed and how *my* lip curled. As I saw my mother in her, I could also see myself, a weary, bitter, hard version of myself.

Draelyz was hunched over, and with the tattered edges of her tunic riding up her thighs, purple and green bruises were now visible on her pale skin.

"You beat her," I said, pointing at Draelyz's legs. Her face and arms were untouched, and my dinner congealed in my stomach.

He'd only beaten the lower half of her body. Was it so I couldn't see until now? Or because he didn't want to see her mottled skin while he ate? "Why did you beat her?"

"Why do you think?" he asked. He pulled her hair back, revealing her beautiful face, her blue eyes glistening with tears. "Betrayal."

His favorite word.

But he couldn't kill them. They were Drae.

In a blur, he brought his hand back and swept it forward, his fingers turning to talons as he sliced.

I shouted in warning.

Draelyz managed a half-whimper before Draedyn's talons sliced through her chest. Her body pitched forward, and her head bowed.

Draedyn glanced at one of the Druman and pointed at Draelyz. The mule pulled a knife from his belt and a bead of silver dripped to the black stone. I sucked in a breath, my body stiffening, but before I could yell out a warning, the Druman drove the blade through her back. Her body jerked and then crumpled. She fell on her side, seizing.

Draedyn sauntered over to the writhing female kicked Draelyz over the edge of the balcony.

I stared at the spot where she'd disappeared, listening to the flap of her clothing as her body fell below. How could he—

Draedyn straightened with a deep inhale and looked at me with bright eyes. "Before you ask, no, that is not my favorite method of execution. There is something inherently satisfying to seeing heads roll, but I have to work around my limitations."

How could he kill another Drae? How was that even—

"Possible?" he asked, raising his eyebrows. "Technically, heir-daughter, I'm not delivering a killing blow. The Druman, who you'll recall do not have such limitations, can wield a blade with Phaetyn blood to kill a Drae, and I'm merely pushing the Drae over the edge. The ground and the Phaetyn blood are doing the killing."

My stomach churned, and I averted my gaze, desperate to not lose my dinner. I locked on my aunt's panicked face. *Drak.*

"Now," Draedyn said. "It's your turn."

"My turn for what?" I asked. He was going to kill me too?

"Draeryn has not only betrayed me but you, her kin as well. She deserves to die." He frowned as if considering his next words and then added, "She deserves much worse, but I'm willing to forgo the torture to watch you take revenge."

I glanced at the Druman, but none of them even moved. I stared at the unmoving mules and then at my father who merely raised his eyebrows, as if waiting . . . I shook my head, bile rising in my chest. "I won't."

A slow, cruel smile spread over his face. "You will."

I braced myself for the mind-invasion, only it didn't come. Aunt Ryn frowned, and I glanced at my father.

"You're not going to make me?" I asked, scooting closer to my aunt, and then thinking better of it, I backed away. "You're not going to take over and make me?"

He shook his head. "Then I would be doing it, not you."

Something about the way he said it made me more nervous, not less.

Ryn remained on her knees, tears falling down her cheeks.

"No," he said. "But I can force you in some ways."

My nails on both hands elongated, becoming deadly blades, and I quickly flung my arms behind my back even as my fangs extended and my eyes narrowed to Drae slits. I fought his control over my body, but the tips of my talons bit through my skin.

"There now, all ready," he said.

I shook my head, refusing to do what he wanted as long as I was in control.

"No?" he asked. "Then you can watch. If you'd acted, you could've spared her this."

A blast of his energy hit me in the chest, expelling the air from my lungs and pushing me against a Druman. He wrapped his arms around me, holding me still. I turned my head away, and another Druman forced my head back toward my aunt and my father. I closed my eyes.

"Even if you do not watch, you will hear every cut, every scream, every time my talons run against her bones. And you will know, heir, you could have spared her pain if you'd acted."

He was right. I could've given her mercy. I couldn't even shake my head, so I spat. "Don't blame me for your actions. You're the one killing her, regardless."

"Killing? I'm not killing her. I *can't*. But you could have. So don't blame me for your *inaction*," he replied, his tone no more riled than if we were discussing the weather.

Ryn screamed, and I clenched my teeth and closed my eyes. Another scream, and another. I whimpered with her, but refused to look as Draedyn mutilated and tortured her.

"Please," she begged. "Ryn, please."

I choked on my refusal of a few minutes prior, filled with a new awareness and even a small amount of appreciation for why Tyrrik had moved so quickly when killing Arnik so long ago. Her wet, strangled cries continued, until I couldn't take her suffering any longer. "Al'right," I shouted. "I'll do it."

The Druman released me, and I collapsed to the dark stone, pounding it with my fist. Tears streamed down my face, blurring my vision, and I let them fall unchecked, hoping they would obscure a bit of the torture Draedyn had inflicted on my aunt already.

I hadn't even had time to know her.

I struggled to my feet and raised my gaze, hunching back over as I threw up all over the balcony.

The tang of Ryn's blood saturated the area, and when I stood upright, I was more prepared—if that was even possible—to see my aunt's flayed body suspended by Draedyn's grip. His hand was buried in her hair, and she dangled limply in the air. Her chest still moved. She was alive, and her wounds were slowly knitting back together.

"Do I have to cut off her head?" I asked him, choking on another sob.

Draedyn shrugged, and my aunt's body swayed. Her eyelids fluttered, and her bloodied lips moved in incoherent pleas.

"I don't care how you do it."

A mercy. That's what Tyrrik had said, and now I could see it. My talons emerged again, and I whispered to my aunt, "I'm so sorry, Aunt Ryn. Go to the stars and be with your sisters. Please tell my mother I love her."

I sliced into my leg, and Draedyn watched, transfixed. "Yes," he said, his voice filled with eager anticipation. "Taste the reward of vengeance, daughter."

I glared at him.

"Do it," my aunt coughed on the ground.

I tore my gaze from the emperor and closed my eyes, sliding my talons into her chest cavity like a hot knife into butter.

Draedyn released her, and her body slid from my talons and crumpled to the stone. I squeezed my eyes shut, listening to the drip of her blood from the end of my talon. I choked on a sob and coughed, opening my eyes to see one of the Druman plunge a dagger, slick with Phaetyn blood, into my aunt's chest.

"A bit too slow," my father said with a frown. "I'll leave a contingency of Druman to make sure you've learned your lesson. You will stay with her until she's dead."

"No," I gasped as Draedyn whirled on the spot and left the balcony.

I blinked, disconnected from the scene around me. The Druman moved, time didn't stop, yet I existed in a muted bubble. There was my vomit. There was my aunt, the woman I was named after, her broken body trembling as her life bled from her. As black cracks marred her face, reacting to the Phaetyn poison in her bloodstream.

Twilight descended, and the air cooled. The Druman retreated into the dining room, leaving me and my aunt on the graphite platform.

My breaths came in rapid, shallow gulps, and I crawled over to the female Drae, my kin. My real kin.

"I'm sorry," I whispered again. I wanted Tyrrik here.

I wanted someone to make this better.

I didn't want to have my aunt's blood on my . . . I swallowed, stunned with the craziness of the idea that flitted through my mind.

I looked inward, covering my thoughts with my Phaetyn veil and double-checking my Drae-thread.

Aunt Ryn's power was completely unsullied by Draedyn's slick green energy. He'd pulled his power back at some point, leaving me a perfect opportunity. I stretched the mossy web over my aunt slowly, first covering the vibrant turquoise still around her heart and then pulling the power of invisibility over her entire body. I hunched over and whispered, "Please work."

I'd healed Tyrrik. Ryn was my aunt, so I could totally do this. Couldn't I? I pushed my healing-mojo into her. I imagined the edges of her skin knitting together, the Phaetyn poison burning away like Drae fire, her blood multiplying, replacing what she'd lost, and her heart pumping her power back through her. I watched the mossy green, turquoise, and lapis lazuli dance and tangle and play like old friends.

When I felt her stir beneath my hand, I opened my eyes wide and shook my head as I pressed one hand to her mouth and the other to my own, indicating we couldn't talk. I pulled my Phaetyn net over her energy and whispered in her ear, "Don't move."

I pulled her body toward the ledge, doing my best to pretend to be sobbing while I huffed for air. Turning her so her feet dangled over the edge, I knelt down and focused on the bubble in my mind, whispering to her again. "I'm going to push you off the edge. I've got your body invisible right now, so as soon as you fall, shift and fly to Azule. Find Tyrrik."

Her eyes widened, and she mouthed, "I can't."

"You have to or you'll die. Give Tyrrik information. He knows."

She swallowed, pain-filled eyes set on my face, a flicker of regret in their midst.

"I'll hold the veil as long as I can," I breathed into her bloodied, torn ear. "Please live."

And then I shoved my aunt off the ledge of Draedyn's palace.

34

I stumbled back into the dining room, my hands bloodied and mind still reeling with the acute memories of my aunt's shredded body. The Druman lined the interior walls of the dining room they waited in to ensure the job was done.

"I pushed her body off the side, like Draedyn did. Is that good enough?" Unless they sent someone to check if my aunt's body had landed below, my subterfuge would work. I glared at the mules, and when no one answered, I wondered if they were mute like in Irdelron's castle. "Do you animals speak?"

"Done yet?" one asked, his voice rough.

I don't know why I found it creepier that Draedyn left his Druman with their tongues, but somehow I did.

I narrowed my eyes, disturbed by how normal he looked. They all wore tunics like mine only bigger, but most of the bastards were filthy and grimy, their long hair matted with unkempt beards and broken nails. But the one who spoke had his hair pulled back, and his clean-shaven face set him apart from the others. That and his apparent language skills. "Yes," I replied. "All done."

"Wait," he said and then ducked out of the door.

Was he kidding? Wait for what?

I stepped toward the doorway, and two of them closed ranks,

their wide smirks only slightly less disturbing than the sadistic gleam in their eyes. Nice to see them taking after my father . . . Ew. *Our* father. That thought and their hulking bodies stopped me in my tracks.

My lip curled, and as I scanned the Druman, I realized I was no longer afraid of them. I wasn't intimidated by their strength, speed, and violent tendencies. Somewhere along the line, I'd stopped reacting as a human.

I studied the sneering mule, his cruel grin matching his brother's next to him. I glanced around the room, seeing the same expression on nearly all of the other Druman. How easy it would be to end their sadistic existence, especially with the violent energy coursing through me, begging for any outlet—to run, fight, to lash out. I could destroy them, but really I wanted to hurt the person who'd caused my aunt's anguish. Only, I couldn't. Not yet.

So lashing out here wouldn't help me right now.

I sneered back at the Druman and had the satisfaction of witnessing a quiver of uncertainty momentarily unsettle his smirking façade. If the emperor wasn't his father, the Druman wouldn't stand a chance, and we both knew it.

Druman got off on violence at the best of times, but my father's minions *could* be a real danger to me if they became vindictive like Jotun, jealous of Draedyn's attention on me. While Irdelron had raised Tyrrik's Druman to be violent, Jotun's jealousy drove him to be excessively cruel. Though my half-bros couldn't kill me, if they managed to pin or tie me down, I could be tortured for a long time, possibly eternity, if properly restrained.

My angst and frustration morphed to simmering anger as the Druman continued to loom around the outskirts of the room in silence, smirking, leering—grunting like animals, filthy and vile.

Instigating a fight wouldn't help me right now, so clenching my fists, I stepped to go around the two blocking the door. After the day I'd had, if I couldn't obliterate my father, I needed the privacy of my chamber. Or even just a plain ol' empty corner would do.

The two Druman shifted, continuing to bar my way.

"Not a great idea," I said, clenching my teeth. "If you don't move, I'll have to kill you." If I hadn't been itching to sink my talons into them, the extension of my father, I may have tried harder to restrain myself. I wanted to fight, to do anything I could to hurt him, and the Druman had fought for him and would again at his whim. Destroying a few now would be less to kill later. I leaned forward and whispered, "What's the matter? Cat got your tongue? Or do you move as slow as you speak?"

Instigator? Yeah, just like my mum. Before my Drae transformation, I couldn't fathom Jotun's supernatural speed. Now, craving vengeance, my mind seemed to process their movements as if in slow motion. One raised his arm, lifting the end of his spear, and the other swung wide with his fist closed as I instinctively knew their trajectories. Aiming for my crotch and my face! Dirty move.

I wouldn't have felt bad killing them before, but the talons were out now.

I crouched and stepped left, evading the strike, and grabbed the Druman's spear. I yanked on the staff, and when he held fast, I jerked upward, snapping off a large piece. Spinning back toward the first mule, I plucked his dagger from his waist and sliced through the meaty part of my forearm. I turned the blade and sliced again and then dipped the jagged piece of wood into my blood before shoving it into the stomach of the Druman still holding the other end of the spear.

Kicking the now seizing mule to the side, I faced the rest of my foes with a grim smile. I had no idea how my instincts had improved, but I knew they had. Not only could I do this, I would.

Several of the other Druman drew weapons, and others tensed, but I had no time to analyze their hesitation.

To my left, the one who'd thrown the first punch reached for me, and I slid closer, taking advantage of the proximity to slit his throat.

He screamed, a gutteral bellow, and doubled over before slumping to the ground. Bent to retrieve the shortened spear, I dragged it over the closing wound and buried it in another Druman's solar plexus.

My rage flared, and I ducked under a heavy swing and thrust the knife into the Druman's armpit.

The sound of weapons being drawn made me smile because it indicated their admission to the fray of death. I yanked the blade from the dying Druman and sliced through my arm again. I would kill them all, every single one of them. For me, for the female Drae, the captured Phaetyns in this palace, and for the whole realm. These dark creatures had no place here.

I threw my head back and roared, a combination of challenge issued and accepted as the thrill of the fight burst through me. I yanked the broken spear from the Druman's stomach, dipped it in my oozing wound, and then I spun and hurled the poisoned weapon. The wooden weapon grazed a mule before bouncing off the far wall. Not perfect, but death was death.

I was done waiting for them to come to me, done taking them one by one, so I moved. Twisting and spinning, I wound between the Druman, grunting when one of their hits connected, but my adrenaline sang with singular focus as I drew the dagger across their skin, poisoning them with my blood.

Phaetyn blood.

It would kill their Drae side. Some would die from their wounds now, but those that weren't lucky would live, like Jotun, to be torn apart by those they'd abused. Justice.

I spun and cut, dipping the blade into my blood before striking at a Druman. Over and over. I sprinted around the room, knowing time was short, *knowing* I had to get to as many as possible before . . .

A roar shook the foundation of the palace.

Those still standing, including me, froze. The floor was littered with spasming Druman, black webs spreading beneath their skin as my Phaetyn blood poisoned them. Only three remained, and I leapt to finish them.

Pain exploded all down my right side, and bright lights burst behind my eyes. The momentary reprieve of being pushed through the room ended as I collided with a wall. Draedyn was my first and only thought as I crashed faster and harder into the graphite wall on the opposite side of the room. *My* mind couldn't fathom the speed, and had a human watched, I doubted they would have seen anything until I fell from the wall to the ground in a crumpled, albeit smiling, heap.

Dad wasn't happy with me. He picked me up by the back of my neck like a kitten.

Several of my bones were still broken, and I sagged in his grip. The coppery tang of my blood made me spit through my busted lip, but I lifted my gaze to meet my father's and sucked in a breath at the endless rage still burning inside of them. My glib *sorry, not sorry* retort died on my lips.

"I got angry," I said instead. Vague, but maybe it would work?

"You betrayed me," Draedyn snarled. "You killed my Druman."

Eek, maybe not. I'd pull on his heartstrings instead. "I don't like Druman. They used to torture me."

He shook me, his face still contorted with rage. "They made you stronger."

"Yeah?" I scoffed, trying to ignore the bruising pressure of his fingertips digging into the bony protrusions of my neck. "What if I'd rather be untortured and weaker?"

Fury hung upon the emperor like a thin coat, like he'd washed with soap that had irritated his skin. Whatever my reasons for killing approximately two-dozen of his Druman, he would try to make me regret it. Not going to happen.

I hoped.

Draedyn didn't lower me, continuing to stare into my watering eyes. "I had thought, my daughter, your ignorance may fade with time. Had hoped you would see we are not enemies, and yet . . . You just killed a sizeable number of my elite fighting force."

"A sizeable number? How many are we talking?" Oops, too happy, Ryn. Pull back on the happiness.

Draedyn's face screwed up, and no sooner had I felt relief from the release of his punishing grip than that *small pain* was replaced by the crushing impact against the far wall.

Wheezing, I rolled away from the wall but stayed on the ground. If he wanted to throw me again, he'd have to come pick me up.

"I am *displeased*, daughter." His volume increased with his nearing footsteps. "I find myself wondering if it is not better to neutralize you until the—"

I flopped my head to the side to squint up at him, wondering why he'd cut off mid-sentence. The emperor had shifted, half turned toward the balcony, and his body tensed. In the next moment, Draedyn blurred outside.

What was he looking at?

With a groan, I pushed my still-healing body upright. Best case, if he threw me from the cliff, I could disappear before I shifted Drae. Bolstered by this confidence—what with recent developments of private bubbles and the like, I hobbled after him.

Draedyn faced west toward Azule. I didn't know what he could hear, but my insides burst with joy with what I could see.

Lani's golden net covered a massive army. Men spread over the entrance to his personal lands, covering the valley, a stunning beacon of armor, fluttering banners, and glinting spearheads.

The battering from my close encounters with recent walls did nothing to stop a wide grin from stretching across my face. Elation rose within me, forcing me to clamp my Phaetyn veil over the emotion as I struggled to hold back a shout of joy. They were here. My friends were here to fight.

The sight burned into my mind, and I blinked the tears from my eyes. A fist tightened in the area beneath my ribs; the fierce determination to see the battle through to the end grew and became a *calling* unlike any I'd felt before. The resolution flooded through me, filling my mind and body. I'd be fighting with them. Maybe not beside them, but I'd do whatever it took to help them.

My attention returned to the room's only other occupant to see Draedyn's gaze was no longer on the valley but on my face.

I raised my chin although my grin faded at the impassive expression before me.

"We are back to the start, daughter," he said, his gaze narrowing.

I frowned despite myself, having fully expected to be flying off the edge of the cliff sans wings.

A cruel smile curved his lips. "I see I am not being persuasive enough."

WHEN I DRANK an entire bottle of honey syrup one time, I expected the backlash. I knew my mother would find the bottle eventually unless the world was upturned in the interim. I understood there would be repercussions, but the sweet taste, all to myself, was worth it.

When I'd killed my father's Druman several hours ago, I'd known the act of defiance wouldn't go unpunished.

And yet it had. The room had been cleared of bodies and scrubbed clean, although that didn't completely remove the slight rustic tang of Druman blood in the air.

I cut into the morsel of roasted chicken on my plate after everyone was served, struggling to ignore the fierce glares aimed at me by the other female Drae. To them, my aunt and Draelyn were dead and gone. Two women they'd known for at least one hundred years. And while they were wrong about the former, they were right about Draelyn. Considering, I could handle a few glares. With how they were feeling, angry dark looks were pretty justified.

In fact, their attention was the least of my concerns. I was frantically working to figure out Draedyn's next move. He'd killed Kamoi because he'd betrayed *me* and the Phaetyn. He'd nearly torn Aunt Ryn apart because she'd acted against him. How much of my betrayal was he aware of?

I wasn't lured into false hope by the delay between the deed and the reaction, but the dragging time slowly chipped away at my forced nonchalance. My sleep had been restless, and despite the time in my chamber, I still didn't feel collected.

I closed my eyes against the Draes' glares and studied the ring of my father's power around my mind. My private bubble was there, the wisp of my Drae power safe within. I still had these things. I didn't wish to use any of these untested defenses against Draedyn yet, but if whatever payback he was cooking up was more than I could bear, I had *something*.

I hoped.

I took a deep breath, but my shifting attention snagged on the ring of Draedyn's power as it began to pulse, the dark, emerald green contracting and expanding repetitively. But that wasn't—

The sound of a chair scraping back brought my attention to the room, and I wrenched open my eyes to see the emperor on his feet, staring at me, his eyes wide. What the hay? I wasn't doing anything. *Drak*, I hadn't let something slip had I?

The barrier of power imprisoning my Drae energy steadily thinned and weakened. I doubled over as a wave of sadness and desperation flowed over me—my bond with Tyrrik hitting me for the umpteenth time that day.

I gasped, staring at my plate, but my attention was consumed by my need for my mate.

The doors of the dining room crashed open, and I glanced up to see Druman filing in. My eyes narrowed at the numbers, *so many* of them, and I planned to kill all of them, if possible, before they got a chance to attack the army of my friends.

My mind and soul were swallowed by rich, onyx black, my senses bathed in the color and scent of my mate's Drae power. When it ebbed, the ring around my mind disappeared, and I slammed back in my chair as the connection to my blue tendrils pummeled me, thrashing through my body, laying its claim with full force. I growled, my eyes narrowing into slits, and my talons sliced through the table as I struggled to control the shift.

I pushed back, stumbling to my feet, and whirled away from the audience, nearly falling flat on my face as a gentle onyx tendril stroked my awareness.

Tyrrik, I called, my ache for him swelling. I sobbed at the pain of our trembling bond.

My love, he answered.

I felt him then. The surroundings, everyone and everything, were forgotten as the Druman pouring through the doorway parted, and darkness flowed into the room.

My darkness.

Joy, relief, and excitement, all tinged with horror, caught in my throat. My battling emotions competed to make a sound, but I couldn't wait. My heart pounded, brought to life, and I launched myself at Tyrrik. He sliced through the last Druman to get to me, their bodies falling to the ground as Tyrrik stepped forward. I jumped and locked my legs and arms around him, pressing my body against his. Shaking. Babbling incoherently. Pressing my nose to his neck to inhale his familiar pine and smoke scent.

He stroked my silver hair, and I soaked in the warmth of his touch. The vibrations of his voice stirred my soul, and all I knew, for those few precious, flawless breaths, was the feel of his body, the smell of his skin, and the warmth of his love.

"Mine," I growled.

I pulled back, or he nudged me, and then his mouth was on mine or mine on his. The flesh of his neck turned to scales under my hands as the ferocity of our reunion consumed us. One of his hands pressed on my back, the other underneath my thigh pulling me hard against him.

"Mate," he managed to say when we separated for air.

I certainly planned to.

But the partial glimpse of a Druman over Tyrrik's shoulder provided enough water to put out the burning hay field.

"Audience," I murmured, kissing him again.

His lips moved against mine. *I know.*

He knew. Of course he knew.

I unhooked my ankles and slid down Tyrrik's body until my feet touched the ground, the only distance either of us allowed. I blinked and began coiling my Drae powers around my mind, allowing the bubble of Phaetyn power I'd been hiding to flood my mind and coat *inside* my lapis lazuli energy. Time would tell if this combination was any more effective against Draedyn, but I had a good feeling about it. Compared to erecting my Phaetyn powers *outside* of my Drae powers, doing it the opposite way had taken the blink of an eye.

"Emperor Draedyn, I assume," Tyrrik said, the embers of his voice reverberating through me.

I tensed. The palace was the last place I wanted Tyrrik to be. We were stronger and happier together, yes. But I'd just royally betrayed Draedyn, and he was yet to take his revenge.

What if he sought retribution through Tyrrik? My stomach seized with the thought.

Draedyn still stood, far more composed than when my mate had first begun to push him out of my head. Lips curling into a half-smile, my father said, "My daughter's mate, I assume."

Calling you daughter, already, huh? Tyrrik asked.

Tell me about it, I answered. *Even Dyter doesn't call me that, and he is like a father.* I choked on the question I wanted to ask.

He's not with the army. I'm sorry, love. We don't know where Dyter is.

My stomach sank, but I forced the emotion away. I'd find out the truth and then deal with it.

I scanned the female Drae and caught them exchanging weighted glances. I couldn't glean what they were thinking though. Their expressions could mean *maybe Ryn did get a message to Tyrrik,* or *she has a mate and we don't; let's ruin her life in vengeance,* or something else altogether. I didn't know any of them well enough to get a solid read.

Draedyn moved, and I gripped Tyrrik's arm, digging my nails in unintentionally. I would not let my father hurt my mate.

If he attacks, we fight our way to the balcony and escape. You'll have to cover us with your Phaetyn veil, but it'll work.

Kamoi is dead, but he still has Kamini. Once we leave, he'll never let us return, I replied with utter certainty. *No way.*

Hopefully not.

I kept my face smooth. *I guess it's easier to take him out if we're here.*

Yes, Tyrrik replied. *And while we're here, he'll be less likely to attack the army.*

You hope.

Draedyn rounded the table. "I have not seen mated Drae in over one hundred years. I confess, despite myself, my heart is glad to see the sight once more."

Right. *Where is he going with this?*

"I'll not be parted from my mate," Tyrrik said, his growl rumbling long after his words.

Phew, going in early with the demands. Not that I felt any less strongly, but there were almost two dozen Drae in the room and at least that many Druman, and *all* of them answered to my father's call except for the two of us. The energy in the room was all-but crackling and sparking.

"You will stay then?" the emperor asked, stopping before us. He extended his hands, palms up.

A tiny warning growl slipped through my teeth at his proximity, and Tyrrik sent a pulse of comforting warmth to me through our bond.

Draedyn observed us for so long without blinking that I was *nearly* tempted to relax my fighting stance.

"You misunderstand, heir-daughter," he said mildly. "I find absence has softened my memories of the mating bond, and I beg your pardon. How could you have been happy here without your mate? His presence is of paramount importance. I no longer wonder at your joy upon seeing the army."

I blinked. What the hay?

What's he doing? Tyrrik asked, his confusion mirroring my own.

No idea.

The emperor pivoted toward Tyrrik, my father just slightly taller than my mate. With a nod, Draedyn said, "You will both stay in the palace."

He then swept back to his place, and a servant hurried to set a place for the Drae glued to my side. Draedyn picked up his goblet and, staring at me over the rim, said, "I hope now you will be open to what I offer, heir."

Back to heir, was I? I made no answer.

As Tyrrik and I sat at the table, Draedyn spoke again, "Yes, you are most welcome here, mate of my daughter." He smiled and took a long sip, letting the fluid trickle down his throat with only the smallest swallow. "*Most* welcome."

Tyrrik dipped his head in the emperor's direction, no more than courtesy demanded, and then dug into his food. My mate was way better at this acting game although I was fully aware of the tension radiating from him through our connection.

The game hadn't shifted in our favor, not really. My mate would help with my defenses against my father, but now Draedyn knew I controlled my thoughts and had access to my Drae power. So while I'd be able to protect myself by shifting, Draedyn had removed both Drae from the army, *and* there was the possibility Tyrrik might be used against me despite the emperor's professed love of the mate-bond. Which I didn't believe one bit.

Even with all those worries, Tyrrik was right. The palace was where we needed to be. The war against Draedyn only ended when he was dead.

We have an emperor to kill, I said to Tyrrik conversationally as I cut through a potato and popped it into my mouth.

He swallowed his mouthful and poured more gravy onto his chicken. *Yes, my love. We do.*

I'm pretty sure all the female Drae hate me now, I complained, really only mildly irritated because honestly, I had bigger potatoes to fry. I'd filled Tyrrik in on the events of the last few days as we walked back through the graphite abode of the emperor.

Ask me how much I care right now when all I can think about is you, Tyrrik said as I closed the door to my chamber.

His onyx energy swirled behind me, relief and desire blending together in a tangled mess. My back heated as he drew closer. The desire I had for him was just as strong, but confusion about my father's game tainted my want.

Don't you want to know why he's so willing to have us both here? Why work so hard to separate us if only to bring us together? I asked.

Tyrrik brushed my hair away from my neck and over my shoulder. He stroked his thumb from the base of my neck up to my hairline and then trailed kisses over my exposed skin. *Mate.*

I trembled. The force of his drive nearly overwhelmed me. *Yes,* I replied. *But don't you think we should figure a few things out first? Like why Draedyn is so eager to have you here?*

I was missing something, I knew. He'd removed both of us from the fight outside, but I knew there was more.

Mate. He circled his hands around my waist, gripping the sack-like tunic in each fist on either side of my navel. His restraint disappeared, the tension he'd held at bay burst, and his fangs lengthened, pressing on my skin with each kiss. *Mate.*

My mind clouded, and I waded through it, grasping onto the confusion holding me back. *You are not only monosyllabic, but you apparently have the vocabulary of a single word.*

He pressed the length of his lower body to mine, rotating his pelvis as he pushed into me. Okay, that felt good. Maybe a little Tyrrik and Ryn time was necessary. Now.

He gripped my hip bones and growled. *I've missed you so much. Please?*

I gasped and tilted my head to give him better access.

He nipped me, just the tips of his fangs grazing the soft skin of my neck at our mate mark, and midnight fire pulsed through me. I shifted, turning toward him. His talon grazed the soft flesh of my abdomen as he tore through my tunic. Holy pancakes.

In one fluid movement, he turned me and pressed my back to the door, pushing his lower body to mine. Through the torn tunic, he explored my body—my waist, the underside of my breasts, my hips. His caress was followed by a bruising kiss. He slid his knee between my legs and tugged me closer until I was flush against his hard body.

I trembled as I fumbled blindly with the ties of his aketon.

The remaining shreds of my clothes fell to the floor as well as his aketon. Apparently, I could multitask.

Ryn. Please, he begged. *I need you.*

Yes, I breathed. My own need to feel him just as strong. *Mate.* Now we were both monosyllabic.

His hands slid under my thighs, and then he lifted me.

The world, and all of the problems in it, disappeared. The bands of our bonds danced together, entwined, melding as our passion and bodies became one.

Time ceased to have meaning.

We lay staring at each other in the aftermath, sheet drawn up to our hips, our legs tangled together beneath it.

I felt so strong when Tyrrik was by my side.

I was not made to be parted from you, Ryn. He shuddered with the words, his desperate relief echoing through to me.

Hush now, love. I traced my fingertips over his exposed chest which shined from our recent love-making. He captured my hand and held it to his lips.

A moment later, he tugged me closer, tucking me under his arm so I was pressed against his side. I wrapped my arm around him, and emboldened by the lingering fear I felt in him, I climbed on top of him. Trailing kisses from his abdomen to his neck, I sent small pulses of healing energy through our bond to buoy him, replenishing him in every way that I could.

He responded, and his frantic movements quickened my own.

This time, after we'd both shuddered with release, his eyes closed and a small smile played at the corners of his mouth. He whispered, *I love you.*

I pressed close, our chests together as I sent him another burst of healing power with my kiss. *I love you too. You rest.* Before he could protest, I pressed my fingers to his lips. *We need it, you more than me, just for an hour or two. Then we'll plan.*

Al'right, he said, making me grin. Tyrrik's breathing soon evened into a slow rhythm.

I was not such a fool to believe my father had changed his intentions. But I didn't know his plan either. With another kiss for Tyrrik, I rolled out of bed. I pulled a clean sack tunic on and grabbed a second one, intent on a short bath if the halls were clear.

Lucky for me, they were. I checked my powers, grinning as I saw my lapis lazuli happily entangled with Tyrrik's onyx energy, and there was my Phaetyn web. No oily green nastiness in sight. Good, good.

A Druman stopped me before I reached the stairs, his eyes narrowing in a glare. I returned the look and said, "Don't mess with me. I have no problem severing your head from your neck if you get between me and my bath. I'm not aiming for trouble, so go back and report to Daddykins."

The smart mule stepped aside. In a blur, I grabbed his knife as I passed. Not that I needed it, but I didn't want him to have it either. I ducked into the dark stairwell and started down. If I put on the Phaetyn veil, I was afraid Draedyn would come looking for me, and I hadn't lied. My intent had been a bath, but as I approached the sulfurous pools, I thought I heard someone behind me and turned. I studied the dark, shifting enough to bring my Drae eyes forward. There was a Druman standing there. Why?

As soon as he turned away, I decided to take the risk. I put up my Phaetyn veil and snuck after him. He'd disappeared into an alcove in the corner, and I creeped to it on silent feet.

I waited another couple of minutes, reaching my Drae power through to feel Tyrrik's peace through our bonds, and with assurance of his current safety, I darted to the alcove, pursing my lips at the narrow stairwell. Even with my Drae vision, I couldn't see to the bottom, and my gut churned a gentle warning. What was down there? Decision made, I ran down the stairs.

At the bottom of the stairwell, a long hall extended into the mountain of graphite. There was no light, and even with my Drae vision, the misty darkness made it difficult to see. The smell of sulfur hung heavy in the moist air, and I rotated my arms to trail my fingers along the walls on either side. Only a couple dozen feet down the hall, a gap opened up on my right. I peeked through the doorway and froze when I saw the bars. Cold iron rods, just like in Irdelron's dungeons, made my stomach roil. I blinked, but the vision didn't change. These were Draedyn's dungeons.

The Druman was here, inspecting each cell, and I stood back, safe in my veil as he finished and walked back up the stairs to the top.

I inched forward to see the occupant in the closest cell.

My heart tripped as I looked into the lavender eyes of an emaciated Phaetyn curled in the back corner of the cell. Vivid images from my past assailed me, and I reached a hand up to touch my forehead where a sunflower had once woken me in a dungeon much like this.

I reached out another Drae tendril to my mate for reassurance.
Ryn?

I'm al'right. Just a bad memory. I was outside the cage, at least for
now, anyway.

Do you want me to come to you?

No. I'll be back in a few minutes. Let me take a bath.

I could join you.

I snorted in my mind. *Then I wouldn't bathe. Let me be.*

"Who are you?" the Phaetyn asked, the high pitch of her voice
declaring her a female.

Right, she would be able to see through my veil.

I stretched the mossy-green webbing over, covering her and our
conversation from the Druman above.

"Ryn," I whispered. "Who are you?"

"Ash. Are you here to drain me?" When I shook my head, she
sagged, smiling slightly, or maybe that was a grimace. "I haven't seen
a female Drae for probably twenty years."

I swallowed the emotion that clogged my throat, sure I couldn't
have heard right. "Twenty?"

She shrugged, her sack-tunic sliding off her shoulder. "Maybe
more, maybe less."

"Ryhl?" I asked, my heart fluttering with anticipation. "Did you
know Ryhl?" I pressed my face between the bars.

The Phaetyn straightened. "Did you know her?"

I nodded. "She was my mother."

The Phaetyn stood and hurried over to the bars. "Is she still
alive? Has she come—"

"She . . . died," I said. "But she sent me." Maybe not in as many
words, but because of her, I was here.

The woman's gaze narrowed as she studied me. "To end
his reign?"

I gave the tiniest nod in answer. "With my mate. The Phaetyn
queen, Lani, Luna's daughter, is outside the mountain, fighting with
the others of your people."

She smiled. "How would you kill him?"

This time, I grimaced. "Permanently. That's the plan. I'm Phaetyn and Drae," I joked, weakly. "Draedyn doesn't stand a chance. I'm actually referred to as Most Powerful Drae in some parts of the realm."

Ash reached through the bars, slapping her bony hand to my mouth. "He can hear you."

I shook my head and pulled away so her hand dropped. "I have the ancestral power from Queen Luna. I've covered us. He can't hear a thing. No one can."

"How do I know I can trust you?"

I shrugged. "You don't," I answered honestly. "Anyway, I wanted to know if my friend is here. I'm looking for Kamini. Do you know her?"

Ash sucked in a breath, and her eyes widened, making her cheekbones more prominent, and her entire frame appear even more wasted. "How do you know Kamini?"

I rolled my eyes. Hadn't I just said she was my friend? Ryn the magnanimous needed to make an appearance here in Draedyn's dungeons. Al'right. I could totally do that.

"Yep. I met her in Zivost a few months ago. Is she here?"

Ash shook her head. "No, Draedyn took her to his private prison a few days ago. Up by his rooms."

Dungeons were commonplace, I supposed. But surely owning a private prison near your personal rooms meant for sleep and relaxing was a sign you should check your sanity levels. "Where's that?

"In his tower."

Of course it was. "Umm, any chance there's a prisoner named Dyter here?"

Ash shook her head again. "Is he Phaetyn or Drae?"

"Neither. Human."

Her lavender gaze darkened. "The only humans the emperor tolerates are the ones willing to work for him. If this Dyter is human and against the emperor, Draedyn wouldn't have him here. If he found him, he'd kill him."

"He doesn't keep human prisoners?" I asked, my voice catching. "Ever?

She pursed her lips. "Not in the seventy-five years I've been here."

Drak.

"Let me have your knife," she said, pointing to the Druman's blade.

"It's not mine. I pulled it off a Druman."

She waved at me to give it to her.

"Just don't cut yourself," I cautioned. "It might have Drae blood on it."

This time it was Ash who rolled her eyes. "He wouldn't waste his blood, and the mules' blood isn't strong enough to hurt us."

I handed over the blade though my skin crawled at the wide-eyed excitement on her face. I gulped in horror as Ash buried the blade into her belly, all the way to the hilt.

"What the hay!" I shouted.

"Don't," she snapped, hitting my hands away as I reached through the bars to heal her. "If I'm lucky enough to die, it would be a release from this place, a blessing from the stars."

She wrenched the blade from her body and then held the hilt out to me, shaking the dripping knife when I didn't take it right away.

"What are you doing? What do you want me to do with it?" I asked, my voice hoarse with shock.

"Stab him. At some point you'll be close enough, and I would love to have my blood help poison the emperor."

We'd been talking just seconds ago. I'd given her the blade to protect herself. Shaking, I accepted the weapon, holding the grue-some knife between my thumb and forefinger. I didn't have the heart to tell her I didn't need her sacrifice, that I had everything I needed inside. "I'll do my best—"

Ash reached through the bars and yanked me to her, hissing in pain with the movement. "Don't do your best. Your best won't be good enough. You need to stab him in the chest, right near his black heart. Kill him for all of us. Avenge us."

Ryn! Tyrrik bellowed.

"I'm sorry," I said, pulling away from her desperate clawing, trembling as my eyes took in the silvery blood covering the ground.

"Go now and do it," she shrieked.

I backed away, my eyes wide.

"In the heart," she screamed after me, followed by a wet cough.

Gasping for air, I sprinted out of the dungeons, up to the bath chamber, and up the stairs to the main hallways of Draedyn's castle. The castle seemed eerily empty; everyone was probably asleep. The moon's silvery light seeped in through the windows, highlighting the blood on my fingers and the knife.

Retracing my steps to my room, I asked Tyrrik, *Is everything okay? What's happened?*

He didn't respond, but I could feel his urgency through our bond.

Not that I needed the extra motivation. The walls became hazy as I released my Drae power to aid my speed. I burst through the door, and Tyrrik blurred as he leapt from the bed to meet me.

I dropped the knife just before he crashed into me, the force throwing us several feet back. He cradled the back of my head, preventing it from crashing into the stone as he pressed into me.

Whoa.

Tyrrik muttered under his breath, and I only glanced at his heated gaze before he crushed his mouth to mine.

Surprised by his desperate drive, I struggled to respond. He growled possessively and then trailed kisses down my neck while he inched the edge of my tunic upward with his hands. He stroked up and down my thighs, kneading from my hips to my waist as he repeated, "Mate."

"Wait, Tyrrik. What's wrong?" Chills danced over my skin with his feral want. He'd always been measured and careful with me before, but this . . . This wild need felt animalistic.

He nipped my lower lip, and I opened my mouth to him. Our tongues tangled, and he pulled my arms overhead, trapping my wrists in his grip. Foggy desire pounded through our bond, clouding my mind with his singular focus.

He pushed my neck to the side.

"Tyrrik," I gasped. "What's happening?" This wasn't him. Something was wrong. I felt the pressure of his fangs on my skin, not just anywhere but on the exact space where he'd first touched me. Over our mate mark.

He bit hard and I shrieked, his teeth piercing my skin. Hot fire coursed through me, making me moan with the surging swell of desire.

Mine, he growled.

"I-I." I clung to the wrongness of a moment earlier and pushed back. "No, Tyrrik. Stop."

Tyrrik stilled.

Holy-drae-babies. I blinked through the fog and croaked, *What's going on?*

Ryn?

Who else would it be? I clutched the side of my neck and swam through some serious waves of I-want-to-jump-Tyrrik. *You just bit me!*

His mouth dropped. *I bit you?* He seemed genuinely horrified.

The tremor in his voice made me freeze and my heart pound. An ominous weight pressed on my chest, and terrified of what I might find, I turned my attention to his Drae energy, my abdominal muscles clenching as my stomach turned. I studied his onyx power, comforted when I saw only rich black. Even so, I said, *Please tell me you remember what just happened.*

He ran his hand over my hair, stroking my head and back. His heart pounded in his chest, never slowing, even minutes later. "Yes, at least I think so."

What's the matter? I asked. *Talk to me, please.*

Look over my powers again, Tyrrik said suddenly. *Scour every twist of my energy.*

Al'right. I turned inward to my lapis lazuli energy and followed the glorious strands of onyx to Tyrrik's Drae. *Why are you so worried that you bit me?*

I bit you on your mark? he said to himself. *What was I thinking?*

His question made my stomach flip, and my attention on his strands sharpened. *And just what does that do?*

Draedyn is alpha. If he got in somehow, he replied, hedging. *Then he was behind that.*

I stopped looking for the oily green energy of my father and pulled my vision back. I couldn't find any trace of him, but that wasn't to say he hadn't been and gone. *Why would Draedyn want us to dance the maypole?*

I put myself in my father's disgusting shoes, trying to reason like a sick tyrant. Why would he want me and Tyrrik to dance the maypole?

The answer hit like Jotun's fist.

"He wants us to have Drae babies," I gasped. That was the entirety of his plan, I was certain of it! Not only did he want Tyrrik and me out of the fight, he wanted us to grow the Drae population.

My voice shook with fury as I asked, *Take me back. What do you remember?*

yrrik flashed images through our bond. He'd been asleep. His guard was down. He'd awoken at the first intrusion in his mind, at the powerful "suggestion" from the alpha. Tyrrik's initial call for me had been in the split second he'd known what Draedyn was doing, and then I'd burst through the door, and Tyrrik's only thought, *compulsive instinct*, had been to make little Tyrriks and Ryns.

All of that was replaced by Tyrrik blaming himself for being too weak to resist.

Anger, fiery hot, pulsed, and in an instant, turned into a roaring inferno of rage.

"Draedyn," I yelled, seizing the emperor's emerald power in my own. What did he plan to do if Tyrrik and I did have children? Take them for his own? Raise them in his soulless image?

I followed the strand of emerald power to his core and hurled a blast of my raging fury at him, going further than I'd ever dared to go. Returning to my mate, I wrapped our Drae energy in my Phaetyn net.

"It's not your fault," I grumbled, opening our bond wide to let Tyrrik see the only anger I had was with my father. I scooted to the edge of the bed. The knife was by the door, and I picked up the blade and waved it at Tyrrik. "Phaetyn blood on this one and not mine, so be careful."

I stormed toward the door. This wasn't over. I could count on one hand the amount of times I'd been so murderously enraged. He'd gone into my mate's mind. And I'd left Tyrrik alone as he slept, vulnerable. Not only that, I felt wild protectiveness surging through me at the thought that Draedyn might try to control any future family we had.

I couldn't let this rest.

Wait—

Don't tell me—

I just need to get dressed. In a blur, Tyrrik stood by my side, dressed again in his black aketon. He opened the door, his features hardened, and said, "Let's go."

We charged through the castle, side by side, my mind tracing Draedyn's emerald power through the palace like I'd done a moment before. I couldn't feel the core of it like before, but the traces were strongest from the levels above.

Doors slammed, and the sound of footsteps pounded behind us.

Druman, Tyrrik said to me.

We both ignored the mules.

The dining room was empty when we arrived. I glared at the rough-hewn table and the otherwise empty space. Where was he?

"Out here," Tyrrik called from outside on the terrace.

I blurred out to join him, noting the sun halfway up the horizon with its daily climb. Tyrrik pointed to the sky, and I swore, my fury over personal grievances settling into horror for the entire realm.

In the pale-blue-and-gray dawn, two dozen dragons were flying toward Azule.

My insides twisted in horror, and I grabbed Tyrrik's arm. "He's heading for the army!"

My terrified shout was superfluous, but the dread spilled out.

Dyter was out there. He *had* to be! And Lani and my Gemondian friends. The entire rebellion would be on fire.

"Lani has the shield up over most of the army," Tyrrik reminded me. "We're not fighting this alone."

But his eyes scoured the ground, and I followed his gaze. Hundreds of Druman scrabbled out of the mountain like ants, leaping and bounding along the ground toward Azule after their father and master.

The emperor was making his move. I'd been so upset about *what* he'd just tried to do I missed the *why*. That he might've had another layer of motive to his action hadn't even occurred to me.

If I'd surrendered to Tyrrik's bite, we'd have been none-the-wiser to Draedyn attacking the army. And he'd lied about the number of Druman he had.

My talons and fangs lengthened. "What do we do? They've got a head start."

Tyrrik and I stared into each other's eyes, our bond swirling around us.

"Draedyn is away from the palace," Tyrrik said, gripping my hand. "It's the perfect chance to destroy his base."

"But the army," I whispered, pointing out to the valley.

"We'll have to trust Lani and the others. We'll light his palace up—"

"Which might turn him back anyway."

"And then give chase. Leave him nothing to come back to."

"Wait." I gripped his arm. "The prisoners. There are Phaetyn down in the dungeons."

His gaze darted back inside, toward the maze of hallways and stairs of Draedyn's lair. "Okay, don't worry. I'll get them out now."

I didn't have a chance to tell him no before he was gone.

I didn't want to lose sight of Tyrrik, not even to save others. I felt out of depth, unprepared. I wasn't ready to come head to head with Draedyn. I was on the cusp of understanding how I could take advantage of my half and half powers, but I hadn't had time to test anything.

The next few minutes were among the worst of my life. The duration multiplied tenfold as I imagined every possible harm befalling Tyrrik.

But he blurred back into the room.

The Phaetyn? I blurted.

On their way out. If they want to save themselves, they will.

After seeing what Ash did to herself, I had no trouble understanding his comment.

I feel like there's so much more to do, I said as we walked out onto the balcony.

My love, you cannot prepare for this. None of us can.

Tyrrik pulled me over the edge of the graphite cliff.

I tumbled with him into the open air, unafraid.

Hurtling downward, our gazes locked. All our regret and fear and hope pressed between us, but those emotions would drown us if we let them. We let them go. The air sucked them away greedily, and then we pushed away from one another.

And shifted.

My neck lengthened, and my spine elongated with the size of my Drae, the bony protrusions extending into deadly spikes. My tailbone stretched, and barbed spines burst around the end of my clubbed tail. With a powerful beating of my wings, I surged into the air in tandem with my mate. We unleashed our roars, combined, shaking the very stones of the graphite mountain.

I'm going to light this place up, Tyrrik said, sounding a mite bit too pleased with the idea.

The realm should be worried that my mate not only possessed the ability to breathe fire but enjoyed it. Pyro.

He swooped to the bottom of the cliff, and I noticed a massive entrance carved into the side I hadn't seen before, being mind controlled on arrival here.

As Tyrrik dove, the inferno in his chest glowed, showing through his scales as his chest expanded with the pressure building within.

I maintained my high position, scanning the ground. Human

soldiers were gathered beneath us, close to the palace. I blinked and noticed the golden powers coating their arrows and spears.

Phaetyn blood on their weapons, I cautioned Tyrrik. *Don't get hit*.

Then I smiled. Because arrows and spears were nothing against me. And neither was Phaetyn blood.

I'm taking care of the soldiers, I told my mate as a jet of his lapis lazuli flame, *our* flame, licked the entrance, dissolving the doors within seconds. The rest of his fire shot inside.

Be careful.

I spread my hind talons wide and circled to the jutting cliff balcony outside the dining room, ripping off a huge chunk of graphite. And then I dove on a steep incline and headed for the thick army of human soldiers.

If they'd hidden in their huts, I would've guessed they were unwilling accomplices to the emperor, vulnerable, hence controlled and afraid. But to rally against me and my mate with weapons? These men were a danger, an enemy I wouldn't hesitate to kill.

Coming in from the side, I launched my oversized boulder at the army below, roaring as it catapulted through their midst. Men screamed as the massive stone broke apart, the pieces crushing many in its path. Returning to the cliff, I dug my talons in again, repeating my tactic with the relatively soft stone.

I blinked through an image from Tyrrik, and he systematically worked along the base of the cliff. The fire would rise, but as he climbed from the base of the mountain, a massive detonation shook the entire range.

I dropped the chunk of graphite in surprise, and my mouth gaped open as Draedyn's castle, and the whole cliff he'd built his home in, imploded. As the black stone mountain collapsed in on itself at the base, the top third of the peak broke away and fell forward, spilling death for hundreds of feet into Draedyn's lands.

The humans with their Phaetyn-dipped blades were buried, along with their uniform houses.

Tyrrik flew through the gray dust billowing out from the implosion and subsequent collapse, his Drae eyes reflecting none of the shock raging through his body.

Uh, nice work. I take it you didn't know you were going to do that?

No idea. He shook his head. *I can't hear anything except when you speak in my head. That explosion is making my ears ring.*

Do you want me to heal you?

No time. We have Druman to kill.

He sent me a flash of giving chase, and hot-potato-pie, was I ready. This was just a warm up although even better than I could've imagined. We roared together, and I pushed up through the air to race by his side as we hurtled after my father's Drae army. They were nearly upon the rebellion but remained together as a group, their pace slow compared to our desperate flight. When I'd sent the surge of fury at Draedyn after Tyrrik bit me, my father had still been inside the palace. I'd felt his core. And now, they could only be ten minutes or so in front of us.

No, less. We were gaining fast.

Pumping my wings, I flattened my scaled body to cut through the air as I scanned our army ahead. Lani's barrier was up, reminding me to put up my own. I allowed the Phaetyn power to flood my mind first, inside my Drae power, and then I worked on wrapping my blue Drae powers around my head before finally erecting another level of my Phaetyn powers to cover our physical bodies. Three walls of my power now protected my mind. But it wasn't until Tyrrik added the fourth layer of his onyx power over my blue tendrils that I felt invincible.

Now I was ready to take my father down.

Ryn, Tyrrik said. *Is there any way to break Draedyn's hold on the female Drae?*

What? I have no—idea. But then I realized . . . I did. Draedyn's powers coated their minds in the exact way he'd coated mine. The females wanted to be free of Draedyn, and if I could separate them from his power, they could either fight with us against him or at least get out of the fight.

We've got to try. You saw how quickly we dealt death to the men he left behind. Those outside of the Phaetyn barrier don't stand a chance against twelve Drae.

I focused my Phaetyn eyes ahead, my pace slowing as I attempted something I'd never tried. I'd only discovered I could even see Draedyn's hold over the other Drae in the bath with my aunt the day before.

Focus, my love. If this can be done, you will do it.

Tyrrik's belief bolstered my courage, and I stared ahead to the blaze of Draedyn's emerald-green powers, vibrant in the early morning Draeconian sky, surrounding the others' Drae energy. Doing my best to blink through the intense glow, I traced his power to the female closest to me and farthest from him. His power covered her mind like a blanket of rocks, just as he had with me.

Do I break it with my Phaetyn or Drae powers? I asked Tyrrik.

Can you attack with both?

His answer was so simple, and yet for a moment, I could only gape at the epiphany. Why *not* layer both for an assault? I'd been layering them for my defense. Why try to keep the two powers apart? That wasn't in my nature. I was both races.

I narrowed my already slitted eyes further as I concentrated. I threaded a tendril of my Drae power outside of the veil, siphoning a wisp of the Phaetyn veil to wrap around the tendril. If Draedyn saw what I was doing, he'd fight me. Better to blast away his control of as many of the females as I could before we had to face him.

Ready? I asked. *I'm going to slap them with a pancake of power. It will work.* I hoped.

As long as you don't ask me to call you a potato, I'm with you, love.

I snickered or made a noise that vaguely sounded like it. *Al'right. I'm going to hit as many as I can*, I said. *You need to tell me I should stop if anything bad happens to them.*

My wings continued to beat, but the heavy rhythm slowed as I focused on my Phaetyn-Drae beam of power and set my intention. I didn't just *want* the beam to break Draedyn's hold; I was going to shatter his control over my kin.

I set my gaze on the same female on the outskirts as before, her pale-yellow energy almost completely swallowed in the emerald green. With my next exhalation, I shot my powers out like a spear. They blurred forward too fast for me to see, hitting the ring of emerald power encircling the Drae's head. I didn't stop to watch what happened; as soon as I felt Draedyn's control splinter, I moved to the next Drae, blasting my power out to her. To the next, blast. The next, shatter. The next, fracture. And then once more, only this time as I severed Draedyn's powers, they fought back, blasting through the sky like the sun exploding, flinging both me and Tyrrik back in the air.

I clung to my defenses as I righted myself, glancing at Tyrrik to make sure he was okay before we continued our desperate flight without delay.

Where are they? I asked, searching for the six Drae I'd blasted free. Below us, much of our army lay slaughtered, those first to absorb Draedyn's display of Druman strength.

Falling to the ground, Tyrrik said. *They're out cold.*

I immediately altered my trajectory.

No, Ryn. Let them fall. They will not die, but Dyter and Lani's army will. Can you do the same again?

He'll be expecting it.

Then don't hold back. Tyrrik's anger with Draedyn leaked through our bond. *Not just a pancake, hit them with a stack.*

I hesitated because we were closing the distance, and as I paused, Draedyn and his harem reached the army of my friends. I roared as the females dived upon the exposed portion of our soldiers.

Still minutes away, I watched in horror as Draedyn's chest expanded, just as Tyrrik's had at the palace. Screams filled the air, lending an erratic beat to my flight.

Blinding white-green fire exploded from the emperor's mouth.

Tyrrik! I screamed, my eyes widening in horror.

Draedyn wasn't aiming at the exposed portion of the army. He was aiming at Lani's shield. He shouldn't have even been able to see it!

On his back, Tyrrik said. *Kamini's on his back.*

I scoured my father's form and saw Kamini there, a Druman holding a knife to her neck. Two Phaetyn children were also there, probably dragged up from the dungeons. Two more Druman held knives to their throats.

She's showing him where the army is.

You have to stop the other Drae first, Ryn! Tyrrik shouted. *We're nearly there. Just delay them.*

The emerald-green power licked the sky in every direction, filling me with a heavy weight. Who could compete with such raw power? I was eighteen, thousands of years younger than Draedyn with thousands of years less experience. And yet I was the first of my kind, the most powerful Drae as I'd told Zakai, and the only one who could do this. If I failed, we would all perish.

I dropped my external Phaetyn veil, pointless against Kamini anyway, and then unravelled half of the lapis Drae bands from around my head and slapped my green Phaeytn mojo alongside them, merging the powers as tightly as I could.

Without pausing to think, I blasted the interwoven force at each female in rapid succession. For the first three, I did okay. I even braced for the rebound flare of Draedyn's energy as before. I caught an image from Tyrrik of three more of the Drae toppling from the sky. Screeching, I funnelled all of my might through the band of his control around the remaining three, but the last flare of Draedyn's power was tailored to resist my efforts.

I can't get through, I called to Tyrrik.

Keep trying. I'm flying ahead.

No! I screamed at him, fear clawing at my heart. *We stay together.*

I could feel his answer, but before I could respond, shock stunned me. Through his eyes, I watched a turquoise Drae rise from within the rebels' ranks.

It's my aunt, I choked as emotion overwhelmed me. My Aunt Ryn.

Untangling a strand of my powers, I threw them like a net to cover my aunt who was circling above Draedyn. The net settled around her just in time, and then Draedyn and I were both locked in two battles. Not only did I need to keep my aunt's mind free as she attacked him to give the rebels a fighting chance, but Draedyn and I fought for power over the remaining Drae still under his control.

Draedyn unleashed a second bout of white-hot fire on Lani's shield, the crackle of power singeing the air.

Despair flooded me as the green power swallowed her gold veil, and then the Phaetyn barrier began to shrink, exposing more and more of our army.

I glanced up just as my aunt dove.

I wasn't sure whether I felt Tyrrik holding his breath or if the tension inside was all mine as I did the same.

Aunt Ryn closed the gap, plummeting toward the emperor, and I pounded against his control of the female Drae, gaining an inch.

Draedyn cut off his flame and twisted in a circle in the air, whipping his spiked tail high and wide.

A vice squeezed my chest, and I screeched aloud as his tail connected with my aunt's head. She rolled upside down over his back, her wings scraping over his ridged spine, and then she toppled, plummeting to the hard ground.

I couldn't waste the opportunity she'd given us. I threw everything I had into breaking his hold. Triumph surged from within as I felt his grip loosening on one of the Drae, feeding my confidence and my power. She fell and then a second. I couldn't fathom how my aunt's move had distracted him so much, yet I refused to let that distract me as I drilled my powers at the last barrier, shattering the final ring of control on the female Drae.

Ryn, Tyrrik said. *Your aunt took the Phaetyn from Draedyn. Kamini and the children are no longer on his back.*

Yep, that would've distracted him.

I grinned at my mate, but my breath caught as I faced the massive green Drae before us. Draedyn was monstrous, and my stomach turned.

You did it, my love. You freed them.

I hoped my mate was right, but I was too fearful to share his elation. I cast my powers to the eleven females, checking first that they were unconscious and no longer a danger. Unwilling to risk them joining the battle again, I wove a thin layer of my powers around each, hoping it would be sufficient to give me a warning, even if the barrier couldn't keep Draedyn out entirely. My aunt was still conscious. I darted a look at her and saw her fighting the three Druman who'd held Kamini and the children at knife point.

I hate Druman, Tyrrik said. He blew out a breath of flame, torching the Druman farthest from the Phaetyn.

It was all the help we could give her. We'd have to rely on my aunt and Kamini to kill the others.

What's our plan? I asked. I'd felt him assembling a strategy as I freed the females.

Draedyn unleashed another jet at the army, and my heart wrenched with the cries and screams as the rebels caught in the flame disintegrated into ash, their lives over in a single breath. Druman attacked the front lines of Phaetyn, and roots burst from the ground, spearing the Druman on the spot. Swords and arrows and spears coated in golden Phaetyn blood flew through the air at the mules.

As I watched, a catapult launched from our side at the Druman, and countless throwing stars dipped with Phaetyn blood soared through the air, killing the Drae side of any Druman they scratched.

The plan is that I attack him physically and you attack him mentally, Tyrrik said in a rush. Get your Phaetyn veil up again.

I did so in a second.

Keep it around me if you can, he said. *It gives me an advantage against him.*

I will, I said, my heart thundering. My mate was about to go into battle, and I so desperately wanted to tell him no, to go in myself, to force him away south to where we could hide.

But we'd both made the decision to fight. To be here with those we loved.

We were in this.

I'll need you to watch my energy levels, he added as the remaining distance closed with awful finality.

I will, I said firmly. *And I'll attack his mind. As best I can.* This was it. Fear coated my insides.

Ryn, Tyrrik whispered as my father turned to face our attack.

Draedyn's emerald scales and sword-like fangs glinted in the morning sun.

Tyrrik's determination was set, but his nervousness leaked through our bond too. *I love you more than my life.*

My heart shattered; to hear him say such things felt like accepting failure. I couldn't bear to hear it. This talk of love and lives when we were here on the cusp of losing everything we'd fought so hard to achieve. Without Tyrrik, I had no love, I had no life. My future was with him.

Always with him.

He knew that. He would feel my anguish, my pain, just as I felt his. But his courage to act in spite of fear made me love him more. And so I told him simply, *I love you. You are my mate, my soul, my life. You are my future.*

I banked sharply to the right, peeling away from Tyrrik's side, diving to a position from afar, and hearing dreadful twin roars at my back and the whining groan of talons and fangs locked in battle.

37

I didn't dare speak to Tyrrik, only sending images of Draedyn's spiked tale when I thought my mate might not see it coming. Draedyn was a third larger than Tyrrik, but my Phaetyn power gave Tyrrik an advantage. While Draedyn could see through my veil because of our familial bond, like Tyrrik before we fully mated, judging by my father's delayed reactions, he was having trouble. Keeping the veil completely over Tyrrik with his constant unpredictable movement was impossible, so Draedyn was still attacking, but we'd evened the playing field. I hoped.

Now, I planned to tip it in our favor. I couldn't spare a thought for what was happening below, despite the cacophony of battle. I could hear them, but every ounce of my attention was finely attuned to the person who meant the most to me. I could only see, feel, think of the danger to my mate.

Circling around the fighting Drae, I flooded my mind with Phaetyn power and then coiled my Drae and Phaetyn tendrils as before.

This time, I aimed for my father.

I'd never attacked him. As I blasted beam after beam of my power at him, I felt like I was slamming my energy against a brick

303

wall, and I realized with stone-cold certainty the enormity of our task.

His power was smooth. I couldn't find purchase. My powers were like hands trying to scramble up a slippery, vertical wall. I groaned as my mind screamed with protest, but renewed my efforts as I noticed, finally, they were having some physical effect.

Draedyn's movements slowed, and he faltered as I continued the assault on his power. That was encouragement enough. I roared in triumph, and Tyrrik slashed his talons over the base of Draedyn's wings. Black blood sprayed from the wound, and my father's pain-filled screech was deep, outraged.

Tyrrik spun, whipping his tail across Draedyn's snout.

I continued blasting the slippery wall, desperate to see this through. I wanted a life with Tyrrik. I wanted it so bad that I would do anything to make it happen. Draedyn sunk his fangs into Tyrrik's side, and I screamed with my mate, immediately diverting some of my power to healing my mate until I felt his energy return to full capacity.

As Tyrrik righted himself, the emperor dove for the ground behind his lines of Druman.

What's he doing? I asked, feeling safe to do so as my father landed.

Changing tactics, Tyrrik panted. *Are you okay?*

Never better. I tried to roll my eyes and snorted at myself. How can Drae not have the eye-roll? *Do you need more energy?*

Not at the moment, but I have a feeling this is just beginning.

I had to agree with him. Hours and days could go by as they slowly chipped away at each other's strength.

The air around Draedyn's form shimmered. *He's changing!* I said. *Why would he do that?*

Tyrrik and I circled above.

I'm . . . not sure. It doesn't make sense. He's hiding behind his Druman.

Yes, we need to take them out. Just be careful. They fight dirty.

My stomach twisted with the gruesome fight, and surprise punched me in the gut. Hundreds of Druman swarmed through the ranks of humans. Men from Verald and Gemond mixed with the silver-haired Phaetyn as they battled.

Let's end this.

Of course, Khosana.

Tyrrik twisted, and I followed suit, angling toward the battle below. The stench of smoke and fire grew, burning wood, metal, and . . . flesh. Screams mixed with the clash of steel, the chaos beating mercilessly against my ears, growing in intensity the closer we came to the mêlée.

Look at that group of Druman to the left, Tyrrik said, sounding a mite too pleased about seeing them clustered in a convenient group for execution. *I'll blast them. There's a contingency of Azuli behind them. If you land there and put your tail to good use, I'll mete punishment to the mules.*

I glided past him, catching the glowing heat in his chest out of the corner of my eyes. A moment later, he bellowed and then spewed liquid-blue death on my father's progeny.

I landed, my legs colliding to the earth, and roared at the humans siding with Draedyn. Enemy. I swung my spiked tail through the clustered groups of men, not pausing as I stomped my way deeper and deeper into their ranks to administer justice. Men screamed as I sliced through their paltry armor. Like hay ready for harvest, the Azulis fell under my wrath.

My deafening roar carried across the plain, and suddenly, the ground reverberated with the pounding steps of a mass of humanity. A giant troop of young men crested the horizon, shaking their weapons in the air, and I grinned wide and toothy as I recognized the assassins at their head. These soldiers were the young men returned from the emperor's offshore battle. They were here to help us!

I batted away a small number of the persistent Azulis. Ahead, a shimmering golden web reappeared, and I chuffed, recognizing Lani's shield. Everyone was here.

I continued my advance, confident that Tyrrik had my back. My triumph radiated through our bond, and his bounced back to me.

Whatever plan Draedyn had no longer mattered. I surged forward, knowing the scales of justice had tipped our way. To my left, the assassins and our young men from Verald and Gemond washed over the few remaining Azulis as they fought for freedom.

Surrender. Their chant tickled my ears, the song of Draedyn's defeat thrumming through my veins.

But where is Draedyn? Until my father was dead, the war still raged.

Up ahead, Tyrrik replied. *In the center of his minions.*

I turned to see where my mate was looking, and my breath caught. A Druman loomed behind Tyrrik, wielding a dagger dripping with silver. *Tyrrik! Behind you!*

The Druman swung his dagger downward in a slow arc. And sliced through my mate.

Blistering pain stabbed through our bond, and my vision wavered. *Tyrrik?* I gasped. Frozen, panic pressed from all sides as I felt the poison course through his body. I screamed, *Tyrrik!*

I reached through our bond as desperation flooded me. I screamed his name over and over. Phaetyn poison pumped through him, carried by his bloodstream to kill him. I screeched and lashed my tail wide as I spun in a circle, leveling everyone within reach. I crouched and then bounded into the air as I extended my wings, pumping as hard as I could.

Tyrrik's pain consumed me, yanking me to him. I tried to focus through the blinding panic. Tyrrik *needed* me to focus. *Hold on, my love,* I begged him.

At the bottom of the valley laid my mate, right where Azule met with Draedyn's lands. Throughout the area, only small skirmishes remained. The army might think the battle was won. How wrong they were.

There. In the center of a mixed cluster of Phaetyn and humans were three Drae. In a blur I could barely decipher, my mind absorbed the scene. Tyrrik and Draedyn were in their human forms. And one of the female Drae lay still in the dirt. The once vibrant amethyst color of her scales was now gray and ashy. The lack of movement from her rib cage indicated the end of her suffering, and as I drew near, the coppery tang of blood wafted into the air from the gaping wound on her side. Druman surrounded her body, their weapons dripping with her blood.

They were killing my kin. And yet, despite what I knew through my bond, that my mate was dying, a small part of me hoped I was wrong, that only this female had been slaughtered and not the other half of me.

Three Phaetyn were on the ground . . . Two of the three silver-haired healers lay prone and unmoving, their skin sliced to ribbons and their heads twisted at an unnatural angle. Kamini knelt between her two dead compatriots, her face buried in her hands as her small frame shook with her sobs.

I didn't care. If my mate was safe, I would've felt grief on their behalf. But my heart lay torn and exposed on the ground, and as my gaze fell to Tyrrik, what was left of me disappeared.

In front of Kamini was my mate, his back riddled with small blades.

High in the sky, my vision tunneled, a strangulated groan escaped through my snout, and I swept closer, vicious determination filling me. He would not die.

I would save my love.

I had to save him.

The closer I flew, the more the crowd funneled in. As if they believe that by closing ranks, they could prevent my landing. I bellowed in warning, but the group refused to heed my caution. Red crept in on the edges of my vision and then flooded my every sense. I barreled forward, pulling up at the last second.

Only one thing could have stopped me in that moment. How had Draedyn known?

Terror squeezed my heart. Dyter stood in the midst of the cluster and, next to him, the Verald servant he'd disappeared with, clinging to his arm. Behind Dyter, a Druman hovered, holding a knife to my oldest friend's throat.

And yet, Tyrrik was dying.

I pulled up when the Druman inched the blade over Dyter's neck, and he cried out. I couldn't make sense of my thoughts. Instinct screamed at me, and my mind was desperately, *furiously,* attempting to figure this out. Or maybe my mind knew there was no solution.

I circled wide, and the Druman released his pressure on the blade. Keeping Dyter in my line of sight and Tyrrik in my periphery, I angled to the left and landed. Swinging my tail wide once again, I cleared the area around me.

Empty space surrounded me for a heartbeat, and then the crowd converged on me. I roared and whipped my tail in figure-of-eights, the mace-like weapon plowing into the Druman and humans alike. Screams rent the air, and the tang of blood increased as the spikes tore into my attackers. Crimson warmth splattered as I raked my talons through a group of humans foolish enough to attack now, when my mate was breathing his last breath and my true father was at knife point. I'd kill them all!

Weapons bounced off my vibrant-blue scales, impenetrable without the aid of Phaetyn blood. I lashed through the foolish and stubborn mortals, ending their existence without remorse. I turned my pain and anguish upon them; they'd been complicit in Draedyn's reign.

A sharp sting pinched my back, followed by a bolster of energy. I reeled to see who was so foolish and couldn't stop my broad smile as I faced several dozen of my father's mules. I charged.

Lunging forward, I snapped my jaws through two of the men and rose up on my hind legs to toss their bodies wide. I roared again and swung my forelegs in an arc, letting my talons carve through those who remained. I brought my front legs back to the ground as a group of Druman moved as a pack toward me. Wielding my head as a weapon, I reared back and then hurtled down. The horns atop my thick skull hit the group, impaling three of them and sending two more airborne.

I stomped the ground and bellowed, challenging anyone. Everyone. I would not stop until I reached my loved ones' sides.

I could feel my mate as I shifted back to my Phaetyn form. I couldn't see him, but he was still alive, his pain consuming. His vitality was draining rapidly. I tried to burn out the golden Phaetyn blood, but with the number of distractions to still deal with, I couldn't give him the singular focus needed. I sent waves of my healing power to him during the brief silence as additional enemies sprinted to attack, but they were too far away to stop me. I shoved more power at him and pleaded, *Hold on, Tyrrik. Hold on . . .*

I had to kill Draedyn. Only then would this madness stop. I stepped in the direction of his emerald power, my fangs and talons lengthening on their own accord as I prepared to fight.

My father stood in the center of the clearing. I froze as the scene before me bludgeoned my chest; my breath completely stolen. To Draedyn's right were Kamini and the two dead Phaetyn; to his *left* Dyter stood with the Veraldian woman, a Druman behind him with the knife.

And in front of my father was my mate. Tyrrik lay face down, unmoving.

"No," I cried. My heart shattered, and I screamed, "*No.*"

"Ryn?" Dyter moved his head slightly to the right and flinched. His face was covered in bruises and dried blood. The Druman pressed the blade tight against Dyter's throat, and he froze. His split lip oozed fresh crimson horror to mix with all the other evidence of pain he'd had to endure. Next to Dyter, the servant from Verald wept incoherent pleas for assistance. Behind the Druman holding a knife to Dyter stood a row of Azulis, their weapons aimed at the Druman.

I blinked, trying to understand . . . Was this a stand off? If so, why were the Azuli's turning on the Druman?

My gaze returned to Dyter again and saw what I had not seen before. The gore smeared over Dyter's face was merely the remains of his now-empty eye sockets. I growled and swung my attention back to my father.

His talons lengthened, and I screamed.

The Azulis released their arrows into the Druman, and the

Veraldian woman pulled Dyter into the dirt as the mules fell behind them. I had no idea why the Azulis were helping, but Dyter was out of immediate danger.

Draedyn turned, his neck elongated, and his head morphed as he opened his mouth and blew a stream of molten flame at the archers. The men disappeared, and their ash gusted, rising and falling on the breeze as the wind swirled around us. Eerie silence fell as the powdery residue of the men settled.

Then there were the six of us. At the end, Draedyn, Kamini, Dyter, and the Veraldian servant, me, and my dying mate.

Draedyn grinned. "Hello, heir-daughter."

I couldn't answer. My voice was twisted and hiding in the mess that was my heart, and I couldn't be bothered to find it for him.

"I did my best to save your mate." Draedyn kicked the assassin's body back with his foot and waved me forward. "You better heal him."

Was this another trap? Probably, but it didn't matter. The compulsion to heal Tyrrik was overwhelming. My body trembled with the need to go to him. I dropped to my knees and pulled the blades out of his back, letting the Phaetyn blood buoy my own power. As I started to burn the golden power out, I gasped as Tyrrik pressed images into my mind. Draedyn shredding the Phaetyn children's bodies with the small daggers before giving them to his Druman to finish Tyrrik. Even now, Draedyn was trying to keep me at his side with his lies. Rage swelled within me. He'd hurt my mate.

I shifted the talons on my right hand, driving them deep into my thigh, just like I'd done when I'd almost killed my aunt, and then I rotated my entire torso as I drove my talons back, slashing through my father's tunic and deep into his chest.

He stumbled to the ground and then straightened and shook his head. "I merely wanted to watch. Your lack of trust is disheartening. I had no choice but to incapacitate him to win, but that does not mean I want his death."

I glared at Draedyn. "Liar."

I waited for my Phaetyn blood to poison my father. Kamini was now unguarded, as was Dyter. Soon enough, Draedyn would succumb to my Phaetyn power while I stabilized Tyrrik. Soon.

Draedyn shook his head, still upright. "Stand up."

I ignored him and sent another wave of power into Tyrrik, my chest swelling as he clung to life. *Hang on, Tyrrik. Please don't leave me here alone.*

"Have it your way," Draedyn said calmly. "I think we have everyone here."

My flash of confidence waned. Why wasn't Draedyn reacting to my blood? Maybe because of his age it would take longer to affect him, but I knew it was just a matter of time. Distraction . . . I could do that. I'd play along. "Everyone for what?"

"Everyone you care about, heir-daughter," he said and then laughed, a cruel grating sound. "Did you think your blood would affect me? Why do you think I made you poison your aunt? I had to know my risk. Now, Queen Lahr, if you will . . ."

W-what? My mind reeled, and I struggled to process what that meant with the activity in front of me. Queen Lahr? The queen of Azule? There was no queen here . . . Someone moved, and I glanced at the Veraldian slave. Her makeup was smeared across her face, but her eyes gleamed. How had I ever thought she was a Veraldian slave? I blinked and remembered the woman standing next to Mily, just before Draedyn disemboweled the former queen. Queen Lahr yanked a blade from inside her tunic and stabbed Dyter.

My world stopped.

38

The only man I'd ever considered a father gasped. Dyter's hands rose to rest on the blade protruding from his chest. As his knees buckled, my vision blurred.

"No," I screamed, leaping at the Azule queen. I raked my talons not only across her body, but all the way through her. I blinked as her blood sprayed me and then spilled to the ground, mixing with Dyter's, and her body dropped in large chunks to the dirt.

I fell to Dyter's side, shrieking for help. "Kamini!"

The Phaetyn princess screamed as Dyter writhed on the ground. I reached for her as Draedyn sliced a short sword streaked with black Drae blood through Kamini's leg. Blood gushed from the wound in her thigh, and she crawled toward me, her eyes wide with terror.

"Kamini, please, you have to help him," I begged. "You have to heal him—"

Black lines webbed her face, and her movements slowed. "Ryn," she whispered, her voice hoarse. "You need—"

I choked on my emotions as a fresh wave of agony tore through me. "No!"

I reeled to see my father, *still alive*, standing over my mate. The emperor held a long knife in his hand, dripping afresh with Kamini's Phaetyn blood. He stood over Tyrrik and met my gaze.

Emerald surrounded me, and I screamed as I scrambled for my powers. It was happening too quick, all at once, everything in a mess. Draedyn's power pinned me.

Ryn! Tyrrik shouted, his voice echoing from far away. *Be ready!*

I blinked through the crushing weight of my father's power and watched as he drove the blade through Tyrrik's abdomen.

"No!" I mouthed as Draedyn's force flooded into me.

Onyx strands chased the emerald green down; Tyrrik's strength coursed through my veins. Tyrrik pushed his energy into my body, bolstering *me* on his deathbed. Tyrrik's power slowed to a trickle, and I gasped, unable to even clutch my chest as I felt our bond wither. Tyrrik's onyx bands turned to threads then tendrils, fading into wisps. Tears spilled down my cheeks, and my heart gushed with agony as I watched the wisps turn to smoke. Then the smoke floated up into the sky to be lost among the dust and ash.

Tyrrik! I screamed, throwing up my defenses. *Tyrrik!*

No, there still had to be time. My soul, my very being couldn't accept anything else.

I filled my mind with my moss-green power as Draedyn pummeled his emerald tendrils against my mind. And an epiphany blasted through me.

Draedyn shouldn't have ever been able to get through my veil. He shouldn't be standing before me now after I'd stabbed him. Drae repelled Phaetyn and vice versa, but he'd *never* had too much of a problem with me after my Drae transformation. I stared at my moss-green powers as though seeing them for the first time. I'd always seen my powers as different entities, my green Phaetyn power totally different than my lapis lazuli Drae. But Phaetyn powers were gold, not green. Whatever I possessed once, before my Drae transformation, had changed. I no longer had pure Phaetyn power. Blue and gold . . . *made* green. My Phaetyn power was a mixture, tainted by my Drae nature. *That's* what he'd meant.

Just like I couldn't kill Tyrrik with my blood because of our bond, my blood hadn't killed my father. Draedyn was my kin, which meant we had a bond. Whoever I was bonded with had some immunity to my Phaetyn blood.

I needed . . .

I writhed with the force of Draedyn's energy. He left the blade pinning my mate to the ground and walked to me.

"I knew your mother had lied, and when the Phaetyn queen died, I knew you would live. But I was content to bide my time. I've bided my time since the very beginning. Baeyn refused to see it, but Drae were never meant to serve. I was meant to rule. I was always meant to rule them all, Ryn. And you will help me."

I shook my head. "You're wrong. It's why your brother wouldn't give you help in your sick pursuit."

"Aedyn?" He laughed and then bent down to look me in the eye as he spoke his next words. "I am Aedyn. I don't know what story of our history you've heard, but let me tell you the truth. I left the Drae. After millenium, I found there was a difference between peace and pleasure. A difference between strength and power. I left. Baeyn and I disagreed, so I left."

I clutched my head as his anger beat against me.

"And when there is no one else, daughter," Draedyn continued in his calm voice, "you will turn to me. I will be *all* you have left. And you will be all I need."

I couldn't access my powers. He had me trapped.

"The interesting thing when you're the oldest of a mostly extinct species, you can say whatever you want about your kind, and there's no one wise enough to refute it. You can create the history you want, the very world you want. You just have to be patient. And I am very patient." He nudged Tyrrik's body. "I'll tell you a secret, heir-daughter . . . you won't die when your mate does. I didn't die, though at the time, I wished I had. You'll get over it and be stronger alone, just like I am."

I wasn't stronger alone. I didn't *want* to be stronger alone. I wanted Tyrrik by my side, his strength and his kindness, his humor and his patience. I wanted his arms around me and his love inside me. Without my mate, I felt like half the person I was meant to be. I tried to move, but I couldn't break through. *Tyrrik,* I sobbed. *Tyrrik* . . .

Draedyn crouched next to me. "One day, you'll become everything I want you to be. I will make you into an indestructible weapon. No one will stand in my way ever again."

Hatred burned deep within me, and I stoked the flame as I struggled against the slithering green. I needed to find a break, just a small one. But only two things had ever been able to break Draedyn's powerful hold.

"I bet your mate begged for death just to be away from you," I whispered to Draedyn, wielding the first. *Distraction.*

He blinked, and I barely processed that despite his words, he still loved his mate. I focused, gathering the onyx power Tyrrik had given me, the second. *My mate's power.* I shoved through the oily green force pinning me down.

I grabbed the blade at my waist and twisted as I drove the blood-coated knife from the Phaetyn in the dungeon deep into Draedyn's heart. "My blood may not work," I said through gritted teeth, "but I'm not the only Phaetyn. And they all hate you."

The emperor reeled back, falling to the ground.

I leaped to my feet only to kneel on his chest as I pushed the blade deep. I followed the receding emerald power into Draedyn's core while I pulled my energy, not separated but coiled about each other, blue and moss-green, and then I shrieked, blasting all of it at Draedyn's core.

Thunder rolled overhead, and Draedyn bellowed in pain, his hands scrabbling for purchase on the blade. Smiling maniacally, I knocked his hands away, shoving the blade in farther, driving the weapon all the way in to its hilt.

He gasped, eyes wide, and I soaked up his demise, vindicated by knowing that his death was right. I would never tire of seeing the life drain from the man who had hurt so many.

"You will never take from anyone again," I snarled. I hurled another blast of power at the monster who'd ruled Draeconia for centuries. Over and over again, I pummeled him, and Draedyn's emerald core splintered and then shattered, and I nearly fell forward as it evaporated, giving me unfettered access to his mind.

"Daughter," he choked.

I wanted no part of him. Especially not his sick mind. "I am no daughter of yours."

I collected everything left of myself and Tyrrik, and for us and all of those I loved, I blasted my power into Draedyn, wave after wave, not stopping even when his body numbed and his thoughts ceased. I continued to beat him even when his mind was void and his soul had departed to whatever black abyss it might belong. I didn't stop my assault until every last spark within me knew he was gone.

I rose, my legs trembling, and stood, staring down at the man who'd ruled in terror, his eyes glassy, forever fixed unseeing at the sky overhead. Yet there was no triumph, only a hollow ache in my chest, a void nothing would ever fill.

Turning, I looked at the still form of my mate. My soul reached for him with trembling fingers, searching over and through his body and soul for any wisp of onyx energy remaining. My hunt started tentatively, afraid to confirm, desperate to negate.

Chaos moved around me, sliding through my awareness. Lani dropping to Kamini's side, a small group of Phaetyn sprinting to Dyter, rings of Gemondians, Veraldians, men, women, kings, and queens gathering in silent circles to stare upon the emperor's body.

And to witness my grief.

A wracking sob worked up my throat as I stumbled to my mate. Another cry followed the first as I fell to my knees by his side. I ran my hands over his body, my heart rending when my palms rested on his still chest. His silent heart. I threw back my head and screamed in agony. I screamed until my throat was torn raw.

I would scream until my last day in this cold, hard realm.

Tyrrik was gone.

THE INTENSITY with which the Drae studied me cocooned us, and the rest of the world disappeared.

"You can see me." Tyrrik studied me, his gaze intense and penetrating. In a low voice, almost to himself, he murmured, "It can't be."

I blinked and then glanced around, smiling as I realized our location. We were in Verald, in the courtyard inside Harvest Zone Seven. This was the exact place where we'd first met.

I lifted a hand to my mate's face. "Of course I can see you. And you can see me."

He brought his hand up in tiny increments, his expression rapt as he circled the back of my neck. His warm palm connected with my clammy skin, and fire licked where we touched, the warmth spreading from where his hand tangled in my hair, sending tendrils of pulsing energy all over me.

I closed my eyes, basking in his onyx power. I sighed as his dark bands slid and danced over my lapis lazuli swirls, our energies twisting and binding with one another. This was right. This was how we should be. Together. I fell into him, pressing my body against his length.

He ripped his hand back and stepped away, glaring at his palm with a look of betrayal as I fell to my knees.

"Tyrrik?" I said in confusion, getting back to my feet.

He swore long and hard again in the guttural Drae language, shock tinging his voice. But he knew me. He knew me, and I knew him.

I squeezed my eyes closed. "What's happening, my love?"

"Where are you going right now?" he asked in a different tone. Gone was the shock. Something very different took its place in his expression. His gaze darted behind him, and then he turned toward the fountain, scanning the dry space.

"Where am I going?" I asked, completely confused. "Don't you mean where are *we* going?"

I blinked and the memory disappeared, swallowed in a heavy gloom, and Tyrrik pinned me with his dark gaze. He shook his head, his lips turning down in a sad look of pity.

I rubbed my chest, trying to rid myself of a hollow ache spreading through me.

"I know where I am," my mate said.

My love. I reached for the bottom of his black aketon, fingers shaking. Why was he talking like this? "You're here with me," I whispered urgently. "You're right here."

He untangled my fingers, brushing gentle caresses over my skin as he removed my hold on him. I reached frantically for him. "Please."

Tyrrik stepped back, and I followed. But every time, I made to close the distance between us, he moved away again, just out of my reach. Why couldn't I reach him?

"Tyrrik," I said, my voice rising as panic clawed up my throat. "Tyrrik, come back with me."

"Oh, my love. I cannot. You know I cannot. I am here, and you are there." Tears trekked down over the planes of his features.

My eyes burned, tears spilling over the brim, and I dashed at them if only to see him better. "What are you saying?" I asked, clutching my head. "Stop saying such things."

"Move on, Ryn."

"Stop!" I screamed.

"I'm already gone."

I fell to my knees, raking my nails through the stone. "Stop," I pleaded. "Stop!" I repeated my chant without break, rocking back and forth as I wept. "I won't let you leave me. I won't let you go."

He reached for me, dropping to the ground to pull me into his arms.

Is that what it took for him to touch me? If so, I'd gladly repeat my anguish until my last breath.

He held tight, his long fingers encircling the entire width of my bicep as he pulled back to look me in the eye.

"Do you want to die?" he whispered. He leaned forward and traced his nose up the side of my face as he inhaled me. He pressed his lips to my ear and said, "You are not meant for death, my love."

Shivers erupted then, and a fierce desire took the place of my shaking sobs.

"You need to be gone. Right now."

"I'll never leave you," I swore. "Never." I stared into his face that not so long ago, in this very harvest zone, I'd seen as stone-cold. But now I knew better. The wild edge to his eyes was fear. For me. Always for me.

My mate had always thought of me.

"Please, Tyrrik? I'll . . ." I stared up into his face, tracing his skin with my fingers, my heart expanding. I had no quip. Nothing but raw honesty would do here. "I love you. There is no one else, and there never will be. I need you with me. I want you . . . Please?"

My throat clogged as he pulled away, my hands falling to my lap. But as I bowed my head in defeat, a thread of onyx power brushed against my palm. I closed my fist around the wisp of midnight, hope tickling within my chest, and I tenderly wove my lapis Drae power around the onyx strand and opened my heart to my mate.

The warm darkness swallowed us both.

"You've already left me," my mate whispered.

And then fire erupted, encasing my body. As the blaze raged, consuming me, I wept. More painful than the physical burn was the realization that his flame was a myriad of yellows, oranges, and reds.

A normal flame.

Not the lapis lazuli blue that he'd always breathed in my presence.

Not our flame.

Yet I wouldn't release the onyx tendril and let him leave me forever.

J flailed, fighting off invisible flame as I wrenched upright, sending black sand flying everywhere. The sand was hot, like Drae fire. Too hot.

Drak, I rubbed a hand over my stinging eyes and then reached for my nearby waterskin—a must in the desert at the very southern point of the realm. After a year here, I'd learned the wisdom at having one handy. I squeezed the remaining liquid into my mouth, swallowing painfully, one foot still inside the horrible remnants of my nightmare.

I sighed and got to my feet then hobbled to the top of a black dune. Looking out over the endless desert, my gaze fell over the tents spattering the area beneath me. The bohemian material was strung out to provide shelter from the beating sun, but all in all, the Drae liked minimizing the layer between them and the twin moons, especially at night.

I didn't blame them.

I scoured over the area, and my attention snagged on a lithe Drae as he pulled off his aketon.

He leaned over and returned to his effort, digging what appeared to be a massive hole in the ground. His tall frame was all lean muscle, and his skin, the color of Mum's burnt sugar, smoothed when he stretched. Although currently, he dug through the sand and rock with his talons. Sweat glistened and beaded, rolling down his back, disappearing into the top of his black trousers.

He was perfection.

Having a good look? Tyrrik asked.

I grinned, not the slightest bit ashamed of being caught. Well, if you're going to put on a show . . .

Tyrrik wiggled his hips slightly, and I snorted, his antics chasing away the last remnants of my bad dream—as he'd no doubt intended.

Same nightmare? he asked even though he already knew the answer.

Yep . . . I wish you would've moved me out of the sand.

I wish you would've walked another six feet to our tent before you lay down for a kip, Khosana. I don't like when you go flying without me.

I winced. *Is that why you didn't wake me?*

No. He brushed his hand over my face, wiping off the residual sand. *I was focused on our cave.*

What he meant was he hadn't noticed I'd fallen asleep until the nightmare was almost over. Otherwise he would've done something to help me. I eyed the hole he was digging. There was a natural entrance to his old treasure cave two dunes over, but apparently *that* entrance wasn't big enough. Probably because he knew I wanted a sapphire the size of a Drae. *Yep, yep. Keep digging.*

I flicked my gaze over the rest of our kind. All but two of the females in Draedyn's harem were here as were five males Tyrrik had found in the emperor's dungeon before blowing it up.

Draedyn had told me I was only meeting *most* of our family when I met the female Drae, and I'd never put two and two together —even after he told me the extinction of our species had never been his design. On some level, underneath all of the cruelty and depravity, he'd still possessed some loyalty to our kind. I was grateful for that, no matter what elitist belief his loyalty had stemmed from.

Three of the males found their mates in the group of female Drae and were making a shockingly rapid recovery. The other two males were coming along, just not as fast. Starvation and dehydration might not kill the Drae or Phaetyn, but it could still weaken us. I was grateful Tyrrik found them and they'd been strong enough to get out before the mountain blew.

All in all, we had the makings of a nice little family although I was finding my Drae kin were a bit more serious than I was accustomed. I was one hundred and ten percent certain all of them thought I was six short of a dozen, but I'd killed Draedyn, so they accepted my eccentricities even if many still kept their distance. We had time. Lots of it.

The area under the left side of my ribcage pained with a blossoming ache of loneliness. More and more, I missed my friends, human and Phaetyn alike.

I *was* the Most Powerful Drae. But after a year here in the realm of the Drae, I wasn't sure what that meant.

Do you want to talk about it, my love? Tyrrik asked.

I tilted my head back to the sun and took a cleansing breath. *I'm fine*, I said, both to assure Tyrrik and because it was the truth. *The battle just comes back to me at the weirdest times.*

I wasn't sure I'd ever get over the feeling of staring at my mate and believing him dead. Nor would I forget the anguished search and soul-crushing confirmation of his passing. I'd knelt at his side, despite the void I'd felt in Tyrrik and the panic in me, and scoured him for any hint of life that I could cling to and use to drag him back into being.

In another existence, whether in my head or a spiritual realm only mates could access, I'd found an onyx wisp of life, or maybe it found me. I'd latched onto that strand—not knowing if it was real— and I'd refused to let go. I'd poured everything into my mate, even more than when I'd obliterated Draedyn, for Tyrrik's life was more meaningful than even my own.

If he hadn't come back, I'd still be there now—wherever *there* was—with him. *I can't believe I found the last trace of life in your little toe.*

Everyone you tell that story to is aware you're making it up.

I bit back a smile. *When the scholars write our history, they'll say little toe. Because that's what happened.*

Tyrrik continued his laborious digging. *We won't be in any history books. At least not that part.*

No, we wouldn't. Only a handful of people knew the truth.

To the rest of the realm, Tyrrik and I had died in each other's arms. That was the decision Tyrrik and I had made, our hearts sick of the conflict, desperate to just be with each other. In the aftermath of the war, I'd known with single-minded surety I wanted a life with my mate. No more banquets, politics, platitudes, and discussions about what everyone else needed. Our duty was done; the realm was saved. We'd sacrificed so much, and now it was time for us.

A year ago, that decision felt so easy.

It's a bit hard to turn pages with talons anyway, I joked halfheartedly.

I'd been so focused on removing the emperor from the throne I hadn't really thought of what happened *after* the war was won. I mean, I'm sure the leaders of each realm did in the back of their minds. They might have even discussed it amongst themselves. But I'd never thought beyond Draedyn's death. When I came through the darkness of death with my barely-alive mate on the ground and the stench of fresh blood saturating the air, *my* path forward had been clear.

What was most important? Draedyn hadn't known. He'd never gotten past the 'necessary' part. He'd never gotten to see that living a necessary life, void of life's pleasures, was not a life at all. Draedyn had never learned that merely surviving was just death dressed up.

I planned to live. I planned to do more than what was necessary.

And yet here I was in the southern desert.

Are you getting anywhere? I asked Tyrrik, watching the sweat bead on his back. Really, I almost couldn't appreciate his body any more than I did. Because *mine.* But also . . . just hot. A lot of hot.

Soon, my mate will have an underground cavern fit for all her treasures. Even big sapphires or rubies.

I grumbled, but his thoughtfulness made my heart soar. Even though I didn't enjoy how long it was taking to expand his current treasure trove in the Draeconia Desert. I was waiting until Tyrrik was finished before undertaking a stealth mission to dig up my pillbox and gems from the Gemond palace.

Just inside the passageway here, there is a staircase down, he continued. *Shelves will line all the way down for display pieces. I can't wait for you to see what I've done.*

Neither could I. Tyrrik had kept vigilant about not showing me anything until the cavern was complete. Likely another Drae custom or maybe instinct meant to drive the female crazy. Like his other question game or even watching him sweat in the desert. Once he was done with our lair, I could move everything here to where I'd eventually have our children in a bajillion years or so. Then I would have all my treasures in one spot.

You look very animalistic digging like that, I told him. *Like a wee doggie who can't reach his bone.*

Sand erupted as Tyrrik blurred up the dune to stand before me. I pursed my lips, trying to hold back the smile as I waited.

He leaned over me, his onyx gaze studying my face. I felt his inhale as he took in my scent just as I was soaking in his pine and smoke smell.

"You want to rethink that statement?" he asked, his voice low and menacing.

My heart skipped a beat at the sound, but I stood on my toes and reached up, using a finger on each hand to press down the tops of his ears so they stuck out. "Nope," I replied, raising my eyebrows as I shook my head. "Just like a wee doggie." I inched closer to him and said, "Arf."

Tyrrik chuckled, his joy threading through our bond. Grinning, he leaned in to kiss me. Just like the first time, fire licked my skin with his touch, and with the bonds between us, our blue-and-onyx energy danced around us. His mouth moved over mine, and my tongue met his stroke for stroke. I gripped his arms to drag him closer, and he wrapped me in his embrace.

"Mine," he growled, breathing hard as he rested his forehead to mine.

I inched back and brushed my thumb over his bottom lip. "Mine."

He squeezed my waist and then tugged my hand. *Sit with me.*

We sat in the sand and watched the Drae below in content silence, our observations of their happy faces and strong bodies bouncing between us so quickly it was hard to tell which thought originated with who or who was finishing it.

Do you think they'll be okay now? I asked.

"My love, they'll be fine. The Druman are gone, Draedyn is gone, Azule isn't a threat anymore."

Azule. The country had received the dawn rooster wake up of their life. Queen Lahr's position had been filled by one of our own. After the war, the Azulis were made to live a time in Gemond and Verald so that they could *see* how their fellow human beings had suffered. They heard the young men speak of the horrors experienced at the overseas war. They listened to tales of starvation, of oppression, of cruelty. And then the Azulis were given the option to return to their home if they desired.

Under Dyter's rule, their frivolity reportedly dwindled to tolerable levels without even the hints of an uprising, nor did there seem to be a risk of it. Azule could hardly fight back against an alliance uniting the rest of the realm. And their alliance was fierce.

Are you ready to talk to me now? Tyrrik asked.

What do you mean?

You're not happy, mate, Tyrrik stated, turning to study me.

I glanced at him. *What? Of course I am. I'm with you.*

He shook his head. *I can feel it here.* He pressed his hand to my chest, making my heart pound. *You weren't raised a Drae. You were raised human. Your friends are human and Phaetyn. I know how much you miss them.*

Yeah, I'm not sure seeing them twice a year is cutting it. I sighed heavily then hesitated before continuing. *Do you think we made a mistake, cutting ourselves off from the world? I miss my friends, but . . . More and more, I feel isolating ourselves isn't right, even if it was all we wanted at the time.* I paused, taking a deep breath to gather my thoughts, determined to make Tyrrik see my way.

He nodded. *I agree.*

We want our children to experience cultural divers— I blinked at him. *You . . . agree?*

Tyrrik snorted at my shock. *You needed to come to this decision on your own. I've had similar doubts; Drae are guardians of the realm, after all. We needed time to recoup—and we've had it—and nearly finish a really big cave. Plus, I'm happiest when you're happy.* He cupped my face and pressed his lips to mine in a brief kiss. After pulling away, he added, *You need the realm, not just this desert, Khosana.*

He stood and brushed off his butt.

My heart swelled with love, and I admired his backside. *And you. I'll always love you most.*

That's a given.

He looked at me gravely, and I laughed at his serious expression. *You're pretty al'right. For a broody-Drae.*

Just trying to stand out from the rest. He shook his hips again and cracked a rare smile.

Could we really do it? Reveal ourselves to the world after hiding for a year? I couldn't really change my mind if we did this; dying was pretty much a once in a lifetime thing.

"If you decide the answer is still yes, we should leave for the Zivost forest tonight," Tyrrik said, watching me closely.

I straightened, my eyes narrowing. "Tonight? Wait . . . How long have you been waiting for me to come to this decision?"

He turned and stepped away. *Got digging to do.*

"How long?" I called after him, ignoring the glances of the other Drae milling below.

How long is a piece of string?

Tyrrik's amusement radiated through our bond, and I rolled my eyes, making sure he could feel me doing so. I was mated to the funniest Drae in the entire realm.

One who made his choice about stepping out from the shadows and taking risks back in Verald. Had he ever looked back since then?

The truth resonated through me. Life wasn't about looking back. Life was about looking and *moving* forward.

Hey, I want to land here. Just for a minute, I said, flying beside Tyrrik. He suffered this—I knew—he really wanted to be in front, protecting me from the list of enemies we still had in the night sky. Clouds.

You're sure? he asked. *The night is still young.*

I am. My Phaetyn veil made us invisible to human eyes, so I wasn't afraid of terrifying anyone by accident.

With my Drae vision, I scanned the kingdom far below, clear to me despite being swathed in darkness. Verald. In what felt like another lifetime, it had been my home. From my vantage point, the alterations in the kingdom were plain. The castle still sat in the center—Calvyten's abode. The ring of quota fields in the valley below was lush and green. I inhaled the abundance of growth, and an approving rumble sounded in my chest. The market circuit road was still there, but the three rings beyond had changed drastically over the last year.

Even with my keen Drae eyes, I could spot no difference between the Money Coil, the Inbetween, and the Penny Wheel, *no* noticeable sign that one house was significantly wealthier than another; all three areas appeared to be prospering now.

I had to give that King Cal his due. I liked what he'd done with the place. But the most sentimental things were the fields of lapis-blue flowers. My chest puffed with pride as the tyrs waved with the breeze, a rich sea of blue. That was all me.

Come with me?

Of course, Tyrrik replied.

We circled down toward a large field of my flowers, and I shifted mid-air and landed on my feet. Totally had that badass trick down-pat.

Tyrrik did the same, landing at my side.

We crossed the field and into the Money Circuit, approaching the square.

"Recognize this?" I asked with a soft smile.

"Where we first met," he said, sliding his hand into mine.

I'd taken us just outside the courtyard where I had so many memories. The best of them included my mate. And my mother. Tyrrik turned toward me and closed the gap between us.

"Why didn't I just tell you we were mates back then?" he mused, studying my face.

The dark cocooned us, and I rose on my tiptoes, bringing my lips near his, intentionally teasing him.

"Why didn't you tell me we should stop hiding from the world two months ago?" I replied.

Tyrrik pulled back and grinned, his white teeth gleaming in the dark. "Feisty. But I'm not telling you how long I waited."

I'd get it out of him eventually.

His grin dropped. "Humans are coming."

Probably not the time for a *Heeeey, we're baaack* moment. Following his lead, we blurred to the buildings bordering the court-yard and melded into the shadows in a crouch, watching as a woman and a young girl entered the clearing. I snorted as I pressed my back to the brick wall of the alley and reminded him, *Phaetyn veil.*

Two females crossed to the middle of the courtyard, to the foun-tain. One appeared to be in her twenties and the other no more than five or six. As I turned to pulled Tyrrik down the alley, my breath caught at the gleaming metal piece reflecting the light of the twin moons. *My welded flower.*

Tyrrik looked at me, and I sent him my memories of the flower. Of how my mother had lifted me to touch it each day.

I didn't think it survived when Irdelron ordered you to burn Zone Seven. I swallowed the lump in my throat.

The woman spoke, and I blinked back the mist in my eyes to listen.

"Do you see that cluster there?" she said to the young girl sitting beside her on the edge of the fountain. "Those seven stars to the side of the moons?" The woman held the girl's hand and lifted her arm to trace the constellation.

I didn't bother looking up. Gazing at the stars and moons from the ground was kind of overrated after flying amongst them. Instead, I watched the young girl and her mother, thinking of the numerous times I'd sat on the edge of this very fountain with my own mum.

"Caltevyn named that cluster Ryn's flame," the mother said. "Because of her and Tyrrik's sacrifice, we are free."

Extra points to Cal for not calling me Tyrryn. Glad to see that one hadn't followed me to the fake grave.

"The one on the top looks blue," the little girl said, swinging her feet off the edge of the fountain as she pointed. The child stared up at the night sky with wide-eyed intensity. Her auburn curls had escaped her braid, and the wisps framed her face, catching the moonlight.

"Yes. That's why our king chose it. Blue was the color of her fire."

The young girl narrowed her eyes. Clambering up, she stretched, just managing to touch the stem of the welded flower inlaid in the middle of the stone pillar. "I thought Lord Dyter said Ryn didn't breathe fire. And why didn't Tyrrik get a bunch of stars?"

I'd like to know that too, my mate thought gruffly, making me snicker.

"I'm sure he *helped*," the mother muttered, "He kept her safe from Irdelron, so he wasn't all bad. But he caused a lot of harm around here . . . for a very long time." She took a deep breath and kissed the young girl's head. "Come now, it's time for bed."

"That's dumb," the young girl huffed and slid off the fountain edge. "Ryn made tyrs. And that's the start of Tyrrik's name. She must've loved him a lot to make flowers for him. *I* think he was good."

I like that kid, Tyrrik said. *They're not all that smart.*

I bit my lip to stop from laughing. The girl's mother ambled toward the opposite edge of the courtyard. The young girl scampered after her but stopped at the entrance of the alleyway and turned back to look at the night sky.

As she looked down, a sudden notion struck me, and I stepped from the shadows, dropping the veil as I dragged Tyrrik with me.

The girl startled at the sight of us, squeaking. I heard her gasp as she looked at the stars again and then down at us.

I held my finger to my lips and winked.

Her eyes widened.

Would it be cooler to shift and take off? I asked my mate. *Or to blur out of here?*

"Arwyn!" the girl's mother called.

The girl glanced over her shoulder and half turned. But rotating back she lifted her hand and, with a shy smile, waved.

Tyrrik and I waved back.

I crossed the now empty courtyard and jumped up onto the lip of the fountain. Chest bursting, I brushed my hand over the welded flower and then looked to the night sky to the blue star, blowing a kiss to my beautiful mother. *I love you, Mum.*

Then I got down to business.

Prying the welded flower from the stone without bending the metal was difficult, but I'd had a lot of practice in Gemond; the metal *tyr* would be the crowning treasure of my hoard.

You're taking that? Tyrrik asked, his shoulders shaking.

I covered their kingdom with flowers; I get this one.

The welded flower came free, and I leaped back down, glaring at my hooting mate. With a deep breath, I peered once more around the empty town square. *I'm glad we came here. I feel settled somehow. Like what we're doing is the right thing.*

You still had doubts?

I lifted a shoulder. *Sure. A little.* But I was determined to embrace life—all of it.

And you shall. I'm glad we came, too. Now, I don't have to pretend to stay asleep when you fly here at night. He kissed my forehead, and before I could protest something we both knew was true, he added, *We should get going so we can reach the forest in time.*

"In time for what?"

He paused. "A surprise."

"Is the surprise revealing ourselves to people who think we're dead?" I asked.

"No."

"A huge diamond carved in your likeness?"

His lips curved. "I'm afraid not, my love. Don't bother trying to guess."

Pretty sure I'd spend the entire journey to the forest doing so. A thrill shot through me, and I exhaled, a slow smile crossing my face. *We're going to be part of this realm, live among the people and make things better.*

We are, Tyrrik answered, reaching for my hand. *And you will inspire many to do the same.*

I gave his hand a squeeze, the welded flower safe in my other hand.

Letting go of residual fear was hard.

But residual was all that was left. I'd fought my horrors, and I'd won.

I'd conquered my fear.

EPILOGUE

*T*hose who knew we existed were small in number but integral in the restoration of our realm: Lani, Kamini, Caltevyn, Zakai, and of course, Dyter.

Tyrrik and I circled the middle of the Zivost, my stomach a bundle of nerves. Lani didn't bother to keep the gold veil up these days. No point when there was a treaty between our kinds. That, and I could get through the veil anyway. My Drae ears made it impossible to ignore the gasps and screams from the Phaetyn below as we descended. The gaping Phaetyn pressed back to the outer edges, trampling each other. I chose to believe they were giving us space to land.

"They're alive—"

"But I *saw* them die—"

"Impossible."

I think they're taking it pretty well don't you? Tyrrik asked me.

I chuffed with nervous laughter as we landed. My gut churned, and I hesitated before shifting.

Don't forget your surprise is waiting, my mate said.

Shifting, I grumbled, *Sometimes I get the feeling you just bribe me to do everything.*

Does it work?

Yes.

Then why would I stop? he asked.

Straightening, I cast a furtive glance around the forest clearing. In my bid to avoid the shocked Phaetyn, my gaze snagged on the banner strung overhead.

I read aloud, "Biannual Potato Growing Competition." I grinned at Tyrrik. "For *real?*"

He nodded, his smile as wide as mine, radiating love. "Surprise!"

Holy pancakes. "I love it." I cracked my knuckles. "This competition is mine."

"As it'll be every six months now, my love."

Too true. Now I'd come out of hiding, I wasn't rolling over for anyone. Not that there was much competition. I'd kick up a fuss about Lani competing because she had a crown that amplified her powers. If she wanted to grow big potatoes, she should have thought about that before accepting *responsibilities*. Which was exactly why I wasn't a queen or empress of anything other than potatoes and soap. All the other titles were overrated. But this? Totally worth coming back to life.

A crowd of people strode toward us, and I saw my friends, those who knew and a few who'd been kept in the dark after our faked deaths.

"Rynnie!"

My smile widened, and I approached Dyter and said, "Hello, Father."

"What?" he said in confusion. "Who said that?" He reached for me, his hands grasping at the empty air.

A length of material covered his eyes. The battle against Draedyn had left Dyter with his life but not his sight. He had learned the lesson of trusting blindly just because a person played on his empathy, or worse a common nationality. Queen Lahr had played him from the moment we'd stepped into her kingdom, acting the part of a helpless Veraldian woman. But the harsh lesson had served him well in the early months of his rule, and he hadn't been caught by the same ploy again.

"Whatever, old coot," I said, stepping forward and enveloping him in a hug. I'd last seen him three months ago. Our separation made me appreciate the time I had with him even more. Even with his endless blind jokes.

"You've decided to rejoin the realm?" he asked, squeezing me tight.

I nodded against his shoulder. "We have."

"That took courage, my girl. Ryhl would be proud."

Had this been what my mother always yearned for? A life where she didn't have to hide in fear? Smiling, I said, "Yes, I believe she would have."

"Drae," a woman said.

Pulling back from Dyter's arms, I cocked a brow at my friend *Queen* Lani. "Phaetyn."

I hugged her next and then Kamini, who Lani had nearly killed herself to save.

"You're competing?" Kamini demanded. "That's not fair . . . *really* not fair. You have *ancestral* powers. Lani isn't competing."

"She has a crown," I said quickly. "I don't. It's totally fair." Okay, so maybe I had a small edge, but then maybe this really was my calling. Besides, I'd be setting a standard and inspiring others to reach for the stars, in my humble opinion.

Kamini grumbled under her breath, and I felt Tyrrik's amusement echoing my own.

I waved at King Zakai who was sitting down at the far end. He lifted a hand in greeting, busy conversing with a young woman. The death of Zakai's son had dealt the king a blow he'd never quite recovered from. To have lost so much in his realm and then his only son made me want to cry on his behalf each time I saw him. He'd aged decades in the last year, although he smiled as the two assassin boys took seats to his left. Rumor was he was training one of them to be the next ruler. I had my money on non-smiley. Neilub set a plate of chocolate in front of the young woman before saying something to Zakai, making the old man laugh. I hoped the king would find some measure of joy until death led him to the moon and stars.

"They're about to begin," Tyrrik whispered in my ear, his breath warming the sensitive skin of my neck.

I shivered and felt his approval of my reaction vibrate through me. But there was potato glory to defend. Even if that meant moving closer to the *still* staring Phaetyn. Seriously, had they never seen someone come back from death before? *They* were supposed to be healers. I sucked in a shaky breath as Tyrrik ran his hands up and down my sides, and his low rumble of desire clouded my thoughts.

"Potatoes first," I managed to gasp. "And then—" I cut off, glancing at the present company. *We'll have sex*, I finished silently.

"I'm going to pretend I don't know exactly what you meant to say." Dyter shuddered. "Drak, I wish they'd taken my ears, instead."

Oops. Poor Dyter really did have rotten luck when it came to me and Tyrrik's maypole dancing and card playing.

My motivation to claim my title and move on to *other* things had me sprinting over to the plot of freshly overturned soil.

The other Phaetyn were already in the starting position, their heads turned to me, eyes the size of saucers. Ignoring them, I dug my hands down into the rich, brown soil and drew my moss-green power forward. Concentrating, I extracted the blue from this, leaving only pure, golden power behind.

Oh yeah, I was going to grow a potato taller than this freakin' forest. They'd be *Phaetatoes* when I was done. Enough to feed the entire realm.

Always a pleasure to be in your head, my queen. Tyrrik's laugh echoed in my head and aloud.

Up to my elbows in dirt, I lifted my head to look at him standing next to my father, my Phaetyn sisters on his other side.

How had we come to this moment when all had seemed hopeless? All this happiness might've slipped out of my grasp or never even been attained. So much risk . . .

And here we were filled with so much joy.

My family.

I grinned, my heart bursting with love. The word seemed pathetic to encompass all I felt. Love didn't account for all the bad things it had taken to get here, but it was only because of the contrast of darkeness that I could appreciate the light. My joy was so great because I'd not only passed through pain and loss but triumphed over it. Together, with Tyrrik and others I loved, we'd fought the despondency and misery of fear, the control of a tyrant, and we'd won.

Tyrrik smiled back and then quirked a brow. *Phaetatoes? I can't wait to see one.*

A call went up.

The Phaetyn either side of me tensed, and I did the same, turning my focus inward as their queen shouted, "Go!"

KELLY'S ACKNOWLEDGEMENTS

Wow, what an experience. It's hard to believe that less than a year ago Raye was telling me about a dragon shifter who was three people but really only one in the end (:O), and that book one in this series only released in November last year. Raye, did we even sleep for the last eight months? #worthit

Thank you to my friends and family for their massive and continued support of my books. I loved sitting and listening to you guys discuss The Darkest Drae. Including how the title of book one should be Bloody Oath instead—sorry, it's probable only Australians and New Zealanders will get that one.

The manuscript team for this series has been absolutely incredible. The deadlines for each book have been narrow and I am totally appreciative of the last minute work each and every one of you did for us. A round of applause for Krystal Wade, Jennifer Jeray, Dawn Yacovetta, Michelle Lynn, and Daqri Bernado. We couldn't have done this without you gals.

To my husband who has benefited hugely from this co-authorship in the way of pretzels, lollies, and a shiny new nerf gun. He shot me in the head a couple of days ago, Raye. Your fault. Also quite an impressive shot, if I'm honest.

Finally, to my Draebae, Rayetato. There is so much I could say about the fun we've had, and about our calls that span many hours. You are a strong, honest, and loving person—and you have hair like sunshine. Never change. The world needs more people like you.

Kelly St Clare

RAYE'S ACKNOWLEDGEMENTS

Whoa! One year ago this week I picked Kelly up so she could stay with me for Utopiacon 2017. At the end of the week together, I bullied her (or bribed, or maybe a bit of both) to co-write this series with me. Happy Draebae-versary! I'm still thrilled you said yes. I've enjoyed so much of our journey together (late night calls, memes about potatoes), not to mention the care-packages of yummies, the thoughtful words, kindness, and helping hand. You've brought laughter, light, and organization to this mad project, and you've become a dear friend as well as fabulous co-author/partner. Let's do it again sometime. ;) #Draebaes

We had such an amazing team on this project. Thanks, hugs, and kisses to Krystal, Dawn, Michelle, Daqri, and Jennifer. The Darkest Drae is as good as it is because of your help. Hallelujah for your awesomeness. #muchappreciated

Jason, I still remember finishing telling you about this "idea" and you saying, "But is there a book out there like that?" Hahaha. Nope! Although you were 100% right about the cover, and that definitely counts for something. Thanks for all you do to support me and this mad hobby of mine. I'm SO glad we have eternity. #stuckwiththe-craycray

Jacob, Seth, and Anna. I don't praise you nearly as much as I should and definitely not as much as you deserve. Because each one of you has more strength than you think, more power than you can comprehend, and as you battle whatever storms, dragons, or evil kings life tosses your way, you have everything you need to come out on top with a happily-ever-after. And I'll always be nearby cheering you on. #momlovesherlittles

Mom and Dad, any success that I have that's significant, is because you taught me what matters most. I will love you to the moon and back, for all eternity. I'm so blessed to have my parents as two of my best friends, as well as my siblings, their spouses, my nieces and nephews, and aunts, uncles, and cousins. #blessed #nooneelsewouldtakeus #wefooledenoughtogetmarriedhaha

And my bestie pals: Katie, Alli, Annie, Kathy, Cassy, and Melissa. You get me, even when you don't get me, and then you still put up with me. #bestiepals #davethelaughismine #yesyoucanborrowmylippy

Finally, to my enthusiastic readers, thank you. A million times, thank you. #gratitude #waituntilthedesertdemons #diditellyouaboutzivrune

XOXO,

Raye

KELLY ST. CLARE

When Kelly is not reading or writing, she is lost in her latest reverie. Books have always been magical and mysterious to her. One day she decided to start unravelling this mystery and began writing.

The Tainted Accords was her debut series. The After Trilogy and The Darkest Drae are her latest series.

A New Zealander in origin and in heart, Kelly currently resides in Australia with her ginger-haired husband, a great group of friends, and some huntsman spiders who love to come inside when it rains. Their love is not returned.

Visit her online and subscribe at:
www.kellystclare.com

ALSO BY KELLY ST. CLARE:

The Tainted Accords:

Fantasy of Frost

Fantasy of Flight

Fantasy of Fire

Fantasy of Freedom

The Tainted Accords Novellas:

Sin

Olandon

Rhone

Shard (2019)

The After Trilogy:

The Retreat

The Return

The Reprisal

The Darkest Drae (Trilogy) Co-written with Raye Wagner

Blood Oath

Shadow Wings

Black Crown

RAYE WAGNER

Raye Wagner grew up in Seattle, the second of eight children, and learned to escape chaos through the pages of fiction. As a youth, she read the likes of David Eddings, Leon Uris, and Jane Austen. As an adult she fell in love with Percy Jackson Olympian series (shocker!) and Twilight (really!) and was inspired to pursue her dream of writing young adult fiction. Raye enjoys baking, puzzles, Tae Kwon Do, and the sound of waves lapping at the sand. She lives with her husband and three children in Middle Tennessee.

RAYE WAGNER

Visit her online and subscribe at:
www.rayewagner.com

ALSO BY RAYE WAGNER:

The Sphinx Series

Origin of the Sphinx: A Sphinx Prequel Story

Cursed by the Gods

Demigods and Monsters

Son of War: A Sphinx Companion Story

Myths of Immortality

Daughter of Darkness: A Sphinx Companion Story

Fates and Furies

Sphinx Coloring Book, Vol. 1

Forthcoming:

Phaidra's Story

Birth of Legends and The Lost Curse (2018)

The Darkest Drae (Trilogy) co-written with Kelly St. Clare

Blood Oath

Shadow Wings

Black Crown

Curse of the Cytri co-written with Rita Stradling

Magic of Fire and Shadow

Magic of Talisman and Blood

Fantasy of Frost
(The Tainted Accords, #1)

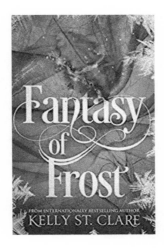

I know many things. What I am capable of, what I will change, what I will become. But there is one thing I will never know.
The veil I've worn from birth carries with it a terrible loneliness; a suppression I cannot imagine ever being free of.
Some things never change...
My mother will always hate me. Her court will always shun me.
...Until they do.
When the peace delegation arrives from the savage world of Glacium, my life is shoved wildly out of control by the handsome Prince Kedrick, who for unfathomable reasons shows me kindness.
And the harshest lessons are learned.
Sometimes it takes the world bringing you to your knees to find that spark you thought forever lost.
Sometimes it takes death to show you how to live.

COMPLETE SERIES NOW AVAILABLE

Cursed by the Gods
(The Sphinx, #1)

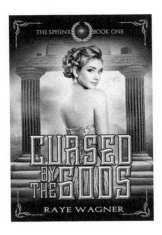

Hope has a deadly secret...

Hope has spent her entire life on the run, but no one is chasing her. In fact, no one even knows she exists. And she'll have to keep it that way.

Even though mortals think the gods have disappeared, Olympus still rules. Demigods are elite hunters, who track and kill monsters. And shadow-demons from the Underworld prey on immortals, stealing their souls for Hades.

When tragedy destroys the only security she's ever known, Hope's life shatters. Forced to hide, alone this time, Hope pretends to be mortal. She'll do whatever it takes to keep her secret safe— and her heart protected. But when Athan arrives, her world is turned upside down.

With gods, demigods, and demons closing in, how long can a monster stay hidden in plain sight?

Join Hope on her unforgettable journey to discover what it means to live and her daring fight to break Apollo's curse.

COMPLETE SERIES NOW AVAILABLE

CPSIA information can be obtained
at www.ICGtesting.com
Printed in the USA
LVHW09*2257200918
590876LV00002B/20/P